Praise for *A Lot of People Live in This House*

"A smashing debut novel about love in the time of COVID! *A Lot of People Live in This House* broke my heart and pieced it back together page by page, character by character. What does it take to recover from trauma? In her beautiful book, Bailey Merlin makes a convincing case for applying liberal amounts of friendship and laughter."

--Mary Kay Zuravleff, Author
Man Alive! and *American Ending*

"How do we balance our need for community with our need for privacy? How do we heal from loss and trauma, and from the pain of loneliness and isolation? The COVID-19 pandemic has raised these old questions anew, and Bailey Merlin's warm, witty, and original novel offers some answers. I fell in love with the characters in *A Lot of People Live in This House*, and they will stay with me for a very long time."

--Suzanne Koven, Author,
Letter to a Young Female Physician

"Most of us live our lives buttoned up in apartments or in homes, and if we're lucky with a special few whom we love. Bailey Merlin imagines a different life, one in which her richly detailed characters cope with living together through the COVID pandemic in a communal household. Enter Rachel and Job, a married couple, reeling from the loss of their only child, searching for solace from a motley crew living together. Sharing a kitchen and sharing the intimate daily details of one's life with strangers is at first more than Rachel can bear, but when Job is marooned in India, seemingly with no way home, Rachel must turn to her new family for emotional support in order to find strength to face some harsh facts about her own privileged life. *A Lot of People Live in This House* challenges us to rethink what family means in these stormy times and offers hope that there are many ways to live a fulfilling life."

-- Neal Baer, MD, Executive Producer of
ER, *Law & Order: Special Victims Unit*, and
Designated Survivor and Co-Director of the
Master's Degree Program in Media, Medicine, and
Health at Harvard Medical School

"A woman alone in a new city during a pandemic, mourning a number of devastating losses, discovers that true families, the kind that will save you, can be created through proximity, shared ritual, and kindness. I finished reading this moving first novel with a renewed belief in human nature and the power of real community. It's a book that heals."

–Susan Neville, Author
The Town of Whispering Dolls: Stories

"Bailey Merlin's wonderful debut novel, *A Lot of People Live in This House*, is a freshly told and compelling description of a young couple attempting to cope after the loss of their unborn child. Set in Boston on the brink of COVID, Rachel moves into a group house with a large cast of characters while her husband travels to India to grieve privately. When COVID hits, complications arise in efforts to get Job home. And Rachel, ever adaptive and quick to solve problems, saves the day at the novel's biggest crises. An original voice, not afraid to look at life head-on, with a lot to say!"

-- Donna Gordon, Author,
What Ben Franklin Would Have Told Me

Bailey Merlin is a talented writer with a rich background in fiction and media, medicine, and health.

She holds an MFA in fiction from Butler University and an MS from Harvard Medical School, and her writing has been published in numerous literary magazines, *The Lascaux Review*, *ellipses...*, *Honeyfire Literary Magazine*, *Bandit Fiction*, *Anti-Heroin Chic*, *Chantwood Magazine*, *Drunk Monkeys*, *Dime Show Review*, *Streetlight Magazine*, *Into the Void*, *Crack the Spine*, among others.

In addition to her writing, Bailey has co-performed a spoken word short story album, *Bug Eyes*, with award-winning jazz guitarist Richie Smith. She is also the librettist of the opera *¡Dime! An Opera in Four Acts*.

Based in Boston, Bailey lives in an intentional community with a dynamic cast of humans, a toddler, a dog, a cat, and a friendly ghost. You can find her thought-provoking and creative work on baileymerlin.com

A LOT OF PEOPLE LIVE IN THIS HOUSE

BAILEY MERLIN

First published in Great Britain in 2023
by Book Brilliance Publishing
265A Fir Tree Road, Epsom, Surrey, KT17 3LF
United Kingdom
+44 (0)20 8641 5090
www.bookbrilliancepublishing.com
admin@bookbrilliancepublishing.com

A CIP catalogue record for this book is available
at the British Library.

ISBN 978-1-913770-64-8

Typeset in Sabon.
Printed by 4edge Ltd.

For The Bond House,
where I learned to live again.

CHAPTER ONE

888 IS A GOOD NUMBER for a house, Rachel thinks as her Lyft drives off, leaving her at the end of the driveway of her new home. *Temporary home*, she resolves. In many cultures, the number eight is seen as a sign of prosperity because, turned on its side, eight is the symbol for infinity, of perpetual new beginnings. Prosperity aside, living with ten strangers isn't her idea of a good time.

She stares up at the great white house, and the great white house stares back, its many-windowed eyes framed with black shutters. She thinks it has too many eyes and that its bright red front door is too big. But what else can she expect with Federal-style architecture, especially in this part of the country? Nothing but symmetry and friezes. In a way, it is comforting to Rachel to know what to expect of the inside: high ceilings, curved open staircases, maybe the rogue Palladian window. The almost-architect inside of her breathes a little more freely. A little.

Rachel reaches into her thin snow coat—a poor panic purchase made in Atlanta after reading the Boston weather report the day before—and fishes out her cell phone. She calls Job. He answers right away. "Hello?"

"Do I have to do this?" she asks without ceremony.

"You made it!" he says, voice bright and more than a little relieved.

"I made it," she says. Her backpack feels heavier than it did when she got off the plane, and her roller bag's handle is awkward under her palm.

Snowstorm remnants cling to the bushes and brick steps, reminding her of an old life and bitter Chicago winters. Even still, that life was predictable. Whatever they're trying to do now is something else entirely. "Are you sure we *want* to do this?" she asks, fighting hard to keep her voice from trembling. It was easier to be brave for Job when they were saying goodbye to one another in Egypt because bravery is easier to muster in warmer places.

Job hums, a patient sound. "Sweetheart, we've been over this. The rent is reasonable, it's furnished, there's enough space for all my shit, you liked Ted and Daniela. And, most importantly?"

She sighs, knowing he's right and hating him for it. "*And* they have pets."

"Exactly. Are you inside yet?"

"No, I'm on the driveway."

"You're just standing outside like a crazy person?"

She chuckles, breath fanning into a mist. "Yeah."

"Cool. So...are you gonna go in?"

"We found this place on Craigslist," she reminds him.

"Yeah, but we interviewed and met all those people. They were legit. Social media certified and everything."

Rachel's anxiety grasps at straws now, trying to find a way to back out of this deal.

"What if I get murdered? Serial killers have social media, too, y'know."

Job is patient, though; he specializes in walking her through her anxieties. "There's only a small chance that you'll get murdered."

She eyes the upstairs windows with suspicion. "Still a chance."

"But like, there was a chance you'd get murdered on the way there. Hello, you got into a car with a stranger. And, you know what? You could even get hit by a car right now."

The grotesque "what-if" game is enough to calm her nerves, it usually does, and Job has known that longer than she has. With the most ridiculous possibilities out in the open, seen for their ridiculousness, reality is easier to grapple.

Rachel's gaze turns back down to the driveway. "I guess that's true."

Job's voice is gentle again. "Then you better get inside, huh? At least you can fend off an attacker there. What are you going to do against a car?"

"Yeah."

Her snow boots crunch against the asphalt as she takes the first step.

"Sweetheart? Take a breath."

She stops and listens. He's taking care of her from a million miles away, even though he was the one who needed to stay in India to learn to better cope with himself. Even though he's the one who needs tenderness from her. Rachel stands taller and resolves not to be selfish; she resolves to be brave. She looks at the house head-on, daring it to scare her. It doesn't blink. "Okay, I'm gonna do it. I'll call you when I get to my room. Okay?"

"Of course, sweetheart. I love you."

"Love you." She hangs up and opens her email to find the message chain from the owner.

Hi Rachel, we're all so excited that you'll be here on Sunday! There will definitely be some folks around the house when you get here. If you have any trouble finding a ride and/or don't want to take the T, let me know—I'd be more than happy to pick you up! If you get here by other means, come around to the side. We don't open the front door in the winter because it's too drafty, and I'm pretty sure the doorbell is broken (joy of old homeownership!). So just come around to the mudroom door (right side of the house) and call me. I'll let you in! xx Ted.

As she rolls up the hill, she wonders if his enthusiasm is a persona or if Ted really is just this jazzed to be alive. After meeting him and six of her soon-to-be roommates on a video call three weeks before, she's inclined to believe the latter. She follows his instructions all the same: up the driveway around the right side of the house, casting sidelong stares at the three-story building. She mumbles to herself, "How many rooms did they say this place was? Nine bedrooms? Ten? God, it must have cost the earth." Compared to all the other multi-family homes and four-story apartment buildings, this place is a veritable palace. Plus, from what she can tell from the outside and aged brick wall, it's well on its way to being a part of some historical society's next walking tour. It's hard to put a price on history, but something in the way of two million is probably about right.

She is careful walking up the stairs, opting to drag the roller bag behind her instead of bending down and picking it up—too top-heavy. When she gets to the door, she finds her phone again to call the number provided. Ted picks up halfway through the first ring.

"Hello, hello! Are you outside?" Ted's voice is as bright as it had been over Skype all those weeks ago while Rachel and Job were in Egypt. She assumes he always sounds like he's done a rail of coke.

"Oh, yeah, hi. I think I'm in the right place. Outside?"

"Fabulous. Two seconds! Ciao."

Rachel looks over her shoulder towards the street and into an empty wooded lot that surprises her. Not too many empty spaces left in this part of the city from what she can tell. Scraggly oak trees burst out of the frozen ground, their branches already tall enough to tangle. She wonders how long developers have been trying to slap some condos into that bad boy.

There's not much time to wonder about zoning board logistics as the door swings open to reveal a gregarious, well-dressed businessman in his early thirties.

"Hi! Welcome, welcome! So good to finally meet you in person!" There is no ceremony before he slings thin arms around her neck in a quick embrace, kissing Rachel on one cheek and then the other.

She stiffens but does not pull away. "Thanks, same to you."

Ted steps back, still smiling, and puts his fists on his hips. He looks good in his expensive, navy-blue sport coat. "How was your flight?"

She shrugs and pretends she's not horrible at small talk. "Pretty good. The flight out of Atlanta's short."

"Yeah, totally." His face turns curious, the way faces do when someone wants the latest gossip but was raised better than to ask for it outright. "Were there any issues with the coronavirus thing? I saw on the news that flights were getting canceled in Europe."

Rachel shrugs again, thinking about the two-hour wait time just to get through American customs after arriving in Atlanta. Everyone seemed tense, more than just jet-lag tense. It frightened her. She doesn't say this, though, doesn't know *how* to say it. Instead:

"Lines were long. People were trying to get home earlier, I guess, but it didn't affect my flight. There haven't been any cases reported in India."

"That's good, that's good. Hopefully, Job will have the same experience." Relieved, his smile returns. "Well, come on in out of the cold!" He steps out of the house to reach for the bulky roller bag. "Here, let me grab that for you."

She leans beyond his reach, unwilling to relinquish her anchor. This is the bag that Job packed, which means that it is of him—that he is, in a way, with her. As long as he is with her, nothing can go wrong. "No worries, I've got it."

Ted's expression falls slightly. "Sure! Is that everything?"

"Yeah, this is me." Rachel gasps in remembrance. "Oh! You mentioned that our other stuff arrived a few days ago?"

Ted lights up at the prospect of being useful. "Yep! We put the crates out in the garage, which I will show you whenever you want. And the boxes marked 'House' are up in your room."

She blushes at the thought of someone making such a fuss over her. Traveling with Job has made relying on the kindness of others and accepting favors a more daily practice, but this generosity from total strangers makes her feel guilty in a deep way. "Really? I'm so sorry. Y'all didn't have to do that."

He waves her away. "No trouble at all! With all the hands we have around here, it only took a few minutes."

"Well...I appreciate it." She knows firsthand how heavy Job's woodworking equipment is. It had taken them four weeks to get his whole workshop packed into storage.

"Of course. If you need any help with moving stuff one way or another, let us know." He puffs out his cheeks and jokes, "That bench is something else, though. I didn't realize they were so sturdy! But of course, they are. They have to be, right?" Ted laughs.

Rachel's blush deepens. "Job will be happy to know it got here safely." She quickly adds, "And, if it didn't, we paid for the insurance."

Ted bobs his head in enthusiastic agreement. "Good, good!" He claps his hands again and reaches for Rachel's carry-on before she can stop him. Before she knows it, her piece of Job is in Ted's grasp. "Well, let me grab your bag, and we'll head up to your room."

The red door swings into a small room full of snow boots, coats, umbrellas, reusable bags stacked into one another into infinity in the corner. Despite the grandiosity that the house had displayed from the road, it is obvious that regular people live here. This is a home. What strikes Rachel, though, is the smell: a sharp scent of onion and bacon. Her mouth waters as

Ted puts his hand on another doorknob, smiling over his shoulder.

"Some folks are in the kitchen, which is good. You can meet everyone in stages. We can be a lot all at once."

CHAPTER TWO

THE KITCHEN IS LARGER THAN it has any business being. What Rachel notices first, of course, is the massive copper-topped island. It is littered with cutting boards, knives, spoons, towels, a bread box, two-wire baskets full of fruit, laptops, books, and a loaf of bread so fresh that it is still steaming. She looks at the far wall lined with its shabby cabinets. She sees the giant kitchen table beset by at least ten chairs and a small bench; she marvels at the stainless steel refrigerator and the double-stacked ovens. Her eyes feel wide before she even notices the two people at the range, looking back at her with expectation.

The first is a tall Black woman with hair that's short on the sides with a shock of sapphire blue corkscrew curls on top. Her smile eats half her sharp face as she sets a skillet into a deep sink. It hisses and smokes upon contact with water.

The second is an even taller man with a well-groomed beard, glasses, and dirty hair in need of a cut. He smiles, too, though the look is made mischievous by a scar that splits his left brow. Though turned to greet Rachel, he continues to stir a giant pot. They both say hello.

Rachel closes the door behind her as Ted plops her luggage down and launches into introductions. "Hello, hello, everybody. This is Rachel. Rachel, this is Markeya—she's an ER nurse at Beth Israel." She waves. "And this is Vernon. He says he works at Google," he leans into Rachel's shoulder to loudly whisper, "but we're all pretty sure he works for the CIA." Markeya chuckles at whatever inside joke the three of them share.

"Why's that?" Rachel asks as her right hand holds her left arm in uncertainty. There is a history here that she doesn't know.

Markeya rolls her eyes and leans her hip into the counter. "He's secretive for no damn reason. Always been that way. He won't tell them when his birthday is, so they think he works for the government."

"But you know when his birthday is?" Rachel asks, trying to determine relationship lines.

Markeya shrugs. "More or less."

"That's cryptic."

"Yep!" Vernon rejoins, pleased while he reduces the heat on the stove. "Hey, Rachel, have you ever had an aspic?"

She flicks through her mental lexicon and comes up empty. "A what?"

The tall blonde man's face blooms with joy. "An aspic is when you take a good food, such as beef chili," he points to the pot with a meat-stained spoon, "and you chill it up with gelatin until the consistency is questionable and then you attempt to recover it by making it pretty. For some aspics, that means adding flowers or fruit. In this instance, it means covering it with molten cheese."

"So, you're making lukewarm chili?"

Vernon chuckles. "Yeah, but in a heart mold." He picks up a piece of silicone to show her. The empty plastic shell is already so grotesque looking in its anatomical correctness that Rachel refuses to imagine it full of meat.

"We're all looking forward to it! But anyway, I'm going to take the newest addition up to her room so she can get settled," Ted announces as he leans down for Rachel's bag, but she recovers the handle and wheels it close to her legs. This is the first frown he gives her, and it looks foreign on his face. "Are you sure I can't get that for you?" he asks.

"It's really no problem," she says, knuckles nearly white with effort.

"Sure thing." The smile returns. "Follow me."

"It was nice to meet both of you," Rachel says, bowing her head over her full hands.

"You, too. Looking forward to chatting later," Markeya says so sincerely that Rachel almost believes her.

Rachel waddles with her suitcase past the tall chairs into a long hallway, at the end of which she can make out the bottom of a large chandelier. She glances up and sees just how high the ceilings are. No, the Craigslist photos had not done this place justice.

Ted pauses and gestures to doors like a flight attendant. "On the left is one of the communal bathrooms. House guests on the first floor use the shower here. On your right is the door down to the basement. If you have anything that needs to be stored, there's plenty of room in the back left corner." They take a few more steps to the second set of doors, both closed. "There's the library here, and across is the informal sitting room." He pauses to listen at one door and then the other. "Shoot. They're both being used right now. That doesn't usually happen. Okay if we look at them later?"

Informal sitting room, Rachel wonders ruefully. *How the hell did we find this place on Craigslist?* "Sure, that's fine," she says, already overwhelmed by the doors and the people and the aspic. "I'd be happy to just head up to my room, too."

"Oh!" Ted turns with a hand on his chest while the other successfully snares Rachel's luggage once again. "I am so sorry. I'm sure you're exhausted. Yes, of course, we should go up to your room! Follow me."

Rachel frowns as her host insists on hospitality and lugs her suitcase up a narrow staircase designed in the long-long ago when servants being seen going up and downstairs was a primary concern of the day. She admires the engraved spindles that hold up the handrail. *Expert craftsmanship.* "When did you say this place was built?" she can't help but ask.

"Late 1700s. Y'know, an architect that designed quite a few of the churches in Boston actually designed and lived in this place. Of course, that's probably why the house has aged so well. Good bones," Ted replies with a little chuckle, and Rachel can tell that he has a curator's tour speech down pat, lame jokes and all. There's no doubt she will hear it in full at some point.

Ted looks over his shoulder, expecting a laugh with so pleasant a smile that Rachel finds herself giving in with a muted chuckle. She averts his gaze, drawn instead by the sunlight coming from above. Glancing up, she finds a skylight. The snow covers its glass, obfuscating the world outside with milky white.

"Your room is here at the end of the hall," Ted sighs winsomely. "So glad you got here when you did. The light is so nice in this part of the house in the afternoon."

They step onto the landing, and Rachel can appreciate that these ceilings are tall too, and the hallway is wide and white, and there are so many closed doors. The air smells like fresh laundry laid out in sunshine. *Eat your heart out, Martha Stewart*, she thinks as a hinge squeaks.

"Come on in," he says as he swings her luggage around and places it just inside the door.

Pulled almost by a magnet, Rachel follows him inside. The room is stunning. The bed is made with fresh linens, a chandelier, and matching wall sconces over a bricked-up fireplace. The walls are white, the curtains black, the outside light divine. It is spacious, certainly more spacious than any of the other rooms she saw online, even with all of their boxes stacked on the far wall. Her eyes are caught by the small doorway that leads to a full bathroom that she won't have to share with anyone, and she is in disbelief.

"This is mine?" After sharing a toilet with twenty other people for the last month, this is a paradise.

Ted is beaming yet again. She's pretty sure he smiles in his sleep. "All yours! Do you need some towels? We have plenty."

She gestures to her bag. "I brought my own."

He nods again and again. "Sure thing. If you ever need extras, let me know. There are stacks in the basement." He claps his hands together, onto the next thing. "So, in lieu of a tour, can I get you a drink? Some tea, perhaps?"

Rachel's head is swimming with information, smells, and the boundless energy that Ted exudes. "No, thank you."

"Well, you settle in, then. We'll be in the kitchen if you need anything." He spins on his heel and heads back out, closing the door behind him. His footsteps are soft, but the wood still creaks. It is an old house, after all.

Properly alone, Rachel wraps her arms around herself and spins in a slow circle to take in every detail she can. The floors have been recently refinished, gleaming chestnut in the sunlight pooling in from the far window. The white walls are without a single suggestion of a previous occupant. There are things that don't belong to them: large bed, white metal desk, side tables, two lamps, linens, all courtesy of Ikea. Nothing is broken or shabby. Just as the post had stated. It seems like this place wasn't a scam after all. She enters the bathroom and is astonished by the size of the shower and the cleanliness of the mirror. It's a far cry from hostel life.

Placing her hand on the bathroom window, she's pleasantly surprised by the giant oak tree that waves its branches outside. Though mostly leafless now, it will be beautiful in the spring. She almost believes her luck. She calls Job. He answers after one ring: "Not dead?"

His voice reels her back into herself. "Not yet."

CHAPTER THREE

RACHEL HUGS HER FREE arm tight around her middle, trying to smother the loneliness that her husband's voice evokes. Job is a million miles away in an ashram. She reminds herself that the trip is a good thing for him and that to mention her missing him now would be selfish. Because, of course, he would come home if she wanted. That's what Job does. Instead, she says, "You're never going to believe this place. There's so much space. Way bigger than the pictures."

The bugs are buzzing so loud in India that Rachel can hear them over the phone. "Oh yeah?" Job asks, excited. "How's the room?"

"Good." She looks up at the ceiling, eyes drawn to the chandelier in the center. "Bigger than I thought."

He chuckles softly, no doubt trying not to alert anyone to his cell phone's presence. It's hard to be spiritually present when you're focused on your phone, or so Jon's guru had told him when he arrived in the small village two hours north of Kerala.

"That's because you don't have good dimensional awareness. I told you it would be big enough."

Rachel rolls her eyes and takes a seat in front of the desk. "You were right."

"I'm sorry, you broke up a little bit there." Job's tone is playful. "I'm what now?"

She sighs dramatically and gets up to pace to the window, peeling back the gauzy inner curtain. Below there is a wide yard covered in snow. Too much snow. Rachel shudders and steps away from the glass. "You were right. As usual."

He snorts. "Okay, okay, let's not fluff my ego too much. What else?"

Rachel is glad for his questions. Moving in without him is overwhelming enough. At least with his partial presence, she can begin to catalog her new reality. "Um, let's see...it's very clean. Smells like Murphy's Oil and lemons. There's...a bed."

"King or queen?" he asks. Nothing is ever too small a detail for Job. He prefers to know everything.

Rachel tucks the phone into the crook of her shoulder so she can hold out her hand and close one eye, trying to mentally measure the mattress. "A queen, I think. Maybe a full." She straightens, returns the phone to her hand. Something is amiss; she knows that already. She feels herself frown. "The bedspread is different than the one in the photos." Everything is ruined.

Job, of course, will not allow his wife to spiral. His voice does catastrophize but instead teasing, "Oh my God, pack up our shit and call the police!"

Rachel ignores him and goes to stroke the top comforter with suspicion. It is soft to the touch but she hates it. "I liked the blue stripes better. This one has little red and yellow flowers."

He gives a stage gasp. "I am shocked. Shocked, I tell you!"

That, at last, breaks the comforter's spell. Rachel blushes, grins, and sits at the end of the bed. "Shut up!" she says, inflection high. It's like she's fourteen again, talking on the phone with some high school crush.

He chuckles. "What else is different?"

Her attention drifts to the fireplace, and she is struck by a painting that rests on the mantel. She squints. Surely she isn't seeing what she's seeing? "Um, there's a life-sized Mona Lisa replica with, um, googly eyes glued on."

"No way! Take a picture."

She peels the phone from her face and snaps a photo. It will be good to have him confirm that this strange bit of art is real. "I'll email it." Suddenly, she sits up and remembers that Job is across the ocean. "What time is it there?"

"Um...around one."

"Oh my God." Guilt runs hot in Rachel's face and hands. She shouldn't expect Job to hand-hold her like this. He's the one who needs consideration right now. "I'm sorry, you go—"

He cuts her off. "No, no, I wouldn't be able to sleep without knowing whether you made it okay or not."

Heat travels to the back of Rachel's neck. "But I don't want to keep you up."

"Honey, we talked about this. Everything is okay. I can stay up for a bit longer and will still have plenty of sleep before Sun Salutation. Okay?" Job's voice is tender because he knows better than anyone how guilt can get under his wife's skin and run amok. "Tell me more about the house. Please."

It's been a long day, and her emotions are running high. She recalls what her therapist said about getting in front of panic. "Okay." Rachel takes a deep, steadying breath with one hand on her heart. She focuses on the facts. "There are a lot of people in this house. Like, a lot. I came in and met, like, four people down in the kitchen making an aspic." Well, perhaps the facts are a little exaggerated.

"A what?"

She stretches out on the bed to stare up at the ceiling. There's something about the blankness that's comforting. "It's Jell-O with stuff inside of it. Like a whole fish or something. Served cold."

Rachel can almost hear her husband wrinkle his nose. "Ew."

"Right? Some sort of curiosity that Vernon—do you remember him? He was the bearded guy with glasses. Anyway, it's something he's into right now. The flavor of the month, I guess. Remember Ted said they do that vegan month thing once a year?"

"Oh yeah! That sounded cool. That aspic thing, though," his voice turns incredulous, "I'm not sure about that."

Rachel is silent, gaze fixed on the ceiling as the scene in the kitchen swells around her. Even after spending a year traveling the world with Job, she still has a hard time meeting people, no matter how welcoming.

Job is sensitive to this shift in mood, as usual. "Are you okay, honey?"

She closes her eyes and sighs to coax her busy brain back into her skull. "It's nothing, really. Just tired." A deep sigh, a shuddering breath. "There are just so many people here, and not everyone is even here yet. It's...it's a lot."

"You don't like it." He's matter of fact.

"It's not that, I'm just..." She places the back of her free hand against her forehead. "Why did we decide that this was a good idea?"

They've had this conversation before. Many times. His words are familiar. "Because we just moved to a big city, and neither of us is good at making friends." That's kind of him to say. A lie, but kind. Rachel's the one who's bad at making friends, not Job. "Because we spent months in Chicago without talking to anyone outside of work. Because we need to do something different if either one of us can hope to be happy." He pauses, and she can hear a smile creep into his voice. "And because they have a cat."

She's silent.

"All we have to do is try it for three months. If you hate it after that, we can find something else." His tone is softer now, more cajoling as he paints a picture: "A little studio apartment near your work, and I'll find some sort of coworking space. We'll find a new Thai restaurant. Just three months."

"Three months."

"*And*, if you really hate it," his smile sounds big now, "you can blame me for *everything*."

She chews on the inside of her cheek. If Job was here in the flesh, she wouldn't feel so anxious. But he isn't, so she is, and she's thinking about the airports and the news and the virus.

The afternoon's pleasantness melts away under this new stressor. What if Job can't come home to her as soon as they think? "Do you think you'll be able to get a flight back?"

"What do you mean?"

Sitting up, Rachel surges with new worry. Her brain reaches for catastrophe with more ease than it has for breathing. "The airport was swamped coming into Atlanta, and Ted said he saw on the news that flights were getting canceled in Europe. Remember I told you how weird the airport was?"

The bugs are almost deafening on Job's side of the phone. "I do, and I get that people wanna be safe getting home. But, honey, everything will be okay. If it gets too bad, I'll get on the next flight out of Kerala. I promise."

Images of grounded planes, of breaking news coverage, flash out across Rachel's vision. She's almost to the point of no return. If that happens, she will find refuge underneath this new bed and stare at the wall until she can feel like a person again. "But what if you can't get a flight out of Kerala?"

Job seems to recognize the panic in her voice. He's talked her off the ledge many times over. "That's not going to happen, sweetheart," his voice is stern enough to get through the panic fog. "I'll finish up here in two weeks, and then it's home to Boston. To you. Okay?"

Her anxious brain does not want to believe him, but she still says, "Okay."

CHAPTER FOUR

AFTER PROMISING JOB THAT she will email the photo of Mona Lisa and her googly eyes, Rachel decides to take a shower. After a year of backpacking, a private shower in a private bathroom in a private bedroom is the zenith of luxury. For a moment, the anxiety subsides in place of excitement. With a grunt and some muscle, she plops the roller bag on the bed. A little travel dirt gets on the red-patterned blanket, and she does not dust it off. The left zipper is stuck in its corner, which forces the right zipper to pull double duty. After the lid flops back onto the mattress, Rachel is relieved to see that Job's packing job has not budged. Marveling at the way the shirts are rolled tightly and at how he's used her books and journals as a means of maintaining the bag's structural integrity, she allows herself a chance to miss him properly. Pragmatism is a love language; it says so here in this fastidious bag.

Rachel picks out some underwear, fresh jeans, a green sweater that reminds her of spring. Her heart flutters at the reminder, but then reminds herself that Job will be here by then. She won't have to do spring alone. It would be easy to sink into this particular anxiety sand trap, but Rachel refuses and takes a moment of pride in herself. Three years ago, the thought of spring would have sent her under the bed for the remainder of the afternoon. But she's been to therapy, she's had her *Eat, Pray, Love* moment, and she knows better. *Take a shower*, she tells herself. Tasks bring focus. Focus brings peace. *Wax on, wax off*, she thinks, though it is Job's voice she hears.

Towels are easy to find. There are two of them, both microfiber and folded as small as handkerchiefs. She holds one of them to her nose and can still smell incense on them. Smiling, Rachel leans her whole face into the roller bag and inhales deeply. Sandalwood is the aggressor amongst the lighter scents of sweat, dirt, a bottle of mouthwash that soaked everything through in Egypt. Underneath it all, of course, there's Job lingering on everything. Sawdust is hard to get out of fabric, not that she wants to; she is happy that he is here.

For now, she feels safe enough to bathe. With everything clutched to her chest, Rachel back-steps out of her sneakers and creeps into the bathroom, half-expecting someone to be there. After sharing countless bathrooms with countless strangers all these months, she half expects someone to give her a wave from the toilet as they continue doing their business. There isn't. Instead, she is free to use every inch of space alone. And even though the bathroom is small, it has a window and is big enough for a shower stall, sink, toilet, and laundry hamper. When she turns on the sink faucet, the water runs clear. This place may as well be Shangri-La.

Looking up, Rachel watches as her reflection begins to frown. The first thing she notices is how oily her skin is and the two—no, three—pimples that have cropped around her chin. She hates traveling for many reasons, but the acne might be the worst. After she turned thirty, she thought that her skin would settle down the way it did for most women her age, but it didn't. Any amount of stress makes her break out like any other hormone-riddled teenager. And her hair—her poor brown hair that she drew back tight into a spite-bun because she didn't know what else to do with it—is greasy.

Rachel leans in and tries to use her nubby nails to pop the biggest pimple, bringing only pain and probably further infection. She wants to dig out her comedone extractor, but that's packed away somewhere in a box marked "Bathroom: Rachel." It is in this moment, with both arms held aloft, that she becomes aware of a strong onion aroma wafting from her pits. Even though she is alone, Rachel still blushes and jerks her arms down. *It was a three-hour flight, for Christ's sake. Who smells this bad after a three-hour flight?*

Scrambling back to her rooms, she digs out her toiletry bag to find the deodorant stick that she is pretty sure she should not have been able to get by TSA and slathers it on. "What are you doing?" she asks aloud as she spins on her heel back from the bathroom. "Just go take a shower." Of course, when she speaks, she becomes aware of her travel breath and the fact that it must have wafted all over Ted's smiling face. She trips over her own shoes. Steadying herself on the nearest door jamb, she thinks, *Kill me.*

Slinging the toiletry bag onto the bathroom counter, she looks for her toothbrush. This is the only bag she packs, so naturally, it's a disaster. When Rachel is in charge, nothing is where it should be, ever. She does find the toothbrush, though, but it's Job's, which means that hers is still in India. While gross, there is no denying the flutter of happiness in her stomach at the intimacy. Still, she runs the bristles under scalding hot water before covering them with the last little bit of Colgate and starting to scrape at her teeth with fury. *Never drink coffee or soda on the airplane. Water and tea only. Fucking rookie.* Rachel continues to chastise herself as she scrapes the brown film from her tongue and spits it into the sink. She makes a horrible face in the mirror, inspecting her teeth before frowning at their slight yellowing. A new mental note files itself away: *Find a dentist.*

For now, though, she pulls a t-shirt off over her head. Or she starts to before she is interrupted by a knock on her bedroom door. Her frown deepens before she covers her belly again. "Rachel?" a voice she does not know asks in the hall.

"Just a second," she calls. Her reflection is still a sight, but at least her breath isn't strong enough to peel paint. She takes her hair out of the rubber band, shakes it from side to side, and flips it back into some semblance of shape. While she tries to fluff it out, it's not much better.

"Fuck it," she whispers before bounding to answer her door.

An elderly woman not much shorter than Rachel stands with a stack of towels tucked under one arm while her free hand holds a steaming cup of tea. "*Hola,*" the woman says, beaming with crooked, browning teeth. It is hard to say how old she is. Even though her brown face is wrinkled and she wears big circular glasses, her hair is shiny dark brown and cut into a fashionable lob.

"Oh, *hola.*" Rachel tries to remember if she saw this woman's face on the Skype call all those weeks ago.

"I brought you some towels," the old woman announces. Her accent is hard to place.

"That's okay. I have some...travel towels."

The old woman shakes her head and thrusts the stack into Rachel's arms. "These are very nice. Clean, too. I meant to put some on your bed, but I forget. Here, I brought you some tea. I'll put it over here." The small force of nature brushes into the room. "You had a good trip?"

"Yes, um, very nice." Rachel closes her eyes to concentrate. "Um, so sorry, but I don't remember if we've..."

The old woman laughs once, jostling the tea but not enough to spill any as she sets in on the mantle. "Sorry! I've heard so much about you that I feel like we know each other. I'm Francesca. Daniela's mom."

"Nice to meet you. I'm Rachel." She extends her hand to the woman who looks more at home in Rachel's room than Rachel has ever felt in her entire life. They shake long enough for her to feel Francesca's strength.

"So good to meet you in person. Do you like tabbouleh?"

"What?"

"I made some this morning before I made up your room. Daniela told me you'd been to Lebanon, and I thought maybe you would like it."

All of the information makes Rachel blush. "I do like tabbouleh, yeah." She shifts her weight to her left leg, feeling every bit a child. "Thank you very much for making my bed and stuff. You didn't have to do that."

Francesca shakes her head again and zips up her light grey hoodie before pointing to the bed with a swollen finger. "We had a big blue comforter in here for a long time, but I thought you wouldn't like it. So, I brought the red one up from the basement. Have you been to the basement yet?"

Rachel fights off a shudder when she looks at the comforter. It makes her double uncomfortable to know that the old woman had schlepped up two flights of stairs for her. "Not yet. Ted said he would show me around later after I'd settled in." She hopes this hint is enough to get the old woman to leave.

"Good," Francesca says, the word chopped off with a grin so big that forces her small brown eyes shut. "Were you going to shower?"

"Yeah, I was headed that way."

Francesca starts walking towards the bathroom before she speaks, "Let me show you."

Rachel darts after, practically wringing her hands. "Oh, you don't have to do that."

"This shower has a trick the first time. You've got to turn it all the way to the right and then to the left."

"I'm sure I'll figure it out," Rachel protests, trailing after the woman's confident stride.

Francesca is either hard of hearing or is choosing to be. She is already pushing the shower curtain to the side. "Come, come, let me show you."

Rachel swallows down a sigh as not to be rude, the way her mother taught her. "Yes, ma'am."

The old woman's hand, which Rachel now notes in the bathroom light as severely arthritic, clutches the metal handle and pulls hard to the right. Water bursts from the shower head. "And now, all the left for heat." She demonstrates, and steam starts to build almost immediately. "If you don't do it all the way to the left first, it won't get hot at all. But now you can make it as hot or as cold as you want. Sounds good?"

"Yes, ma'am."

"Good. I'll go make you a bowl of tabbouleh." Francesca leaves before Rachel can protest, closing the door behind her.

"What the fuck just happened?" Rachel asks aloud before shutting off the water.

She follows the vapor trail left by the small woman, looking at the closed door, back to the bathroom, and then at the cup of tea on the mantle. She does this a few times, her mind still trying to puzzle out what, in fact, just happened. Eyeing the tea with the most suspicion, she approaches as though the beverage were a bomb. Coming upon it, Rachel peers down into the amber liquid. The tea bag bobs in the center of the cup, anchored by the string wrapped three times around the handle. Tazo is printed plainly on the paper tag. *Probably not poison*, she thinks. Lifting it gingerly, she sniffs and is pleased by the scent of lemon. Still, she decides not to drink and returns instead to the bathroom.

Glancing in the mirror, she finds her hair to be even more of a mess. Francesca is probably in the kitchen now telling Markeya and Vernon what a disaster she is. Frustrated by the prospect, Rachel starts to tear off her shirt again. At least she can be a clean disaster. As the stinking black t-shirt flutters to the ground, there is another knock on the door.

CHAPTER FIVE

RACHEL DOES NOT GROWL, but she wants to. "Just a second," she says, her voice comically high. Putting back on the damp shirt, she reminds herself not to stomp as she answers the door.

Rachel's visitor is a woman about her age, pretty with a barrage of freckles on her face, barely over five feet tall. She has heaps of red hair braided into a style that a shield-maiden would approve of. She wears blueberry scrubs with a Patagonia vest. She holds a cup of tea. "Hello! So nice to finally meet you. Do you hug?"

"Uh, not really." Rachel crosses her arms, one-part defensive gesture and one-part infinitely aware of how bad she smells.

The woman does not bat an eyelash at the rejection. "I brought you some tea—chamomile, for your throat. With all the traveling you've been doing these last few days, I figured you would want something soothing." The small burst of energy thrusts the hot cup at Rachel, expecting her to take it.

In fact, there's no other option than to take the cup. "Um, thanks."

"You're welcome! I remember my flight back from Ghana being miserable. The air was so dry. I thought

I'd cough up dust at the end of it." There is a hint of what Rachel thinks is some kind of Southern accent lingering in her guest's vowels.

A little annoyed at the intrusion and out of over-politeness, she says, "I'm Rachel."

"Oh my god, of course." The tiny woman gently smacks her own forehead with her palm. "So, sorry. We didn't get to chat the other week. I was working. Night shifts all this month. Anabelle." She extends a cool, delicate hand. They shake. "It's so nice to meet you. Vernon mentioned that you're from Georgia?"

Rachel rolls the hot cup between her palms. There is no denying the pleasure in its warmth, even if she didn't exactly want yet another cup of tea. "Yeah."

Anabelle leans against the doorway. "What part?"

"Marietta." Rachel immediately clarifies, "It's a little north of Atlanta."

"Oh, yeah, I know Marietta! Some friends of mine went to school there." Anabelle is even more animated now. She takes a step back into a sunbeam cast down by the skylight, and her red hair shimmers. "I can't tell you how great it is to have another Southerner in the house."

Here it comes: the assumed comradery of geographic closeness. Rachel has done this dance before, especially when she and Job were living in Chicago. Meeting a Southerner in the middle of winter meant that she must share lamentation over the snow, despite the fact that she used to like it. But telling a Southerner that you *like* snow simply isn't done. "What about you?" Rachel asks, wishing that she were better at asking for space and worse at people-pleasing.

"New Orleans, born and raised." She beams, displaying perfectly straight and white teeth. Rachel briefly wonders if it is a requirement to smile at least six times an hour in the place. "Maybe the two of us can make a proper Southern supper one of these nights."

The idea isn't too bad. After months of eating flatbreads, Rachel thinks it would be kind of nice to have some proper cornbread. "Yeah, that'd be cool. Though I'll admit that I'm not much of a cook." This isn't true, she just doesn't like it.

Anabelle waves her off. "Don't worry about that. Sometimes having a co-conspirator in these sorts of things is key. Everyone eats pretty health-consciously around here, so I'll feel better about making it if I know you want it." Before Rachel can thank her, the red-haired woman launches onto the next thing, "Hey, do you need some help unpacking?"

"What? No, I'm—" Rachel glances back at the formidable stack of boxes at the far side of the room. It will take her weeks to get everything sorted. "Well, I couldn't ask for the help."

Anabelle's voice remains kind, if a little insistent, "You're not asking for help. I'm asking if *I* can help *you*. Let me get changed out of these gross scrubs, and I'll be right back."

The sound of heavy footsteps on the stairs catches both of their attention. Rachel fixes her eyes on the violet-haired youth trotting onto the landing wearing black thigh-high platform lace-up shoes that make them about six feet tall. They wear a black mini-skirt and purple tights, a lacy black top with drop sleeves, an elaborate leather corset that cinches their chubby waist, a ferocious cat-eye, and purple lipstick. Without a doubt, this is one of the most interesting people Rachel's seen since returning to the States. The young person is holding a cup of tea.

"As long as you don't sit down," the young person jokes, though it seems more good-natured ribbing than anything. Yet another inside joke beyond Rachel's comprehension. Before she can be anxious about it, though, the young person turns to her and explains, "Anabelle can fall asleep literally anywhere. Once, she fell asleep sitting at the kitchen island. Mid-conversation."

Anabelle sticks her tongue out at the young person. "Okay, well, I'd been up for thirty-six hours." She holds up three fingers like a Girl Scout. "But I solemnly swear to change my clothes, wash my face, and then come straight back."

The young person rolls their eyes. "Sure you will. Anyway, I'm Wren. They/Them. It's really nice to meet you."

Rachel works hard not to furrow her brow at the pronouns so that she can seem hip and in the know, like using pronouns is first nature to her. "Uh, yeah. I'm Rachel. She...Her. It's nice to meet you, too."

Wren smiles a little but not as wide as everyone else, which is a relief to Rachel. Wren offers up the cup in their hand and laughs when they notice that Rachel's hands are preoccupied. "I brought you some ginger tea, but I see someone got to you first."

"Twice, actually," Rachel says, leaning to one side of the doorway so her guests can spot the other cooling cup on the mantle.

Both of them chuckle. "Let me guess..." Wren hums. "Anabelle, obviously. I don't think Daniela is home yet...so I'd guess Francesca was here first."

"Yeah, she wanted to show me how to use the shower."

"You let her, right?" Anabelle asks.

"Like she had a choice," Wren jokes.

With that out of the way, Anabelle again moves onto the next thing. She turns to Wren and says, "Are you gonna help?"

"With what?"

Anabelle huffs, overdramatic. If not for the fine lines on the small woman's face, it would be easy to believe that she was still a teenager. "Rachel's unpacking."

"If she wants."

"Of course, she wants." Anabelle turns and starts to jog down the hall. She calls over her shoulder, "Y'all get started. I'll be back in ten minutes."

Wren and their purple lips turn to Rachel. They smile anew, a gesture that seems sage. "It'll just be you and me then. May I come in?"

Rachel flushes, embarrassed by the prospect. "Oh, you don't have to help."

But Wren's face is sincere, earnest-looking around their brown eyes. "I'd like to. Moving is such a pain. It'll go faster if we work together."

And Rachel, not wanting to do the job at all, relents with a solemn nod. She sips her chamomile tea, which is still hot and overly sweetened with honey, and makes room for Wren.

They lean down and start to unzip their shoes. "You lucked out with this space, y'know. One of the biggest rooms in the house. Perfect for two people, I think. Last guy who lived here had way too much space."

Rachel goes to the mantle and places the second cup of tea next to the first. "Oh yeah?"

Wren deposits the giant shoes outside the door before coming into the room, revealing that they are, in fact, a little short and pudgy. "Yeah, one of Renato's classmates. You met Renato on Skype, right?" Rachel nods as she remembers the boxy young man who laughed a lot. "Yeah, that guy was only here for a semester-long certificate course. Played the piano like you wouldn't believe."

Rachel leans against the wall, unsure how to approach the mess in her room at all. She settles for small talk. "That's cool. There's a piano downstairs, right?"

"Yes, in the front living room. It's just a keyboard, though." Wren comes into the room and gestures to the open suitcase. "Should I start taking stuff out of here, or do you want to start with the boxes?"

Her gaze flicks between the bed and the boxes. "Um, I don't know." The anxiety starts at the base of her spine, creeping up towards her skull.

Seeming to sense this, Wren places their hand on the suitcase. "Why don't we start here? Probably a bit more manageable than all of those boxes."

Rachel smiles sheepishly, thankful for direction. "That's a good idea."

"Should I start taking stuff out, and you hang it up? Or the other way around?"

"Um, if you pull stuff out, I can hang. Oh..." She sends an uncertain glance at the many cardboard boxes. "I don't know where any of my hangers are."

Wren plods—a shocking movement to Rachel after the graceful display in those platform boots—to the sliding door that reveals a modest walk-in closet with dozens of hangers, sturdy ones with felted gripping, a sure sign of wealth in Rachel's book. "I think we've got you covered."

"Wow," she whispers, going to inspect the new space. Even the Chicago house hadn't had this sort of luxury.

Wren returns to their post at the roller bag and begins to remove shirts. "This is some pack job," they say.

"Oh, yeah." Rachel chuckles with pride as Wren removes the creased pants and dresses. "Job is kind of a neat freak. It's his superpower."

"I'll say! I'll have to ask him to pack for me next time I go anywhere. Damn." They begin to organize the piles of clothes by type.

"He'd be thrilled," Rachel says, knowing the truth in her words and halfway hoping that Wren does eventually ask Job to help them pack. The morning after their fourth or fifth date, one of the ones where it had become socially acceptable for them to sleep together, he had spent the better part of their breakfast reorganizing her refrigerator. Had it been anyone else, it would have been weird, controlling, uncomfortable. But it hadn't been because it was Job, and Job was genuine, and he loved to fix. Rachel sighs with longing as she retrieves a handful of hangers.

"So," Wren snares her attention again, "Ted tells me you're from Atlanta."

No need to clarify with a Northerner. "More or less. You're going to school here, yeah?"

Wren hands Rachel a red blouse to hang. Almost everything is out of the bag now. "Boston University. Social work. Going for the Ph.D."

"Right on." Rachel winces right after she says it, feeling about a hundred years old. She tries to gain back some of whatever cool credits she had with Wren by asking, "Are you specializing in anything?"

They nod a few times while folding a pair of jeans over a hanger. "Violence and trauma."

Rachel's stomach does a strange flip, though she does not know why. After all, she has a therapist that specializes in the same thing. "Impressive."

Wren shrugs. "I'm minoring in gender studies." They turn their full cat-eye attention to Rachel. "What do you do?"

"I'm starting my new job at Harvard Medical School this week. I'm a grant manager for some of their hospitals."

They whistle as they take out the last sweater from the bottom of the roller bag. "Whoa, Harvard? Now *that's* impressive."

Rachel takes a few of the hung clothes back to the closet, trying to decide whether she wants the left or right side. "So, are you a Boston native?" she calls over her shoulder. "Or are you a transplant like everyone else?"

"My mom is from Puerto Rico, but I grew up with my dad's family in Rhode Island. When I moved to Boston, Ted wanted me to live with him. Pretty sure my parents made him. Him and my dad are cousins. Guess that makes us second cousins." Wren pauses, and Rachel can hear the bag's zipper scrape against something. "Oh my gosh, I love this. Is this your family?"

The floor might as well have come apart underneath Rachel's feet. Her heart begins to race, but she makes sure that she moves slowly when she turns around, walks up to Wren, and gently tugs the frame out of their hands. "Yes."

Confusion is written all over Wren's face as their voice fights to remain curious and nothing more. "You have younger brothers?"

Rachel does not look down at the picture but knows it well enough from memory. Her smile is tight, not a smile at all, really. "It's an old photo."

CHAPTER SIX

WREN FURROWS THEIR BROW, trying to decide what to do about the defensive tone. There is no doubt in Rachel's mind that Wren is empathetic to a fault. Like most empathetic people, they can probably sense that something is off but know that it is too soon in their acquaintanceship to talk about trauma. In the end, all they say is, "It's a nice photo."

Rachel cradles the frame as she approaches the left bedside table where she settles it, which is where she settles the frame wherever she goes. "Thanks," she whispers.

Still standing at the end of the bed, Wren looks on with distinct concern, with a deep crease between their eyes and their violet lips pulled into a sympathetic frown. "You okay?"

"Yeah, sorry." Her laughter flutters, insincere. "Just tired and cranky."

Even though they both know it's more than that, Wren does not press. Instead, they nod with understanding. "For sure. You've been traveling all day. Do you want some alone time to settle in before dinner?"

"Dinner?"

"Yeah." Wren starts towards the bedroom door. "We have a house meeting tonight around seven. It's where we sort of talk about what's going on with everyone, air out any grievances, and then make plans for the month. Shouldn't take more than two hours."

"Oh…" Rachel does not much care for the idea of meeting even more people. She feels scooped out, overwhelmed.

Wren's tone becomes even softer than before: "Try not to worry about it. Everyone is super nice and excited to have you. How about you take a quick nap, a shower, unpack, whatever? Have a little alone time, and then I'll come get you before I head down. Sound good?"

Rachel looks past Wren's shoulder at the closed door at the end of the hall. "Will Anabelle be upset?"

"Huh? Her?" Wren shakes their head. "Rachel, I promise you that she's asleep right now. Like, dead asleep. She's getting off a forty-eight-hour call. It'll take a miracle to get her out of bed for dinner. You can relax and take your time. I'll tell Francesca to leave you alone."

Rachel feels herself smile a bit at the offer. "Thanks, Wren."

"Sure thing." They squat down to pick up their platform boots. Before they leave, though, they say, "Did Ted give you all the apps and stuff? August, Signal, whatever?"

She recalls the laundry list of things that were supposed to make running the house easier. Job, of course, had downloaded everything the day they had received the acceptance email from Ted. "Yeah. I haven't made accounts yet."

"No worries. Vernon will help you with that."

"Cool." Rachel follows her guest to the door.

"See you in a bit." Wren's smile is encouraging, perhaps even promising that everything will be okay.

"Thanks." Rachel closes the door and is properly alone once again. She turns her back to the wood and slowly slides down until she sits with elbows on knees, remembering how to breathe. *Calm down. You've only been here for an hour. You can go more than an hour without having a total fucking breakdown. Get it together.*

She rolls her forehead across the coarseness of her jeans a few times before letting herself rest and stares at the framed photograph on her bedside table. It's not that she won't talk about her family; it's just that it's hard. And hard things are better left undone in Rachel's mind. The ends of winters are always hard because that means another anniversary is approaching fast and ruthless. This coming spring marks a decade since Rachel's father lost control of the family RV during a cross-country move, careening himself, her mother, and two younger brothers into a ravine that they never came out of.

Now, ten years later, the only surviving member of *that* family is sitting on the floor of her new bedroom on the verge of a panic attack because the only remaining piece of *her* family is halfway around the world. There's nothing she can do about that but be supportive. Because Job needs to be halfway around the world. Because Job had been on the verge of leaving the world a year ago. Dear, sweet Job, unconscious from gas fumes when she got home from work. Her Job. The Job that was always there, almost never was again.

So, she has to get up and do something. She must move so she doesn't bother him in India, at the ashram where he is trying to get himself together so they can move forward. So they can heal. She gets off the floor and lets her leaden feet lead her to the piles of boxes and starts to unpack with abandon. Boxes marked "Job" and "Rachel" soon have no delineation as she digs through books, art, shoes, pillows, sheets, piling things in a way that could only possibly hold any meaning to her. She finds Job's record player and sets it on the desk before promptly tearing through cardboard until she can find a portion of his collection. The records are carefully wrapped in foam peanuts; these are the only thing among all their belongings not wrapped in scarves or sweaters. Right on top is Job's favorite: *A Love Supreme*.

Wading through the mess, she plugs in the player and gets it going before gingerly adding Coltrane, knowing that Job would shudder to watch her place the record without first carefully dusting it with that funny little broom he keeps next to the player. She's gentle enough, though, and soon, the fluttering brass comes through the built-in speaker, which is fine for her. She turns back to survey the mess.

It is a disaster, which makes her feel guilty. The space was so pristine, so thoughtfully put together before Hurricane Rachel tore through. All the thoughtfulness that Francesca had shown her? Wasted. Oh, yes, the guilt is very heavy. So heavy, in fact, that she must recall the breathing technique her therapist had given her in Chicago after a particularly bad night she had spent locked in a closet with baby clothes in her lap and had knocked her forehead against the wall until she bruised. Not even Job had been able to calm her.

Placing one hand on her heart and the other on her stomach, she closes her eyes and takes a couple of deep breaths. "I am safe," she whispers. She knows that guilt over the mess is only a secondary emotion. The real root is the fact that she is unpacking, and unpacking makes her scared. Because luggage is a painful reminder of clothing strewn across a Wisconsin highway and her brother's light-up sneaker blinking on the side of the road like a safety flare.

No, she doesn't like unpacking at all. She wishes that Job was there to do it for her. In the near decade they have been together, she can count on one hand the number of times she's had anything to do with their luggage. The panic refuses to bend to the breathing exercise and begins to radiate in her fingertips, earlobes, and toes. I can do small things, she thinks and then convinces herself that it would be better said out loud. "*I can do small things,*" she repeats to the empty room.

She steps over her maddening piles and finishes emptying the roller bag and her backpack, finding homes for every article of clothing she finds. The socks, underwear, and bras find their way into a built-in organizer on the left side of the closet, which is the side she picks. If Job had been here, they would have done rock-paper-scissors for it. But he isn't, so the left side with the better organizational sense is hers. She will still hang up his clothes for him because that's her job, a job she can do.

Little by little, the boxes empty and are broken down into flat shapes that will stack nicely in a recycling can. Pieces of their lives, fake succulents, abstract brass sculptures, and wood carvings, are placed about on available surface areas. She makes notes of bookcases that she might want Job to make when he comes home to her. Her wooden desk is somewhere in storage with the rest of the woodworking equipment. So is her favorite chair and her favorite lamp. As the mental list grows longer, she decides to break out her tiny memo pad and pen. These things can wait a day, things that will make this place feel like home, as temporary as it may be. When Job comes back to her, she wants this place to feel warm, inviting. A place where he would want to stay.

Whenever Rachel grows the faintest bit overwhelmed, she remembers Job and says, "I can do small things."

She flips the album once in the middle of her unpacking and continues to find new places for new winter clothes.

The coat rack is unearthed and screwed together with ease, the way Job designed, and Rachel sets it up next to the door to hang her purse, scarf, and hat. Looking at it, she can almost remember what it was like in Chicago when they first moved there. Warm summers full of concerts in the park with homemade potato salad like her mother used to make. She smiles at that memory before life got too hard and messy for both of them.

A Love Supreme fades out on a prayer. It is easy to walk through the room again, and Rachel remembers that she needs to shower. She takes a clean towel that Francesca brought her and goes to do just that. Because she can do small things.

CHAPTER SEVEN

AT FIVE TILL SEVEN, RACHEL opens the door to Wren, whose hair is now acid green and cut into a fierce bob. They're wearing a black evening coat with a full-on pine green waistcoat that matches their lipstick. The outfit is complete with a pair of sensible leather platform boots, only four inches tall. "I'm a total wig fanatic," they explain upon seeing Rachel's expression as if the hair was the only thing that needs explanation.

"Um, am I underdressed?" she asks, looking down at her white button-down shirt patterned with tiny cacti and her black jeans. Her slippers now seem wildly inappropriate.

"Nah." Wren waves her off with a friendly smile. "I'm overdressed, which is how I prefer to be at all times. Ready for dinner?"

The smell of the evening meal catches Rachel off-guard, and her stomach growls loud enough for both of them to hear. "Yeah, I guess so."

"Excellent." With a flourish, Wren offers their arm to Rachel. "May I escort you to supper, madame?"

Despite herself, Rachel laughs and takes the youth's arm. There is something rather charming about Wren.

She did not expect to like anyone so quickly. "Did Anabelle wake up?"

"Her light is on, but that doesn't really mean anything. She'll either be there, or she won't." Rachel wishes she could be dismissed so casually. She wishes that she could sleep through this, too. "Watch your step on this first one coming down; it's steep," Wren warns, demonstrating the right way to plunk down off the landing, a delineation that Rachel had not noticed when coming up the stairs.

A lot of sounds are coming from the kitchen: laughter and overlapping conversations. Thankfully, Wren does not force her to interact with everyone yet. Instead, their steady arm leads her to what appears to be a foyer where the chandelier that she saw peeking out earlier is now in full view. It is quite a sight with several dozen strands of crystals gathered in the center to make for dazzling light. There is a large circular mirror across from the chandelier, making the light loom ever larger. Beneath the mirror is an end table tastefully decorated with a small metal statue of a woman dancing, a potted purple orchid, and a blue book with the word "Guest" emblazoned in gold on its cover. Rachel releases Wren's arm to flick through the pages, caught by stray phrases that thank Ted and Daniela for welcoming so-and-so into their home. Some notes are addressed to individuals in the house, and Rachel quickly realizes that they are goodbyes from residents. Sentimentality at its peak.

Wren points to the open door before walking inside, prompting Rachel to pause on her investigation and follow. In truth, the dining room is only a portion of a giant room, pocket doors splitting it into halves.

The decorating is impeccable, done the way rooms in Wayfair catalogs are done. There is lots of blue velvet, brass fixtures, concrete-topped tables, and many big leafy plants. The furniture is probably worth more than Rachel's student loans.

The table, which is a concrete slab sealed in lacquer and has bright brass legs, is set for eleven. Matching white flatware and silverware are placed on top of pristine cloth napkins. There are serving platters and bowls full of sundries. Six taper candles burn in matching crystal holders, while others burn on the mantle and in the fireplace. There is a brass chandelier, something decidedly more modern than the rest of the house, with its light dim enough to act as its own pseudo-candle flame.

She is impressed, maybe even a little overwhelmed, as she approaches the table and chooses a seat at the end.

"Oh, no, no," Ted's voice interjects. Rachel turns to see him hurtling towards her with a bottle of wine and a new navy-blue blazer. "You've gotta sit in the middle seat. The most important person sits in the middle."

She flushes and cannot find the words to graciously reject his offer. Instead, she allows herself to be ushered to the seat in front of the fireplace. The soft candlelight backlights her with something akin to a halo. "This is too much," she says.

"Not at all. It's your first night with us. Can I get you some wine?" Ted holds the bottle out for her inspection like a server. "Or maybe you're feeling water instead? I bet your flight was dehydrating. What would you like?"

She doesn't know much about wine except that some are red, others white, and some still are pink. This one appears to be red. "Wine would be nice."

"Fantastic, be right back." Ted dashes off back down the hallway.

Rachel is exhausted just watching him go. "He's always like that," Wren says at the end of the table without looking up from their cell phone.

"Oh yeah?" It's hard to believe.

"Oh yeah."

In the hall, Rachel can hear one door squeak open and then another. Then comes the scrambling sound of clawed paws on the ground. "Cornelius!" someone calls from the kitchen, and the sound skitters that way. "Who's a good boy?" comes the chorus.

Rachel's interest is piqued to the point that she stands up and leans to look down the hall. She had seen the dog, a gorgeous red and white Australian Shepherd with big blue eyes, during her interview. It was ultimately the reason she agreed to move into the house. She loves dogs, especially because she's never lived anywhere that's allowed its tenants to have one. For a while, she thought about getting a fake note from the doctor about needing an emotional support animal but ultimately had never found the time.

Someone in the kitchen throws something, which sends Cornelius, the dog in question, racing down the hall towards Rachel. Her heart swells at the sight of such focused joy as the athletic creature jumps to catch the projectile before it hits the ground. "Good boy, Cornelius, good boy," a new woman's voice calls.

"Dani, is that you?" Ted's voice cries from the other end of the house.

"Yes."

"Rachel is in the dining room!"

A gasp of delight, and then an average-sized woman with a not-so-average-sized stomach swings herself around the corner. "You're here!" she says, positively glowing.

Daniela had not seemed so pregnant over the video call. Now, she is so pregnant that it physically hurts Rachel to look at her. Goosebumps explode all over Rachel's skin, her mouth dries out, she feels ill. She knew that being around a pregnant woman would be hard, but she never imagined it would be this hard. She wants to vomit. Instead, she manages to say, "Hi."

Despite her size, Daniela maneuvers herself to Rachel's side of the table in a moment. She draws the new addition into a brief embrace. Contact with the pregnant belly is almost enough to destroy Rachel. She struggles out of her host's arms, and Daniela pretends not to notice the discomfort. "It is such a pleasure to have you here! Is everything set up in your room? Do you need anything at all?"

Rachel focuses all her attention on Daniela's left eye, dark brown in color and framed in a thick fringe of black lashes. It's easier to breathe that way. "No, thank you. Francesca brought me some towels earlier. It is lovely."

Daniela is still smiling, her teeth perfect and white. She reaches out to touch Rachel's arm. Rachel keeps staring into Daniela's left eye. "I think it's safe to say that we're all happy you're here. This is the biggest the house has ever been."

Wren interjects, "Except for last summer when those Ghanaian drummers lived here for a month. But once Job arrives, we'll hit a new record."

Ted enters with a stemless wine glass and an open bottle. Smiling, of course. "Isn't it great? Ugh, I'm so happy to see a full table." He sets the glass in front of Rachel's placemat and pours generously. "Does anyone know if Yukiko is going to make it on time?"

The man with glasses and blonde hair—*Vernon*, Rachel reminds herself—comes in with a steaming metal pot that he puts in the center of the table on a cork pad. "She texted the group. Said she'd be back in twenty or so but that we should start without her."

"Sounds good." Ted shifts back to Rachel. "So sorry, I can't remember. Do you have the messaging app yet?"

She shakes her head. "Not yet."

Vernon raises his hand and waves. The gesture is vaguely endearing, though Rachel wonders if that's because he's wearing a cardigan with elbow patches. "I'll get you set up after dinner."

"Thanks very much." Rachel takes her seat and a hearty swallow from her wine glass.

Ted claps his hands together. "Okay, then we'll get started. Vernon, you ready?"

"Yep. Let me go get the cheese." Vernon starts but then makes a short stop, throwing an incredulous look over his shoulder. "You eat cheese, Rachel? I should have asked when you got here."

She raises her glass to him. "Sure do."

He nods once. "Great. Be right back."

"Dinner!" Daniela cries down the hall.

Somewhere upstairs, doors open, and footsteps can be tracked as they descend the stairs. Anabelle is among the first to arrive, her red braids fraying at the ends.

She looks tired but still waves and takes the seat across from Rachel.

"So, how was your trip? Did you fly right in from India?" Daniela asks.

Before she can answer, the scrabbling footsteps catch her attention as the dog trots out in front of Francesca, who carries a full platter of asparagus spears. He wags a stump of a tail as he keeps his eyes trained on the plate.

"He's so cute," Rachel whispers.

Daniela, still within earshot, claps with delight. "That's right, you haven't met Cornelius in person yet. Come here, Cornelius."

Attention diverted, the Australian Shepherd makes a beeline for Daniela underneath the table. He sniffs about until he comes upon Rachel, realizing that he does not recognize her scent. Excited, he shoves his nose underneath her nearest hand, to Rachel's delight. "Hi, gorgeous, hello, hello."

"Cornelius, this is Rachel. Rachel, this is Cornelius," Daniela says.

"It's a pleasure to meet you, Cornelius. I've been looking forward to this for weeks," Rachel says. The dog stops sniffing and looks at her, just looks at her with blue eyes that are actually brown at the top of the pupils. For a moment, she swears they are breathing at the same time. She strokes the top of his head and whispers, "Good boy."

Cornelius sits and leans his head into her thigh. She scratches behind a dappled ear.

"Looks like Cornelius has a new best friend," a new voice says. When Rachel looks up, she sees Markeya taking a seat near the door. The two women wave at one another. "He's a good dog, y'know. Shit at snuggling, but a good dog."

Rachel looks back down at Cornelius and smiles. "Oh yeah?"

"He knows when people are sad," Daniela says affectionately. "If you have a bad day, he'll sit at your feet."

Then I guess he'll never stand up around me, Rachel thinks as the dog continues to press his head into her leg. She looks back up at the table, which is now nearly full, and there are few faces she does not recognize. Instead of focusing on that, she focuses on Anabelle, who is still waiting for an answer, as she pours a bit of wine and hands the wine bottle to Francesca.

"Sorry, got distracted," Rachel says.

"Totally understandable. Just look at that face."

"Right? But anyway, someone was asking about the flight?" Anabelle nods. "I didn't fly straight from Kerala. I stayed with a friend in Atlanta for a couple of weeks to get my bearings. The flight out of Atlanta to Boston is super short, but the traffic was horrible. Accidents in both directions." She does not add that she saw those accidents as omens. "But it was okay when my Lyft got off the interstate and into the neighborhoods. We made good time, I guess."

"Oh, good!" Anabelle says.

"Who hasn't met Rachel yet?" Ted asks.

"Me," says a woman at the far end of the table. She has softly curled hair that hangs around her shoulders and a neat snub of a nose. "Lorelei."

"Hi." Rachel can't quite place the accent, but she thinks it's German.

"And me," says the boxy young man to the left of Daniela, which forces Rachel to look around the pregnant belly. "Renato."

"Nice to meet you," Rachel says quickly so she can return to looking at Anabelle.

"Yukiko should be here soon. She was finishing up with some recordings," he explains in accented English.

Ted stands up at the end of the table and claps. Everyone quiets down to watch him. Vernon's hard-heeled shoes clomp against the wood floor well before he appears in the doorway with a steaming pot. "Well, with that all being said, I'd just like to get this dinner kicked off real quick by raising a toast to our newest addition." Everyone raises a glass of wine or water. Vernon raises the cheese vat a little higher. "Rachel. I think I speak for all of us when I say that we are glad to have you here. It's exciting to welcome someone to Boston, especially after such a long and interesting trip. And we're excited for Job to join us and get his workshop set up out in the garages and bring that space to life. It is a pleasure. Welcome!"

They all echo the sentiment and reach out to touch their glass to hers. Rachel flushes at the attention. When everyone is in their seat, Vernon scoots by Anabelle to hold the pot aloft when suddenly he says, "Shit. Hold this, please," he shoves the handle into the red-haired woman's hand and jogs down the hall.

Everyone watches the doorway for his return. His footsteps hurry back.

"You forgot the aspic, didn't you?" Markeya clucks her tongue.

"I didn't forget it," he tells her as he carries a cutting board with the mold on top, his hand steadying both. "I wanted to make a dramatic entrance. Rachel, would you move that pot a little to the left for me?"

"Sure."

Vernon places the cutting board down, gets his fingers around the edges of the silicone, and gently lifts. A disgusting squelching sound ricochets through the room. Cornelius lifts his head off Rachel's leg to twitch his ears. The plastic comes away free and clean. There is some polite clapping.

The gelatinous heart wobbles but holds its form out of the mold. Though the meat makes the object opaque, she can make out the ventricles and valves and other parts she learned about biology. Everyone holds their breath as Vernon pours the near-boiling nacho cheese atop the aspic and the cold heart melts to meat.

CHAPTER EIGHT

THE HEART COMES APART completely in a matter of seconds. In its stead is a steaming pile of meat and cheese. Vernon holds Rachel's gaze and grins; the candlelit scar on his eyebrow makes him look even more mischievous than earlier. "Welcome," he says.

"Thanks so much. It's really nice to be here." She means it, mostly. This wiggling mass of food has her second-guessing some things.

"Okay, Vernon, will you tell us what the hell that thing is?" Wren asks, their green lips twisted in disgust.

"It's an aspic," Markeya supplies.

"Meat Jell-O," Daniela explains to her mother.

"Why?" Francesca asks, leaning forward to pin Vernon with an incredulous look. "It wasn't good in the seventies."

Vernon chuckles as he sets the leftover cheese on a trivet in front of the empty seat to Rachel's right. In all the excitement, she had not realized that the soft-spoken woman with curly brown hair, whose name she has already forgotten, has left an empty seat between them. For a moment, Rachel wonders if she still smells. After a discreet sniff, she knows that is not the case.

"Well," Vernon continues, "there's plenty to eat for people who aren't interested in the aspic. Markeya made the chili for the mold but help yourself to whatever is in the big pot. Then I put together the vegan nacho cheese."

"He used his potions, so it will stay creamy," Markeya rejoins.

"Potions?" Rachel mouths across to Anabelle, who rolls her eyes.

"Francesca made the potatoes," Vernon says, pointing towards a piled-high platter at the far left of the table. "Ted made the salad, Renato sautéed the asparagus, and..." His quick blue eyes scan for anything he has missed. "Somebody poured tortilla chips into a big bowl."

"Me," the quiet brunette says.

"Thanks much, Lor," Vernon says as he sits. "I think that's everything."

"*Bon appetit*," Daniela says, mimicking Julia Child.

Hands move quickly then, seizing upon plates and serving utensils, taking out reasonable portions to ensure that everyone has enough to eat, passing to the next person. Rachel receives tray after tray until her plate is full of color and texture. "Did anyone want some aspic?" Vernon asks, waving a big spoon.

"I'll try some," Ted says, standing up with his fork. "Just a bite." He rounds the table to lean between Anabelle and Vernon and selects a well-cheesed portion. He puts the fork in his mouth. Everyone watches for his reaction, which is immediate. Disgust first, then forced enjoyment as he comically rubs his stomach and says, "Mmm."

Even Rachel laughs. Soon after, the dinner party settles back into itself, conversation splitting off in ways that make sense to the diners.

There are no more takers on the aspic, though the chili's consensus is very good when hot, made nearly perfect by the nacho cheese. Rachel wonders if Vernon's feelings are hurt that no one is eating what must have taken at least a day to complete. Still, even he only has a discreet bite before moving onto the hot version. She cocks her head to the side and wonders what the aspic's purpose is if no one eats it.

"Rachel, are you all settled into your room?" Francesca asks.

"Not quite, but I'm getting there. Thank you again for setting up the space," she says before taking a sip of wine to wash down the rich chili. "It's cozy."

"So, where are you from?" Markeya asks, leaning one elbow on the table as she reaches for the chip bowl. "I missed your interview because of work. Everyone says you're lovely, of course, but when those crates started to arrive, I got excited."

"Yeah, what does your husband do again?" Renato asks. Rachel rather likes the sounds of his voice; it's deeper than his body suggests.

Rachel flushes with pride, though her tongue gets twisted with it. All she can manage is, "He's a woodworker. Cabinets, chairs, tables—that sort of thing."

Ted claps the tips of his fingers together. "We're so grateful to have had the space to accommodate his work."

Rachel nibbles on the garlicky asparagus as she thinks about her husband's excitement upon finding the listing on Craigslist. With Rachel's job start date looming over the couple, it had been a huge relief to find a living situation that was perfect for him and suited her well enough. "Job is over the moon. It would have been a whole thing to find, like, a maker's space or something. The rent on the storage space was so high that we may as well have lived in it."

"Honestly might have been a better option than a lot of studios in Boston," Vernon says.

She scoffs as she recalls looking at one-bedroom apartments hardly big enough for a dog, let alone a person in Allston that was going for nearly thirteen-hundred dollars. "You ain't lyin'," she says, then blushes. The wine has relaxed her tongue. She catches Anabelle's gaze across the table, and both women smile.

"I'll show you tomorrow, but the space needs some work," Ted says, and everyone's eyebrows go up in agreement. Rachel worries that it will be a lot more work. "But I've got no doubt Job will make good use of it."

"He was going to make some cabinets, right?" Markeya asks.

"Oh, yeah. He's got plans. He sketched out some designs during a long layover." Rachel recalls a stack of cocktail napkins, along with a whiskey sour, liberated from the Delta Members Lounge. "Probably red oak or mahogany. We had a great supplier in Chicago that would ship to us out here."

Markeya flings a dramatic hand to her chest. "Yes, please. With a light stain? Ugh, that would brighten up the kitchen so much!"

"Are you and Job both from Chicago originally?" Daniela asks, though Rachel is not tipsy or brave enough to look at her.

She shakes her head and works on the roasted potatoes on her plate. "No, we lived there for a couple of years. We're both kinda from all over."

"Military brats?" Wren wants to know. There is a question about the picture frame lingering between the two of them.

"Not quite," Rachel replies.

Before Wren can ask another question, Markeya launches into a new line of thought. "Vernon and I lived in Chicago for a while. Gorgeous city. Super queer. Where were you?"

Rachel recognizes already that Markeya is a talker, the type of person that does not really need anyone else in the room to speak but prefers an audience whenever possible. A drama kid. A fundamentally good person, but the kind of person that Rachel finds exhausting if forced to socialize for extended periods of time. "Eagleton—not Chicago proper, but it's easier to say."

Markeya nods, which makes those blue corkscrew curls on top of her head dance. "When my contract ends at Beth Israel, I'll go back. Great communal living situation."

"You lived with a bunch of people there, too?" Rachel asks.

She grins. "Oh yeah. Nine folks. Everyone was super into gardening and sustainable living, which I loved. I lived communally all throughout college, on and off after that."

Rachel frowns in thought as she finishes her chili and cheese. "Does living 'communally' mean something other than roommates? Sorry, this is all really new to me. I had roommates in college, but we were basically just haunting the same room."

Vernon immediately comes to her rescue. "Communal can mean a lot of things. So yes, we are roommates, but this situation is more intentional, more about sharing resources and building community."

"Which is especially important in a big, international city like Boston," Daniela adds.

"Yeah, I don't think any of us are even Massachusetts natives," Wren says.

The investigation into this truth is interrupted by the sound of a door opening in the kitchen. Moments later, a young Asian woman dressed in all black, whom Rachel remembers is the pianist, enters the dining room. The two gazes meet, prompting both to nod in acknowledgment.

"Sorry I'm late," the young woman nearly whispers.

"Not a problem, Yuki. There's plenty to eat," Daniela soothes in a motherly tone.

"Have a seat next to Rachel. You two remember one another, right?" Ted asks.

"Yes. I'm Yukiko." She bows slightly, an overly formal gesture that Rachel finds classy as hell. "It is nice to meet you, Rachel."

"Likewise."

Yukiko scampers silently to the other side of the table and sits to Rachel's right. People begin handing her platters, and she fills her plate. The young woman smells like old books and rosin, a smell that Rachel remembers well from her days in high school orchestra. While Yukiko places the chili pot back in place, she speaks up to say, "My director told me how things are really bad in Italy right now. Does anyone know anything about that?"

Vernon nods with some insistence. "My sister is backpacking there for a month, but we think she should come home ASAP. Flights are already filling up."

Rachel does not know what everyone is talking about, not really. She just knows that the airports were full of scared tourists. She has done her best not to watch or read the news for the last year. Life is hard enough without everyone else's problems.

Ted's face shifts into one of unnatural concern. "What about Job, Rachel? Is he going to fly back as soon as he can?"

Rachel sets her fork aside and begins to twist her fingers in her napkin. "Um, well, there haven't been any reported cases in India yet, so I'm hoping he can finish out his two weeks then fly back."

"What's he doing there?" the woman with the serious face asks at the end of the table.

What is he doing there? Rachel repeats to herself. It is a good question with a good answer, but it's hard to tell strangers: Um, he tried to kill himself last year because we lost our baby and he didn't really know how to deal with it, so we packed up our lives to help him find a reason to live again.

"It's, uh, a spiritual retreat," she says. "A little bit of Buddhism, a little bit of yoga, chakra stuff, veganism to cleanse the soul. You know how it goes."

"Why didn't you stay?" Anabelle asks; the question is curious and not combative.

Rachel reminds herself that the world is not out to get her but does not look up from her lap. "Well, it was his turn to pick a thing to do. We went to Norway for two weeks for me at the beginning of our trip. He wanted to round up things with this thing in India. It made more sense for him to do that by himself while I was setting up here, y'know?"

"Nice!" Francesca says. "How was Norway?"

Rachel wants to whisper, *Barren.* Instead, she says, "Beautiful."

CHAPTER NINE

THE ROOM IS WATCHING HER now, and Rachel is well aware of their curiosity. She looks like the kind of person who has a secret, of course. She wonders if now is an appropriate time to excuse herself from the table.

"You don't think he'll have any trouble getting back to the States?" Vernon asks.

"Well, things seem okay right now. His flight is on the twenty-first, so he'll be here in two weeks. He needs to finish up his..." She can't find the right words. "He needs to be there."

Ted's voice softens. "We'll be happy to have him home."

Rachel smiles a little to herself. "Me too."

"Now that everyone has had something to eat, shall we move over to the meeting portion of dinner?" Ted asks the group. Some people nod, and some people bring out their phones. Daniela sets her cell close to Rachel so she can see the screen. There is a bulleted list under the title: *House Agenda.*

- Empty dishwasher/clean kitchen after use
- New bike lock?
- Garden planning

- Snow considerations
- Update group calendar
- Planned maintenance

For some reason, this is the thing that makes living in the house real to Rachel. Her stomach drops, worried that there will be some sort of fallout from the conversations around these points. She does not like conflict, much less when it is between people she does not know.

"Life updates first, Ted?" Daniela asks.

"Oh, right. Silly me! Yes, let's get started with life updates. Anyone want to go first?"

The table is silent. Rachel inches one eyebrow up in query. "I'll go," Markeya offers. "So, things are going well, more or less. My new unit is kind of a nightmare, but I'll get used to it." She twirls one of her curls. "My mom is on a new medication, which seems to be helping with her symptoms." A few people offer their second-hand relief. "Dad is still stressed about her, but she's optimistic. Time will tell, of course. Fingers crossed. Oh! The seed catalogs came yesterday, so if anyone wants to look at some seed porn, let me know, I've got you covered. I'm hoping to put in some orders for the garden in the next two weeks or so. I'm thinking at least six different types of tomatoes this summer." Markeya trains her dark brown eyes on Ted.

"Yum," he says at the head of the table. "Well, for me, things are going great. Nervous with all the baby prep, of course, but mostly excited. My project in the South End is moving forward pretty smoothly. The team hopes to start construction by the end of the month." He looks over to Rachel and explains, "I've been fighting to get an old building remodeled for a year now. We finally got approval last month, and we're now moving to the demo phase."

"Is it a knock-down-the-old-building kind of remodel?" she asks. She understands the purpose of this life update now and is terrified to give hers. Self-sharing might as well be torture.

"No, no. A gut, definitely, but not a knock-down. At any rate, that's mostly what's on the plate right now. Hopefully, we will have some renovations on our own property now that Rachel and Job have joined us. Whenever you guys are ready to talk changes, let me know."

Rachel gives a thumbs-up.

"I'll go next," Francesca says, moving her plate to the side, so she cab clasp her hands together. "This month is the eighth month I've been here since Venezuela. I've grown accustomated—"

"Accustomed, Mom," Daniela corrects.

"Accustomed to the way things happen here." Francesca shrugs, then smiles. "I still like things my way, but I am not as upset as I would be before. Having so many young people to talk to is good for me, and my English and talking to you people makes me feel young. I have a new job at the BMC that I like and am excited to be a grandma again. That's it."

A beat of pause before Wren picks up the gauntlet. "School is going well for me. My classes are challenging this semester, which is good. I have to write a lot of papers in the next few weeks, so you may not see as much of me as usual."

"The same for me, as well," the German woman says. It's all she says.

"Renato and I have a performance coming up in three weeks," Yukiko announces. Despite the softness of her voice, it still shocks Rachel to hear. "If anyone wants to go, let me know so I can get tickets."

"Yuki didn't tell you that she is going to compete in a competition in New York next month," Renato says.

Daniela claps to Rachel's left. "That's incredible!"

"We will see," Yukiko says. "The competition will be very hard."

"You'll do great," Renato says, leaning forward so he can beam down the table. Rachel wonders if the two of them are together.

The young woman blushes at the compliment. "I will need to practice a lot. I hope that is okay with you all."

"Of course," Vernon assures. "I hope it's okay to sit in while you practice sometimes."

"That would be very helpful. It's easier to prepare for an audience with an audience." Yukiko sets her knife and fork to one side of her empty plate.

"What about you, Vern? Any news?" Daniela asks.

"Nothing interesting, really. I got into some Twitter beefs with a couple of lawyers based in D.C. Read a book about irrigation systems in Ancient Rome that I do not recommend. Made an aspic. That's about it." His body language is stiff, cagey, ready to move on. He shrugs. "Yeah, that's about it." Rachel senses a kindred spirit in him.

Anabelle suddenly straightens in her chair, and Rachel realizes that the red-haired woman has been close to sleep this whole time. "Okay, so residency is slowly killing me." Her cornflower-blue eyes are a little wild. "And I love it! I got to do a really cool surgery today that I will talk about later with Markeya since the rest of you are so squeamish."

"For good reason," Wren mutters into their water.

Anabelle either does not hear or chooses to ignore the comment. "I'll be starting a new surgery rotation in two weeks! In the meantime, lots of baby delivering, preventative care, blah, blah, blah. Super ready to go with Daniela to her next OB visit, though!"

"Oh yeah! Baby is growing fast these days. Only a few more weeks before D-day. Right, little baby?" Rachel refuses to look at Daniela's happiness.

"How are you feeling?" Anabelle asks, sounding like a doctor now.

"Oh, just fine. Sleeping is a little tough."

"I'll say," Ted joins, chuckling. "I've been sleeping on the couch in our room."

"I run too hot," Daniela explains, though no one has asked for an explanation.

"When I was pregnant with her," Francesca says, pointing a knobby finger at her daughter, "I did not sleep a full night for nine months. She danced all night in my stomach."

"I'm suffering the same now, Mama." Daniela grunts. "That was quite a kick. Do you know that we are talking about you, little love? Does anyone want to feel?"

"I do!" Anabelle cries and jumps out of her seat to come to their side of the table with renewed vigor. The red-haired doctor squeezes in between Daniela and Rachel. "Excuse me. Where's she moving?"

Heat presses into Rachel's chest. The room is shrinking.

"Here."

Anabelle cups the top of Daniela's stomach. "Wow, what a kick. Do you want to feel?"

It takes a moment before Rachel realizes that the doctor is talking to her. She meets her gaze for a moment then reverts to staring at her napkin. "No, thank you."

Anabelle teases, "Oh, no, are you freaked out by pregnancy, too?"

Rachel stands up quickly, jostling both Anabelle and Daniela, clattering her fork onto the floor where it gets tangled up with her napkin. The dog scrambles to search for any fallen treasures. "I'm so sorry," she announces, her voice sounding far away. "I need to excuse myself. I'm not feeling well."

Somehow, she's already on the other side of the room when someone calls, "Do you need us to bring you anything?"

"No." She remembers her manners: "No, thank you."

Rachel trips upstairs with a few tears already running from the corners of her eyes. The bedroom door is barely closed behind her before a sob pops out of her mouth. Her legs cave in slowly, allowing her to fall to her knees in a gentle motion. "You're okay, you're okay," she chants to herself, trying to break through the black haze. But she and the part that her therapist calls her "higher self" are not okay; all parts of Rachel want to call Job. They can't call Job because Job is asleep somewhere else. They can't call Job because Job needs them to be brave and strong on their own.

Sometimes, when a heart is breaking, it is easier to heap on the hurt than it is to feel better. Right now is one of those times. Rachel finds the smallest cardboard box among the packing, the oldest among them all, and undoes the tape. Inside are tissue paper-wrapped mementos from what feels like another life. Love letters from Job. Poems by Rachel. A photo strip of her and Job from an aquarium photo booth. An invitation to a friend's wedding they did not attend. A sonogram marked *Little Bean 3/3*. That photo alone is enough to scald Rachel's hand, but it does not hurt nearly enough. She keeps digging all the way to the bottom.

The frame is wrapped up neatly with a pink tissue bow. It rips, and then Rachel is carefully unfolding her prize. No, not carefully. Reverently. Out she comes, just like the day she was born: slowly at first, then all at once. Their baby girl stares up at Rachel with her milky brown eyes, perfectly shaped lips, and upturned nose. Everything beautiful in her daughter is surely Job's doing. Everything broken, everything cursed inside of Siobhan's fragile body is all Rachel's doing. She knows that. She knows.

Stumbling to her feet, Rachel cradles her daughter's photo in her arms and collapses into bed. The tears come, swallowed up by a freshly laundered pillow. She is silent and allows the picture frame's corners to bite into her palms. Nothing hurts as exquisitely as this.

CHAPTER TEN

RACHEL WAKES UP EARLY the next morning to take a shower and change into an outfit that helps her resemble herself. She puts away another box of clothes in the closet and packs her daughter's photo back into the old cardboard box. It will be some time before she dares to look at it again. She emails Job the photo of Mona Lisa like she promised and does not tell him about her breakdown. At half-past seven, her stomach rumbles hard enough for her to venture downstairs. With any luck, no one will be in the kitchen this early in the day.

When she opens her bedroom door, though, the smell of baking bread hits her square in the face. She feels like a cartoon character enticed and lifted by an enchanted wind all the way down the stairs and into the kitchen. The small German woman, Lorelei, sits at the giant island with a book in one hand and a fat cat in her lap. She looks up at Rachel upon entry but says nothing. The two settle into silence until Rachel can no longer stand the quiet. "Good morning," she says.

"There are bagels," the woman replies. She gestures to the bread box, a double-decker affair, and Rachel finds it stuffed with bagels dotted with seeds. "They're fresh."

"I could smell them upstairs. Where did these come from?"

"Made them."

"Really?"

She hums. "Couldn't sleep."

Rachel can sympathize, but she is impressed. "Oh. What, um...what flavor are they?"

"Regular? They've just got poppy seeds on them."

"Oh, right. Okay, if I have one?"

"You live here, yes?" Her mousy face draws into confusion.

Rachel wraps her arms around herself in a gentle hug. She feels so little in this big kitchen. And, after last night, she feels every bit a fool. "I guess so."

"Then have a bagel. They'll be gone soon. As soon as Renato wakes up. I have mine with cream cheese and salami. In the fridge." She returns to her book.

Rachel thinks that Lorelei's suggestion is a good one, so she goes to the industrial-sized fridge and must use both hands to swing open the well-sealed door. Considering how many people live in this house, it is surprisingly organized. This is no hostel fridge. There's one gallon of milk, not four. There are glass containers neatly labeled with titles and dates aside from a lunchbox with Markeya's name stitched into the side. There is no ownership here. At the front is a huge tub of cream cheese, the size brunch places buy. The weight is awkward in her hands. A package of sliced salami rests nearby.

She turns, uncertainly eyeing the teak wood cutting board settled on the nearest corner of the counter.

Depositing her ingredients, she plucks a bagel out, slices it with a serrated blade, and pops it into a toaster oven next to the sink. Rachel begins to search for a plate.

"Far-right cabinet," Lorelei comments softly.

Following the advice, she finds the matching flatware. She plunks a plate down in front of the toaster oven and wills the three minutes it will take to toast the bread to speed. The silence is deafening. To distract herself, she allows her gaze to wander over the shabby-looking cabinets. *Are these particle board? In this place? Job is going to have a field day.*

The kitchen island is of different craftsmanship, something more recent. The pounded copper top is a more fashionable phenomenon. She rests a hand on top of it and hums.

"Do you need something?" Lorelei asks.

"Huh?" Rachel glances up and realizes that the German is looking at her. "Oh, no. Just thinking about how old this counter is. Seems so different from the rest of the room."

"Ted could tell you," Lorelei replies, still petting the orange cat in her lap.

"Who's that you've got there? I saw Cornelius on the call, but that little fella didn't make an appearance."

"Klimt."

"Like the painter?"

"Mhm." Lorelei strokes the cat in question behind the ears. Rachel can hear it purring across the kitchen.

She looks closer at Klimt and decides that he is kind of ugly. His white nose is smudged with orange fur like a grease stain, he is fat, his tooth is snaggled, and his right ear is tipped. *Where on earth did they find such a beast?* "Who does he belong to?" she asks.

"Daniela's, but he belongs to everyone." Lorelei sets her book down and picks the fat orange and white cat up so that his arms and head are swung over one shoulder. "He gets lonely sometimes, so you might hear him in the hallway. I let him sleep in my room most nights."

The toaster oven timer beeps three times. "That's nice of you," Rachel says as she snatches the hot bagel off the rack.

"Not really. He cries if he's in the hallway alone, and that keeps everyone awake."

"So, more pragmatic than anything." Rachel takes the plate to the cutting board. She opens the top drawer nearest her and is relieved to find the silverware. The cream cheese spreads easy, the salami is then affixed. When the two halves meet again, they come together to form an excellent sandwich.

Rachel rounds the kitchen island, feeling wildly out of place, and takes the seat opposite of Lorelei, creating a distance that feels safe between them. With both elbows on the table, she picks up the hefty breakfast and takes a bite. The crunch of the toasted bread, the creaminess of the cheese, the salt of salami. It is divine. "Mmm." Lorelei is silent. She probably already knows how good it is. She had the same thing for breakfast herself, after all. Rachel still feels compelled to say, "This is incredible."

"I'm glad you like it."

Silence returns, and Rachel worries if she has already branded herself as a total nutcase that can't even get through a dinner without crying. She worries if she's already ruined Job's chances of enjoying his time here in this place. She worries if everyone hates her. She keeps eating, focused on the air holes in the back of the breadbox. Her face is hot with anxiety, but she fights to stay in control of her emotions.

"Change is hard," Lorelei states quietly. Rachel turns to look, finding both the German and the cat staring back at her. The young woman has intense brown eyes that seem to blaze in the blooming morning light. "It's a little easier when you don't have to do it alone."

Weight rolls off of Rachel's chest. For a moment, everything seems manageable. Before she can say *thank you*, they are interrupted by footsteps bounding down the front staircase. The dog enters first, his white and red body hurtling into the mudroom door. Rachel jumps at the sound. When she turns, she sees Cornelius dancing on his hind legs. Ted follows, dressed in a soft gray button-down and black slacks.

"Good morning, good morning," he greets. He pauses next to Rachel and places a hand on her shoulder. "Feeling better?"

She blushes. "Yes, thanks."

"Glad to hear it. Shall we tour the house when I get back with Cornelius?" Ted offers.

"Take her now," Lorelei says, setting Klimt in the middle chair. "I can walk the dog."

"Are you sure?" Ted asks.

"Yes," she replies as she gets up and takes her plate to the dishwasher. Moments later, she and Cornelius are out the door and headed down the drive.

Ted smiles out the window as he watches them. "That's so cool. When Lor moved in, she was terrified of dogs. Now, look at her." Animated once more, Ted spins on his heel and rubs his hands together. "Shall we get the tour started?"

Though Rachel wishes she had some coffee, she agrees.

"Fabulous. Okay, so here we are in the kitchen. Like I said, this is where we spend most of our time. Over here are all of the dry goods." He dramatically flourishes towards the shabby cabinets and then begins to open all of them, starting with the far left. "Snacks, cereal, Asian sauces and spices, liquor are here. Then we've got our canned goods, aluminum foils, and parchment papers, dried beans. Then the flours, sugars, oils, and baking ingredients. The far-right has all the spices, broths, giant bags of rice. The shelves are all labeled in case you have a hard time finding anything. If you ever think we are out of anything, head down to the basement. That's where we keep run-off."

Rachel marvels at the bursting larder. The only place that she has ever seen such stocked shelves is the grocery store.

"And then, over here, we've got the fridge. Everything inside is fair game unless otherwise labeled." He reaches up and grabs a fancy-looking label maker. "We use this for names and dates. We do try to date everything to limit spoilage. We do compost." He points to a copper can on the windowsill over the sink.

"That makes sense."

"Um…" Ted scans the counters. "Oh yes, here is where we keep the tea and coffee, right over the coffee pot." He opens the cabinet to reveal dozens of glass jars full of tea leaves and four giant bags of coffee beans. "Microwave here, dishwasher here...oh, and the laundry room is right here." He practically skips to the small laundry room, where a new washer and dryer sit stacked together. "This pantry area is where we keep all of the kitchen gadgets. InstaPot, stand mixer, blender. You name it, we have it."

Rachel's head swims with information, and they have barely gotten started. Ted seems to notice the overwhelmed look on her face. He says, "It's okay! I know it's a lot. Just ask anyone what you're looking for, and we'll find it. That's the only way to look after this place. It's just too big for two people. Ready to see the rest?"

What other choice do I have? Rachel wonders. "Lead the way."

"Excellent!" He heads full force down the hallway but stops at the closest door. "Are you a basement person or no?"

"Not really, no." People being underground before they die is highly unnatural, in Rachel's opinion.

"Then we'll skip that for now. Nothing much down there but storage and extra groceries. We'll just look at the fun stuff." He winks and opens the doors that were closed the day before. "So, here's the informal sitting room." The room has a good deal of morning light in it, tastefully furnished with blues, blacks, and grays. There's a desk and chair, a loveseat, a small coffee table, a plethora of green plants, and a plush armchair. The curtains are pulled back, and look onto the snow-filled front yard. "It makes a good room for conference calls, casual conversation. I use it as an office space from time to time."

"Everything is so neat," Rachel observes.

"We try to keep tidy, so everyone can enjoy the space. It just works better that way."

"'It' being the house?" She wonders how the owner of a communal house must trick their tenants into behaving.

"More like the community as a whole. Neatness begets care, or at least I think so." He grins and gestures across the hall to the room that Rachel knows will become her favorite. One wall is composed entirely of bookcases, and those shelves are packed with paperbacks and hardbacks alike. Across from it is a fireplace that looks like it might, in fact, be in working order, as evidenced by the fire screen and ash pail. The hardwood floor here is covered by a massive Oriental rug, which is, of course, blue and white. There is a small desk with a green glass shaded lamp, like the ones in old libraries. A divan and a well-loved armchair and ottoman are available for seating. Two windows point towards the backyard, one of which is a small stained-glass affair with a blue, gold, and green mosaic. This room makes her feel holy.

"Wow," is all she can muster.

Ted makes a sound of pure pleasure, and she finds him, once again, beaming. "Do you love books?"

"How could anyone look at this room and not love books? I feel like Belle in that scene from *Beauty and the Beast* right now."

He smacks his lips. "Well, unfortunately, this library isn't two floors."

Of course, he knows Disney details. He's probably one of those adults who likes to go to Disney World for a vacation with his friends once a year. Or, a more likely scenario, he pays an obscene amount of money to see *The Lion King* on Broadway whenever he's in New York on a business trip. He's naïve about life, and Rachel tries not to judge him for it. It's not his fault that his life has been easy.

"In any case, feel free to use this room as much as you want. I only ask that if you use the fireplace, you make sure it's out before you go to bed." Ted places a dramatic hand on Rachel's shoulder, face drawn into mock seriousness. "I have this horrible fear that a hot log is going to roll out and catch, like, all the books on fire."

"You've got it," Rachel says, shrugging away from his touch. It's not Ted; it's her. Too much sensory input after a night like last night equals even more crying.

"Let's check out the formal living room next," he says and starts to the foyer.

Rachel shakes her head as she looks up at the massive chandelier again. "It's so funny to be in a house with a formal and informal living room."

Ted looks over his shoulder at her as he puts his hand on a new doorknob. "Why funny?"

"Like, what even is informal living?" she asks as he opens the door. "Do we have to dress up to be in the formal living room?"

"Only if you want to. I encourage you, really," he teases.

Rachel smiles. For all his puppyish energy, it's hard to not like Ted. She steps past him into the living room, which she saw in shadowed light the night before. The formal sitting room has the blue velvet theme that's echoed in the dining room. The same brass fixtures. A fireplace to match, complete with a dozen or so burned-down candles. Lots of natural light flows in from the French doors that point at a snowy patio. The large plants in here must be very happy. There is a nice electric keyboard tucked in the corner with a variety of sheet music stacked on top. It is easy to imagine a candlelit concert taking place.

"This is really nice, Ted," Rachel says. "Everything goes so well together."

He holds up his hand to reject the compliment. "I can't claim credit for any of this. My former business partner actually designed the space. Each room has a theme, too. I think yours was..." Ted squints his eyes together, "spring, maybe."

Rachel shudders with memory but does not speak to it. She pretends instead that she is cold by wrapping her arms around herself. "Yeah, with all that light, I guess so."

"So, all of those double windows act as doors in the summertime. They go right out to the patio. But, with the cold, we keep 'em sealed with the plastic wrap stuff." His smile turns apologetic. "After you spent so much time in better climates, I feel obliged to tell you that it does get warmer here."

"Can't say that I believe you."

He chuckles. "That's understandable. Do you feel up to braving the cold long enough to check out the garage?"

The idea of checking on Job's stuff brings her a tiny sliver of happy expectation. "Sure thing. Let me just go grab my shoes and coat."

"I'll do the same and meet you back in the kitchen in three minutes."

Three minutes later, almost to the second, Ted joins Rachel, who is fixing herself a cup of coffee with the miraculous manifestation of the stuff that greeted her when she came back downstairs. Whoever buys the coffee in this house has good taste. "Ready?" Ted asks.

She raises her cup at him. "Ready."

"Follow me." He opens the doors that lead from the inside world to the outside.

The cold is a slap in the face. Rachel quickly zips up her winter coat, knowing that she will have to purchase something heftier immediately. She misses her Chicago wardrobe, but sacrifices had to be made. There is a light, fresh snow on the ground that melts when touched by their boots. Instead of taking a right towards the street, Ted rounds the left corner, and Rachel is immediately arrested by the size of the squat, gray house fraying at the seams. It's not a garage at all, more of a carriage house with a giant barn door on the front with a smaller human-sized door built into it. This door is padlocked and quickly unlocked with a key that Ted fishes out of his fine snow coat.

"Be careful on the step," he warns as he disappears into the dark. Rachel follows. Inside smells a little of mildew, a little of wood, a little of fresh paint, a little of age. "Give me a second to hit the light. No idea why someone thought putting the switch on the other side of the room was a good idea." He adds quickly, "We can have that fixed if you want."

Rachel's eyes struggle to adjust to the dim, though they don't have to strain long. Two industrial fluorescent bulbs start to sizzle awake, shining down on the great open space and all their crates. She sighs in relief. Job may not be in the house, but he is in this room. She does not run to the crate that contains his workbench. Almost, not quite. When she finally touches the roughly hewn wood, she thinks, *A great many things need to be fixed.*

CHAPTER ELEVEN

"SO, WHAT DO YOU THINK?" Ted asks, his voice nervous. With the lights on, Rachel can see why this place barely cost them an extra $200 a month. The wooden floor is warping in its corners, suggesting some long-ago water damage; the walls are splitting at the centers, displaying at least three different paint colors; all but one window is cracked. She does not imagine that the plumbing works. In sum, it is a shithole.

"It's ..." she chooses her words carefully, "...rustic."

Ted laughs louder than Rachel has heard before, and she wonders if this one or those that came before it is the genuine article. "You're too kind." His fancy shoes with the hard heels click across the wasteland until he is standing at her side, looking with her at the closed crate. "It needs some attention, that's for sure. We never spent much time with it because there was no real interest in the space. I tried to rent it out a few times to maker's spaces. Nothing ever stuck."

Goody for us, I guess, Rachel thinks as she turns to Ted. "And you think we'll stick?"

Ted smiles serenely. "I hope so. This place deserves to be used." He points up at the ceiling, which sags in some places. "Don't get me wrong, I know that this thing will take time. But, after all the time is spent fixing it up, think about how nice it'll be."

Rachel crosses her arms, frowning as she looks up at the off-white stains that populate the space above her. "You're an optimist," she says, trying hard to not sneer. For her, people who maintain their optimism just haven't experienced enough of life.

"Eternally," Ted says. He takes a seat on a smaller crate, patting the space next to him. Rachel drags her feet a little but ultimately joins. The two stare out the door to observe the settled snow on the driveway. "Optimism gives me vision, y'know? When we bought this place, the whole thing was gray. I mean, literally gray. Gray exterior, gray interior, gray furniture. Gray. And that's not even mentioning how dirty it was." He gives a conspiratorial look from the corner of his eye. "Seriously, Daniela and I spent three weeks just scraping dust off walls. My parents thought I was crazy for buying this place. They thought it was a total teardown."

Rachel glances back up at the ceiling and thinks that Ted's parents may have been right.

"Even Daniela wasn't completely on board by the time we closed," he confesses.

"Really?" It is hard to imagine Daniela anything less than enthusiastic.

"Yeah." He pauses long enough for Rachel to observe a pensive look on the dark-haired man's face. "But she trusted me. She trusted me about the house, the community, the money. Everything. Her trust in me was, and is, the biggest honor of my life."

Despite her bitter inclinations, Rachel's heart softens towards the man. It's hard not to like him when his love for his wife is obvious. "Why do you think she trusted you so much?"

"That's an excellent question. We talked about it a lot that first year, about why she trusted me and went ahead with my crazy scheme." He inclines his head. "I fully acknowledge that buying an old house to stuff full of people is a crazy scheme. But she told me she trusted my instincts because I trusted my instincts. And I know that I'm impulsive, but I do things that I think will benefit others in the long run. Because when I walked into that gray, gray kitchen, I saw people in it. I saw someone cooking at the range. I saw someone making soup. I saw people living their lives. Together."

Her smile catches Rachel off-guard. "I guess I understand that." She leans back on her elbows, puffy coat material whispering against rough wood.

Ted mirrors her. "Do you want to know what I see when I look at this place?"

There is no denying the appeal of optimism now. "Sure."

He sits up and frames the room with his hands. "So, I'm thinking that we rip up this wood floor and put down polished concrete instead. Makes more sense for the woodworking aspect, and correct me if I'm wrong, it would also add a really cool industrial lounge vibe."

Ah, yes, the industrial lounge vibe that all woodworkers long for, Rachel thinks, amused. She will let Ted take her on this ride because Job would be ecstatic to hear all about it.

"We'll knock out that bar area for more space. Unless you want to keep it." He looks over to gauge her reaction.

"No, no, this is your dream. Conjure away."

He grins. "Okay, so we knock out that bar, which leaves us pretty much with a perfect rectangle. We group up the tools however you and Job want them. Definitely need one of those wall things with the holes in them so he can hang up his equipment. Do you know what I'm talking about?"

"A pegboard?" Rachel guesses, thinking of the garage in Chicago.

"Sure!" Ted bounds to his feet and hurries to the far wall. "We'll hang the pegboard up right here so all of his tools can be in one place. And then, we'll line up the tools along these two walls and put the giant work table here." He jumps back, stretching out his arms and legs like a star. Rachel laughs, realizing that Ted prefers to be seen as a performer, maybe even a clown. "We can get some roller chairs, some toolboxes, some plants."

She rolls her eyes at the prospect. Imagine getting sawdust all over a succulent. "Yeah, what if we just got a big tree to put in here?"

He pivots on his heels, striking a Superman pose. His eyes are almost childish with glee. "I *love* that idea."

He looks so earnest that she does not have the heart to tell him that she was joking.

"We could probably get a decent size fig or something. Put that right over here in the corner?" He whips out his phone and starts typing away. Before Rachel can get another word out, he says, "Done, I love it."

Rachel is horrified. When the plant arrives and dies, it will be her fault. She imagines Ted, crouched in the corner of a room, holding the last remaining leaf at the base of a luckless fig, staring at her with a face that asks, "Why?"

"Uh, did...did you just buy a plant?"

He shoves his phone back in his pocket. "No, not yet. I'll ask Markeya what she thinks would be a good fit. We have some time to think plants."

Rachel sighs in relief.

"Let's see..." Ted taps his chin. "We'll also remodel both bathrooms. I won't even want to have you look at those. Disasters, believe me."

She does. "Wait, two bathrooms?"

"Oh, yeah." He points to a door that she assumed led to a closet. "There's a whole upstairs loft situation. I'd take you up there, but there isn't a floor."

"I think I'm beginning to understand why you didn't bother remodeling this place."

He returns to his seat on the crate. "Like I said, I was waiting for the right incentive. Now that you and Job and all of Job's things are here, a picture is starting to come together."

"Glad to hear it," she offers politely.

Ted hums, leaning his elbows onto his knees. After a minute of nothing but the sound of the breeze outside, he turns his head towards her and asks, "Rachel, is everything okay?" He isn't smiling now.

Her brows draw together in consternation, looking over all of Job's belongings, the space, the peeling paint. "Yeah, everything is fine. We shipped twelve crates, and I see twelve crates. All in perfect condition."

"That's good to hear, but I don't mean right now... last night?"

She blushes, prepared to be cast out of the house for being a total nutcase. "Oh. With dinner. Yeah, it's..."

Ted's voice is patient, kind even. "It's a lot. It's okay to be uncomfortable."

The blush deepens. "What gave me away?"

"Nothing. I just...it's a lot," he repeats. "Moving alone into a place with a bunch of other people who know one another really well is, I imagine, very overwhelming. It doesn't help that we're loud."

A sharp snort of laughter blows through Rachel's nose, surprising them both. "Sorry."

"There's no need to apologize. Really." He pats her shoulder twice before standing. "You're allowed to take your time to warm up. And if you don't wanna be as loud as, say, me or Anabelle, that's fine, too. There's no need to rush. How about I leave you in here for a while in case you want to unpack or whatever?" A grin touches his lips. "I only ask that you don't go upstairs because it is really fucking dangerous."

She nods, still embarrassed by her actions at last night's dinner. He inclines his head and leaves the carriage house, closing the door behind him.

The first thing Rachel does, of course, is open the door to the upstairs. A part of her still believes that this is a murder cult and that whatever sketchy shit they're doing is surely hidden in the attic of the decrepit mausoleum. The door reveals a staircase that hooks to the left five steps in, up into some mysterious place that smells like mildew and old cigarettes. Ah yes, the place where secrets are kept.

Maybe I should have 9-1-1 dialed and ready to go in case there are cultists or something up here. Ultimately, she goes without her phone at the ready in case she needs to grab onto something to keep herself steady. Standing on tiptoes, she distributes her weight on each groaning stairstep, more and more certain with each passing one that she will fall straight through to the first floor. These walls are peeling, too, though they are more yellow here than they were downstairs. *Guess the guy who owned this place did all his smoking in the attic.* There's a loosely bolted handrail to her left but grabbing it seems both gross and pointless.

At the top, she is met with silence. No cultists or misdoings. He hadn't been lying. There really is no floor, only beams and exposed wires. Ted was right; this place is fucking dangerous. There is a lot of light, though, which makes the loft less ghoulish and more haunted. There are a couple of closed doors and slanted ceilings, but that's about it. Nothing to write to Job about; no monsters, just mold.

She makes her way back down, taking a few photos of the crates for Job, which she promptly attaches in an email. He has not yet written her back about Mona Lisa's googly eyes. She types out a brief message about the garage and Ted's plans for it. She shuts off the light and stands in the gloom long enough for her vision to adjust. When they do, she goes to sit on the crate again and stares up at the ceiling. Closing her eyes, she tries to imagine the sound of the bandsaw, the hammer, the gentle jazz. She tries to imagine the space finished. She tries to trust Job's crazy scheme. When she opens her eyes again, the yellow water stain is still there.

CHAPTER TWELVE

IN THE BRIGHT FEBRUARY morning light, Rachel's phone rests face up on the bathroom counter. A beauty influencer chirps on about her simple twelve-step up-do tutorial. After the sixth step, Rachel's arms grow too tired, and she releases her hands before angrily brushing her hair. She wishes she had more patience, wishes that she had learned to do her own hair years ago, but that hadn't been something her mother had taught her. *Hair left down or put up in a ponytail is as good as it needs to be,* she almost hears her mother say. So, Rachel leaves her hair down, flicking it back over her shoulders and shellacking it with hairspray. In a maroon button-down shirt with its white flowers, her reflection seems serviceable. Nervousness has brought color to her cheeks without blush. It has been a few years since Rachel has had a first day of work; the nervousness is familiar.

Her phone pings again, the tenth time in about as many minutes. The night before, in the kitchen, Yukiko prepared ginger pork, and Renato distracted her with his dancing. Vernon sat patiently beside Rachel as she downloaded all the apps she should have downloaded when Job had. Vernon does not comment on this and instead helps get her profiles up and running on Signal,

Google Calendar, Splitwise, August, and Todoist. Vernon isn't quiet, but he is secretive, as Markeya had suggested. He asks about her job, wanting to know whether or not she is excited to start at Harvard but doesn't offer much about his own job at Google. Rachel decided that maybe Vernon does work for the CIA.

But now, her phone is inundated with notifications and text messages from the house group chat. She picks up her phone and clicks in, surprised that there are so many people up already:

Wren:	Anyone seen my platforms?
Daniela:	Which ones?
Wren:	Red with silver studs
Daniela:	Mudroom
Renato:	Anyone have dinner plans tonight?
Vernon:	Not me. Fair game.
Renato:	We still have that grouper?
Daniela:	Should be in downstairs freezer
Renato:	Who's feeling ceviche?
Lorelei:	Me.
Anabelle:	ME ME ME
Vernon:	Need some limes from the store?
Renato:	L I M E S
Vernon:	I'll go around noon. Drop small stuff on Todoist before, and I'll try to pick it up.
Daniela:	Thanks, Vern!

Rachel chuckles once to herself then sets her phone to silent. The constant beeping will be the death of her. An email notification pops up at the top of the screen.

It's Job. Her heart flutters the way it did when they first started dating. Leaning against the bathroom sink, she reads it at once:

Hey Honey Bunches,

Who knew Da Vinci could be improved with googly eyes? Wouldn't mind seeing more pictures of the room if you had the time to take them. Everything is okay on this side of the world. I only want to eat steak, though. Haven't told the guru that. Might want to keep me at the retreat longer. A lot of people are starting to head home, some of them leaving pretty early. I'll keep my ears open about whether or not I should leave early, too. Are you okay? You didn't call me yesterday, and I was getting worried. Will you email me before you head off to the big first day? I'll be up late so we can talk after.

Love you,

J.

Though she worries that other pilgrims are leaving the ashram ahead of schedule, she cannot deny how pleased she is to hear from him. Of course, Job would stay up to ask about her day. His constant consideration was one of the main reasons that Rachel had agreed to marry him. Warmed by his concern, Rachel hits reply:

Hi Sweetness,

Still alive! Everything and everyone is super nice and accommodating. Ted took me to the garage where all the crates are. Wow, what a shithole. Honestly, a lot of work (see attached photos). He seems game to do something about it, but we'll see if that's bullshit or not. Maybe when you get here, you can decide how much work needs to go into the place for it to be worth your time. I think you'd like Ted. The two of you are very...enthusiastic. He was going off about all of his ideas and then latched onto this joke I made (I told him he should put a big tree in the corner), and I'm pretty sure he's going to buy a tree. Kinda crazy, right? Anyway, I'm okay. It's all just a lot. Big group dinner on Saturday, brunch on Sunday, another meal together last night. Wren is cool (they go by they, not she). They were kind enough to help me put away some of our stuff. And Anabelle is nice. What am I saying? Everyone is really nice. Do you remember the German woman? She's quiet but kind, sorta deep. Haven't gotten to know the students yet. Not sure if they're interested. Anyway. Yeah. Finishing up my hair and makeup now. Google says the walk should take about 20 minutes, so I'll be headed out soon, so there's plenty of time to get there. I'll call around five my time. If you don't answer, that's totally fine. Sorry that this is a lot. I miss you.

Love always,

R.

After hitting send, Rachel wonders if she should mention her panic attack about Daniela's baby update at her first dinner. No, it's better she didn't. No need to cause Job any undue stress. Besides, they both knew that a baby in the near future would be a reality. They had agreed to the terms. With any luck, at the end of three months, they will live somewhere else without baby updates, or sonogram photos, or anything like that. She can only hope.

She turns off all the lights in her room and opens the door to the hall, where she nearly trips over Klimt. His fat body is stretched across her threshold and does not move as Rachel recovers her balance; he merely watches then yawns. "Jesus," she mutters, glaring at the cat. He gives her a slow blink, struggles to his feet, then waddles into her room. Rachel starts after him but stops—she does not want to waste time rummaging through her room for that orange beast. She has no love for the creature after spending all night with her head under a pillow to drown out his yowling in the hallway.

At one in the morning, she had opened her door to him, trying to lure him in. After all, her roommates had warned her that he got lonely in the night. But he did not seem to want anything to do with her at all. Instead, the iridescent globes of his eyes had watched her in the dark, totally still, until Rachel grew too tired to wait and returned to bed. Moments later, the yowling started back up, and she had to seek refuge underneath the Ikea pillow.

Klimt will not make a fool of her. She trots down the staircase and joins half a dozen others in the kitchen. The smell of coffee is hot in the air. Underneath that acrid scent is a cinnamon note that Rachel finds wafting from a half tray of roasted sweet potatoes on top of the stove. "Good morning," Lorelei greets softly from her seat at the island.

"Morning," is Rachel's sheepish reply.

Daniela, Renato, Ted, and Francesca greet her with a jubilant: "Buenos!"

Yukiko merely waves.

"There's coffee in the pot," Francesca says as she starts to get up with an empty plate. "I'll show you where the cups are."

"Oh, that's okay. I know where they are." Rachel starts for the cabinet between the sink and stove. Francesca beats her there, pulling out a large glass coffee cup. "Thank you," she says.

"Here, I will get you some coffee. Do you take cream?" Francesca asks as she goes to the fridge, opening it with much less resistance than Rachel had met with the day before. Maybe the old woman is simply stronger than Rachel. It seems a distinct possibility.

"I do," she replies while splashing her cup full. She checks the time on her phone, relieved to see that there is enough time for breakfast.

"Good. Here's sugar. You like sugar?" Francesca wants to know.

"I do."

"Good." Francesca plops a sugar caddy in front of Rachel, pats her on the butt, then puts her dirty plate in the dishwasher.

"Can I make you some eggs?" Ted asks from the kitchen table.

"No," Rachel says quickly. Her face is bright red from the butt pat.

Ted is on his feet, too. Apparently, no one in this house takes her protests seriously. "It'd take two seconds," he tells her. "I poach a mean egg. My scramble is even meaner."

"Let him poach an egg for you," Daniela says, nodding vigorously with a hand on her stomach. Rachel looks away. "Then put it on top of some of those sweet potatoes."

"Seriously, there's no need for such a fuss," Rachel says, crossing her arms and wishing that Ted and Francesca weren't so close to her.

"No fuss at all," Ted says with a wink. He's already filling a small pot with hot water. "It's not every day that someone starts a new job at Harvard Medical School."

"First day, huh?" Renato turns to face Rachel. He is a handsome young man with dark facial hair, a long thin nose, large eyebrows, and a gold hoop earring in his left earlobe.

"Yeah." Rachel fixes her coffee, sweetening it with three heaps of sugar and too much cream.

"Nervous?" he asks.

Caught off-guard, she glances over at him. "A bit."

"You'll be great." Renato's grin is dimpled and sincere at the same time.

"Thanks," Rachel replies, secretly pleased.

The hood over the oven clicks on, wind roaring at first and then adjusted to a reasonable level. "Poached, right?" Ted asks as he plops a water pot onto the stove.

Rachel checks the time: Google tells her that she needs to leave the house in fifteen minutes so she can be fifteen minutes early to the new office. "Oh no, I've got to—"

"Do you have a route to work?" Daniela interrupts. Not meaning to, Rachel looks at her. If not for the swollen belly crammed behind the table, no one would suspect that she is pregnant. Her straight black hair bobs at her caramel chin, which has not doubled with pregnancy weight the way Rachel's had. Dressed in a black turtleneck made of some expensive cotton, Daniela is as regal as a queen. As if Rachel needed more reason to resent her. But Daniela does not know this, and so her kind smile remains as she says, "You're on the Longwood campus, right?"

"Yes." Rachel's attention refocuses on her coffee.

"Hm. Looks like you'll want to head down Cedar to Columbus. Do you know where that is?" Rachel shakes her head, watching the swirl of cream as it becomes chocolate brown. "That's the street you turn down to get to the house. If you take a right and walk all the way down the hill, that's Columbus." Rachel's head swims with the instructions.

"Walking through the neighborhood is faster," Renato rebuts. There is the tinkling sound of a knife against a glass jar.

"I'll take you," Lorelei says, and Rachel returns her attention to the kitchen. The German dusts her hands free of crumbs over her plate. She finishes chewing her bagel before continuing, "My lab is in Countway Library. Where are you working?"

"Gordon Hall?"

Lorelei nods and says again, "I'll take you."

"Thanks."

Ted places a hand on Rachel's shoulder. He smells expensive, like the way fancy department stores smell. "Go, sit. I'll bring you a plate."

Rachel grips her coffee cup. "Oh, no, that's okay."

"Go, go." He shoos her with all the affectation of a Southern grandmother. "This will take two minutes."

Renato scoots closer to Yukiko at the table, waving Rachel over. Her eyes dart to Daniela, stomach flipping. To reject now would be rude to the whole table, not just Ted. Resigned, she holds her coffee with two hands and sits at the very end of the bench. All eyes are on her. "Um, so…" She stares straight ahead, noticing that

Francesca sits right across from her, playing some kind of matching video game on her phone. "What do you do, Francesca?"

"Huh?" The older woman looks up, readjusting her glasses. "Me?"

"Yeah. What do you do?" Rachel asks, second-guessing herself now. Is it okay to ask an elderly immigrant woman what she does to fill her days? Should she have asked something else? Would it have been better to ask Renato about his work?

"Oh, I water the garden, walk the dog, those sorts of things."

"That's not all," Daniela interrupts, but Rachel still won't look at her. "Mom works as a translator at BMC."

"Oh, wow, that's really cool. Do you go to patients' rooms?"

"If they ask me. Mostly I am on the phone. Someone calls me to talk to a patient about this or that, and I talk to the doctor or nurse or whatever."

The sound of stomping upstairs startles them all, and everyone watches the kitchen door. Vernon enters, blonde hair sticking up at all ends. He wears faded plaid pajama pants and a gray t-shirt stained to hell. "Has anyone read the news?" There is an edge to his voice.

"Not this morning. Why?" Daniela asks. She places a hand on her stomach.

He looks down at his cell phone. "The virus made it to Boston. Two people who attended a conference over the weekend tested positive."

"What does that mean?" Ted asks from the oven as he cracks an egg over the pot.

Vernon's expression is dim; the scar on his eyebrow looks more sinister in the morning light. "That means that two people tested positive and that a lot more people have it."

Everyone is still for a moment. Yukiko is the first to speak. "Are they quarantining them?"

"Yes, at Beth Israel," he says, and everyone understands his seriousness now, his borderline panic. The virus that lurks in the lungs is tearing its way through China and Italy, killing hundreds, and has found its way to them. And now that virus is lingering in the air that Markeya breathes.

"She'll be okay," Daniela says as she starts to scoot out from around the table. Francesca stands so that she can get up and place a comforting hand on Vernon's arm. "She'll be okay."

Vernon stiffens, turns on his heel, and disappears up the hallway. His steps are quiet as they retreat.

No one seems to know what to do or what to say. Ted moves first, going to the fridge to take out a plastic box of greens. Daniela stands in the kitchen doorway with one hand on the frame and the other still on her stomach. Rachel thinks of Job, wondering if the virus has reached India, praying that it has not. Francesca asks Renato something in Spanish that Rachel does not understand. He responds in kind, which has the older woman nodding sagely.

Ted rounds the kitchen island with a plate, placing it and a fork in front of Rachel with a flourish. "One poached egg á la Anabelle on a bed of baby spinach, for the lady."

The poached egg, covered in a familiar red and orange powder, sits in a green nest of stems and leaves. She leans closer to inspect, not quite believing. "Is this Tony's seasoning?"

Ted leans around Lorelei to produce the green can. "Anabelle is addicted to the stuff, and I'll admit that it tastes great on eggs."

Despite the news they've all received, Rachel can't help but smile. Her father, born and raised in Louisiana, had kept a giant canister of the stuff on the kitchen counter. No other seasoning would do, and he would get into pointless, long-winded arguments with anyone who dared to use some other seasoning salt. She closes her eyes in a sort of prayer as she thinks of him before cutting open the perfect poached egg. The yolk coats the leaves, acting as the best sort of dressing. Such a simple meal has done much to cheer her.

"This is delicious," she admits to an expectant Ted. His smile widens so much that she could count just about every tooth he has.

"Good!" Ted then gets to the business of washing dishes.

"Should I go talk to Vernon?" Daniela asks over her shoulder.

"No, he will want his space," Lorelei replies as she gets up with her dish and takes it to the dishwasher.

Yukiko starts to slide out around the side of the table and glides to the fridge. Despite her size, the door opens easily to her touch. Rachel is certain there must be a trick.

"Ready to go?" Renato asks Yukiko.

"Mhm," she replies as she takes out three colorful Tupperware containers.

Renato does not ask Rachel to move, sliding around the whole table to get up and join Yukiko. When she hands him one of the containers, he kisses her cheek. A dull red spreads across her face. "Is this one for Rachel?" Renato asks.

"Mhm."

Renato brings the lavender container and places it in the center of the kitchen table. "For today," he says, giving her a meaningful expression.

"Chicken curry, rice, and fruit," Yukiko explains.

Rachel raises an eyebrow at the gift. "You made me lunch?"

"No first day of work should go without a homemade lunch," Renato says. The sun catches the gold in his earring loop.

Her face is hot. She feels embarrassed but does not know why. "I could have picked something up at the office," she replies.

"Now, you don't have to." Renato rejoins Yukiko, picking up two satchels from the floor.

"Uh..." Rachel remembers her manners. "Thank you. Very much. This is very kind."

Yukiko waves. "Have a good day."

"Have a good day," Ted and Daniela reply.

The couple disappears into the foyer; the sound of two doors opening and closing follow them. Meanwhile, tears prick Rachel's eyes as they consider her breakfast and lunch. This is all too much. "Will you be ready in ten minutes?" Lorelei asks from the other side of the kitchen.

"Yes," she replies curtly, not capable of saying much else without crying.

"I'll finish getting ready, and then we can go." The quiet German woman sweeps out of the room.

Rachel starts shoveling the egg and spinach into her mouth. She will not leave one bite behind. Hospitality such as this must be met with the most politeness she can muster. She fights from throwing up the whole time.

CHAPTER THIRTEEN

THREE DAYS INTO HER NEW job, Rachel cannot help but confess that she likes Boston, the little of it she has seen at least. Everyone minds their own fucking business here. She walks the twenty-three-minute route to work with Lorelei and the twenty-three-minute route back home alone—both are spent in complete silence. When she accidentally syncs her stride with another pedestrian, the two do not exchange pleasantries. The two lunches she has taken alone in the Courtyard Café, a three-minute walk from her office, have gone uninterrupted by a friendly staff member asking whether or not she enjoyed her meal. It is bliss.

Her co-workers are all nice enough, leaving her alone to figure things out unless otherwise asked. The first few days are all about passwords, permissions, identification cards. She schedules her orientation for late the following week, irritated that she must go to the main campus across the river in Cambridge for something that surely could be as simple as a pre-recorded message.

Rachel's office is quiet, punctuated by the occasional husky voices as a member of her team tries to convince some philanthropist to donate a couple thousand dollars for this or that. Almost all the grant officers are women, which she is certain is purposeful. This place is basically a million-dollar version of a phone sex call center. "Oh yeah," someone murmurs a few cubes over, "that kind of a donation would be a *big* tax credit."

She decides that she will like working here better than at the University of Chicago, if only for the fact that no one wants to chit-chat. Her new space is isolated, with hardly any clutter. Two screens, a standing desk, a comfortable chair, an empty filing cabinet, pens galore, and three donor profiles neatly stacked near her office phone. Her new email address is very official-looking with hms.harvard attached to the end. While she's never put much stock into collegiate elitism, it does feel pretty cool to have a business card with a lion on the back. She takes a photo to email Job from her work computer.

Midway through the second day, however, Rachel's boss had taken her aside and asked how comfortable she was with remote work. Never having had the chance, Rachel isn't sure how she would handle it; but she's not stupid. Those two cases at Beth Israel have tripled, and Italy is exploding. The word "lockdown" has entered her lexicon. It seems the direction things are going. It would be unwise to do otherwise. She knows that.

And so, on Wednesday, when her phone pings around seven with a very official-looking email from Harvard's president, she is not surprised. *"Dear Members of the Harvard Community..."* Quickly, she learns that classes will be online by the end of next week. Moments later, an email comes from her boss that details the move to online work as soon as possible. The *"as soon as possible"* is bolded and underlined. There is a long section about IT training, about how to gain access to the server from far away, and then there is a smaller section about maintaining good mental health with links to counseling services provided by Harvard.

Rachel sits up in bed and feels the weight of reality settling around her. She turns on her table light, cradling the phone in her hands. What does this mean? Does this mean that she must go to the office and carry the computer with its monitors back home? How long will this last? Glancing up at her bedroom, now free of moving boxes, she is cast in a sickly yellow light. She does not like this at all. She fidgets with her phone, thinking about calling Job but deciding instead to email. If she calls, he will hear the panicked tone in her voice, and they will have to pay the cell phone company too much for the pleasure.

Hi Angel—

Just got the email from HMS that I have to go get my things from the office. The city isn't on lockdown yet, but it probably is just a matter of time. Whatever that means. I'm okay here but am thinking about what we should do. Should you come home?

She pauses at that and considers deleting the question. It seems like since there are no cases reported in India, that he should stay there indefinitely. Now Boston is the danger. She deletes the whole message and starts again.

Hello, my love—

My boss emailed me this morning to come in and get my things. It looks like Harvard will be moving its classes online for the rest of the semester and that I'll be working from home for a while. Seems big. I am a little worried, but I am sure that everything will sort itself out. How are things in India? Have any of the Americans talked about their plans? I imagine there will be a lot of travel in a couple of days. What are you thinking?

Always and always,

R.

Rachel sends that copy off without rereading it. *I guess I should go in now before everyone else gets there*, she thinks. Her phone screen blinks at her: new group message.

Vernon:	Anyone else been asked to work remotely?
Renato:	Last day of in-person classes for us by the end of next week.
Wren:	BC got the same. Wondering how they will do classes online.
Renato:	Students are getting mics from the department this afternoon.
Wren:	Wow.
Lorelei:	Have to clear out today.
Daniela:	Same.

Her stomach swirls, making her feel sick. It made sense for a school to go online if a highly infectious disease was making its way through the city, but Google moving its operations to their employees' homes is disquieting. She texts: "For me too."

Markeya:	I think we should all meet to talk about this today. Figure out protocol.
Daniela:	How is the hospital?
Markeya:	Busy.

Daniela: Who needs to get their stuff from the office?
We can take the car and caravan.

A few people drop a "thumbs-up" emoji on the text. Rachel follows suit, relieved that she will not have to trudge through the snow with her monitors. Even from upstairs, she can hear people talking over one another in the kitchen. She can smell coffee and bacon and bread.

*

Hours later, after making a circuit through Boston in a car increasingly full of computers, parts, papers, boxes, and office plants, Rachel tries to organize her new workspace into a semblance of "workable." She almost gives up twice because the desk is clearly not large enough for her monitors, pens, or case files. This is not how things were supposed to go. She was supposed to have her office with its quiet and plentiful space, not have to settle for this cracker-sized square of a desk and all the noise coming from downstairs.

Her skin feels hot and achy, like she has a sunburn. *Am I sick?* she wonders. The pen holder in her hand falls to the floor with a metallic thud. She starts Googling her symptoms, which makes her feel worse. The news reports are at the top of the feed, with both *CNN* and *The New York Times* fighting for real estate on the Google News front page. There are claims of where the virus originated in China; assumptions about how to stop the spread; advisements about safety; a call for people to stop stockpiling toilet paper, bread, and milk. No one actually knows much of anything. The news only seems to know the body count in Italy and China, and even that doesn't seem too reliable.

As she reads, the heat and ache start to fade, and she realizes that it's just her anxiety that is getting the better of her. She should probably call her psychologist in Chicago to renew her Klonopin prescription but does not want to go through the uncomfortable part of actually *talking* to her psychologist about the last year. If she could travel the world without medication, then surely, she can do the same thing in a comfortable house in Boston. For now, she puts a hand to her heart, closes her eyes, and takes several breaths. Resettled, she opens her eyes and sees that her phone screen is glowing again.

Daniela:	Emergency house meeting at 7. Everyone should attend, if possible. Thank you!
Anabelle:	Stuck at hospital tonight. I will try to call.
Daniela:	Any news from the hospital?
Anabelle:	Not yet. Meeting with my chief later today. I'll keep everyone updated.
Daniela:	Please do.

Right at seven, Rachel goes downstairs to the kitchen and finds it empty. She redirects her path after she hears the voices coming from the dining room. Unlike the night of her arrival, the table is empty, and there are no candles twinkling in the fireplace. Most of the house has gathered; everyone looks tense. Rachel takes a seat between Vernon and Wren.

"Hey, how's it going?" Wren asks her. Their cat eye is not as intense today, but the shadow is crimson red.

"Oh, you know, regular day," she replies, and they both make a smile that's more a grimace than anything.

Francesca, Daniela, and Ted come in together, taking three seats on the other side of the table; the seat at the head remains empty. "I'll call her," Vernon says, gesturing to the space where Anabelle should be. Everyone is quiet while he dials. Cornelius's toenails can be heard in the hallway before he joins everyone, huffing as he finds a spot under the table and lies down.

"Hey," Vernon says, "free to talk?" A moment later, he places the phone down on the table. "You're on speakerphone."

"Hi, everybody," Anabelle's high voice calls, sounding tired. Rachel realizes that she has not seen the red-haired woman in days.

They all respond, even Rachel.

"How much time do you have?" Daniela asks.

"A couple of minutes before I've got to get back." Various beeps and muffled intercom chatter accompany her voice.

"How's it there?" Markeya asks, leaning into Vernon's side to get closer to the microphone.

"Not as bad as other units," Anabelle replies.

Daniela asks the question everyone wants an answer to. "Bad in what way?"

A doctor is paged in the distance. "Supplies are being reallocated. Gloves, gowns, and N95 masks, surgical ones, are being taken to the ICU and ER."

"Are ICU beds full up?" Markeya wants to know.

"Not that I know of."

Rachel leans over to Wren to whisper, "What hospital does she work at?"

"BMC," they reply.

"What should we do?" Ted asks, directing the question to Markeya and Anabelle.

"We should get some masks for everyone to wear if they have to go out. But really, everyone ought to stay home," Anabelle says.

Rachel glances towards her end of the table and finds Yukiko and Renato clasping their hands tightly on top of the table. Yukiko's dark brown eyes catch hers; Rachel can tell how scared the young woman is.

"We'll need hand sanitizer and good hygiene practices," Markeya picks up. "I'm talking, you come inside from outside, and you wash your hands with hot water and soap. We should probably be thinking about this thing like scrubbing in and out of surgery."

"You're right," Anabelle says. "Everyone should change their clothes when they get home, maybe even shower."

"Really?" Francesca balks.

"Doesn't hurt to be overly cautious," Markeya says. "You, of all people, need to be vigilant."

"What do you mean?" The older woman sounds offended.

Markeya points at Francesca. "Look, you're over seventy, and you smoke. This is a virus that gets into your lungs. If Italy has proven anything these last few weeks..."

"Okay," Daniela says, holding onto her mother's shoulder. "We will *all* be smart."

"Hey, guys, I'm getting paged," Anabelle says, diffusing the situation. "Markeya and I need to talk about what we want to do about the house. We are definitely a liability."

"Agreed," Markeya says.

"See you tomorrow, Anabelle," Ted calls before the line goes dead. He takes a deep, shuddering breath. Suddenly, he claps his hands together. "Well, it looks like we will all be together for the time being."

Vernon chuckles wryly.

"We want to be safe and conscientious of one another, so let's talk about it." Ted puts an arm around Francesca and Renato, drawing them close. "Obviously, even though the house is big, office space is a concern. We have the library and living rooms for private work. We can probably make the dining room into a communal workspace. Who needs what?"

"I need the piano," Yukiko whispers.

"You got it. We'll close the pocket door, and Yuki and Renato can have the living room. Is that fair to everyone?" Ted releases his friends and pulls out his phone, typing on a new note sheet. "Anyone else need space or have a preference?"

Daniela says, "I'll need office space."

"Great, you can have the library."

Vernon says, "I can work upstairs."

"I can work from my bedroom if needed." Ted looks around at the table. "I'd rather take the informal living room, but I can split it with anyone who wants in."

Lorelei says, "I can work with other people in the dining room."

"Wren? Rachel? What do you need?" Ted asks, fingers poised over his screen.

"A bigger desk," Rachel blurts.

He smiles a little. "No problem. I've got something in the basement bigger than the glass one in your room."

Rachel squirms in her seat, knowing what it is she really wants. "My desk is in one of the crates outside."

The smile widens. "Even better. I'll help you unbox."

"Thanks…"

"What about you, Wren? What do you need?"

"I'll take space in the dining room, but I may need privacy for meetings or whatever." They cross their arms tightly over a brown leather corset. "Not sure how this is going to impact my learning."

"A lot of unknowns right now, that's for sure," Ted soothes. "When you have a meeting, we can juggle space. Best practice is probably to text the house chat when you need space. Fair?"

"Fair," Renato and Lorelei say simultaneously.

Ted nods a few times. "Great. Okay, what next?"

Daniela has her phone out now. Rachel watches as the pregnant woman furrows her brow, takes a breath, and then unfurrows. She is still touching her stomach, the gesture increasingly protective. "Everybody put what you want on the grocery list now, okay? We'll do a big haul. Probably the last one for a while. We'll get canned foods and the like, just in case."

Markeya stands up, the chair scraping on the hardwood floor with a sudden sound that most of them jump. "I'll go ahead and clean out the fridges."

"Thanks, Markeya."

She turns to go but stops before she's taken a step. "What about Job?" Markeya asks.

It feels like a rock has dropped into Rachel's stomach.

"He should come home?" Francesca asks.

Markeya frowns. "I'm not gonna make that call. But, if I was him, I'd be on the first flight back to Boston."

"There's no word of spread in India yet, right?" Renato asks Vernon as if the sandy-haired man was as good as the CDC.

Vernon answers delicately, turning to look over at Rachel instead of Renato. "Not that I've read, but I'm sure it's just a matter of time. Better for him to be here than there."

Rachel's mind races with the implication. *If he gets sick in India, it's a death sentence, right? Because aren't hospitals in America better than hospitals in India? Because wouldn't he have a better chance here?*

She does not say any of this, though. Merely mumbles something about having sent him an email earlier in the day and hoping to have an answer soon. The group disperses after that, each person cobbling together their own version of dinner before disappearing into their bedrooms for the remainder of their night. Each person picks through their fears that suit their needs best.

Sometime after Rachel falls asleep in an exhausted, fully clothed heap on her bed, Job sends an email that she will not read for hours yet.

Honey-love,

Glad to know that Harvard moved quickly on a decision. I'm sorry that you didn't get to stay in the office longer, but it is probably for the best. This won't last too long. I'm hoping that you are already set up in the room and have made it your own. It's okay if you haven't. Don't force yourself into anything. Take it easy. As for India, things are pretty much the same...people are leaving, though. Mostly Americans and the English. I should probably go ahead and move up my flight. I'll let you know what I can snag. A little bummed to leave earlier, especially since I've acquired a taste for tofu, but so happy to be with you soon.

Missing you,

J.

CHAPTER FOURTEEN

THE FIRST MORNING OF quarantine, breakfast has everyone downstairs around the same time. Vernon cooks pancakes at the range in his work slacks and blue button-down covered with a green Starbucks apron. Rachel rolls her coffee cup between her palms as she alternates between reading the news and Job's email. Beside her, the stinky cat Klimt purrs in Lorelei's lap. Behind them both, Renato and Ted hash out summer plans for a volleyball court. It is a cozy din, and Rachel cannot deny that.

Daniela sweeps into the kitchen in a pale green dressing gown. Her hair is swept up into a silk scarf. Despite the purple bags under her eyes, she is glowing, and Rachel hates her for it. "Costco is completely out of toilet paper," she announces.

"What?" Renato's voice is higher than usual. "Completely?"

Vernon turns towards the group, casually flipping a pancake in the pan. "I read on Twitter that there are toilet paper, Lysol, and mask shortages already."

"What?" Francesca asks.

Renato says something in Spanish, and Rachel assumes that he has repeated Vernon's words for her.

"No good," she reports. "We only have a couple of rolls downstairs."

"Well, shit," Lorelei says.

Everyone laughs, even Rachel. In the last week, she has observed two things about the German woman: she is quiet, and she is funny.

Vernon brings a full stack of pancakes to the kitchen counter. His eyebrows are especially devilish today. "How does everyone feel about bidets?"

Rachel brings Job's email up on her phone and reads it again, lingering on the last sentence about his coming home. She wants to tell everyone the news but is sidelined when Ted says, "What about them?"

"Markeya and I have one in our bathroom. It's great."

"You have a bidet?" Yukiko asks.

Vernon moves the pancakes onto the kitchen table as Ted stands up to let Daniela scoot behind the table next to her mother. "We have an attachment that goes right on the toilet. All you have to do is hook up the waterline. Takes five minutes to install. Totally removes the need for toilet paper."

"Really?" Renato asks.

Rachel repositions herself to watch as plates and pancakes are doled out. Ted hands her two plates, one for her and one for Lorelei. "Pancakes?" he mouths. Rachel nods, and he holds out the plate for her to pick up two fluffy discs. Lorelei does the same.

Meanwhile, Yukiko sighs. "I miss bidets."

"But how..." Renato looks over at Francesca to gauge her reaction. "How do you get your butt dry?"

"The one in my apartment back home had its own heater," Yukiko says as she splashes a giant dollop of syrup over her pancakes.

"Markeya and I have one with a dryer, too," Vernon says, taking a seat at the kitchen island. He quickly thanks Renato for the plate of pancakes. "But people I know keep little washcloths in a basket on the back of their toilet. You use one to dry off, drop it in the hamper, and launder once a week."

"No toilet paper," Renato says, mystified.

"And you like yours?" Ted asks Vernon, incredulity littering his face.

"It's great," Vernon states with the syrup container dangling from his long fingers with their stubby nails.

Ted turns the question to the table. "How does everyone else feel about getting bidets?"

"Yes," Yukiko says at once.

"It would remove the need for toilet paper..." Daniela muses. "I like bidets; I think they're great. How much are they?"

Vernon takes out his phone and starts to scroll through Amazon. "The one we bought was expensive because of all the features. Let's see how much a regular one costs..."

"How much is expensive?" Ted asks.

"Over three hundred."

Ted whistles low.

"A regular one will cost about thirty. Yeah, here's the one." Vernon offers his phone to Renato and lets everyone at the table look. Yukiko is already shaking her head. "It's a bit of an investment because we'd need what, five or six?"

Francesca takes the phone and says, "Woooow. So sophisticated."

"Easy to install?" Daniela asks as she scrolls through features and product comparisons.

"Absolutely. I'd be happy to install them myself," Vernon says.

Rachel is finally given the butter and syrup. She continues listening as the bidet debate continues. "Is it hygienic to share one?" Ted asks.

"The spray part is always covered, so yes," Vernon replies.

"Well, I'm for them. More eco-friendly," Daniela determines.

"And we won't have to worry about toilet paper shortages," Renato says. Rachel is amused by his fascination. She herself is interested in using a bidet again and knows that Job will be delighted. After six months of almost exclusive bidet usage, it felt gross to go back to the rough scrape of toilet paper.

"What do you all think? Do you want bidets?" Ted asks Rachel and Lorelei.

"Did he finally get y'all with his bidet propaganda?" Markeya's voice asks, shocking Rachel into straightening. Behind her, she finds Markeya clutching a terry cloth robe closed tight. Her blue curls have disappeared under a colorful silk bonnet. She looks tired. The dark purple bags under her eyes are not as glamorous as Daniela's.

"We're deciding about it," Ted says.

Vernon is up on his feet, grabbing a mug out of the cabinet and pouring in the last bit of hot coffee from the pot. He hands it to her, and she thanks him quietly. "I think it's a good idea," she says.

Rachel's shoulders fall a little at being talked over. But Ted does not forget her or Lorelei. "What do you think?" he asks again.

"I want one," Lorelei says, moving Klimt from her lap and onto the floor. He gives a single grunt of displeasure before racing to his metal food bowl and begins to chew loudly.

"I'd be okay with it," Rachel agrees.

"Settled, then," Ted says and takes out his own cell phone, quickly going to Amazon and dropping a half dozen bidet attachments into his cart. "Some washcloths and baskets, too?"

"Baskets, yes. Washcloths, no. We have all of those Ikea ones in the basement," Daniela tells him, leaning into his shoulder to watch what he does. Rachel envies their intimacy. "Will Wren be okay with this?"

"If she—they..." he corrects himself, "If they aren't okay with it, they can use the toilet paper we do have, and we will try to get more."

"What about Anabelle?" Rachel finds herself asking, surprised by the consideration.

"Anabelle has been preaching the bidet gospel for about as long as I have," Vernon says as he finished up the last pancake bite on his plate. "It was easier for me to make the switch because all I had to do was convince Markeya."

"And I admit when I'm wrong." Markeya takes the remains of the pancake plate for herself. "The damn thing changed my life."

Renato laughs, resting both hands on his stomach. "I'm so excited."

"I'm not sure anyone has ever said that about a bidet before," Vernon says through a chuckle, wiping a tiny tear from the corner of his eye.

Outside the window, Rachel's eyes follow a fast-moving hooded and scarved figure as it makes its way up the driveway and up the backstairs. The door opens, and someone stomps their feet in the mudroom.

Francesca checks her watch. "Anabelle," she says to herself.

A half-second later, the red-haired woman barrels into the room. Anabelle looks thinner than the day Rachel met her, definitely more exhausted. When she sees everyone watching her at the door, she beams, but the expression seems off. There is a hint of pain in her eyes. Rachel pays close attention.

"Hi," she says.

"Hello. How was your shift?" Vernon asks. "Can I get you something to eat?"

"All the food, please," she replies cheerfully, then catches herself. "I need to go change, though. I'm gross." Her small face becomes pinched. "And I should probably eat in my room."

"Why?" Francesca asks. The lines between her eyebrows become ever deeper.

"Because I could make you all sick," she replies simply. Sadly.

Rachel observes Markeya and Anabelle exchange a meaningful look of some kind. She realizes she is not the only one to notice. Ted squirms.

Then, Markeya says, "Anabelle and I talked about it. We think it's best if we move out."

There is clamoring. Panic ripples through the table and plays against Rachel. Though she has only just arrived, she would prefer that things not change further. This is selfish of her, and she knows it.

"Move out?" Ted cries. His cheeks are red. "You can't move out. We are at the beginning of a pandemic. You need to be here!"

"We can't, Ted," Anabelle says as she leans back into the mudroom door.

Ever the optimist, he scrambles for words. "What if we converted the library into a makeshift bedroom?"

Markeya sighs heavily. She leans her elbows onto the copper-topped island and cradles her head. "Look, it's only a matter of time before we start working directly with infected patients."

Anabelle picks up the torch as she gestures to the kitchen table. "We can't stay in the house and put everyone at risk, least of all Francesca and Daniela. We don't know how long this will last, and we need to have access to a kitchen and bathroom."

The room is silent. Rachel watches Ted's face carefully. She can almost hear the thoughts springing back and forth in his skull. He catches her watching, and her gaze falls away. "What about the garage?" Ted asks.

Two or three people snort at the notion. "Huh?" Markeya says, lifting her head out of her hands to shake it. "That whole thing is a gut."

Some light has clicked on over Ted's head. His voice is no longer dejected; it's energized. "No, no, listen to me.

It's got the foundation for a good little house. That's what it used to be. The upstairs is a totally open space, more than big enough for two beds. Two bathrooms and the makings of a functional kitchenette. We could flip that thing, easy. You could move out there but not away. Problem solved."

Anabelle sinks a little lower down the door, her legs sprawled out in front of her. "It's a good idea, but we don't have a month to have it fixed up. We should probably be isolating now."

Ted is not dissuaded. "What if it was done this weekend?"

Markeya turns her chair around so she can cross her arms and stare Ted down. "There's no way that's possible."

Rachel's head bounces between Ted and Markeya as they begin to lob rebuttals back and forth like master tennis players.

Ted: "Why not?"

Markeya: "Because that sort of thing takes weeks to get settled."

Ted: "What if it only took the weekend?"

Markeya: "Ted, man, I'm telling you that it's not possible."

Ted: "Why not?"

Markeya: "It's just...it's just not."

Ted taps the top of the table with his fingertips, using them almost like a gavel. "Listen, if the Amish can raise a barn in a day, we can outfit a carriage house in a weekend."

At this, Markeya raises her hands in exasperation, stands up, and goes to pour herself a cup of coffee out of the newly-brewing pot.

Vernon steps in on his partner's behalf. "We don't exactly have Amish know-how."

"What's Amish?" Francesca asks.

Rachel finds herself providing a quick answer. "People who choose to live without electricity or modern conveniences. They build and make all of their things."

"Plenty of people *have* to do that in Venezuela," the older woman murmurs to herself. "It isn't so special."

Ted and the rest are not paying attention to this portion of the conversation, though. "If we get this thing done this weekend, would you guys stay?"

Anabelle and Markeya make some more eye contact. "I guess it would solve the problem," Anabelle says at last.

Markeya rolls her eyes as if to say, *I can't believe you're on his side.* Then she shrugs.

"Great." Ted claps his hands once with delight. "I'll call the contractor and get him over here today. Rachel," he reaches for the back of her chair, "will you ask Job for his opinion on how we should approach this project? We would all benefit from his knowledge, I'm sure."

"Uh, okay." Rachel flushes in pleasure and panic. She is not sure if throwing Job's hat into the ring will cause some unknown friction down the line. Ultimately, she does not want to deny the chance to entice Job back to her faster. "Yeah, okay, I'll email him."

120

So, over breakfast, on the first day of their self-imposed lockdown, the house decides to fix the carriage house, and Rachel misses Job more than she ever has in her life.

At about the same time, Wren enters the room and says, "Hey, what'd I miss?"

CHAPTER FIFTEEN

RACHEL WILL SAY THIS ABOUT Ted: he can be single-minded. When there is something he wants, he goes for it. Her father had been the same way: single-minded, focused, an optimist. Even after losing his job at the electric company for drinking while driving, he had been certain that everything would work itself out in the end. Their lives would be "great"—which had been his favorite word. "Everything's great," had been his personal mantra. Rachel is glad to see that things are working out better for Ted.

About two hours after the conversation in the kitchen, a contractor shows up on their doorstep. A couple of hours after that, a plumber shows up, then an electrician. Daniela explains to whoever is in the kitchen at the time of a new arrival that so-and-so had worked on the house when they'd bought it a couple years back. They are honest.

At least, they are honest enough to tell Ted that a weekend to pull the little house together the way he wanted is not possible. It would take a week for the concrete floor to set properly, a month for it to cure and be ready for polish. In the contractor's personal opinion—Ted later reveals to the kitchen when

Markeya and Anabelle were not present—the little house should be torn down and built from the ground up. But the little house is protected by the historical society, has been for a long time, and no previous owner has wanted to fix it up properly. In the wake of their neglect came about sixteen-hundred square feet of missed opportunity. Rachel conveys all of this in an email to Job that night. By morning, he replies simply: "Let's hope Ted likes a challenge."

Of course, Ted does. By Thursday evening, he has hashed out a scheme with the contractor, electrician, and plumber. If the contractor lays the bones, the electrician and the plumber can fill the little house's wasted body with new life. For a friend like Ted, these things can surely be done in two days. Everything that comes after, though, will be left to the house. As the contractor finishes one section of the room, volunteers follow with insulation. After that, either plumber or electrician will do what needs doing. Then, Sheetrock will seal up the work.

Downstairs is a different story, and at least there, Ted realizes concessions have to be made if he wants Markeya and Anabelle to stay. He will have to do away with notions of polished concrete. There simply isn't enough time. No, downstairs will have to settle for tile. But after that, for Ted, the little house would be ready for the things that make a house a home by the end of Saturday. Surely.

Though the plan sounded crazy to Rachel at dinner Thursday night when Ted revealed it, there is no denying how easy it was to trust him. He made the grueling prospect of laying tile and hanging Sheetrock sound like a fun group activity. A challenge that they could all take on and be proud of at the end of the day. Through them, the little house will have a new chance at life. Even Markeya seems excited by the prospect, and since she had the weekend off, she would be able to oversee the work.

Late Saturday afternoon, though, Rachel drips sweat despite the low-thirty-degree temperatures and wonders how on earth she allowed herself to be conned into this sort of back-breaking labor. She and Renato hold up a piece of Sheetrock as Vernon takes the power drill and fixes the thing into place with screws. Everyone's noses are red and running. Even though the space heater is doing its best in the corner, there's simply too much room and not enough insulation to keep everyone warm. "Bet you didn't think you'd be spending your second weekend in Boston on a construction site," Renato teases.

Rachel likes Renato. He's in his mid-twenties and acts like he is seventeen. He is a burly guy with hairy arms and a burgeoning unibrow. He is getting a master's at Berkeley, majoring in vocal performance, and takes every opportunity to show off his chops.

"No, I thought I'd be at the Symphony or getting sushi somewhere," she replies, not doing a very good job at hiding how irritated she is.

"There's a place called Symphony Sushi, y'know," Vernon says as he finishes off the last few screws at the bottom of the sheet.

"Wish we could go," Renato says wistfully as he and Rachel move for another piece of Sheetrock. "Seems like we will never do anything again."

The looming city-wide shutdown certainly makes it seem that way. In Italy, there are drones chasing pedestrians while a local mayor shouts at them over a Bluetooth speaker: "What are you doing? Go home! There's nothing for you here." In Boston, schools are sending their children home, and restaurants are shuttering. Office space has been carved out inside the house, though Rachel knows nothing of those troubles. She remains cozy in her room, typing at the desk made by Job's hands. Having this anchor reminds her that the house is real and that what rages on outside of this room is real. It is a blessing and a curse.

"We're hanging Sheetrock right now, aren't we?" Vernon asks flatly.

Renato makes a show of rolling his eyes.

"Hey, does anyone need help up here?" Wren's voice asks.

Vernon steps back, holding the electric drill tightly to his chest as they welcome Wren, dressed in black jeans, a flannel overcoat, and sensible shoes. "Do either one of you need a break?" they ask.

Renato raises an eyebrow at Rachel. She feels bad, but she wants the break because the feeling has long since disappeared from her fingertips. "Yeah, I need a minute," she says.

"The Costco order should be here soon if you wanna help with that," Wren says as they slide in to take Rachel's place.

"You sure?"

Wren's face is clean of makeup but full of worry. They look very young. "Yeah, I need to do something with my hands."

"Thanks. I'll be back out in a bit," she promises and then scurries downstairs, careful not to disturb the freshly laid tiles on the ground floor. Somehow between this morning and now, the little house has become more of a home and less of a county fair attraction.

The wind is cutting, but Rachel cannot help but think that she is relieved that she probably will not need to buy a proper winter coat this season. Where would she go? Trotting up to the mudroom, she trips over an empty cardboard box from Costco. Inside, the kitchen counter is laden with vegetables, a double box of cereal, a case of almond milk, fruit, two rotisserie chickens, and about a million other things. Francesca and Markeya are making room in the fridge. Rachel's eyebrows raise a little as she wonders how they will abracadabra everything into an already packed space.

"Oh, hey." She holds one arm when both women acknowledge her with quick waves. "Is there anything I can do to help?"

Francesca does not hesitate to put her to work. "Will you put the fruit in the baskets, please?"

Rachel nearly curtsies but remembers that she is not an extra in *Downton Abbey*. She makes swift work of the apples and oranges, stacking them in neat little piles. While she is investigating a bruised spot on a banana, Markeya manages to sweep half of the hoard into the fridge.

Rachel places her hands on her hips. "Oh my gosh, that's amazing!"

Markeya beams, readjusting the silk scarf on her head with a deft flick of her forefinger. "I always liked Tetris."

"I can tell," Rachel replies, smiling. Deep inside her jacket pocket, her phone buzzes.

It's Job.

"Be right back," Rachel whispers to the women before breezing into the hall. "Hello?"

"Hey, honey, can you talk?" His voice is low, a little husky. If she did not know about the strict rules about alcohol at the ashram, she would have sworn he had been drinking.

"Yeah…" She looks down at the time on her phone, quickly doing the math that tells her that it is very late where Job is. People only call this late when there is bad news. Nothing good happens this late in the night. "What's wrong?"

The buzzing is loud in the background. "Can we talk in private?"

She immediately dips into the guest bathroom, using the flimsy latch to lock it. In the mirror, she can see how panicked her face is. She turns her back to herself. "What's wrong?"

"Rach, honey, it's okay. Take a breath."

"Just tell me."

A pause. "My flight was canceled, and I'm having a heck of a time finding a replacement. The States are closing the borders, and India is grounding its planes." He hastens to add, "Don't worry. We're going to figure this out."

The bottom falls out of her stomach. The floor comes apart. She is falling, surely. Slowly, Rachel crouches, touching her left fingertips to the wood, certifying its realness. *This isn't happening. This isn't happening. This isn't happening*, her mind chants.

"Rach?" Job's voice calls. Then it calls again.

"I'm here," she says, trying to convince both of them. "What are we going to do?"

He is quiet again, which she takes as a very bad sign. "Job?"

"I don't know." He sounds so tired. "Go to the embassy, I guess. Have you heard anything on the news about America evacuating citizens?"

She had not. "Should you go to the embassy? Maybe it would be better to quarantine where you are?" Her voice softens. "Until this all blows over?"

"I'm not sure it's going to, honey."

"Okay."

They are silent together. Out in the kitchen, Rachel can hear Francesca and Markeya murmuring back and forth. Eventually, Job says, "I need to get some sleep. It'll be easier to think about all this when I'm rested."

She starts chewing the inside of her cheek. "Okay."

"Are you okay?"

"Okay." She crunches the tender flesh of her mouth harder, allowing pain to focus her attention. She wants to be there for Job.

"Rachel."

She stands, and the blood rushes back to her legs. "I'm okay. Go get some sleep. We will figure this out. I'm going to do some research tonight."

His voice holds a hint of incredulity. "You sure?"

"Positive. Love you."

"Love you, too."

She hangs up on him and turns to stare at herself in the mirror. "Keep your shit together," she whispers, trying to will the tears that have bubbled up back down. When she feels confident enough to face the kitchen, she unlatches the bathroom door and steps into the hall.

Before she can escape up to her room, Markeya is standing in the doorway. Her face is pinched into concern. "Rachel, you okay?"

She blinks, smiles, and says in a chipper voice, "Job can't get a flight back." Then she bursts into tears.

Markeya tuts her tongue to her teeth. "Oh, honey," she says, moving to draw the crying woman into her arms. Without meaning to, Rachel puts her arms straight out to push. Seeming to sense this, Markeya takes a step away.

Fear overtakes Rachel's body. Strangely, her mind feels detached from the drama of it all. Why is she crying? She remembers now. It's Job. Job. She can see him on his grass mat in the middle of all that sticky heat. The weather across the world never agreed with her. It had not really agreed with him either, but he was affable and would often croon about how good it was to be far away from Chicago and its bitter winters. Wasn't it so nice to be warm? To be honest, she had never really noticed the niceness of the heat. Instead, she had choked on the sun, struggled for breath. Like she is choking for breath now with a limp hand on the doorframe, moments from collapse. Why is she crying again? Oh, right, because Job is stranded, and she is alone.

Markeya makes a shushing sound that grates on Rachel's nerves. "It's going to be okay," she says because that is what people have to say at times like this.

"What's wrong?" Francesca asks, padding across the floor. Rachel cracks open her watery eyes and finds the old woman holding a pineapple and a pensive expression.

"Job can't get a flight back to the States," Markeya says.

"What happened to his flight?" Francesca puts the pineapple on the kitchen counter and shuffles to stand in the doorway.

"Canceled," Markeya supplies.

The old woman sucks her teeth. "Because of the virus, I bet. He can't find anything?"

"No!" Rachel snaps. She wants to push both women aside, knock them to the ground, and flee into the street, running until she can no longer breathe or think or anything. She doesn't, of course. She is better at staying still.

Markeya eyes her with pity, the expression tightening her lips. Rachel has grown accustomed to this expression and hates it; she trembles with resentment.

"Everything will be alright," Francesca says.

"How do you know that?" Rachel says. Tears blur her vision.

The old woman shrugs. "It just will."

Rachel wants to scream at Francesca for her indifference, but Markeya interrupts the impending tirade. "Why don't you come upstairs with me? I'm gonna do my hair."

The sharp change in conversation is enough to give Rachel whiplash. "What?"

"Hair?" Markeya pats her silk-covered head. "I want to clean up the back of my head. Can you use clippers?"

Rachel's face shifts into disgusted curiosity. "Yeah?"

"Great, let's go." Markeya holds up a slender forefinger. "Let me grab some wine."

Before anyone can protest, Markeya is ready to go with a bottle of red and two stemless glasses. She starts for the staircase. "Come on up to the attic. I'll show you our room."

Rachel's brain works to compute. Much better to focus on this than India, right? Francesca offers no assistance as she returns to her previous task of unloading the groceries. "There's an attic?"

Markeya leans over the banister and beams. "God, yes. Took me two weeks to get properly settled. I kept walking into Francesca's room. Come on." Her steps trip lightly up onto the second floor, leaving Rachel to scramble behind her. She feels compelled to see a new part of the house.

"How'd she like that?" Rachel asks.

Markeya shrugs as they walk. "She keeps coming up to my room for some reason, so I guess we're even." She goes to the end of the hall and puts her hand on the doorknob that Rachel's assumed was a broom closet. But instead, there's a staircase. Markeya ascends, creaking steps, disappearing around a tight corner.

Curious, Rachel follows on tiptoes. The first thing she notices is how the air smells different here, more like sage and sandalwood, like a psychic parlor. On the landing, she is surprised by the stark contrast between this and the rest of the house. Where the bottom floor is furnished in blue, white, and trendiness, the attic is faded and comfortable. While no overt scheme holds it all together, there is something charming about the cobbled-together nature of the twin mustard-colored chairs in one corner and a dining room set in another. There is a built-in bookcase full of frayed spines and a small white-washed stepladder folded against it. On the far wall hangs a giant television before a squat coffee table and a turquoise sectional. It may as well be another planet, one where the air is easier to breathe.

"Your room?" Rachel asks, spellbound.

"Common area. Our room's through there." Markeya points to a closed door opposite the staircase as she works her toes into a pair of gray slippers. "I can show you in a minute, though. Why don't we have some wine first? I've got a bottle opener around here somewhere. Gimme a second." She goes to rustle around the couch, picking up cushions and digging in cracks until she holds the silver gadget aloft and says, "Gotcha. Come and sit, babe."

Rachel creeps across the room to take a seat on the couch, both legs tucked under her. She feels very young when Markeya uncorks the wine. Steady as anything, the older woman pours a hefty portion into each glass, sets them aside, and then moves closer to put an arm around Rachel. She stiffens then eases. Tears come after that.

CHAPTER SIXTEEN

AFTER A FIFTEEN-MINUTE crying jag and a glass of wine, Markeya places a set of full-metal electric clippers into Rachel's outstretched hand. "You're sure you know how to do this?" she asks, dark eyes full of sudden uncertainty in the vanity mirror. Vernon and Markeya's bathroom is bigger and nicer than Rachel's, with its fresh porcelain, chrome finishings, and matching mauve-colored towels. A pang of nameless jealousy hits Rachel hard in the gut, and she swallows up the dregs of her glass to soften the blow.

Rachel dabs the corners of her mouth with the back of her hand and sets the glass on the floor. She gestures to the folding chair in front of the sink. "I told you, I've been cutting Job's hair for ages."

Markeya sinks into the chair and says, "Gonna go out on a limb here and say my and Job's hair is a little different."

Rachel takes one of the matching towels and drapes it around Markeya's shoulders, laughing. "I can manage a line-up." She turns on the clippers, letting the buzz rattle her hand. "Besides, if I fuck it up, you'll look great bald."

Her client jerks in her seat, scowling over her shoulder. "Don't play."

Catching a glimpse of herself in the mirror, Rachel is surprised to find a smile on her face. Guilt overtakes at once. How can she be even a little happy while Job is off in the middle of a nightmare? She sobers, bending down towards the task. "Okay, okay. Seriously, I've got this." The metal smooths the hairs back into line.

"So, how did Job wind up in India?"

Rachel pauses, the blade an inch away from skin. "What?"

"Trying to distract myself from my terror," Markeya explains with a grin. "Curious more than anything, really."

"Oh." Both Rachel and her reflection blink once before getting back to the task. "It was the last place on the list he wanted to go, and we had just enough time to do it properly before coming back." She steps away to see how straight her work is. Almost there.

"You said you took a year off? That's a big deal."

Rachel shrugs, determining where the line bows low before scooting it up to meet its friends. "We needed space, so we traveled."

"What about Chicago?"

Rachel doesn't like to think about Chicago. "Do you want me to fade this at all?"

"No!" Markeya shifts away suddenly, protecting the back of her neck with her hand. "No, thank you. I'm gonna curl it. But back to Chicago." Her hand lowers. "Didn't you have work? Friends? Family?"

Rachel turns off the clippers and places them on the counter. "Nothing worth staying for."

"So you just packed up your lives and went..." There are questions upon questions crammed into that lingering space.

"Anywhere."

Markeya rubs her neck free from hair before picking up a hand mirror to check Rachel's work. "And you didn't look back." It wasn't a question.

Rachel crosses her arms tight across her chest, leaning against the bathroom door. "There's nothing there for us."

"This looks great." Markeya sets the mirror aside and moves the chair out of her way. "Here, take a seat. I'm gonna finger-curl the rest." She begins to rummage under the sink, taking out a spray bottle and a series of oils and pomades. After a moment of not finding what she's looking for, Markeya bows forward under the sink and reaches far back near the pipes. "So, tell me," she grunts, "after traveling all around the world, why on earth did you pick Boston?"

Rachel is transfixed as she sits, watching as the pile of potions becomes larger. In theory, finger-curls sound like an easy thing to do. Use your finger and create a curl. But now, she can see that this is too complicated for her, a woman who prefers hairspray above all other products. She wonders if Markeya is searching for a single lost spell component. Eye of newt? Mandrake root? She wants to ask this but does not think that it will come across as funny. Instead, she says, "Boston was hiring."

Markeya glances over her shoulder and says, "You don't sound too happy about that."

She isn't. It would have been easier to stay on the road. She can almost hear her husband's scoff. "Job knew if we didn't plan to come back, we wouldn't come back."

The bottles and jars glow faintly under the iridescent light. "Is that a bad thing?"

"Job has this theory." Rachel crosses her arms tighter and stares at Markeya's reflection as it makes a fierce part with a comb. The methodical nature of the action reminds her of afternoons spent watching Job plane wood. "He says that if you're out in the wild anywhere from one to twelve months, you learn a lot about yourself. But, out any longer than that, you lose your sense of self. Trick yourself into thinking that having a 'real' job is for squares and that you'll never be like that because you're too 'enlightened.'" She snorts, closes her eyes. "Maybe he was right to worry. Met a lot of couples in hostels and farms that had been backpacking for a year and a half or more, and they were all the same."

A pungent sweet scent fills the bathroom. "How d'you mean?"

Eyes open, she watches Markeya work the cream into a section of hair before taking a few strands and working them around her index finger. "Well, take a straight couple."

Markeya laughs in surprise. The women make eye contact in the mirror to share their funny secret. "Okay, take a straight couple."

She holds out a hand, weighing her experiences. "The woman is always super nice and super thin. Always into yoga. Sometimes a doormat, but what are you gonna do?" They grin, both holding twin images in their minds. "The man is the kinda dude that thinks that doing mushrooms makes him deep. He always haggles with locals over lodging even though you know he has Daddy's money. Same kinda guy who tries to get your husband to 'trade models' with him for the night after they buy you a bottle of wine."

Markeya's busy hands pause. "Fucking ew. Has that actually happened?"

Rachel scoffs, thinking of short men with white teeth that don't quite fit their mouths and Ted Bundy eyes. "Oh yeah. People are baseline bold. But for some reason, they get worse every day after a year."

Markeya coils another strand into place. There are two dozen now, and her head is nowhere near being done. "What about the queer couples?

She takes quick stock of those traveling memories for faces already blurred by time. "Honestly? Never came up."

"Makes sense. Not as many of us queers can rely on Daddy."

The women share another knowing laugh. The laugh, though, dies on Rachel's tongue a moment later. Thoughts of Job surface towards the base of her throat. Now he is a wanderer perilously close to his own one-year mark. Perhaps even as perilously close to losing himself as he had been when they left Chicago. They'd both been a little more than lost then.

"Hey now, come on back," Markeya's voice calls.

Head heavy with the past, Rachel must blink a few times to gather herself fully. She realizes that she has an audience now. Markeya stands facing her with hands still in her hair. Heat hits her cheek, which she dabs away fast. Even though she knows why she is crying, the tear is still a surprise. "Sorry about that."

"No need," Markeya says before turning back to the mirror. "I can't imagine how you're feeling." The near-indifference of her tone is a breath of fresh air.

"Job'll figure it out. He always does," Rachel states.

Markeya hums.

Out in the media room comes the sound of footsteps. There's a brief knock on Markeya's bedroom door before it swings open without permission. "Anyone in here?" a voice calls.

"Bathroom, Ana," Markeya says into the mirror, not sounding the least bit irritated. Rachel would have been furious if someone had come into her space so unceremoniously.

"Coming in." Anabelle appears in matching polka-dot pajamas and a surgical mask. She carries two steaming cups with paper tags hanging over the sides.

For a moment, Rachel thinks about hospitals and doctors coming into rooms reserved for people whose family members are dead, but they don't know it yet. That was the sort of place where you could get a Mello Yello for five quarters and news that would change your life for the low-cost of a ten-thousand-dollar deductible. Her throat clenches, she swallows, then blinks. The panic passes for now because Anabelle is offering up one of those steeping cups and asking, "What do you need?"

Reflexively, Rachel accepts the warmth and replies, "Nothing. I'm okay."

Anabelle's thin red brows gather together in concern as she leans against the door jamb with crossed arms. "Honey, you sure don't look it."

Rachel stares down into the darkening liquid. "I'm okay. Really," she whispers.

"Well," the small woman says, "what are we gonna do?"

Markeya swings around as her fingers continue their twirling business. "About what?"

Anabelle huffs with impatience. "About Job."

This is annoying. Who is this red-haired doctor to ask about a couple's plan for extracting one-half of the relationship out of an entirely different continent? Who is she to criticize a wife's efficacy in the face of chaos?

Keeping her attention on the tea bag, Rachel mutters, "Oh, I don't have, like, a plan."

To add insult to baseless injury, Anabelle's eyebrows relax, and she nods. "Gotcha. Be right back." When she heads back the way she came, Rachel tries hard not to throw her teacup. She succeeds, barely.

Markeya chuckles a little as she leans into the mirror to monitor her work before taking a small spray bottle and spritzing her curls. "Now you've done it. You'd better buckle up. She's going to rally the troops."

"What do you mean?"

"I mean, brace yourself for everyone being in your business in about, I dunno," Markeya hums as she taps her phone to check the time, "five minutes."

Rachel takes a sip and resents that the tea is delicious. How did Anabelle know she prefers lemon-ginger with too much honey? How did she know that it is exactly what Rachel needs to soothe her stomach? The red-haired woman has no business being right. Ever. Instead of saying this, Rachel sulks in the chair and watches Markeya move from one section of hair to another, leaving tight blue springs in her wake. Rachel wishes she had the patience for something that intricate, but getting her hair into a simple braid is frustrating enough. Why are things so easy for other people and so hard for her? She crosses her arms tighter, feeling her heart pound resentfully inside. Some small part of her, the reasonable part, tries to soothe, to tell her that everyone has their own cross to bear. Rachel isn't listening, settling a scowl further on her face as Markeya effortlessly curls more hair.

A sullen moment passes before Marekya comments, "Well, don't you look like you just ate some dog shit."

Rachel flushes hot, fingers digging into her biceps as she maintains her gaze with the other woman's reflection. "I don't like people in my business."

Markeya replies, "Then you're in the wrong place."

"Tell me something I don't know," Rachel snaps, regretting it. Now Markeya is going to tell everyone what an asshole she is, and then neither her nor Job will have anywhere to live. *Good going, Rach*, she tells herself.

To her credit, Markeya does not seem to take offense. In fact, she doesn't even stop twirling her hair (halfway done now, even). No doubt she's heard worse as an ER nurse at Beth Israel. "Why don't you go take a minute out on the couch? Give you a second to breathe before everyone else gets up here?"

Mollified, Rachel nods, stands up, folds the chair, and goes out to the media room. She stands in the doorway, taking in the shadowed forms of the overstuffed couch, the tables, the chairs. Why is this room so much different than everywhere else in the house? Is it the fact that nothing quite matches that makes Rachel feel more at home? She imagines it does as she falls face-first into the turquoise fabric, inhaling the sweet scent of what she imagines to be lavender linen spray. Turned in towards the cushions, she lets out a long sigh that turns into a growl. The sound is muffled by the pillow. She growls again, though this sounds more like a scream. She worms in further, trying to dig herself into the couch the way she did as a child when she wanted to disappear. Maybe this time, she'll succeed. *Why does everything have to be so goddamn difficult? Why can't Job just be here? Why did I let him stay behind? Of course, this happened. Fucking idiot.*

It feels safe to think these things with eyes closed. The confessional nature of the pillows makes a lot of things seem safe. Her guilt inbreeds, taking those initial insecurities and birthing things far more monstrous than its parents. Now she knows she could have done better by staying with Job in India. Or by convincing him that Boston was better than a three-week meditation retreat to a fucking ashram. And now, he'll never come back to her because he's going to die in India, she's sure of it. Either from this virus or bandits or his own hands. Weren't they running from Job's suicide attempt after the death of their daughter? Hadn't that been her fault, too? If her body had been just a little more hospitable, then none of this would have happened. If she'd done better, they would still be living in that cute little house in Chicago, building Job's business, and tending their small yet fulfilling lives. Rachel knows this all to be true, and she hates herself more than a little bit for it.

Wallowing in self-pity is an act best done alone; unfortunately for Rachel, this house does not allow much for privacy. The door to the attic swings open, and a wave of voices and footsteps come flowing through. She sits up quickly and forces herself to put away the metaphorical flogger. No, there's not enough privacy in this house at all.

CHAPTER SEVENTEEN

RACHEL TRIES TO STOP trembling with rage but finds it difficult as house members move furniture around to assemble a sort of circle. The couch is pulled back, its ottoman moved, the overstuffed chairs scooted due to cumbersome weight, lighter chairs pulled away from their tables. Somehow, Rachel finds after a quick count, everyone but Job has made it to this impromptu house meeting. Markeya has emerged from her room wearing a red paisley sweater, a head full of playful curls, and a quirked brow thrown in Rachel's direction. Rachel makes a reply by way of watching Vernon as he hauls the last seat into the circle.

Ted approaches, his jubilant smile replaced with a somewhat more sombre version. He puts a hand on Rachel's shoulder. "Just heard about Job. I'm very sorry."

She shrugs him off and backs into the nearest corner. Ten sets of eyes are fixed on her, all of them holding varying levels of pity. She's been here before, in a room like this, and she knows these conversations never go well. With her back against a literal wall, she struggles not to lash out. She says, "Look, I appreciate y'all coming up here, but it's not necessary. Job and I will figure things out."

No one seems to notice all that she has in common with a bobcat, though. Daniela steps towards Rachel with a hand resting on her baby bump like some sort of Madonna. She is all reason, and Rachel hates her for it. Of course, it's easy to be calm when your husband isn't trapped in India and your belly is still full of baby. "We can be more effective as a group. Pool resources, get things moving so that he at least has somewhere to be." Daniela turns to the group as everyone starts to find their seats. "Do we know anyone in India?"

Anabelle takes one of the larger armchairs away from everyone else, crossing her legs up into the seat. "I have a friend from Doctors Without Borders stationed in India." She looks at Rachel. "Where's Job?"

Before she can answer, Vernon says, "North of Kerala on the southwest coast."

Indignant, Rachel wants to tell the blonde man to shut up about her husband but is again interrupted. Anabelle, this time: "My friend is in Mumbai. If I'm remembering right, that's two days by car, at least."

Ted sits beside Daniela on the couch, one arm going around his wife's shoulders. "Is travel even open in India right now? Or are they doing a shelter in place order?"

Anabelle pulls out a bright blue cell phone. "I'll find out."

Rachel could spit; she's so angry at all of these people trying to stick their noses where they don't belong. She collapses into the nearest seat and clasps her hands. Lorelei eyes her warily before taking a seat on the ottoman to Rachel's right. Everyone is seated now, their gazes no longer fixed on Rachel but on one another.

Renato throws himself into the conversation, "I did an exchange program in Bengaluru a few summers ago. That's in the south. I still talk to my host family. It's not close, but if Job needs a place to stay..."

Daniela holds her hand out to the young man, smiling gently. "Thank you, Renato. Let's table the staying conversation for now. Let's focus on getting him on a flight. I have a few contacts that may have suggestions."

Rachel can't for the life of her remember what Daniela does for a living, but she's pretty sure it has something to do with managing other people's bullshit. Probably why she's so good at this conversation. *Oh good, something else she's better at than me.* Inadequacy is a garment that Rachel often wears; it's just never been this itchy before. "Doesn't..." she starts.

Ted interrupts her this time. "I'll call Lori Strutherland. I bet she'll have some ideas about getting him out."

Whatever threads Rachel thought she had a hold of in this situation are swiftly being pulled from her hands. "Wait..."

Vernon speaks over her. "Even though the planes have been grounded?"

"Could we charter a plane?" Yukiko asks.

Wren cackles. "Now, *there's* an idea."

"A *plane?*" Rachel balks. Her face feels so hot.

Markeya leans into the circle with a badly needed dose of reality. "There's probably an emergency extraction order for U.S. citizens. If Job gets to an embassy, maybe there's a waiting list or something. It's just a matter of time before people get moving."

"That's what Australia and New Zealand are doing right now," Vernon adds.

Renato nods. "And how long can flight restrictions last, really? In two weeks, we'll be back to normal. I say we get him on whatever list and then find him a comfortable place to stay while we wait."

Vernon hums, stroking his beard. He looks at Rachel with blue eyes that have lost their mischievous glint and have gained a certain intensity. "He's at a yoga retreat, right?"

Rachel glares at him. "Oh, am I allowed to speak now?"

His whole body jerks. "I'm sorry?"

Daniela reaches out towards Rachel, snaring her ire instead. "We're trying to be helpful."

Anabelle looks up from her phone, oblivious to the room's tension. "We need to get him out of that retreat immediately. If this is an airborne disease, him being around that many people is a threat. How far away was your host family from Kerala, Renato?"

Vernon jumps up, looking eager to have something to do. "Let me get Google Maps on the projector." He is efficient, pressing whatever buttons there are in the far right corner of the room that gets the screen next to Rachel lit up with some innocuous blue and white logo. After Vernon logs in, they are greeted by a photo of the house dog Cornelius wearing a pair of bone-patterned pajamas. He looks ridiculous. "Last Christmas," Lorelei tells her, even though Rachel didn't ask.

"Where did you say your host family lived, Ren?" Vernon asks.

"Bengaluru."

Markeya cocks her head to the side with a curious smile on her face. "What were you doing there?"

"Learning how to sing in Kannada," Renato replies simply.

Markeya chuckles. "Of course."

"Okay," Vernon drawls as Google Maps blinks onto the screen. The blue pin with the white house icon floats over their location before disappearing after Vernon inputs the cities. Then they are all on a different continent, staring at a bold blue line that cuts across the map. Rachel does not see the name of the town where Job is staying, but she knows that he is there. "Looks like Kerala to Bengaluru is eight and a half hours by car."

Wren leans their elbows onto their ripped tights and asks, "What airport was he going to fly out of?"

Before Rachel can respond, Anabelle says, "Must be Cochin. That's the nearest international airport."

"It's Cochin," Rachel says murderously, glaring at Anabelle. No one seems to notice.

"Well, that's no good," Lorelei says into her phone screen. "The nearest American embassy is in Chennai."

"How far is that from where Job is by car?" Ted asks, drumming a fan of his free fingers against his clean-shaven chin.

Vernon half hops over the furniture to get to the projector screen. "Nearly twelve hours. Job's here," he gestures vaguely around Thrissur, "and we want to get him here." His forefinger traces the long line to the southeast coast. "It's only an hour there by plane, which would obviously be better than driving. Not sure if domestic flight is allowed. Or, if it is, for how long. But, if we get him to Chennai, he can get to the U.S. embassy and figure out how to get home."

Ted hums. "It would be a hell of a trip."

Anabelle nods over her phone. "And that's if he could even get a flight to Chennai." She scrolls, frown deepening. "I don't see anything right now. He'll probably have to drive."

Rachel leans her head back into the chair and rubs her closed eyes. *Jesus-fucking-Christ, if all of you could just shut the fuck up.*

"So he drives. Okay? That's no problem," Francesca adds in a flippant tone. "If he drives, he drives. So what?"

Rachel feels more heat rush to her face from some unknown reserve. She's shaking as her glare fixes on the old woman. "So what? So what is that he doesn't speak enough Assamese, Bengali, or Hindi to get him across the country. So what is that he is stranded in the middle of a country where he is completely alone. So what is that even if he by some fucking miracle gets to the embassy, that there is no guarantee that we can even get him back to that States."

Daniela puts a protective hand on her mother's arm. "I understand that you are feeling very emotional right now, Rachel. We are all here to help. Mom has gone through something like this before when she left Venezuela. If she can do it, then we should all have some confidence in Job's abilities to do the same." The woman's face remains politely poised with a delicate smile, but there is no denying the "I-fucking-dare-you" glimmer in her eyes.

Man, oh man, does Rachel feel like an asshole. She lets her gaze sink into the palms of her hands. "I'm sorry, Francesca."

"Oh, think nothing of it," the old woman says in that same flippant tone. Rachel begins to understand that, perhaps, Francesca just isn't fazed by much. "Your husband is stuck. You're scared. But we'll find a way."

What Rachel wouldn't give for the floor to fall in right now and allow her to plummet far into the earth. She's quiet, tears blurring her vision.

Lorelei places her hand so gently on Rachel's shoulder that she barely registers the weight at first. When she, at last, realizes it's been there a full thirty seconds later, it's almost enough to break her.

Ted takes a loud calming breath for everyone. "Even if we can't get Job to the States right away, we could probably get him to Europe. We know a lot of people in Europe."

"So, for now," Daniela clarifies, "we need to get Job to Chennai. Plan A is that he goes to the embassy, books a new flight, and comes back to the States as soon as possible."

"What if there is nothing the embassy can do?" Yukiko asks.

"Then we planes, trains, and automobiles that bitch to Europe," Wren answers glibly, stretching out their platformed feet. "There's no reason why he has to stay in India if we're all sure that's the best idea."

"Wait, what about staying with my host family?" Renato asks, sounding vaguely insulted.

"Yeah, isn't that a solid Plan C?" Ted asks Daniela.

Daniela strokes her stomach. "I think we'd all feel more comfortable if Job was nearer to people who could help us get him on a plane."

"Gotcha." Ted claps his hands together. "Okay, so let's get cracking on this. Rachel, can you call Job so we can let him know about the plan?"

"It's really late there," Markeya says. "How about we try and nail down some options with travel, maybe see if there's a domestic flight through some other website, and let him know what we can do later tonight?" Rachel looks up at Markeya's rationality. "If you called him around nine, that would be okay, right?"

"Yeah, I can do that," she replies. At least this makes sense.

"Cool." Markeya stands up with her cell phone already in her hand. "So, I'll look for flights. Renato, can you look at car rentals? Yukiko, why don't you check out if there is some kind of bus system. Not ideal, I know," she throws a sympathetic look to Rachel, "but we want options. Vernon will work on contacting the U.S. embassy to see what we should be doing to move the request along. Is that okay?"

"Fine. Happy to help," Vernon replies before going to shut off the projector.

"What about us?" Ted asks.

"I think it would be best if the three of you started reaching out to your networks. Find out who he could stay with depending on whatever route we need to take. If he's going by way of the Middle East, we'll need people to meet him along the way. The language barrier can be tough."

"Yeah, it can," Vernon says, chuckling at some shared memory.

Markeya points to the remaining task list. "Wren, Lorelei, Anabelle, if you could collate all of the info we get, that would be super helpful."

Rachel marvels at Markeya's control of the situation, feeling every bit of irritation and fear fall away under such competency. If emergencies were an art form, then surely Markeya would have been in the leagues with Renoir and Monet.

"Aye, aye," Wren salutes with a quick wave of two fingers.

"Good. Let's try to get as much of this done by nine tonight as we can. I think Anabelle's right in thinking that it's dangerous for Job to be around that many people, so we should get him out ASAP. Sound good?"

"Sounds good," Francesca parrots.

Ted stands, crosses the circle, kneels in front of Rachel, and stares deep into her eyes. "This is going to work. We're going to get him home. I promise." His expression is earnest, so much so that she can't quite bring herself to call him a liar.

In the face of such relentless optimism, it seems better to remain silent.

CHAPTER EIGHTEEN

TWO HOURS LATER, RACHEL sits with her whole body squished into her desk chair, endlessly scrolling through news articles on her phone. None of it is good, and her back is beginning to ache. She hasn't heard from Job since he called earlier in the afternoon, and she hopes it is because he is getting some sleep and not because internet connection is no longer possible in India. What will she do if that is the case? Charter a plane like Yukiko had suggested? Was that really such an outlandish idea? After all, what wouldn't she do for him? She searches "charter private plane to India cost" and turns to a new page in her journal, printing "EMERGENCY OPTIONS" across the top. Anxiety is mostly horrible, but Rachel rather likes how organized she is in a pinch. There is comfort in the preciseness of her handwriting.

That comfort swiftly departs as she discovers the one-way cost of chartering a long-range jet from San Francisco. "Well, if I convince my twelve closest friends to take this once in a lifetime trip, it'll only cost twenty-thousand a person. What a deal," she grumbles as she puts her phone down and scratches out the heading at the top of the page, ruining it forever. Chucking the pen across the room, Rachel rests her chin down on stacked fists before muttering "fuck" six times, then once more for good measure. "What are we going to do?"

There's a knock on her bedroom door. It's as if people in this house are lying in wait behind door knobs, listening for the opportune moment to bother Rachel. She stomps her feet down on the floor, already whipped into a whispered tirade, "Silly me thinking I could go twenty god-damned minutes alone."

Her frustration builds as she gets closer to the door. She's ready to give whoever is beyond it a piece of her mind. A glint of light catches the corner of her eye, throwing Rachel off-guard. Turning, she is pierced by the photo on the bedside table. Rachel's mother stares at her from the frame, chastising from beyond the grave. "You mind that 'tude," she can hear.

"Okay, fine, whatever," she says out loud with all the petulance of a teenager. Nevertheless, she pauses to take a deep breath. She counts to five, then lets it go. Feeling a little less like flying into a rage, she opens the door to Anabelle holding a top hat.

"Hey!" the red-haired woman chirps, smiling so big that it crinkles her huge eyes. "It's *Chopped* night."

Rachel blinks, taking in the dichotomy of Anabelle's jeans and t-shirt against the blue surgical mask that covers her mouth. It seems strange. Then again, plenty of Asian countries do this regularly. Then again, there's this whole top hat business. What's that about? She realizes that she's gone too long without speaking. "Sorry. It's 'what' night?"

"*Chopped.* Y'know, like the show?" she leads. "Every month or so, we clean out the fridge and pantry and do a cooking challenge to see which team can make the best dish with the given ingredients."

Rachel blinks again, wondering what this conversation has to do with her.

In the face of silence, Anabelle pulls the hat in closer and rambles. "Vernon was in charge of the baskets this month, so I'm sure they'll be super hard for no reason."

Rachel says nothing.

At last, Anabelle looks a little uncomfortable, her eyebrows pulled together and her forehead creases deepening. "So, are you coming down now or...?"

Half-hiding behind the door, Rachel asks, "Is this something everybody knows about?"

The forehead creases smooth. "Well, yeah!"

"Really? Because I don't feel like I have enough time to prepare." This, at least, is a reasonable excuse to not want to participate in something. There seems to be a little light at the end of this conversational tunnel.

But Anabelle's words bring on the avalanche, blocking off any chance of escape. "It's on the calendar..."

"What calendar?" Rachel asks, but she knows full well what calendar. She remembers deleting the invitation from Ted the minute it hit her inbox.

"The Google Calendar?"

"Google Calendar?" she says, sounding the words out like she's never heard them before.

Anabelle begins to nod in some sudden understanding. "Oh, oh, oh. Ted didn't give you access to the calendar."

As though conjured by his name, Ted exits his room at the far end of the hall and asks, "What didn't I do?"

His sudden appearance furthers Rachel's door knob theory.

Anabelle makes space for Ted at the threshold, accusing with sisterly affection, "You didn't add Rachel to the house calendar."

Already Ted is reaching for his phone for reconfirmation that he is the perfect host. "I thought I did…"

No need to get caught in a lie. Rachel clears her throat, avoiding eye contact. "You probably did, and I forgot to accept the invite." Why attach yourself as deeply as a Google Calendar if you're only going to stick around for three months? Seemed a better idea to bullshit her way through house events than to have a new calendar clash with her pristine, color-coded lifestyle.

Ted flushes with what she thinks is relief. "Oh, no problem! Let me resend it."

"Let's head on down to the kitchen, then. We only have an hour and a half to cook." Anabelle and Ted start for the stairs but pause when they see that Rachel isn't coming. The force of their collective questioning gazes is enough to overpower her reluctance. She follows.

There is commotion in the kitchen as half a dozen of her housemates flit around, clearing the counter of its cornucopias and replacing them with appliances. An industrial blender, an induction burner, a panini press, and a stand mixer are each given a corner of the island and a stack of cutting boards placed in the center. The kitchen table is laden with varying sizes of white plates and bowls, looking like something out of an Ikea catalog.

Despite her annoyance at being corralled downstairs by the two pushiest people in the house, Rachel can't help but ask, "So...who's participating?"

"Names out of a hat style," Anabelle says, shaking the black top hat at her.

Of course, Rachel thinks.

"Six players, three teams. Each team gets a basket, a course assignment, and ninety minutes to work," Ted supplements before taking the stand mixer from Francesca.

Lorelei scoots past Rachel without a word, taking a seat with her laptop at the freshly cleaned island. "Do I have to participate?" Rachel asks, not much caring for the whine in her voice. "There's the Job thing, and my arms really hurt from hanging all that drywall." *Holy shit, that was this morning.* "I'm really not feeling it."

Anabelle thumps her on the shoulder. "If you're picked, you play. A sprained wrist wasn't enough to get Lorelei out of competing."

Without looking up, the German woman adds, "My team won, too. Chipotle cricket and chocolate truffles."

"They were delicious," Francesca says as she fills the dishwasher with liquid soap.

Vernon's plodding steps, which Rachel is familiar with already, hit the top of the basement stairs. She instinctively moves into the bathroom to get out of the way. Then he's in the kitchen with a giant rectangle in his arms. "Can someone grab that plug?" he says, casting a look over his shoulder. "The tail got away from me."

Ted stoops, the two of them walking the unwieldy shape across the room to sit on the fireplace mantle.

Plugged in, the rectangle blazes to life in neon red. It's an industrial-sized timer, like the ones on cooking shows. When Vernon dusts off his hands and rebuttons his coat, Rachel can appreciate how far he's gone for this bit. He's wearing a light blue linen suit with a heather gray button-up, a textured pink tie with matching pocket square, and rectangular glasses. *Oh my God, he looks just like Ted Allen.*

"Should I send a reminder?" Vernon asks the kitchen.

"Go ahead," Francesca replies for everyone.

Ten seconds later, doors open upstairs, and footsteps come flooding down. The mood in this room is different than it was in the attic just a few hours ago. They all seem to be humming with excitement, which makes Rachel resent them all the more. *Happy? At a time like this?*

"Made teams yet?" Markeya asks when she enters the kitchen. Rachel trails in after her, sticking to the cupboards to be as inconspicuous as possible.

"Just about to," Vernon answers. "Daniela, will you do the honors?"

The woman in question waddles across to the top hat, dipping in a perfect slender hand untouched by the bloating so common in pregnancy. *What doesn't she have?* Rachel wants to know before beginning a long, impassioned plea to the universe and any benevolent ghosts to keep her from being picked for this game.

Daniela takes out six strips of paper, making three piles. She takes the hat, and Vernon reads the names, sealing Rachel's fate. No surprise, of course. When has fortune ever been kind to her?

"Alright, alright, everyone, here we go." Vernon adjusts his tie. "Rachel, you're with Wren for the appetizer round. Anabelle, Renato, you're on entrée. Lorelei, you've got Markeya for dessert."

"Oh, my," Lorelei says suggestively, wagging her eyebrows. Everyone but Rachel laughs as the two women put an arm around the other's shoulders. Anabelle and Renato high-five. Rachel finds Wren's gaze across the room.

Wearing platform boots of a sensible three-inch height and a leather trench coat, Wren glides to Rachel's side. Their cat eye seems especially fierce today, as does their black pixie cut. Rachel wonders if the hair is a wig or real. "You ready for this?" they ask.

"Not really," Rachel confesses, drumming her fingers on the kitchen island.

"It should be fun," Wren promises.

Rachel fights the urge to roll her eyes at the young person's enthusiasm. How could they know that she loathes to cook? No sense in being rude, especially after she's spent most of the day doing just that. "Hope so."

Meanwhile, Yukiko distributes three identical leather baskets in front of each team, and Vernon takes his place in front of the timer. Rachel has to admit that these people commit.

"Six chefs, three courses, only one chance to win." Rachel's eyebrows shoot up in response to the spot-on impersonation of Ted Allen's voice. She's only seen *Chopped* a few times over the last decade, but it's an immediate match. "The challenge: create an unforgettable meal from the mystery items hidden in these baskets before time runs out. Our distinguished panel of chefs will critique their work, and one by one, they must face the dreaded Compliment Block. Who will win the privilege of not cleaning the kitchen for a week, and who will be CHOPPED?" Vernon's blue eyes make contact with all of the contestants. "There are ninety minutes on the clock. Chefs, you may...begin!" The numbers roll backward. The onlookers applaud before taking a seat at the kitchen table, waiting for the unboxing.

Wren pulls the basket labeled "appetizer" close, opening the lid, and begins to pull out their ingredients: a box of Zatarain's Jambalaya rice mix, pistachio oil, jarred chutney, and a can of Spam. "Oh, fuck yeah!" Wren says.

"Baba ganoush?" Markeya squawks at the same time, pulling out a gray glass jar with a bold golden label. "Vernon, you put jarred baba ganoush in a *dessert* basket? A fennel bulb? Were you feeling particularly sadistic when you did this?"

"Okay, okay, okay," Rachel murmurs to herself, trying to tune out the noise as she picks up each ingredient. She can't remember eating any of this, not even as a kid. "When's the last time you had Spam?"

"So, fun fact: I fucking love Spam," Wren says as they open the rice box.

Rachel hates the phrase "fun fact" and thinks that people who say it, for the most part, are obsessed with themselves. When are those facts ever actually fun?

"I love it so much that I told Ted that I needed to stop eating it. Hypertension runs in the family, y'know?" Wren catches Rachel's expression. "Anyway, that's why we have it. If you were wondering. But you probably weren't wondering."

She softens. Making her partner feel shitty at the beginning of a competition probably isn't the most tactical of approaches. "I was wondering."

Wren nods. "So, what are you thinking we do with it?"

"Not sure yet. Guess we're lucky that the Zatarain's is only rice, huh? We'd be in for a bad time if they were beans."

They point to the opposite corner of the counter. "We do have a pressure cooker, but I wouldn't fuck with Anabelle over it. She's really competitive. Like, *really* competitive. Two months ago, she had an absolute freak-out when Yukiko was using the mixer. 'She's doing it slow on purpose. She's trying to sabotage me.' She got benched for two games."

The red-haired woman glares them down as she removes the machine's lid and pours in the dried black beans from her and Renato's basket. The metallic clink the pot makes is almost threatening. Rachel decides to ignore it as she tries to orchestrate some semblance of an idea. "We have time to cook the rice. Will you get some water started?"

"Sure thing."

Rachel opens the Spam tin and thinks about her mother. She can't help it, of course. It's just the sort of thing that Mom would have loved. Suddenly emotional, she closes her eyes, takes a deep breath, and remembers why Job does most of the cooking. What is it that she does for them exactly? Besides being a burden? *No, no, not that path. Let's think about Mom.* Mom with the forever clever way of thinking about food and smell and flavor combinations. Yes, yes, she would have thought about the savory heat of the Jambalaya mix playing with some less than ideal grains of rice, the saltiness of the Spam, the chutney's spiced sweetness. The idea is coming now; she can almost taste it. "Smoosh it up," she whispers.

"What?" Wren asks as they return to Rachel's side.

"Let's make a rice cake. We need to smoosh the rice up when it's done, put it in a two-inch mold, chill it, then fry it in the pistachio oil." Rachel opens her eyes and frowns. "Wait, do we have ring molds?"

Wren nods, considering the ingredients. "Use the Spam for a topping?"

"You don't wanna put it in the rice cake?"

"No. What we should do is..." they draw out the word as they lope to the fridge and open it, "is take some cream cheese and make a mousse."

"Mousse?"

"Mhm." They drop a block of Philadelphia on the counter. "Something really rich and creamy on top of a spicy rice cake?"

Rachel's vision shifts and makes room for Wren's. "Then we doctor up the chutney."

Wren snaps their fingers. "Exactly. Put it all on top of a bed of greens? You've got yourself a party."

"That's...that's a really good idea."

"I've been known to have one from time to time." Wren winks.

Rachel can't help but smile. There's something so charming about Wren. Maybe it's their youth or their candor; whatever it is, Rachel likes them. "Okay, so I'll get started with the chutney, and you do the Spam mousse?"

"Let's get on it." They go to the fridge, plucking out green onions, a shallot, salad mix, heavy cream, and eggs. Then, they collect some onions from the pantry. Meanwhile, Rachel explores the cupboards for a pan and a heavy bottom pot.

A moment later, Wren is chopping the shallot with Food Network precision, and Rachel is breaking down a head of garlic. Giving the younger person a sidelong glance, it occurs to Rachel that this teenager might know what they're doing.

"Where'd you learn to cook?"

Wren beams, displaying a gap between their teeth that's never been tamed by braces. "My mom. She's obsessed. But like, not with Puerto Rican food, with '50s American housewife food. You know what I mean?"

Rachel doesn't.

"You know...food that takes all day to make because ladies didn't have anything else to do. Roasts, whole hams, Jell-O salad." Wren wipes the shallots into a small mixing bowl. "She thinks women belong in the kitchen. And, like, she was totally cool with the non-binary thing but could not abide the thought of me not knowing how to cook a five-course meal for my spouse." Wren's voice goes up at least an octave: "'When you marry a man or a woman or whatever, you will not embarrass me, Bernadette Jane.'" Rachel isn't sure if it's okay to laugh at this, so she just snorts before opening the chutney jar. Wren shrugs as they go to the spice cabinet and begin to peruse the three-shelf full affair of glass bottles. "Anyway, I got sent to culinary camp for a summer because my mom wanted to make sure I'd bring honor to the family name. Youngest person in my cabin." They grin over their shoulder with a wholesale container of cumin in their hand. "I can make a mean Beef Wellington."

Rachel purses her lips and nods over the jarred chutney, tasting its overabundance of cardamom, and wonders how best to mask it. "Impressive."

Wren shrugs as they fire up the gas on the range and splash some olive oil into a pan. "It's only an impressive skill to have when you're young. After you turn twenty-five, cooking is just something you're supposed to know."

Rachel smiles again, surprised that she isn't feeling distracted by the din that surrounds them, even as Anabelle fusses over Renato and Markeya continue to complain about her basket. Speaking with Wren feels, well, good. "There are plenty of people over thirty who don't know how to cook."

"And how disappointed their mothers must be."

Rachel laughs as she begins to explore the spice cabinet herself. What a collection it is, five dozen bottles for sure, probably more. Collected food moods of housemates for however long this place has had its doors open. Four years? Five? She can't recall.

"What about you?" Wren asks. "Where does your talent come from?"

There's no need to be modest. Rachel knows she handles herself well in the kitchen. "My mom was a chef," she says as she pulls down mustard seeds and yellow curry powder.

The shallots sweat in the pan. "Like, a chef-chef? With a hat?"

At once, Rachel watches her mother use tweezers to place small leaves atop microscopic piles of caviar. "She had a hat."

"That's really cool."

Rachel clears her throat full of fresh emotion. She covers it up with more subpar chutney, trying to reach for the right balance in her mind. "Yeah, it was."

Wren's frantic stirring pauses and Rachel can tell they want to press but is relieved when they don't. Instead, they steer the conversation into warmer waters. The shallot is joined by the Spam. Wren says, "My mom isn't a chef-chef, just a mega enthusiast. She goes overboard all the time. It got to this point when I was a teenager that my dad just refused to eat anything she cooked. No more buttered escargots or sweet meats or panna cotta. All he really wanted to eat was McDoubles." They make room for Lorelei at the range. "Honestly, so did me and my brothers. Kids, amirite? So, she joined this supper club with some people at the place she used to work at—or maybe it was church? Anyway, do you know what a supper club is?"

Rachel does know, but she's curious for Wren's answer. "I'll try not to be a smart ass and say 'a club for supper.'"

"It's this thing that rich housewives do because they're bored and no one pays them enough attention." Wren pauses to season. "Sorry, that's not kind. Or true. What it actually is, is just a group of people meeting up for elaborate dinners at one another's houses. My mom went for a couple of months and had a great time criticizing other people's food. That lady is a shade queen. Will you taste this?"

Rachel pours the Zatarain's into the boiling water, covers the pot, and reduces the heat. Taking the proffered spoon, she tastes the meat slurry. Salt hits her first, then the cumin. "Add some smoked paprika. No more salt. The cream cheese should smooth that out, and the sweetness of the chutney will soak everything else up." Rachel hands back the spoon. "You were saying?"

Wren nods with approval. "Anyway, my mom's number finally comes up. She has to host, and she has to make, drum roll, a Beef Wellington." Lorelei scoffs as she whisks some milk into her pot. "People always say that karma is a bitch, right? So here she is, my Puerto Rican mother, beholden to the holy grail of temperamental white people dishes. So, she takes me to the butchers with her—because I'm the one who needs to learn how to cook—and we buy this huge fucking beef tenderloin, and it's *so* expensive. Like, bologna sandwiches until next pay check expensive." Rachel feels another bubble of laughter rise up in her throat. When was the last time she laughed this much? Without prompting, she goes to fetch the food processor for Wren.

When she returns, Wren continues their story, and Rachel plops a block of room-temperature cream cheese into the bowl. "It was so expensive that she put a seatbelt on it when we got back in the car. And then we get home, and she doesn't even know what to do with it. Seriously, no idea. All we have are about fourteen cookbooks from the library and my sweet, deluded mother trying to Frankenstein's monster all fourteen into some workable shape."

"Tell me she bought the puff pastry, at least," Rachel says, gesturing for Wren to add the Spam pâté.

"Oh, of course, she did. She's not a complete masochist. Everything else, though, she did to a T. Except, how the hell do you wrap a slippery piece of meat with what is the equivalent of a floured noodle? Imagine this: Puff pastry mounded on top of this piece of prosciutto-wrapped meat. But of course, it won't stick because the kitchen's too warm, and instead, the egg wash is just leaking off the damn thing like a fucking Salvador Dali painting."

Rachel pulses the cream cheese with the Spam, laughing the whole time.

Emboldened by her reaction, Wren lays the story on thicker, gesturing wildly. "And here's my mom, just having an absolute panic attack as she's trying to piecemeal the whole thing together. Sobbing 'Throw it in the oven, throw it in the oven!' at me until she has to go to her room and have a proper meltdown." Both of them start to laugh so hard that the other teams pause to watch before getting back to work. Wren lowers their voice, "You know what the funniest part is? It wasn't even that bad. A little overcooked in spots, but tasty."

Warmth floods Rachel's cheeks, and she realizes that they hurt from smiling. Seriously, when was the last time she felt this good? Even thinking about Job, which she does on purpose to bring herself down, can't dull her high. For a few minutes, the two of them bask in that energy, taking time to finish off the mousse with egg yolks and heavy cream. When she tastes it, she is surprised to find that it is good. Moving then with the elegance of two people who have known one another a long time, Wren places their mousse into the fridge to cool while Rachel takes over the burner with a pot soon fragrant with toasting mustard seeds. She agitates the air with her hand the way her mother did to get the scent into her nose, calculating how much will be needed to make that chutney less cloying.

"Attention chefs," Vernon's eerie Ted Allen calls through the kitchen, scaring Rachel so badly that she almost burns herself. "A few brief announcements! One, the bidet attachments for all of the bathrooms will be here tomorrow. Two, our large Costco order will be here in the morning. Please note that we have ordered a good deal more than we usually do and that it may have to last for a while. And third, there are forty-five minutes remaining."

Rachel throws a frantic look at Wren, wondering how time has gone by so quickly. Wren only smiles, the picture of ease.

CHAPTER NINETEEN

WITH THREE MINUTES TO GO, Wren and Rachel scramble to get their bed of greens laid and topped with rice cakes on plates for the judges. They move with smooth synchronization, arms briefly crossing when Wren pipes the Spam mousse into rosettes, and Rachel uses a small spoon to dollop the chutney. As the clock spirals down into seconds, they take two damp cloths to clean the plates of errant crumbs, the way Rachel's mom did in the restaurant in Atlanta. Miraculously, they finish on time.

When only zeroes remain on the screen, a buzzer rips through the kitchen and summons Vernon back to his stage. "Times up, hands up!"

All six contestants, sweaty and red-faced, comply. For the first time in twenty minutes, Rachel has a look around the room. Piles of dishes sit in the sink and along the counter, the appliances are covered in one goo or another, there are bits of food on the floor. In short, it is a disaster. Her competitors, too, have seen better days. Anabelle's blue mask sports black bean juice splotches. Lorelei's apron is stained orange and gray. Markeya holds her freshly bandaged thumb up for inspection. Wren, having eschewed their leather trench coat fifty minutes in, sweats profusely. Renato seems to have emerged unscathed, though the scowl on his face says that he may or may not be on speaking terms with his cooking partner. Rachel shudders to think what she looks like right now.

"You may take your dishes to the dining room for judging," Vernon tells them, making a gracious gesture towards the hall door.

Following Wren's lead, Rachel picks up a plate then balances a second on her left wrist before picking up a third. Plucking up the two remaining plates, Wren asks, "Server?"

"A couple of years," Rachel replies as they head out into the dining room, the plate on her wrist never faltering. "Started off in an Applebee's before making my way up to some really good steakhouses when I still lived in Atlanta."

"Sounds schmancy," Wren says.

While six of them were working in the kitchen, everyone else seems to have been at work in the dining room. Talk about schmancy. There are lit candles on every available surface, totaling somewhere between forty and fifty wicks waving back and forth in revery. There are eleven identical place settings with white linen cloths, forks, knives, and spoons exactly where they should be. On the other side of the room, four of the five judges sit with hands in their laps, not moving much. In this light, they look more painting than flesh.

When all three teams are in the dining room, Vernon invites the entrée and dessert team to place their dishes on the sideboard before taking his seat. Rachel and

Wren set their work in front of each judge. Ted and Daniela hum in wonderment.

"What have you brought us?" Vernon asks, Ted Allen voice still in place.

Standing on the other side of the table, Rachel and Wren stand with hands clasped in front of themselves. Rachel nods, and Wren reports: "We have a Jambalaya rice cake seared in pistachio oil topped with a Spam-cream cheese mousse and smoked chutney. Enjoy."

Each of the judges picks up a fork, making sure they have a little bit of everything in one bite. There is more humming.

"Oh, this is really excellent," Daniela claims. Rachel tries to push down the rush of satisfaction she has from the words but can't quite do so. "The crunch and spice of the rice cake play well with the smoothness of the mousse."

"It's a little spicy," Francesca complains before taking another bite.

Daniela shakes her head. "A little, but I think the sweetness of the chutney balances it well. There's a tangy note in there that I'm getting. What is it?"

Rachel flushes, pleased by Daniela's sensitive palate. "Toasted mustard seeds."

"Delicious."

"Who did what?" Ted asks as he takes another bite.

"It was very collaborative," Wren replies. "Rachel took care of the chutney. I did the mousse. We worked on the rice cake together."

"Great job. Thank you, chefs."

Rachel and Wren make a weird little bow at the same time, which makes them laugh. The judges push the appetizer dishes to the side to make room for the next course. Anabelle steps into center stage like she was made for it. "Good evening, judges. For our main dish, we have pan-fried chicken thighs topped with smoked mole sauce. Your side dish is stewed black bean and dates seasoned with Lawry's seasoning salt and cumin. Thank you."

With forks and knives, the judges cut chicken and scoop up beans. The reaction is immediate. "Delicious," Yukiko says, surprising Rachel a little. "The chicken is perfect."

"How did you do the beans?" Francesca asks.

"We used the pressure cooker," Renato adds. Anabelle gives him a swift glare.

The older woman eats more beans. "Tastes good."

"I really like what you did with mole sauce," Vernon comments. "It doesn't taste like it's right out of the jar. What did you add to give it so much depth?"

"Good dark chocolate," Renato says, obviously pleased with himself. "My mother sent some from Peru last month, so I grated some in and added in some more dried mild peppers."

"I could eat the sauce on bread," Daniela says as she swirls one finger in the sauce and licks it clean. Her mother swats her arm. "I could, though, Mama, it's good."

"Then use a spoon," the older woman chides.

"Thank you, chefs," Vernon says before the two women can get into any further arguments.

Anabelle's shoulders slump, but she moves back without another word. The judges take a sip of red wine to clear the palettes. Markeya and Lorelei take the stage, their piled plates placed in front of their audience.

"What do we have here?" Ted asks.

"I won't lie to you. What you have before you, is nothing short of a miracle." Markeya throws a sardonic glare at Vernon. "We have a smokey-orange-baba-ganoush-hemp-milk panna cotta with a jicama-apple compote topped with shredded fennel."

"Try saying that three times fast," Wren mutters under their breath. Rachel grins.

"Baba ganoush?" Francesca asks, eyeing the plate skeptically.

"Baba ganoush," Markeya confirms, scowling at Vernon.

Ted is the first to pick up a spoon, saying, "I'll try anything once."

His bravery and surprised hum of delight are enough to spur the others onto try. Yukiko's eyebrows raise as she tries. "Oh, wow."

"This is really good," Daniela says, laughing a little. "I wasn't sure how the baba ganoush would taste with the smoked orange, but it's great."

"Citrus, smoke, cream. What's not to like?" Vernon asks, already finished with half of his panna cotta.

Rachel's hopes of winning begin to evaporate as the raptures continue. "That hemp milk adds a nutty note that just works," Daniela says.

"And not overly sweet, right?" Ted replies as though the two of them are sharing a secret. "The jicama-apple compote balances out the smoked orange really nicely."

"Not too much jicama either. Just the right bright note," Vernon observes.

Oh, yeah, our gooses are cooked, Rachel thinks, her own shoulders slumping. Wren places a hand on her upper arm, squeezing before letting go. It is a comfort, and Rachel feels her body relax.

"This is really very good," Yukiko determines.

"Thank you," Lorelei says.

Rachel thinks she has underestimated the quiet German woman. After all, it takes a creative mind to put chipotle crickets into truffles. Between her and Markeya, it now seems so unsurprising that they would have come up with something so creative. Then again, Spam mousse is pretty creative in itself, and she knows for certain that it tasted good. Maybe there's a chance that they'll win.

"Well," Daniela starts as she pushes the dessert plate away, "it seems like we have a lot to discuss. We ask that you return to the kitchen while we deliberate. Vernon will come get you when we're ready."

The six competitors filter back into the kitchen, which looks even worse now that there are no boiling pots and sizzling pans to justify the mess. Each group plops down in their own camp to either chat or sit in tense silence. Rachel decides to sit on the floor next to the refrigerator, and Wren sits on a stool next to her. They say nothing, just relax into the bliss of not being on their feet under the weight of a timeline. It is companionable, which is a surprise to Rachel. It usually takes weeks for her to feel this comfortable with people. Job has been the only person that level of ease has been possible with since college.

Wren begins to unlace their black platforms. "Are you feeling any better? About Job, I mean?" they ask without looking at her. As though clarification is needed.

"Still scared, but better," Rachel admits. She is transfixed by the shoelace as it unspools itself. *Their feet must hurt like all hell.*

"That's understandable. He's a long way away from home." One platform falls away to reveal a black and white striped sock soaked in sweat. The smell isn't ideal. Rachel doesn't make a face, but she does lean away. Wren sets the boot as far away from Rachel as their short arm will allow. "But Job is a resourceful person, yeah?"

Rachel thinks about her husband and smiles to herself. "He is."

Off comes the second stinky shoe. "Well then, between him, Ted, and Daniela, I'm pretty sure nothing short of a nuclear war could keep him from coming home."

For a brief second, Rachel's mind runs that scenario and throws a chill up her spine. She shakes it away because it is ridiculous, that much she knows. It's better to feed her absurd brain more absurdity to calm it down. "Or India spontaneously sinks into the sea," she says.

"Or Jesus comes back." Wren starts to cackle. Their brown eyes crinkle and sparkle with a delight that Rachel can't help but share.

She rests against the wall with her knees gathered to her chest. "Or the sun blows up."

Wren snorts. "Guess that's always a risk, huh?"

Rachel looks up at the ceiling, finding it not a flat white like she first thought but instead a series of intricate floral tiles painted white; given the age of the house, she imagines they are made of tin. How had she missed that interesting detail? If she ever had a chance to be alone in the kitchen, surely she would have noticed it sooner. Not that being alone in this kitchen will ever be a possibility. "Soooo, you play the 'what-if' game, too?" she asks, curious to know how much in common they actually have.

"Oh, of course, though my therapist doesn't always approve."

She grins. "Thanks, Anxiety."

"Yeah, for nothin'."

Vernon's plodding steps come down the hall, bringing everyone to attention. "Chefs, we have our results. If you'll grab your remaining dishes and come with me."

Struggling back onto tired feet, Rachel dusts herself off and collects the platter of the less than beautiful rice cakes that had been left behind after plating. Wren had explained that after the judging round, everyone else gets a chance to sample each other's dishes for dinner. There's no denying her curiosity about the dessert course, so Rachel hands the mousse and chutney over to Wren before hustling down to the dining room.

Taking a seat next to Wren, Rachel winces when she realizes that she's seated across from Daniela. She wonders if she's done so as an unconscious form of punishment. Her last therapist has suggested that she went out of her way to feel bad as a sort of atonement for feeling good. After an evening that has met every marker for enjoyment in spite of Job's circumstances, maybe she shouldn't be surprised by being dealt whatever justice Subconscious-Rachel deems appropriate. To make matters worse, Daniela smiles at her, which she feels compelled to return.

Once the six competitors are situated around the table, Ted stands. "This has been our hardest *Chopped* judging yet. Because all of the dishes were so good, it was impossible to choose just one winner."

"What?" Anabelle cries at the head of the table. Renato winces.

Ted holds out a hand as if that will assure her. "There are three categories: Best Presentation, Best Taste, and Most Creative. Best Taste goes to Rachel and Wren for a singular experience of crunch, cream, and spice." Everyone but Anabelle applauds. Both of them sit up a little straighter, pleased. "Best Presentation goes to Anabelle and Renato for their upscale version of a delightful rustic meal. And, of course, Most Creative goes to Lorelei and Markeya for their tackling of the meanest basket we have had yet. Congratulations, all!"

The judges clap, and Rachel feels pleased with the results.

Obviously, Anabelle isn't happy. "So there's no winner?"

"You're all winners!" Ted expresses with his signature smile. "Each team will get a week of no dishes, starting with Wren and Rachel."

"So the appetizer won?" The woman's face matches her hair underneath that surgical mask. "That's bullshit!"

Ted frowns. "Now, Anabelle, please don't make us keep you out of the competition hat again. This is what we decided. You and Renato take it home for Best Presentation! The judges thought that…"

"Best Presentation?" she interrupts viciously. "Are you kidding me? That's such a non-place place!"

Renato throws his hands into the air. "Anabelle, this is why no one ever wants to play with you!"

Wren whispers, "Here we go."

"Hey, Rachel," Ted calls as though nothing is happening at the other end of the table, "it's just about time to call Job. I was thinking that we'd chat over dinner. Sound good?"

Feeling put on the spot, Rachel says, "Uh, I figured we'd all talk about it here, and then I'd talk to him in private."

"I think we can be more efficient if everyone is on the same page," Daniela adds.

When Francesca and Yukiko nod, Rachel feels backed into the corner and pulls out her cell phone. "Um, okay. I'll call."

The argument falls away at once, and everyone is quiet, watching as she dials. The phone rings once before Job picks up. "Hey, honey." The sound of morning birds sings out somewhere beyond him.

Rachel blooms with pleasure at the sounds of his voice in the dining room, pretending that he is sitting across from her. Remembering herself, she says, "You're on speakerphone."

"Cool."

"Hey, Job. Can you hear us okay?"

Job clears his throat then says yes. Rachel wishes she had texted him beforehand but knows that the texts can be hit or miss.

"Great! How are you doing over there?" Ted leans forward on his elbows, smiling broadly as though Job could see his friendliness.

Job chuckles once, then says, "Well, to be honest with you, a little freaked out."

Ted's face falls, and Daniela presses for more information: "Are all of your needs being met? Enough food, water?"

"No, no, I'm fine that way. The ashram is self-sufficient."

Markeya gets up to stand behind Rachel, leaning against her chair to ask, "How many people are there now?"

"About half of who were here before. Like, sixty people? Enough to tend the gardens."

Rachel wants to ask about how he's doing, how he's feeling, but Vernon is already interrupting. "Have you heard any advice from the U.S. government? The airline?"

"Not yet, unfortunately. Sorry, who all am I talking to? It's a little confusing on my side."

"Sorry, sorry," Ted says, practically on the table now so he can be heard better. "You've got everyone right now. Ted speaking."

"Remind me of names as we go along, please. Haven't been sleeping very well." Job yawns across the world.

"Of course you haven't," Rachel responds, wanting to reach through the phone and hold him. "We can talk about the plan in private."

"I think it'll be better to have everyone on the same page. Daniela, by the way."

"I agree with you there," Job says, banishing Rachel's hopes of being alone. "What do you have in mind?"

"Hey there, Job, this is Vernon."

"Hi, Vernon. Great to hear your voice again."

Vernon smiles, his blonde mustache curving further at the tips. "You, too. So, to clarify, there are no flights right now?"

"Right. Mine got canceled, rescheduled, then canceled again. I'm waiting to hear back from the airline."

"Markeya here. So, I think we all agree that it's best for you to get to a city with a U.S. embassy, which means getting to Chennai."

"Hi, Markeya. Where is Chennai?"

"Wren. On the other side of the country."

"Daniela, again. You can get there by car, bus, or plane."

"Hi to both of you as well," Job says, then laughs. "It's nuts to talk to all of you like this. Anyway, I've gotta say that the plane thing seems preferable."

"Are in-country flights still a thing?" Wren asks.

"As far as I know. Though, that might not be true for too much longer. The locals don't seem to be bothered by the news, but the tourists are going completely insane. Myself included."

"Daniela. If we could get you on a flight, would you want that?"

"Of course." Rachel notes the relief in Job's voice. Her eyes feel wider than they should be. All of this is happening too quickly. "Where would I stay? Grab a hotel or a hostel?"

Vernon pulls out a tablet from under his seat, already logged in and ready to do what secret spy shit everyone seems to think he does for a living. "We're going to rent you a room at the Accord. It's right down the street from the embassy."

"You're doing that now?" Rachel asks.

"Yeah, we're going to get Job on a plane tomorrow morning at ten." Vernon cranes himself towards the speaker. "Sound good?"

"Wait," Renato says with his arms crossed. "Is it better for him to stay where he is? Hey, Job, are there a lot of people coming and going where you are?"

"No, not really. People are leaving but not coming back in. I don't think anyone new has come into the community in about five days."

Renato continues, "Anabelle says this thing is airborne. Maybe that's a better place for him to be while we wait this out."

Daniela says, "But waiting it out doesn't get him home."

"How long could this really last?" Renato asks.

Markeya says, "The CDC is talking weeks or months, and that's if we get in front of it now. The epidemiology team my friend works with was saying a year."

Renato scoffs. "A year? That's ridiculous."

Francesca points at the younger man, which straightens his back. "It could, though, which is why he should get home now."

Job says, "And, for what it's worth, I'd like to come home."

Ted claps twice. "Then let's get you home."

From there, Rachel's entirely too capable housemates lay it out for both of them. Job flies to Chennai in the morning, he stays in a hotel near the embassy while he waits to change his ticket, he changes his ticket, he flies back to Boston (on a cargo plane if he has to), then quarantines in a local Airbnb, and then he comes home. It's that simple. This plan, they think, will work. And Rachel, despite her deeply laid misgiving about life, can't help but be optimistic. In two or three weeks, her Job will be home. In two or three weeks, everything will be okay.

CHAPTER TWENTY

AFTER DINNER, RACHEL TAKES Job back up to her room, pressing him against her ear so as to not miss a single breath. She's eager to make up for all the words they lost to their roommates. She wants to know how he is, really. The borders closing and global air travel being suspended have exceeded even her greatest "what-if" expectations. If she was still in therapy, her anxiety would have a few choice I-told-you-so's for her therapist. Not that it would help her feel better. Being right rarely feels as good as she thinks it should.

Yes, she knew something would happen while they were apart, but it doesn't feel good to open and close the door to their bedroom without him in it. Any room without him in it doesn't feel quite right, which has been true for going on a decade now. Job just makes rooms better.

She met Job a few months after the accident. She'd spent most of her spring semester in the library, hiding from her roommate, who was a very sweet girl but gave Rachel a hangdog expression that made her want to jump from the clocktower. With each passing day, the thought of being an on-campus urban legend became more and more tempting, so she kept herself tucked in the back corner of the library's first floor, where crying was not so uncommon a sight to warrant concern.

Job had been tasked with repairing a wood buttress that had been damaged in a post-game celebration or post game loss riot; Rachel was never sure one way or the other. She'd seen him on campus a few times, repairing chipped woodwork and replacing rotted doorways with a much older, much shorter man who had a gut the size of a beach ball and a handlebar mustache straight out of the '70s. When she saw the young man in the library that afternoon, she expected to see the old man, too, but he was alone. Not that it made any difference to Rachel, but noticing small things outside of herself was a good way to remember that she was real. Or at least that was what the school-appointed therapist had said after Rachel had mentioned her out-of-body experiences. "Grief can be unkind to the body," she was told, though her body was relaying the same message loud and clear. It had been three weeks since she had been able to sleep for more than two hours at a time. She hallucinated, her head hurt from dehydration, she had lost twenty pounds. Her body was a disaster, a testament to grief.

As she stared down into whatever book was in front of her, the grief let her know that it was not sated with her paltry suffering. Her grief let her know that it would wring proper tribute from her in the middle of this library. It would make itself known over the pages of a borrowed book, smudging words that she didn't recognize. Her throat constricted so tight that it was hard to drink air.

From the corner of her watery eye, she saw a pastel yellow handkerchief placed by her hand. The silent sobs faltered a moment, caught off-guard by the gentle-looking thing. Using the back of her wrist, Rachel wiped tears away to stare down at the intrusion then up at the person who had delivered it. His eyes were deep brown, steady in their gaze as they held her, and she felt them hold her. His lips were quirked up to the right, a pensive crease cleaved his eyebrows, sawdust settled on his faded flannel. No one had ever looked so safe. He was silent, watching until Rachel balled the handkerchief into her hand and felt the sobs well up into her shoulders and into her eyes until they began to shake her harder than before.

Easing to his knees, the young man opened his arms. She fell in, burying her mouth into the crook of his neck where she screamed without noise. He held her with all the familiarity of a friend, passing a gentle hand across her shoulder blades and humming in agreement. Little by little, she slid from the chair into his arms. The weight of grief was too much to bear, but the young man caught it all. Without saying a word, she knew then that he bore the same weight.

Later that night, at a dive bar frequented by underclassmen with fake IDs, they told each other about their personal brands of grief. Yes, Job knew the weight of being an orphan. His parents had gone together, too, in a carbon monoxide accident while he was away at Boy Scout camp. One moment the youngest Eagle Scout in a decade, the next the state's problem. He was the only child of two only children without much family to speak of, which meant he would spend the next year and a half bouncing from group home to group home before aging out completely. After that, he found an apprenticeship at a carpenter's shop in Chicago. It was a good living, he told her, not because the money was decent but because it gave him purpose. It was hard to be sad when your body was exhausted.

She asked him if it got better, the grief, and he told her that it just got different.

They fell in love quickly. In fact, if you asked Job, he would say that he fell in love with Rachel the minute she fell into him. Trust like that is hard to come by, he'd say, and he wanted to spend the rest of his life tending it. Rachel would say that she fell in love with Job a week later when he pulled over in the middle of a rainstorm on the way to the restaurant to help a man change a flat tire. When he got back into the car soaking wet and late to their reservation, he beamed. "A Scout is always helpful, you know."

Sure, Rachel had laughed and called him a dork for still subscribing to something as antiquated as Scouting culture, but there was no denying the charm. He was a good person; that much was certain. He proposed to her in Lincoln Park, six months after their first fateful meeting, though he was firm when he said he wanted to wait to wed until after she graduated. That, she thought, was reasonable. Her senior year, they moved into a one-bedroom apartment not too far from campus and hosted study sessions in their living room. Life was easy. And Job had been right; the grief wasn't gone, but it was different. Some days were hard. The engagement had caused them both to spiral into fresh depression, but at least they were together.

They married the summer after graduation, Job's best friend officiating, and sealed their future in front of a small group of close friends before grabbing a couple of pizzas and calling it a night. Soon, Rachel snagged a job with a non-profit, and Job improved his craft. They were too busy for babies; of course, they both knew that. The years flowed, and they outgrew their jobs. Rachel went back to school for her MBA, and Job started his own business. They bought a house and filled it full of photos of themselves. The grief grew lighter.

A few months before her twenty-ninth birthday, Rachel told Job that she wanted to be a mother. He'd been waiting for those words for a long time. They began to enthusiastically try and fail for months until, rather suddenly, it seemed, Rachel was pregnant. When she told Job, he fell to his knees the way he had the day they met and held her stomach close to his face. Their friends threw them a party with more booze than was appropriate for a baby shower. House jam-packed with supplies, they waited with delight as Rachel's stomach bloomed until it bloated.

Trisomy-18, they were told, as if medical explanation could mitigate devastation.

She carried their baby for eight full months before it turned still. She had to induce labor. She had all ten fingers and toes, you know, and a cleft palate that split her soft lips. Siobhan was perfect, really, resting small in Job's hands. They had to leave her at the hospital, and they had to burn her up. Job built a home for her ashes, adorning it with his mourning. He'd never worked so fast.

The day they came home with her in that box was the day Job stopped speaking. Meanwhile, Rachel took up keening in every room in their house, bundling herself up under their bed and in the closets, wherever she could feel most pressed in. There is no word for a childless couple other than "sad." And they were sad. Six weeks later, Rachel went back to work from maternity leave, and Job returned to his workshop. Very little was said by anyone. Eventually, their friends stopped calling.

Three months after it happened, Rachel came home from work with takeout from their favorite Chinese restaurant. They'd both lost enough weight that a few egg rolls could do them some good. When she came in through the front door, she knew something was wrong. Job wasn't in the kitchen making her evening coffee. He always did, even in the depths of despair. She looked in every room, knocked on the bathroom door a dozen times before going in. She called him, texted, and he was silent.

Every stone unturned in the house, she went out back to the workshop. The lights were off, but she could hear the generator chugging along inside. Her footsteps hastened, and she ripped open the door to a thick toxic haze.

When Job woke up twelve hours later, cocooned in a hospital gown, the first thing he said after weeks of silence was, "It was an accident."

It was the first time that she hadn't believed him.

Two months after that, after too many tense nights of sleeping back to back, they packed up their home and the business and got on a one-way flight, ready for a new way of living. It seemed like the only thing to do.

Now, though, they are further apart than ever. Rachel rests her back against the door and says, "Hi."

Job laughs once. "They're a lot, aren't they?"

She smirks as she sinks to the floor. "I told you."

"They mean well," he tells her. "It feels good to have a plan."

"It does." A silence builds between them. Rachel frowns, gaze fixed on the space between her windows as the sounds of birds swirl on both sides of the phone call. When did conversations for them get hard?

"Hey," he says, "do you know what I'm thinking about right now?"

Rachel removes her ponytail holder and lets her hair go free, rubbing the back of her skull. "Statistically speaking, no."

He exhales with teasing impatience. "Play with me."

She sits up straighter, surprised by the sudden turn. "Oh, it's that kinda conversation?"

Birdsong grows chaotic on his side for a few seconds before he asks, "What if it is?"

Rachel's face goes hot. "I mean...I'm into it. I'm just not...I wasn't ready for it."

"Oh, well," he stumbles, "we don't have to..."

"No!" she asserts. "I want to. Let me just...get into character." She takes a breath, trying to calm her heart. They are rusty at this, but she wants to be better. She tries to remember what it was like to lust after Job when they were young and a little less heartbroken. Her voice lowers, "Okay, so what are you thinking about?"

Job sighs, then hums. Identical shivers run along Rachel's arms. "I love the way your voice sounds on the phone. So smoky. There's something about hearing you and not seeing you that is very sexy."

Someone's footsteps come up the stairs, rocking Rachel's focus. She stands up and goes to the window, moving the curtain back to look down into the dark yard. "Is that what you're thinking about?"

Job clears his throat, letting his voice go husky. "Not quite. I was thinking about our last night in Cairo. Remember?"

Her reflection grins. "It was only a couple of weeks ago." They had spent their last night together in a suite that cost more than a month of backpacking in Nepal. She'd wanted to keep the money in the emergency fund, but Job had insisted on luxury before the temporary separation. The next morning, she felt it was worth the expense.

"That sunset over the Nile was stunning, wasn't it? We'd just gotten back from drinking that bottle of Champagne to celebrate the lease." Her head spins with the memory of bubbles and beautiful things. "You looked so lovely in that green dress."

Rachel recalls the one and goes to the closet to find it. She presses the phone between her ear and shoulder, flicking through hangers. "The one I bought in that market in Marrakesh? I put a hole through the back somehow. It needs mending."

Job sighs. "Do you want to talk about mending dresses, or do you want to talk about what we did after you took the dress off?"

Her hands fall from the clothes. Guilt flushes her face this time, and she wraps an arm across her chest. "Right, right. Sorry. I'm focused."

Patient as ever, Job says, "Honey, you have nothing to apologize for. This is supposed to be fun."

Heart still racing, her words speed too, "I'm having fun. Are you having fun?" This does not feel fun.

"Rachel, it's okay," he says.

"I want to do this," she affirms to herself more than him. She does want to do this and loathes herself for being so anxious around Job. "We should do this."

Suddenly, "Will you lie down for me?"

The request catches her off-guard. "What?"

"Just," he takes a measured pause. "Trust me, please. Turn off your lights, lock your door, take off your shoes, and get into bed."

Now she's trembling, body covered in goosebumps as she goes to lock her door and shut off the lights. The only illumination comes from the salt lamp on her desk. "I can do that." Self-conscious, she asks, "Are you doing that?"

"I'm taking a walk right now, looking for a good place to sit since the weather is so nice right now. I would like to focus on you if that's okay."

Her stomach drops then twists with guilt as she rests one knee on the bed, not fully committed to the idea. "We can do this later."

Job chuckles. "Honey, breathe. Just breathe; that's all you need to do."

It takes a lot of focus to slow down. "I'm breathing."

"Good." She can hear the smile in his voice. "Keep breathing. What are you wearing?"

She laughs outright, which feels good. Natural, almost. "Jeans and my green sweater."

"I bet you look gorgeous right now," he murmurs. "Will you take your pants off for me?"

"Okay." Hot again, she sets the phone on the bed, unbuttons her jeans, and shimmies them to the floor. She picks Job back up and says, "They're off."

Job's breath catches. "I shivered a little bit. I've gotta admit, I'm thinking about running my hands over your bare knees, pushing them up your thighs, trailing my fingertips across your waist. I want to kiss your neck, move my lips up to yours." Rachel shakes as she remembers how he did just that in Cairo. "If I was there now, would you kiss me back?"

"Of course."

"Tell me how."

She does, and their breathing goes fast and in time. Resting back against pillows, she closes her eyes to see his nose tracing her jaw, caressing the points of her nipples, teasing the band of her underwear. He reminds her of the bathtub in Cairo, the way he used his hands to wash every inch of her body, making her stand in front of him with one foot resting on the lip of the tub so his tongue could bathe her so well that it took all her effort not to collapse.

"What I wouldn't give to taste you right now," he tells her hoarsely.

Her body jerks in response. "Really?"

"I want what I want, angel. But I'm not there to do it, so you've gotta touch yourself for me. Keep your eyes closed, and imagine that your fingers are my fingers. Can you do that?"

Hand already in her underwear, she listens and relaxes against her own warmth and wetness. She eases into the feeling, remembering how easy this used to be. Her breathing deepens as he whispers encouragement and love words over the phone. In that moment, he is close enough to touch; she is close enough to be touched.

CHAPTER TWENTY-ONE

IN THE MORNING, RACHEL feels more herself than she has in a long time. Limbs languorous, she stretches in the center of the bed and takes up all the room she wants. Though she misses Job now more than ever, there's no denying the fact that he is a bed hog. *Might as well enjoy this while I can*, she thinks ruefully. It won't be long now until he is invading her side of the bed. Her heart butterflies around the thought. Rolling over, she snags her phone off the charger to see if Job has texted her anything sweet. He has, of course, but what has Rachel's attention is the dozen-plus text messages on the house group chat.

Vernon:	Waffles in kitchen for anyone who wants
Anabelle:	Me! Me! Send them out to carriage house?
Vernon:	Putting them on the tray. Syrup or jam?
Anabelle:	Both! Thank youuu <3
Anabelle:	And butter!
Anabelle:	And fruit!
Markeya:	Coffee too
Vernon:	Aye, aye
Daniela:	Are you both okay out there? Does the heat work?

Anabelle:	It's like a sleepover
Markeya:	Surprisingly pleasant. Little drafty around the windows but otherwise fine.
Ted:	I'll bring up some window cling from the basement.
Lorelei:	Is it haunted?
Markeya:	Definitely.
Lorelei:	Cool.
Renato:	We should do a seance!
Markeya:	No thank you
Wren:	That's a great idea! Talk to ghosts but keep them out of the house.
Markeya:	NO
Vernon:	Anyone else for a waffle before I turn off the iron?

Rachel smiles at the exchange, a bit bewildered by its absurdity. Still, she would like a waffle and sends a text to that effect. Vernon immediately sends back a thumbs-up emoji that prompts her to get out of bed and head to the bathroom. Her step feels lighter as she stands in front of the mirror and notices, perhaps, that the bags under her eyes aren't so deep today either. Amazing what an orgasm can do for one's disposition. Hell, even the light from the window seems kinder today.

Sitting on the toilet, she leans down to open the under-sink cabinet for a fresh roll of toilet paper. As she does, she notices the box of unopened tampons and starts to do math in her head before throwing the thoughts away entirely. International travel has always been confusing for her ovaries, not to mention all of the other cycles that her body is no doubt trying to sync up with for whatever biological reason. No sense in doing period math with so many unknown variables.

The passing thought is flushed away. After, she takes a shower and allows her mind to go to sweeter places where Job is the one washing her hair. Her body warms in response to the idea, though she does not indulge it. Instead, she washes then dresses so she can have her waffle before it goes cold. When she opens the door to the hallway, she nearly trips over Klimt, whose full body is stretched near her threshold. Instead of getting upset, she gives him a quick pat on the head. She is still not a cat person.

In the kitchen, which smells of heated butter, Renato, Yukiko, and Vernon sit at the large dining table, heads bent over a large-print crossword puzzle, forks poised over the remnants of breakfast. Seeing her, Vernon jumps up to his feet to get a plate out of the microwave before Rachel can take a step towards the range. "Just in time," he says with a smile. He's wearing a nice burgundy cardigan over a white button-down. Rachel thinks he looks like the English professors she wanted to have in college but never got because their classes filled so quickly. "There's butter and syrup on the table. Do you want some eggs or bacon?" he asks, blue eyes bright.

"Renato ate all the bacon," Yukiko says, throwing a disapproving look at her boyfriend.

Vernon leans in as though to share a secret: "I can actually bake more bacon."

Even though Rachel would, in fact, like some bacon, she can't bring herself to ask. Instead, she bobs her head a few times. "Just the waffle is fine. Thank you so much."

"Are you any good at crossword puzzles?" Renato asks as Vernon scoots into the bench, leaving plenty of room for Rachel to join them.

"Um, guess it depends on the question," she replies as she butters the fresh waffle.

"Well, that's already way better than us," Renato says, grinning. "Not really fair to ask the non-native speakers to do this sort of thing, but whatever."

"For the record, I didn't ask you to help. You said you wanted to partake," Vernon says.

"That was before you just said 'old townhouse feature.' Like, is that a statement or a question?" Renato says, pointing out the offending clue.

Straightening, Rachel reaches for the newspaper. "May I?"

"Please," Vernon replies, using his forefinger to point out the contention.

Her eyes are quick to find the word's five boxes, one of which is an "e," and tells her all she needs to know about the answer. "It's 'oriel,'" she says.

"Just like that?" Renato demands.

"Yeah, it fits." Rachel scoots the puzzle back to Vernon.

"Do you do these sorts of things often?" Yukiko asks, tucking her hair behind her ears.

After finding that the syrup is a quality brand from Vermont and not the cheap grocery store stuff, Rachel pours it on thick. "Not really. I just happen to know what an oriel is."

"And what's an oriel?" Renato asks.

"Um…kinda like a bay window. Do you know what that is?" Renato and Yukiko look at each other as though their personal dictionaries have identical missing entries. Rachel blushes, hoping that she hasn't embarrassed them. "If you saw it, you'd know what I was talking about. It's a window that sort of pokes out of a building."

"There are a couple of houses on Highland Ave like that," Vernon explains.

Rachel beams, making a mental note to walk down that street, pretty sure it isn't far away from the house. "It was super popular in the 1800s, so there are probably a lot of houses in the older parts of Boston with those windows. I mean, it's an architectural style that's been around a lot longer than that, but anyway." Suddenly, she feels like she's rambling and gazes down into the syrup-filled pockets of waffle. She adds, "It's supposed to help people get more sunlight in their houses in the winter months."

"Not to mention that it was a great way to get around property taxes," Vernon casually adds. When they are quiet, he says, "Because taxes were calculated on a building's foundation width and length? If you add an oriel on the second-floor, you don't have to pay taxes on it."

Renato's eyes widen, and then he begins to nod dramatically. "Oh, of course, of course! An *oriel*." His face relaxes. "I swear, you people make things up to confuse us."

Yukiko elbows him in the side before returning to the conversation. "You both seem to know so much about so many things. Is architecture of interest to you, Rachel?"

Swallowing a divine bite of batter, butter, and syrup, Rachel nods. "I almost got a degree in art history with a specialization in architecture."

"Why didn't you?" Yukiko asks.

Rachel pauses, taking another bite to buy herself some time. When her thoughts are in one manageable place, she says, "I realized that it wasn't the most fiscally responsible thing I could do. I went with a business degree and minored in finance."

"Well, you work at Harvard now, so probably a good call on your part," Renato says.

Rachel's heart drops just a little. "Yeah, you're right."

"But you still get to appreciate architecture as art," Yukiko adds, seeming to notice the dip in her mood.

Rachel struggles for a smile, meeting her eyes and nodding before returning to breakfast.

"What does everyone have planned for the day?" Vernon asks as he closes the book.

"Recital practice," Yukiko says before stacking her empty plate on top of Renato's.

"I should do the same, but I don't want to," he says.

"Rachel?" Vernon asks.

She cuts up the rest of the waffle, casting a look out at the dreary weather through the window. It isn't much of a Saturday. "You know, I'm thinking that unpacking the crates and setting up the workshop before Job gets here would be a nice surprise for him."

"That does sound like a nice surprise. Need any help?" Vernon asks.

"No, no, I can do it."

"Aren't those boxes super heavy?" Renato asks. "I remember them being heavy."

"They were heavy," Yukiko confirms.

Rachel eats another bite and doesn't look at any of them out of sheer embarrassment. "You didn't have to do that for us."

"Of course not," Renato says. "And we don't have to help you today, but we will."

"Seriously..." she starts, but neither Renato nor Vernon are having any of it.

"It's too dangerous to do that alone," Vernon says with surprising firmness. "I'll go get my moving shoes on, and then I'll be over to help."

"Same with me," Renato says, getting up to clear his and Yukiko's plate, holding out a hand for Vernon's. After, the three of them all scoot out of the bench on the opposite side without disturbing Rachel. Despite her embarrassment over their fuss, she feels the warmth of pleasure spread throughout her arms. In fact, she feels downright flattered. Besides, with the extra hands, she'll be able to feather her nest for Job's arrival all the faster.

Finishing up, she tidies her space and heads out to the little house. She hasn't been inside since the day she found out about Job, which was just shy of a week ago. When she turns on the light, she gasps. Literally, the space is so different that, had it not been for the crates labeled "Workshop," she would have thought of herself in an entirely different place.

The warped wood floors have been replaced with large slate tiles; the split walls have been repaired, smoothed, and painted a soft gray; the cracked window replaced with a clean, well-sealed pane; new pendant work lights hang from the ceiling; along the far wall, there is a giant pegboard hung at just the right height for tools. It doesn't even smell musty anymore. Mouth agape, Rachel's eyes track the room and stop at a six-foot-tall fig tree. It is absolutely absurd. Without meaning to, she starts to laugh. The sound is quiet at first, but then it builds into a full belly laugh that feels so good that she wraps her arms around her stomach and folds into it. She laughs until tears well and spill across her cheeks. She laughs so much that she doesn't hear the door open behind her. When Renato asks, "What's so funny?" she has to work hard for her breath.

"It's a-a-a fig tree," she howls, pointing towards the vegetation in question. The laughter doesn't stop.

"Does it tell jokes?" Vernon asks.

Rachel shakes her head. More tears spill. Her chest hurts. "He-he-he bought a tree."

"Yes, a fig tree. Why is that funny?" Renato asks, placing a hand on Rachel's shoulder. "Are you okay? Do we need to move the tree?"

"I'm sorry," she wheezes. "I'll stop in a second. It's just-just…"

Vernon finishes for her, "A very funny tree."

Taking a couple of deep breaths, the laughter turns to humorous hiccups that Rachel manages to tame. She wipes her face free of tears with the backs of her hands. She blinks at Vernon and Renato with a sheepish smile and red eyes. "I can't remember the last time I laughed like that," she confesses.

Footsteps come stomping from upstairs until the camouflaged door swings open to reveal Markeya in flannel pajamas, purple hair wrap, and a sheet mask. "What the hell are y'all doing in here without your faces covered?" Markeya scolds, taking a few steps back up the stairs.

Renato crosses his arms, defiant. "I thought we only needed those outside the house."

Markeya looks at him like he's grown a second head. "Anabelle and I literally moved in here yesterday because we are high-risk individuals. Now you're in here breathing our air. You kidding me?"

Rachel's face goes hot. "Sorry. Didn't think to ask. I wanted to unpack the crates so you wouldn't have to look at them all the time."

Markeya considers this request before giving a single nod of assent. "Well, you need masks. Let me go get a box I stole from work." As she heads up the stairs, she says, "And keep that door open."

"Can do," Vernon says. He props the door open with a brick he picks up outside.

The winter draft is bitter. Hopefully, with three people, the job won't take too long. Then again, there are a lot of things crammed into those crates. Renato claps. "Okay, who's got a crowbar?"

Not long after, the three of them wear blue surgical masks while negotiating with the shipping crates. Rachel uses an electric drill to remove the screws. Renato throws his full weight into prying the boards apart. Vernon catches the sides before they fall to the floor. They move together with the same silent agreement borne out of years of teamwork. Rachel won't lie; their help sure makes things easier.

"Have you heard from Job today?" Vernon asks after they finish tearing apart the last crate and littering the floor with packing materials and about a billion splinters.

She smiles to herself at his rosy reminder of their night together. "A brief text."

"Has he gotten any word from the embassy yet?" he asks.

Just like that, her golden glow evaporates, and she remembers that Job is, in fact, trapped on another continent and that she is, in fact, the most selfish person on the planet. All of the gentleness leaves her shoulders, tightened with fresh anxiety. "Do you think he should have yet?" she asks, hands pausing amidst the shreds of paper they used to cushion Job's equipment.

"No," Vernon says quickly. "Was wondering is all. I'm sure everything's fine."

Do you know something I don't? she wonders, standing too alert.

"Traveling can be such a disaster," Renato laments, cutting the sudden energy shift. "This one time, when I was coming through Nepal, I'm pretty sure I smuggled drugs."

Rachel is grateful for the intervention. She starts hauling workbench pieces together to a section of the room to be assembled. "What do you mean you're 'pretty sure'?"

"Well, I was in line for customs with my own bag. Packed light, of course. I'm a professional." Renato winks at Rachel, causing her to laugh and roll her eyes. She understands why Yukiko would find him charming. "And while I'm waiting, this woman walks up to me and starts making small talk. She's British, just finished up some backpacking, tells me about her trip. Very nice. Then she starts complaining that she's just got too many bags to carry through customs, that she wishes they would let you have the roller carts when you got off the plane, so you didn't have to haul stuff around."

Rachel and Vernon both pause to listen to his story, hands on hips.

"Here I am, a very nice man," he gestures to himself, "thinking that it would be kind of me to offer to help her carry her things through customs. She starts thanking me over and over again and gives me her biggest bag. One of those ones with the wheels. I take it through customs, pop the bag on the moving thing. What's that called?"

"Conveyor belt," Vernon supplements.

Renato grunts as he lifts the heavy top of the workbench over to the pile. "Right. So, I put the bag on the conveyor belt, do my customs check. Do these things screw-in or something?"

Rachel's throat clenches at what happens next. She's heard enough horror stories to know that this story can't have a good end. "They wedge together," she says quickly, already attaching the legs to the base. "What happened?"

"When I went through customs?"

She nods eagerly.

Renato's eyes crinkle, no doubt smiling under that mask. "Nothing."

"Get out," she says, gob-smacked.

"I'm telling you the truth. I got through customs without issue, the lady took her bag, and then I never saw her again. I didn't even think anything was wrong until I told my sister when I got home. She said that I could have wound up in a Nepali prison."

"You certainly could have," Vernon says as their team flips the bench over. It's heavier than Rachel remembers. "Glad to hear that nothing happened."

"You're definitely a drug smuggler, though," Rachel says. "Okay, the counter part is over there. It's really heavy, but it'll slip into the slats easy. I'll use the rubber mallet to secure it."

Renato and Vernon work quickly, huffing as they haul the slab of wood over the structure as Rachel instructs. As she secures the bond, the younger man says, "Which is to say, traveling can be a nightmare, but that everything turns out okay in the end."

Rachel chuckles but gets distracted by the fine wood grain of the workbench. The heavy oak is nicked in places but smooth, a sign of quality craftsmanship. She remembers the time it took for Job to get this thing put together just right. In a few short weeks, he'll be making plenty of other things just right. With the centerpiece of the room done, the three of them make short work of the toolboxes, metal shelves, and power tools. They move so briskly that no one complains of the cold. About halfway through unpacking, the space already looks a mile beyond the home shop in Chicago. The ventilation's better, too.

If she's not careful, she could see them living here for a while. Then again, maybe that isn't such a bad thing. Job would love everyone hanging out in his workshop, chatting about a million and one different things while he worked on cabinets for this client or that. She wants this to be a place he wants to stay, fig tree and all. Despite her initial reservations, Rachel begins to imagine herself sitting at the bar with a book, listening to Job hum to himself in the new space.

She wants to know what it will take to make this work. "Hey, Vernon?" she asks as she bundles a collection of jigsaws onto the top shelf of a freshly put-together cabinet. Renato busies himself with taking their trash to the curb.

"Hey, Rachel?" he replies.

"You've lived in this house for a while, right?"

He pauses as though collecting the weeks and months together into a tidy mental pile. "Guess that depends on your concept of 'a while'."

Why don't you just answer the question? she wants to blurt but doesn't for the sake of politeness. She feels like she's running on borrowed housemate grace after all of her little outbursts this week. No need to set a tense stage for Job's arrival.

She strives for clarity: "You've been here since the house opened."

"Since Ted and Daniela opened the house for communal living?"

Specifics with this guy, she thinks, really trying not to roll her eyes. "Yes."

"Yes."

"Do you like it?"

"Living here?"

Jesus Christ. Rachel's hand tightens around a hammer before dropping it into the big toolbox. It's a good thing there's a mask covering her mouth right now; otherwise, Vernon would get some premium stank face. "Yes. Do you like living in this communal household?"

There is a trace of humor in his voice that Rachel doesn't appreciate. "I do."

Fighting for composure, she asks, "Why do you like living in this communal household?"

"Because there's always someone around to help you unpack a wood workshop." Rachel snorts. Vernon's blue eyes glitter in the early afternoon sunlight streaming in from the new window. He stands up and leans against the workbench. "You want a real answer, I take."

For the love of— "I would appreciate one, yes."

"Okay." He takes another long pause before continuing. "I was in Tokyo a few years ago for an eighteen-hour layover. I left the airport because I wanted to see the city, have a little ramen. So, I get off the plane with my luggage and get on a train. It took about an hour, so I felt like I had plenty of time to explore and get back." Rachel's eyebrows draw together in confusion. "Only problem was that it was pretty late when I finally got into Tokyo, a little past ten, and just about everything was closed. Streets were empty, lights were off. So, I think to myself that maybe it's a good idea to just go back to the airport. Unfortunately for me, the trains stop running to the airport at night."

Rachel crosses her arms and leans back against the nearest cabinet. "So, you were stuck?" *Where is he going with this?*

Vernon closes his eyes and nods slowly. "Yup. And then, to make things worse, it starts to rain. Hard.

Ten minutes in, I'm soaked through. My bag is soaked through. I was freezing, exhausted, and starving. A little past midnight, I stumbled into a hotel that had its lights on and basically begged the front desk person to let me rent a room for a couple of hours, but they wouldn't. Didn't have the right money, company policy, whatever. Probably I just looked deranged, and they didn't want to deal with me. Which, in retrospect, is fair." He shrugs. "At this point, I'm in tears, which no one can notice because it's raining so hard. Bully for me, I guess. I went back to the train station because it was mostly covered and laid down on the bench. I told myself that I would be getting on a plane no matter what in just a few hours. I focused on that fact, even though it didn't make me any less hungry.

"At some point, I guess I dozed off because the next time I opened my eyes, a woman was standing over me with an umbrella, asking me something in Japanese. You might not know this about me, but I don't speak Japanese. Fortunately, her English was good enough to ask if I was okay. I explained my situation, and then she offered to let me come home with her."

Rachel finds that hard to believe. Generosity at that level strikes her as the kind present only in ancient myths about gods in disguise waiting to test unsuspecting mortals. "Seriously?"

"Seriously. She lived a couple of blocks away from the train station, so we walked over to her place. She fed me some leftover ramen, dried my clothes, gave me a place to sleep for the night, and got me on the train the next morning. She asked for nothing in return. It was probably the nicest thing anyone has ever done for me."

Rachel can't help but agree.

They both watch as Renato walks back into the little house, clapping warmth into his hands. Vernon hums with pleasure, then turns to Rachel to say, "Living here is kinda like that. One minute you're wandering through life wet, cold, and alone. The next, someone's standing over you with an umbrella." He hums again, softer this time. "It's special."

As she looks at them both, their faces flushed with cold and exertion, she knows Vernon is right. She feels the truth in her smile.

CHAPTER TWENTY-TWO

LIKE EVERY SPRING, SHE'S told, a blizzard hits after six inexplicably warm days. When Rachel wakes up and peels back the curtain, snow crystals are already piled up on the window ledge. Down in the garden, drifts dance over every available inch, except for the pond where the snow melts on contact with the detritus-rich water just beginning to freeze. It looks like a milky pupil surrounded by all that white. Through sleep-blurred vision, Rachel swears it blinks. Stepping away, she picks up her phone to see if there are any texts from Job. There aren't, but the house is already awake.

Daniela:	Thanks for shoveling the walk, Vernon
Vernon:	I think I salted before the freeze set in, but please be careful.
Lorelei:	I'm taking today off. Going to make pretzels.
Vernon:	Bavarian or Swabian? ;)
Lorelei:	I'll pretend you didn't ask that.
Daniela:	Is anyone else taking the day off?
Wren:	Obviously me
Renato:	Same
Ted:	It seems like a good day to do it. Do we want to plan on anything?

Markeya:	Anabelle and I are off, too. Can we watch a movie?
Daniela:	Are you both okay over there? Heat still working?
Markeya:	We're fine. The window cling did the trick. Anabelle is using the hot plate.
Markeya:	But is anyone interested in watching a movie?
Francesca:	How we do that?
Vernon:	We can all watch it at the same time, on different devices.
Markeya:	We can watch on a laptop in here and you all can watch in the media room
Ted:	Can Job join us?
Vernon:	If he wants. We can watch when it's convenient for him. I'll send the invite.
Daniela:	What are we watching?
Markeya:	If people are interested, the new Cats movie is a beautiful disaster
Ted:	I'm in!
Wren:	Me
Renato:	Please

Outvoted before casting a ballot, Rachel sighs and hopes that Job says no. But, knowing him the way she does, there will be no escaping *Cats*. There's no sense in even contributing to the text chain, so she emails her boss that she will need to take the day off instead. Her boss immediately emails a reminder to enter the time into the timesheet. She rolls her eyes and calls Job. He picks up on the first ring, his voice husky, "Hey, honey."

She plops onto the bed, falling back into red and yellow flowers that aren't so bad after all. "Are we watching *Cats* tonight?" she asks as her gaze holds onto the chandelier's crystals.

"Oh, yeah." He clears his throat. "Vernon just texted me about that. It sounds like a fun idea. The hotel I'm in has Wi-Fi, so I could. You wanna?"

"Not really, but I never want to do anything." She sighs heavily at the prospect of a Broadway musical that was never good to begin with, ruined by CGI. "If you want to, I will."

Job coughs. "Sorry. Tickle in my throat. Anyway, I think it'll be funny. Give me a chance to interact with everyone." Another cough.

Rachel sits up. "Are you okay?"

He clears his throat. "Yeah, just a tickle. Let me get some water."

Rachel hears his barefoot steps slap against whatever tile floor is in his hotel room. A faucet turns on in the distance, then the desperate sound of her husband chugging a glass. Sitting at the edge of the bed now, her hand reaches out to the side of the table to touch the picture frame that lives there. Her father's eyebrows seem heavier-set today, contemplative. Maybe it's the light.

"Okay, back," Job says.

"Better?" she asks as her finger brushes against the tops of her brothers' curly heads.

"Loads," he says. "What are you doing?"

Rachel quirks her eyebrow at the change in topic. "Looking at the family picture."

"How are they today?"

She takes a long look then determines, "Tired."

Job hums, then clears his throat. Rachel feels anxious prickles scatter across her skin. "Hey, honey, I'm going to hop down for a snack. I can watch the movie with you guys tonight if it isn't too late. Sound good?"

"Sure..." She pauses to take her eyes away from her family, focusing on Job. "Do you have everything you need? Stuff to do?"

"I'm fine, sweetheart. Really into meditation right now." He adds slyly, "Plus, I have, like, eight seasons of *The Bachelorette* to watch."

She smiles at that. "Okay."

Job says, "I love you, Rach."

And she says, "I love you, too."

When they hang up, Rachel places her phone on the table in front of her family. "Do you think he's okay?" she asks.

They, as usual, don't have much to say. Without their input, her mind spins into a full panic tilt that she has to tame in the shower with cold water and a meditation video on YouTube. Half an hour later, her hair damp, Rachel creaks her bedroom door open only to find Klimt yet again stretched across her threshold. Upon being disturbed, he cracks open a sleepy yellow eye, meows soundlessly, gets to his feet, and saunters into her bedroom. Before she can catch the ginger beast, he's under her bed and out of reach. She mumbles some unflattering things about cats and leaves the room with the door cracked.

By the time she reaches the bottom of the back staircase, the swell of the house greets her. Voices come from the kitchen, piano from the front room, a sewing machine patters away in the dining room. She follows the latter sound, unsure of the last time she heard one, maybe when she was a child, and her dad made Halloween costumes. There, she finds Francesca at the helm, a small scrap of fabric buzzing under a Singer's needle. Leaning against the door, Rachel watches the older woman's knobbled hands move gracefully as they turn the fabric into some predetermined shape. And with hair that is still more pepper than salt swept back into a loose bun, octagonal gold glasses, and a Patagonia fleece vest, Francesca seems a woman twenty years her junior.

"*Hola,*" she says without looking up.

Jumping, Rachel laughs nervously. "Morning. Sorry, didn't mean to intrude."

"You're not intruding." Her hands pull away whatever is on her altar, snipping the thread.

Without meaning to, Rachel finds herself standing on tiptoes to get a better look. "What are you making?"

Francesca reaches for a piece of cord out of the scrap pile next to the sewing machine, feeding it into a hole at one side of the fabric. "A mask."

"Why?"

"Because they were out of face masks at the store," she explains, eyes never deviating from their task. "I saw online a video on how to make your own."

"Where did you get the fabric?" Rachel asks, leaning forward with all the curiosity of a child. She doesn't remember having moments of peeking her head into a grandmother's craft room or kitchen as they conjured everything from nothing.

"The basement," Francesca says as she threads the other side of the mask. "Leftover from some clothes for the baby I made years ago."

Rachel quirks a brow and smiles. "You've been preparing, haven't you?"

Francesca's hands still, and she looks towards the door with eyes that strike Rachel as sad. She wonders what she said. "If you want, I'll teach you," Francesca says.

Feeling obliged to smooth things over, Rachel nods. "Yes, please."

Francesca pulls out the chair next to her. "Come."

Seated, Rachel's nose discovers a floral perfume going to war with a pack of smokes. Marlboro Golds, if her memory of late nights outside of the school library has anything to say about it. Not that she has to breathe it long because, without ceremony, Francesca holds the new mask up to Rachel's face and loops the strings over her ears. "How's that?" she asks.

Rachel scrunches her nose a few times before using her fingers to get the fabric settled into the right places. "It feels okay," she says, noting the strangeness of having her mouth and nose covered.

Francesca removes her creation. "Good. We can make another. You can help."

"I don't want to slow you down."

"It's easy. *Mira*, give me those scraps." Francesca points to the pile of fabric covered in jungle leaves. "We'll trace around the lid, cut it, sew together, and add the string. Simple." She brushes her soft fingers together as though to snap while the free hand gives Rachel a cooking pot lid. "Trace with the chalk."

Rachel glances between the fabric, chalk, and the lid, nervous. "I don't want to mess it up," she admits.

Francesca tsks. "It's fabric, not heart surgery. If you cut too small, we'll cut more."

"Okay..." Rachel stretches the fabric across the table, placing the lid on top before tracing with a piece of chalk. Then she picks up the scissors. "Just cut along the line?"

The older woman nods.

With shaking hands, Rachel starts to trim around the fabric. Immediately, Francesca reaches to put her hand over Rachel's, stretching it out as wide as the scissors will spread. "Don't be afraid," she demands and leaves no room for question. Seconds later, the fabric is the right size, if not a little ragged around the edges.

Francesca takes the circle and measures it just so, making more chalk marks. She hands it back, and Rachel cuts along them. After, the fabric is laid back on the altar and sewn up with alacrity. A few silent minutes later, Francesca has another mask. "We need a lot," she says. "I think three for each of us. Thirty, do you think?"

Rachel eyes the small pile of fabric. "At least."

"We'll get more," she assures. "There are curtains upstairs that I don't like."

They laugh before Francesca orders Rachel to cut more circles. Something is soothing about the sewing machine's clatter that she wishes were more familiar. She asks, "Have you sewn your whole life?"

Francesca leans in closer and says, "Huh?" Rachel repeats herself. "Oh, yes. A long time now. My mother was a very good seamstress. I learned from her."

"That's nice. I wish I had the skill," Rachel says as she cuts out another circle.

"Your mother never taught you?"

"No," she admits absently while trying to squeeze one more circle onto the last whole piece of fabric. "My mom cooked. My dad was the one who sewed. Never taught me, though."

"Is he alive, your father?"

Rachel cuts over Francesca's lines, not meeting her eyes. "No, they both passed a long time ago."

"Oh, dear." The older woman places a swollen hand on Rachel's back and pats twice before falling away. The maternal gesture is almost enough to make her cry. She refuses to make a scene and ruin the woman's morning.

Silence settles over them as Francesca blocks out shapes and Rachel cuts. Eventually, the sewing machine begins chewing again. Hands clasped between her knees, she watches as rough edges are hidden beneath a neat seam. This mask is even better than the first, its lines more certain and tidier. By mask fifteen, they'll no doubt look professionally done.

"Were you a seamstress like your mom?" she asks after the silence turns awkward.

"Oh, no." The old woman's lips purse in distaste. "I went to school for biochemistry."

Rachel's eyes widen at the older woman. "You what now?"

Her expression shifts to one of delight. "When you get as old as me, you live a lot of lives. After college, I did cancer research in the Mayo Clinic. That's where I met my husband. We married and went back to Venezuela and had Daniela and her brothers. When Daniela was out of diapers, I taught in a university in Caracas." Her seams straighten. "And then, after my children left home, I quit that job and bought a fishery. One of the biggest tilapia farms in Venezuela, you know."

Blinking in stunned admiration, Rachel says, "I had no idea."

She pulls off another mask from the machine and feeds an elastic ribbon through one of the ear holes. "Mhm. No one ever asks me anything."

"Well, if you ever…want to talk about any of that stuff, I'd love to hear about it," Rachel says, meaning it. She regrets not having many things in her life, and not having the wisdom of a grandmother is one of them. Besides, how many people does she know who have actually run a fishery?

Francesca's hands still, she turns to declare, "You're a good kid."

Despite her own age, Rachel does feel like a kid in the woman's gaze. She smiles sheepishly and then gets to her feet. "Thank you for showing me how to do this. I appreciate it."

"Are you going to help Lorelei with her pretzels?"

"Yeah, I'll go see if she needs me."

Francesca returns to her growing mountain of masks, leaving Rachel to decide whether or not she wants to go into the kitchen. Pausing at the main staircase, she scents the air like a rabbit preparing to leave its warren.

The air here, though, smells of fresh bread, which is enough to tempt her. Walking down the hall, Rachel glances into the rooms and finds them occupied with overlapping conversation. It's a nice sight, she admits. Standing at the counter, Lorelei is a burst of sunshine in an orange house dress. She twirls a length of dough into a pretzel and rests it on a tray with a dozen others.

Spinning back to the oven, she opens it and removes a hot tray of golden bread before popping the uncooked batch in. Rachel watches as Lorelei uses a deft hand to flip each pretzel onto a wire rack, brush butter across their thirsty skin, and sprinkle the perfect amount of salt. Each industrious sound brings a fresh shiver of frisson across Rachel's arms.

"Good morning," Lorelei says, breaking the spell.

"Oh, hi," Rachel says and gives an awkward wave from the doorway. Of her housemates, the German woman has been the most difficult to parse. Her chances of Lorelei liking her are probably diminished by this creepy lurking.

"Do you want one?" she asks, pointing towards the cooling tray.

Rachel's mouth waters as she steps closer to the island, no longer a bakery voyeur. "I'd like that." When she sees them glistening with butter and salt, she says, "Oh, neat, they have fat butts." She hates herself.

Lorelei, though, gives a sudden laugh that reassures Rachel that she hasn't put her entire foot in her mouth. "This is how pretzels look in the part of Germany where I'm from. Big bottoms, or 'fat butts' as you say, and tiny arms. They're better this way."

After taking a bite, she can't disagree. Butter swirls with the hint of baking soda, both flavors brought to life by the salt. It's the best thing she's eaten in months, and that's saying something. "Oh my god, this is delicious," she moans as she finds the nearest bar stool and collapses into it.

"Good." Lorelei starts stacking bowls into the sink for washing. "If I were you, I'd take a couple and label them before Renato comes in here."

Staring at the back of Lorelei's curly head, she wonders what thoughts go on inside. During her time in the house, though limited, she can't recall the German woman saying much. With everyone else, there is a sense of how Rachel figures into their thoughts. She's the new one, the one who needs tending and instruction. The German, however, only speaks to her when necessary. And even though she has no plan on staying for however long it will take to become friends, the silence is killing her.

After a big bite, Rachel says, "Can I ask you something kinda weird?" Water pooling into the sink, Lorelei hums. "Do you like me?"

She shrugs over the measuring spoons. "I like you well enough."

This translates to hate in Rachel's mind. "Oh."

"I hope that's not mean," she says over her shoulder. "We don't know each other very well yet."

Stomach in her shoes, Rachel stares hard at the granules of salt glued by butter. She knows how they must feel. Stuck and hopeless. "I understand that... and I haven't exactly been in the best mood since I got here." *You ruined it for Job,* she scolds herself and takes another bite of pretzel. The salt should have somewhere to go. If she's lucky, whatever omnipotent being is holding her in its hand will eat her, too. Of course, Rachel isn't lucky.

Lorelei turns and leans back against the sink, crossing her arms across a faded linen apron. "You just moved across the world, and your husband is stuck in India. I don't think any of us are expecting you to be in a good mood."

Rachel laughs even though it isn't funny. Here's the proof that she has, in fact, been an asshole. Just like she thought. "Sorry."

"Why apologize?" Lorelei's dark eyes are pensive behind her glasses. "It just is."

She licks the last bits of salt from her fingertips before gesturing to the German with a casual wave. "So, is that what you do? Make Swabian pretzels and dispense the occasional nugget of insight?"

"Only on Mondays." She returns to the dishes.

Rachel laughs outright at that because it is funny. Lorelei is funny. Stoic as all hell, but funny. "I'll bear that in mind." When she stands, the chair scrapes unkindly against the floor.

Noticing the preparation to leave, Lorelei points to the tray. "Take another pretzel. Seriously. Renato will be here soon. They will not survive."

Rachel does as bid and smiles to herself. Food is a love language she understands, one taught to her by her mother. Sometimes the words for acceptance and love and caring get lost, but food is universal. "I want to feed you because I care." She takes the still-warm crisscross of yeast and leaves the kitchen in silence. She nearly collides with Cornelius, who is rushing for the mudroom door, when he jumps three feet into the air.

"I'm coming, I'm coming," Ted's voice calls from the front hall. When he rounds the banister and spots Rachel, he beams. Even in a house robe and morning scruff, he looks ready for a meeting with the board. Rachel wonders if that is a genetic trait for people with money. "Good morning, good morning," he greets. "That looks tasty."

"Morning," Rachel says as she gets out of his way. "Looks like somebody is in a hurry."

He chuckles. "I kept telling him that he doesn't actually want to go outside, but he's pretending to not know English. Isn't that right, buddy?"

Cornelius glances over his shoulder, tongue lolling to one side before starting to jump at the door again. He whines. Ted pats Rachel's shoulder as he passes, startling her. "Excuse me," he says, then pauses on the threshold. "Are you joining us for the movie tonight?"

She groans to herself. "Yeah, I guess so."

"Job, too?" he asks, the hopeful tone not missed by Rachel.

"We're going to try."

"Cool," he replies, drawing out the "oo" sound the way people in the North do. There's something about the expression that has struck Rachel as insincere, but it's hard to think that Ted has ever done or said anything insincere in his life. There is something strikingly similar between him and the Australian Shepherd bouncing up and down with laser focus.

"Go, go," Rachel insists, pointing at the dog. "I don't think he wants to wait anymore."

"Me neither!" Ted sings, running to scratch Cornelius's butt, which incenses the dog further and causes him to howl in impatience. Lorelei laughs as the two bound out into the snow.

Rachel starts up the back staircase to her room, where she is caught by the soft strain of the keyboard up in the front room. She pauses as the melody becomes something that Rachel recalls from somewhere deep in her memories. Intrigued, she wanders back up the hall to peek in on whoever is playing. She's starting to understand how easy it is to lurk in corners in this house without meaning to—perhaps this is the answer to her theory that people are always lurking in corners, waiting for the opportune moment to make themselves known.

Yukiko sits at the keyboard with posture so perfect that several books could rest on top of her head. Her hands scatter around the piano in a controlled craze, pulling apart and then coming back together with scales and trills stacked on top of one another. While the music spirals, Yukiko's face never changes. The song slows then begins to build with the fury of an overturned beehive before ending with two powerful cords. Her hands hover over the keys until the sound fades away. When the woman's delicate hands relax, Rachel cannot resist the urge to clap softly.

"I thought someone was watching," the young woman says as she tucks her hair behind her ears. "I always play better when someone is watching."

"You were playing pretty damn well before I came in," Rachel says as she sits in one of the cream-colored armchairs that probably cost more than her mortgage in Chicago.

Yukiko lifts her legs over the bench so she and Rachel can be face-to-face. The morning light shrouds her in a halo. "Oh, that's because the ghost was watching," she says.

"We have a ghost?" Rachel asks, bemused.

"Oh, yes." Her expression remains deadpan. "Haven't you met it yet?"

At this point, Rachel isn't sure if she's being serious. Rachel knows that ghosts aren't real. If they were, she wouldn't have felt so desperately alone most of her life. If ghosts were real, she'd be the first to buy an Ouija board. "Can't say that I have."

Yukiko nods pensively. "Come down here in the morning, and you will. It likes music."

"Lucky for you to have a captive audience then, huh?" Rachel snorts at her own joke.

Yukiko considers this a moment as she steeples her fingers between her knees. Then, "I think people who can't see ghosts can't see them because they are haunted themselves."

Rachel's body breaks out in a cold sweat and her upper arms in goosebumps. It's too early in the day to be seen so clearly. She changes the subject. "So, uh, what were you playing?"

She inclines her head towards the music book. "Beethoven. I'm getting ready for our spring recital." Her tone turns wistful. "If we have one."

Rachel makes a sympathetic hum but cannot contemplate a world in which places are forced to shutter and events are canceled. That's a world where planes don't fly. Wringing her hands together, she finds herself at a loss for words. Without meaning to, she asks, "So...how long have you played the piano?" *Jesus Christ, you idiot.*

"Since I was five," Yukiko says, no doubt used to the question. "Do you play anything?"

"No." Rachel holds her hands up and waggles her fingers. "All thumbs. I admire people who do, though."

Yukiko echoes Rachel's hum. Silence weighs between them. She wonders if leaving now would be too awkward. It's not Yukiko's fault; that much is true. The young woman is collected and accomplished in a way that Rachel has aspired to her entire life. What can she bring to a conversation?

Before she can disappear down that self-conscious rabbit hole, Yukiko asks, "Would you like if I play for you?"

Blushing, Rachel stammers, "Oh, you don't have to do that."

But the young woman is already turning back to her instrument. She does not pause for a request, moving instead to play. Rachel does not know much about classical music, but she knows she likes this piece, that she's heard it before. As Yukiko coaxes sweet trills from the keys, tension eases from Rachel's shoulders. She leans back into the chair and closes her eyes. Music rests on her lids, transforming her vision from red to deep purple. Her breathing changes, deepens and lengthens into places of herself that have been tight for months, maybe even years. They may not have anything to say to one another, but this will do.

Whatever magic Yukiko weaves wraps itself heavily around Rachel's body, lingering there all day. Even in the evening, when she sits on the couch in a corner piece and Wren's knee and Lorelei's elbow both touch some part of her. Even when Job's face pops on the screen and waves at everyone with bandwidth-bound jerkiness. Even when the movie is bad and everyone shrieks with laughter. Even when Markeya pauses the shared video to point out how CGI cockroaches are more terrible when they dance and Anabelle squeals with disgust. Even when Rachel falls asleep, and someone drapes a blanket over her.

CHAPTER TWENTY-THREE

Hi honey,

Just got back from the embassy with a new flight! Ready to head home on Friday. The place was full of people trying to get outta here. Kind of a shit show, if you ask me, but what else were they going to do? The consular officer was nice, tired-looking. Guess "manage thousands of displaced travelers because of a volatile airborne virus" wasn't in the job description. Anyway, they helped me schedule a flight for early Friday afternoon. I'll fly out of Chennai to New Delhi, New Delhi to Newark (woof), then Newark to Boston. Nineteen hours, total, it looks like. Wish the transfer was in Paris or something, but there's no room for being picky. When I get home, I'll quarantine in an Airbnb for two weeks, then it's home to you! Ted is helping me find a spot. We'll be together soon!

Love you,

J.

P.S. It was super sweet to see Wren put a blanket on you last night. It looks like you're fitting right in (i.e., falling asleep in the middle of a movie).

Rachel's stomach loops in joy. She shoots to her feet with her laptop clutched between both hands, shaking it as she rereads Job's email. Saturday! Only days away! And even though seeing him won't be a good idea (and maybe not even legal, she's not sure), knowing that he is in the same city will do a thousand tiny favors for her spirit. The stomach loop shifts to temporary nausea that she sets aside with the laptop so she can pick up her phone and drop into the group chat.

Rachel:	Job will be back in Boston on Saturday!
Vernon:	Whoop whoop!
Rachel:	He's supposed to quarantine somewhere for two weeks
Ted:	We'll get him a spot in Brookline. There's a hotel not too far from the house
Rachel:	Thanks very much!
Vernon:	Are you going to finish up in the workshop today?
Rachel:	Yeah, probably
Vernon:	I'll be down in a little bit to help
Rachel:	You don't have to do that
Vernon:	Be there in 10
Renato:	Me too! Great news about Job
Daniela:	We'll have to plan some meals that we can take to him while he's in quarantine
Anabelle:	That's a great idea! I'll add his meals to our meal list
Wren:	You have a meal list? Why?
Anabelle:	It's for our meals…that Vernon's been making?
Daniela:	I didn't know there was a meal list. More than happy to help prep
Vernon:	I've got it. Gives me something to do
Daniela:	We'll help. Share the link, please

Rachel sets her phone aside, pleased that she isn't the only one who can be bullied into help. Speeding into a fresh outfit, Rachel rips her hair up into a high ponytail rife with lumps. She uses the tips of her fingers to try and push them down into her scalp, to no avail. "Whatever," she mutters, then opens the door only to falter.

Klimt is waiting for her. She heard him through the night, yowling outside her door, but she'd buried her head deeper under the pillow. Now, he sits like a garden statuette, eyes closed. "What do you want?" she asks, not unkindly.

The cat notices her, looks up with those strange yellow irises, blinks slowly, then begins to saunter into Rachel's room. She's ready for him this time, though, catching him around his middle before he can step over the threshold. "Ah, ah," she scolds, pinning his body to hers with one arm as she closes the door with her free hand. "No, thank you, Mr. Smellycat."

The orange beast purrs, pawing at her until he is draped over her left shoulder, back feet perched on her forearm. "What are you doing?" she asks.

The cat, of course, doesn't have a ready response and instead makes a single indignant meow. She tries to take him off her shoulder, but he only hooks his claws into her shirt. "Come on, cat, let go," she demands, and he doesn't listen. She pulls, and he digs in deeper.

Not having much experience with cats, Rachel resigns herself to the walk downstairs in search of someone who can help. Thankfully, Lorelei is in the kitchen with a bowl of porridge and a cup of tea. Rachel knows that Klimt likes the German woman, has seen her petting him on the head a few times. That's what friendship with a cat is like, right?

"Hey, good morning. Can you help me?" Rachel rotates her shoulders to display her burden. "He won't let go."

Lorelei wipes her fingers into a napkin before standing. "Sure. Where was he?"

Rachel frowns as the cat's nails find her skin. "Trying to get into my room."

With a deft hand, Lorelei unhooks Klimt. "Really? That's so strange. He's been sleeping with Daniela and Ted. She told me that Klimt keeps getting in the bassinet."

When the cat is placed on the floor, Rachel is sure he weighs close to twenty pounds. "What better way to make sure that your baby doesn't wind up allergic to cats?"

Lorelei returns to her breakfast. "Good news about Job."

Brightened, Rachel recommits to collecting cleaning materials from under the sink. "Very good!" There appears to be no organizational strategy for under the cabinets, so she pulls out just about every bottle and cloth she can, placing the selected materials into a dish bucket. With all of the machinery and tools out of their boxes and placed into new homes, all the workshop needs is a solid buff and shine before it's all ready for Job. *Two weeks*, her mind chants. She can't believe it's almost been a month and a half since she saw him last. This is the longest they've gone without seeing one another, ever.

Placing her bounty on the counter, she finds the kitchen cabinets staring at her and meets them with a thrill for the future. When Job saw their tattered oak corners during their Skype interview, he told her that "a house that nice deserves maple" then began to source the wood. If she places an order now, maybe he can start working on the project as soon as he gets home. *Home.* She pauses at that.

"What's wrong?" Lorelei asks.

A funny little smile teases her lips. "Nothing. Just a passing thought."

Lorelei scrapes her bowl and nods. "You're not going to work today?"

Fitting the tub into her waist, Rachel heads for the mudroom. "I will in a little bit, just want to finish up in the carriage house while it's on my mind."

"Your boss is okay with that?"

Rachel shrugs. "How's she gonna know? I still get my job done."

"Bold," the German woman observes as she clears her space. "There's coffee in the pot."

"Oh, right, thanks." She pours a cup and takes a deep whiff of morning preparation. Instead of a dose of delight, her stomach turns. "Oof. Is this dark roast?"

"No idea," Lorelei says as she washes her bowl. "It's from Costco. No good?"

"Not for me today," Rachel replies and pours the coffee back into the pot. "I'll worry about it later. Anyway, gonna go work on the workshop. See you." She heads to the mudroom to suit up for the blizzard barren yard.

"Later."

After shoving her feet into her "waterproof" snow boots (really, Rachel is thinking of emailing a complaint to the shoe store in Duluth that convinced her that these pleather puppies are good enough to brave more than a couple of ice cubes), covering her face with a homemade mask, and grabbing the Swiffer, she opens the door. The winter air still bites, but it is warmer today than it was yesterday. She wishes she could find her good winter clothes; those boxes are nowhere to be found. But today is not a day for negativity. Today is for preparation.

In the workshop, Rachel turns on all the lights, deposits her supplies on the counter, and waters the plant. The rest of the workshop looks better than the place in Chicago ever did. Maybe that has something to do with the fact that everything isn't covered in an inch and a half of sawdust, and the walls are actually finished, but Rachel chalks it up to her organization. After a good mop and scrub, this place will be ready for whatever the equivalent of *Good Housekeeping* is for woodworkers.

She imagines Job at the bandsaw with his red bandana and comically large safety glasses. Her stomach flops in response. Scurrying to the counter, she divides out the supplies before taking the tub to the sink, filling it with Pine-Sol and hot water. Bubbles build along the surface. Halfway full, the imitation pine scent crosses some wire in Rachel's brain, and her tumbling stomach kicks up into her throat. Vomit fills her mouth, and she creates a cup under her lips as she rushes to the small bathroom. The cotton mask barely comes off in time.

Leaning over the toilet, Rachel's body purges itself of last night's leftovers. The taste is acrid, which makes her gag out a few spits of bile. Then, nothing. Sure she's done, Rachel flushes, stands, rinses out her mouth, and mops her forehead free of sweat. Her reflection is pale and sallow all at once. *Jesus, I look like shit.* She tries again to smooth the bumps from her hair. Footsteps come from upstairs and prompt Rachel to act like she didn't just barf up a full quart.

Out in the workshop, Markeya is waiting for her in a gray wool sweater, black jeans, and an electric blue face mask that matches her hair. "Hey. Are you feeling okay?"

"Yeah," Rachel says as she returns the mask to cover her mouth and nose. "Little sensitive to smell today. The cleaner didn't agree with me." Remembering the water, she swears and gets past Markeya to turn off the water. Catching another whiff, she gags but manages to keep her stomach in check this time.

"I've got some lemony cleaner if that'd be better." Markeya starts to go to her bedroom door then stops. "Wait, why are you cleaning?"

"I want everything to be nice for Job when he gets home." Rachel nearly rolls her eyes at herself. *Who am I? June Cleaver?*

Markeya's eyebrows pull up and let Rachel know that she's thinking the same thing. "It looks great in here, Rachel." She props a fist on her hip, surveying the workshop. "Seriously, if you showed me pictures from three weeks ago, I wouldn't believe they were the same place. Y'all did a great job."

"Thanks. I still want to get some cleaning done, though, to set the tone for him." She wants Markeya to know that she is not, in fact, a doormat. She needs her to know that her relationship with Job is mutual, like Markeya's relationship with Vernon. She needs her to know that she makes rules, too. "I'd love it if we kept this place, y'know, *not* a disaster for longer than a week."

The front door opens and admits Vernon and Renato in their winter wear. Markeya scoffs at some personal joke as the men remove their layers. "Yeah, that'd be nice," she says.

"Morning," Rachel greets as she takes the Swiffer wipes off the counter and attaches one to the flat mop.

"Good morning," Vernon says. "I brought you some breakfast." He produces two aluminum foil parcels from his pockets and puts them in Markeya's hands. "Bagel sandwiches with poached eggs, bacon, and cheddar cheese."

"Man, I wish I was stuck out here," Renato bemoans. Markeya scoffs, which makes the younger man smile. "How can I help, Rach?"

She flushes at the nickname, pleased. "Um, I guess sweeping first would help."

"What were you going to do with the water?" Markeya asks as she unwraps her sandwich and takes a big bite. The yolk breaks, delicious.

Rachel ignores the new rumble in her stomach. "Wanted to wash the baseboards."

"Vern, would you do that? The Pine-Sol isn't agreeing with her."

Rachel protests and is ignored. Vernon is eager to help, after all. He takes the bucket and rag from the sink and heads to the workshop while giving Rachel a wide berth. "Thanks," she murmurs.

"Do you want the other sandwich?" Markeya offers one of the tinfoil balls, and Rachel takes it. "Anabelle already left."

"Oh, yeah, ladies, enjoy your breakfast while we do all the work." Renato holds the broom aloft. "Shall I get you a little orange juice and Champagne?"

"Yeah, why don't you?" Markeya shoots back. "I'll take mine with a sliced strawberry."

Renato sticks out his tongue but gets back to his task. Rachel isn't sure what to make of their relationship, but she still takes the sandwich because throwing up is hungry work. "Thanks. I'll mop after you're done, Ren." It feels good to use his nickname, too. Then she leans against the bar and unwraps the bagel sandwich, mouth filling with saliva at the scent. Before she takes a bite, she says, "Are you okay out here? I mean, upstairs is a little...antiquated."

Markeya waves a dismissive hand through the air. "I grew up in a log cabin that didn't have indoor plumbing until I was ten."

The sandwich is delicious, bacon perfectly crisped, egg creamy, almost enough to distract her. "What? Really?"

Markeya waggles her brows. "Oh yeah. My parents live in the middle of nowhere in South Carolina. They're off-the-grid people, y'know?"

Rachel can't help but ask, "Are they Mennonites?"

To her relief, Markeya laughs. "No, no, just prefer to live off the land. My dad is an English professor at a college in Spartanburg. Mom takes care of the farm. Chickens, sheep, cows, things like that."

"What, why?" Renato stops working again to look at them. "Did you have internet?"

"Oh, yeah. Dial-up in all its glory. They have high-speed now, but only after me and my sister left for college."

"That sucks," Renato cries, then goes back to sweeping up dust and leftover packaging.

Markeya takes another bite and mumbles through it. "You're telling me. I didn't see any porn until I was in college."

Vernon laughs so hard that he has to put the rag back into the bin while he collects himself. Renato goes bright red and sweeps faster. Rachel finishes her sandwich and mops after him. Little by little, the room shimmers and becomes the place Job will want to stay. When they are through, she thanks everyone and makes her way back to her room, where she promptly vomits one more time and then gets to work. Whatever is in the air, it isn't agreeing with her. That doesn't matter, of course, because Job is coming home.

*

By Thursday night, Friday in India, Rachel is exhausted. Her upset stomach has given way to three sleepless nights. It's hard to say whether that insomnia is travel-anxiety or related to some other nameless pit in her stomach. After a dinner of roasted chicken and kale salad, of which she had two servings, Rachel returns to her room to wait for news from Job. She checks her phone for messages, but there's nothing. She calls, but Job doesn't pick up. His voicemail doesn't pick up either, just rings and rings. This does not assuage her anxiety.

Rachel: Where are you?

His text response is immediate, which pisses her off.

Job: Hey honey
Job: Can't get on the flight today
Rachel: What? Why??
Job: Popped a fever right before I got through security. They've got thermometers

She presses the green call button, and he rejects it. Standing in the middle of the room, she nearly screams. *What does this mean? What does this mean?*

Rachel: Call me.
Job: Can't. Airport isn't good for connection
Rachel: Bullshit! Pick up
Job: Rachel, I can't

Gritting her teeth so hard that her molars hurt, Rachel savagely types.

Rachel: Why do you have a fever?
Job: It's India. It's hot.

Smart ass. This will not do.

Rachel: If you're sick, just tell me
Job: I'm fine!
Rachel: Don't ducking lie to me!

She tries to call, and he denies her again.

Rachel: Answer your phone!

Job: Look, I don't want you to worry.

Rachel: I'm already worried so you might as well tell me
            the truth.

For two long minutes, she watches as the typing ellipses show up next to Job's name. Whatever he has to say, at least he's thinking about it.

Job: Okay. I'm going to the doctor. If I have it, I'll be
            okay. It's easy on young people

Okay, you can do this. We can do this. Her mind goes into crisis mode. She needs to find the closest hospital. She needs to find the best doctor in Chennai. She needs to find a flight to India as soon as possible.

Rachel: Are you going right now?

Job: I have to.

She starts Googling flights, horrified to see that there is nothing available. Nothing. Fuck.

Rachel: Will you call me when you get there? I need to
            be on the same page.

Job: Okay.

All of her anger dissolves back into its essence: fear. She does not know what to do. Standing alone in their bedroom, she does not know what to do. So she just texts: I love you. And he texts: I love you, too.

Then, like that, she is alone. Her stomach flops, and she goes to throw up, chicken and kale mingling in the bowl. After flushing, she closes the lid to rest her head against it. Her brain isn't processing any information. *What the fuck is the matter with me?* She tries to flick through the catalog of foods eaten over the last few days but can think of nothing that would have upset her stomach. And it's not like her appetite has waned, like it does when she's got a stomach bug. In fact, she hasn't felt this way since... She stops pacing. This is a familiar scene. What is she supposed to do? Well, whatever it is, she must do it alone.

At half-past ten, when she's sure no one is up, Rachel creeps into the communal bathrooms to investigate their stores. There's plenty of shampoo and conditioner and even a healthy collection of expensive skincare products in the first-floor cabinets. On the second, she finds hot irons and straighteners. She pulls the third bathroom apart but only comes up with a stockpile of homemade soap. Halfway through the fourth, she is ready to cry until she finds a basket of feminine hygiene products: tampons for every flow, pads, panty liners, and at the bottom: a single pregnancy test.

She takes the hard-won treasure back to her room, where she pees over it with determined precision. Reading the instructions, she caps the end, washes her hands, sets a timer on her phone, and waits. Only she's bad at waiting, so she paces the perimeter of the bathroom, stands in the shower, peers out the window. The timer goes off, and there is no news from Job.

When she leaves the bathroom with the test, she finds Klimt waiting for her on the bed, his front feet tucked into his chest. He blinks slowly at her. They both know how this test is graded; there's no real reason to look.

CHAPTER TWENTY-FOUR

JOB CALLS HER AT SIX IN the morning; Rachel picks up on the first ring because she hasn't been sleeping. Couldn't sleep. Will never sleep again. Klimt rests on the pillow next to her, little face peering into the fabric as though scrying Rachel's future. After the news they'd discovered together, it didn't seem right to kick him out. She didn't, doesn't, want to feel alone. When she hears Job's voice, she hears it full of fatigue and raspiness.

"Hey," he croaks before coughing. Had it been this bad yesterday?

She sits up straight, her hips aching with stillness. Klimt makes a single grunt of an annoyance then falls back to sleep. "Hey," she says, voice raspy, too. "Are you at the hospital?"

He coughs once. "Yeah. Waiting to be seen."

"You haven't been seen yet?" she asks, indignant. Her anxiety, which she always thought had high thresholds for terror, begins to ratchet up to new heights. Fresh sweat beads in her armpits, though it's anyone's guess where the moisture is from given how much she sweated last night. "When are you gonna be seen?"

"Don't know," he wheezes, and Rachel can hear the sound of more coughing and a hum of a language she doesn't understand.

"You're in the waiting room?"

"I said I was waiting," he snaps, breathing ragged. "All of the fucking beds are full, and nobody speaks any fucking English."

Rachel stiffens. In their decade-long marriage, Job has lost his temper four times, all of them when he was raging with fever or grief. If he is irritable already, she shudders to think about how much pain he is in. When he starts coughing again, her throat constricts in sympathy.

"Are you wearing a mask?" she asks, feeling like an idiot a second later.

His coughing goes on for a few more seconds. "Yeah. Yeah. But, if I have it, I have it." He clears his throat and mutters thanks to someone else. Rachel listens as he gulps whatever was given to him.

Rachel hugs her knees into her chest. "When do you think you'll be seen?"

Someone calls Job's name. "Guess now. I'll keep you on the line."

"Thank you," she murmurs, pressing the phone closer to hear a woman with accented English talk to her husband. He answers some questions in a familiar, patient tone. He tells her about his symptoms when they started. The woman's voice encourages him to breathe deeply. He starts coughing before the first breath is halfway down. Each wrack echoes in Rachel's heart.

She hears the woman speak gently, telling him that he needs to be put on oxygen immediately. Right now, please, there is a bed for you through these doors. "Did you catch that, honey?" Job's voice returns, and she can feel its exhaustion.

Rachel stands and paces to the window. There is a light snow flittering towards the ground; it melts on impact. "Yes. Are you going with her?"

"Yeah, looks like she's putting me in a unit with other people with the virus." Other voices begin to crowd around Job's, making it hard to hear.

Rachel catches the window frame. "They know you have it? They tested you?"

He coughs quickly, clears his throat. "I have all the symptoms. They don't need to test me. I don't think they *can* test me."

She thinks about the news and how hard it is for Americans to get tested for the virus. This does not bode well for Job. Rachel strives to keep her tone level. She is the strong one right now. "Well, what happens now?"

"I don't know," he admits, sounding defeated by the fact. "Hopefully, I can get some broth and some sleep."

"Okay. Soup would be good. Or tea," she adds, wishing to be helpful and failing. She twirls a piece of hair around an anxious finger. "Can we text? Do you have energy for that?"

The woman says something that Rachel misses. She pulls the strand of hair hard as punishment. Job thanks her, and then Rachel can hear him put his stuff down before collapsing with a sigh. "Thank Christ."

"Where are you?" she asks.

"Big room with ten other people," he whispers. "Looks like everyone is asleep." A coughing fit erupts wherever Job is. "The nurse told me that she was going to be right back with oxygen and some dinner."

That, at least, brings some relief. Her hand falls from her hair. "You should get some rest. Text me when you feel like you can?"

"Yes, honey, we'll text." More coughing.

When he's done, she says, "I love you so much, Job."

"I love you, too."

Neither one of them can bring themselves to say that everything is going to be okay because lying is poison to a marriage. "I love you," Rachel whispers again and then presses the red button, letting him disappear.

For a while, it's hard to say how long Rachel stands staring out of the window and into the yard. She watches the snow continue to melt; she watches Vernon salt the driveway; she watches a masked Ted leave to take a snow-shoed Cornelius for a walk. Strangely, her stomach is still. The normal anxiety she feels is replaced by an eerie calm. The hand resting on the window does not seem to be her hand, but she knows it is. "I should probably have something to eat," she hears herself say.

Limbs heavy, she goes to the bathroom for her skincare routine, carefully covering the dark bags with eye cream and foundation. She brushes her teeth, flosses, swishes with mouthwash. She takes the time to braid her hair out of her face. Once done, she goes to her closet, ignores Job's empty space, and dresses in black jeans, thick socks, and a wool sweater to match. Suddenly, without really meaning to, she's reaching for the door and pulling it open.

A person who Rachel has never seen before is walking across the hallway in a heavy floral nightgown with a towel over their shoulder. Upon a second look, she realizes that it is Wren without a wig, heavy eyeliner, or a pair of platform boots. Their real hair is dark and cropped close, their brown eyes seem smaller without a fierce cat-eye. "Hey," they say, stopping in their tracks. Their lips form a frown when they get a better look at Rachel. "Good morning. How are you?"

She blurts, "Job's in the hospital."

Their eyes widen. "Oh."

"He's got it," she clarifies, blinking tears.

Wren nods a few times as they absorb the information before saying, "Do you want to come hang out in my room for a little bit?"

Rachel realizes she does. "Yeah."

Wren backs up towards their door, opening it with a flourish. "Come on in."

Taking a cautious step forward, self-consciousness swamps Rachel. Why is she always so needy? First with Job, now with Wren. The guilt compounds. "Do you have somewhere to be? I don't want to make you late."

"Nah. It takes, like, two hours to get this shit show together." Wren circles their face with a lazy forefinger. "We've got all the time in the world."

Drawn by the kind invitation, she slides forward in her socks. Wren's room is—Rachel strives for a kind word—messy. That doesn't quite capture it, of course. Wren's room is a disaster. Clothes, shoes, cords, magazines litter the floor. Their desk is covered in books, more clothes, and takeout cups. There's a bookcase crammed with books on fashion, tarot, psychology, gender theory, poetry anthologies, and a handful of amethyst crystal points. And then, on the left wall, are the wigs. Sweet baby Jesus, the wigs. There are three or four dozen mounted on the mall, each one a different length, texture, and color. For a moment, worry is washed by awe. How much of Wren's college fund has gone into this collection?

"You weren't kidding about being a fanatic," Rachel muses.

Wren closes the door before they start frantically picking up the clothes on the floor and depositing them in a heap on the bed. "For real, for real. Started with boots when I was a freshman in high school, moved onto wigs after my first *Rocky Horror* show." Wren stumbles over a pair of their shoes as they rush to clear the desk chair. "Here, have a seat while I get this crap out of the way. It takes me, like, six tries to find an outfit. Every single day." They huff.

Rachel obliges, settling down and trying to ignore the urge to poke through their stack of books for school. She stares at the wigs instead, counting them. "*Rocky Horror*, huh? I remember going to midnight shows when I was in college." Thirty-six total.

"It's the best!" Wren chirps as they slop their crop tops and t-shirts into a pile. "When I saw Tim Curry for the first time, I knew 'straight' wasn't in the cards for me. Honestly, that may have been the same day I started to realize I was nonbinary. Frank-N-Furter: Man? Woman? Who gives a shit. Hot alien."

Rachel smiles. Wren has such a talent for making her smile. Tension eases from her shoulders for this moment. There is nothing else she can do but sit here and watch the young person as they piece together an outfit from yesterday's discards. "Were you ever in a shadow cast?" she asks.

Wren puts a hand on their hip. "Honey, look at me. I'm a nonbinary pansexual standing in front of a wall of wigs. What do you think?"

Taking this as a joke, Rachel lets herself laugh. "That why you have so many wigs?"

"For sure," they drawl. "I also got *super* into burlesque last year. Which, like, big surprise. *Rocky Horror* is really just a gateway drug for burlesque. One second you're Magenta, and the next, you're doing the *Slutcracker*."

"Slut. Cracker," Rachel tests the words with raised eyebrows. She takes her phone from her pocket to see if there are any texts from Job. There aren't.

"What?" Wren gasps, holding their outfit close in mock horror. "You don't know about *Slutcracker*? It's an absolute Boston rite of passage. December. You. Me. We're going."

"Are you going to be in it?"

"I wish! Maybe I'll try out after another year of classes." They hold out their outfit to her. "Hey, is it okay if I change in front of you?"

"Yeah, that's fine," Rachel replies, taking the time to look down into her phone, scrolling mindlessly through text, email, and social media in search of some answers, but there are none.

"So, do you want to talk about Job?" Wren asks with a grunt.

"Not really," she murmurs, breath hitching. There are still no texts from Job.

"Okay, all done." Rachel looks up and finds Wren wearing an ankle-length black robe, the style reserved for witches and high priestesses, that is cinched at the waist with a brown leather belt. A large ankh hangs around their neck. Honestly, it's one of the more muted ensembles she's seen them wear. They grab a pair of knee-high platform boots before turning to consider the vast wig selection. "You know what I like best about wigs, Rach?"

"What?"

"I like how each one feels like a different person. Like, this one." Wren points out a blunt-cut brunette wig. "She works a nine-to-five for a finance firm, plans out all of her meals for the week, and only has sex with her husband of eight years with the lights off."

"She doesn't sound like much fun."

"Oh, no, she's for sure a drag. *But* she can book a dentist appointment without having a panic attack."

"So, what, they're different aspects of yourself?"

"More like characters. Each wig is a really cool part that I get to play for a little bit. Like this one." They take down a corn yellow wig with pigtails; it reminds her of an anime she liked when she was in middle school and afternoon television was a treat. "This babe is an absolute baddie. She only eats oysters, strawberries in champagne, and caviar. She has three sugar daddies, all of them are named Alan, and she won't fuck any of them."

"I feel like that's just a person you know," Rachel replies.

"Life informs art. And you know what's even better? You put on one of these wigs and just live in another character. You can say whatever you want, true or false, and then just assign them the blame."

"What do you mean?"

Wren puts the yellow wig back in exchange for a violently curly mop of red hair. When they speak, it is in a horrible approximation of a Valley Girl accent: "Like, that one time when I was nine, and my mom, like, sent me to fat camp because I, like, weighed a hundred pounds or whatever. And I, like, wanted to go home so bad that I kept, um, peeing the bed at night, which is super ew. But, like, nobody cared because an ounce out is an ounce out."

Rachel's hand goes up to her mouth in horror. "Did that really happen to you?"

Wren puts the wig back. "Who's to say?" The next wig off the shelf is a dark blue pompadour brushed to gleaming. When it's settled on their head, Wren is four inches taller, which apparently affects their accent because what comes out next is from Jersey: "Yeah, so I met this broad at a freshman mixer a couple months back. We hit it off, have a couple of drinks, then head back to my place. One thing leads to another, bing-bang-boom, I'm face-deep in muff." Rachel blushes, then snorts on a laugh. "I assure you, I am very about this particular downtown activity, but as I'm hittin' my stride, a little bit of TP gets stuck to my lip. I'm like, ay, whatever, it happens. God knows they've got half-ply in the dorm bathrooms. So, I's ask her if she minds freshening up for me, 'cause I don't want to hit my daily fiber intake from pussy lint. She gets up, acts real cool about it, and then never comes back. Won't even look at me in the dining hall the next day."

By the end of it, Rachel is leaning over herself and wheezing with laughter. "How'd you get to be so funny?"

Wren pops off the wig and puts it back up high. "It's definitely not a coping mechanism. Okay, then, your turn. Pick a wig, any wig."

Rachel straightens, feeling lightened by the one-person show before her. "Only fair." She wants to take this seriously and tries to find the cut that will play to her strengths. When she finds her match, she says, "Um, I'll take that short wavy bob on the far right."

Wren follows her gaze. "The '20s number?" Rachel nods. "Excellent choice." With delicate hands, they bring the wig to her, nearly reverent as they place it atop her head. They step away, face alight with expectation. Rachel wants to make them laugh, too.

A strange electricity courses at the crown of her head, one that hums through her whole body. She becomes someone new, someone who always rests one elbow on the nearest surface and smokes with their free hand. She takes an exaggerated pull from an imaginary cigarette. An old memory from undergrad knocks itself loose from a deep part of her memory cave, and that spirit that lives in the wig collects its shards, mining for gold.

"I went to visit my friend's new abode in Manhattan." Her voice reminds her of an old black and white film star: dramatic for no reason. "It was a shabby little thing but in a chic sort of way. I arrived a bit late, as usual, of course, because I had attended a late lunch at an Indian restaurant with an even dearer old friend of mine who had just returned from the Continent and was telling me all about their adventures." A quick puff of the fake cigarette. "Apparently, he murdered his wife and was currently wanted in four countries." Wren goes into hysterics, bracing themself against the bed, which makes Rachel lay it on thicker. "And, dahling, I couldn't be expected to miss out on that juicy bit of gossip. Unfortunately for me, the tikka masala did not agree. It was dreadful. The stomach cramps were worse than when I swallowed that tapeworm for the Met Gala. Of course, worth the pain that time. Versace, dahling, Versace." Wren slips to the floor, face pinched red and watery. "At any rate, there I am, I'm sitting alone, terrified, in this dingy little hole of a bathroom, fighting for my life, dahling. At the end of it, when I go to flush, and I don't mean to be rude, it simply would not flush. I mean, the damn thing wouldn't go down, and the water is rising dangerously high." The cigarette again. "And I certainly don't want to critique anyone on the way they keep their house, dahling, but how do you call a house without a plunger a home? Do you know what I had to do?"

Wren struggles to their knees to find Rachel's eyes. "Oh my god, please tell me."

"Dahling, I had to leave. I moved out of state the very next week. I assumed the identity of my dear old friend's dead wife." Rachel leans towards Wren, smoking again for effect. "Murdered, if you remember. Funny, isn't it? How everything happens for a reason?"

Wren wipes their face dry with a nearby t-shirt. "Let me tell you why I loved that. At no point was I sure what was real and what was bullshit. Whoever this lady is, she sure can smoke."

"Oh, yes." Rachel holds her fingers away from her mouth as if there really was a cigarette there. "One must smoke double when one is smoking for two." She didn't mean to say it, not really, but perhaps whoever lives in this wig is more inclined towards honesty than she is.

Wren's face drops all joy. "I'm sorry, what? Are we playing right now?"

Rachel reaches up and slides the wig off her head. The spirit leaves her. The phone in her lap still holds no texts from Job. "What if we weren't?"

"How?"

Rachel snaps, "Do we need to walk through the mechanics or...?"

Wren rolls with it, barely blinking. "No, but like how? You've been here for, like, six weeks. How are you..."

She knows exactly how it happened, could probably pin it down to the minute if she had to. "Right before I left Job in Cairo, we spent the night together."

Wren's eyebrows can go no higher. "Holy shit!"

Rachel nods. "Holy shit." If only Job would text her, then everything would be okay.

"Well, what do you want to do?" they ask. It's a very good question.

Without meaning to, she places a hand on her stomach and thinks about the last time something lived there. "I don't want to be pregnant right now," she whispers. "It wasn't supposed to be like this. What if he—And then she—"

Wren scrambles around the bed until they are standing right in front of her. "Hey, hey. Breathe. Just breathe. We will figure this out."

Laying in a hospital room as the anesthetic wears off, knowing that Siobhan isn't there. Her throat clenches, preluding dry sobs. "I can't lose another baby."

Wren's hand rests on Rachel's shoulder. They don't say anything. Their touch feels good, the comfort tethering Rachel to her body.

This new life that could be growing inside of her is a tentative wish that feels dangerous, a threat to a future she was beginning to piece together for herself and Job. How can she do any of this without him? She barely got through this the last time with his help.

Wren reminds her that they are still there. "You should talk to Anabelle."

The trembling starts somewhere in her stomach and quickly spreads to her arms. She hugs herself to keep it together. "No, no. That makes it real."

Wren gives her space. "It might be real. You've got to talk to her." Rachel starts shaking her head back and forth, silent. "You have every right to be scared. But you aren't alone, Rachel, not at all. There are so many people here that care about you."

This feels true enough to get Rachel to be still.

Wren gestures to the wall. "Should we pick a wig to wear to go talk to Anabelle?"

"Do we have to go right now? Can we wait?" When Job texts, this can all be real then.

Their arms cross, bell sleeves drooping. "We can, for a little bit. You should tell her sooner rather than later." No one says the words "high-risk pregnancy," but Rachel hears them all the same.

What pain it would be to lose their baby again and to lose Job at the same time? She would die. She wouldn't have to do anything, just let her heart break.

Wren touches her shoulder again. When Rachel looks up at them, they smile and say in an affected tone, "We're going to get through this, dahling. You'll see."

A weary smile touches Rachel's lips. "How'd you get so wise?" she whispers.

"Oh, trauma, for sure." Wren briefly touches the back of their hand to Rachel's chin. "A *lot* of therapy."

Rachel envies them that peace. "You're just so... insightful."

They shrug. "I'm an empath, y'know? I vibe on other people's emotions. Call it psychism; call it a trauma response. Either way, it makes it easy for me to key into what people are feeling."

The bitter-sweetness isn't lost on Rachel. "Three cheers for trauma, huh?"

Wren chuckles. "Yeah."

Taking a deep breath, she meets the young person's concerned gaze. She reaches for their hands. "Will you keep this to yourself for a little while?"

"Of course." They cross their heart. "You have my word."

Rachel sighs in relief. "Thank you." It just has to stay a secret until she knows what to do. Everything will be easier then.

CHAPTER TWENTY-FIVE

JOB DOESN'T CONTACT HER all day. Thirty-five hours and fourteen minutes. The longest they've ever gone without speaking, she's certain of that. Rachel tries to convince herself that he is asleep, resting comfortably, regaining his strength to fight off the virus. She tells herself that again and again as she paces her room, as she stares at a blank computer screen, as she sits in the closet with her face stuffed into one of his shirts, as she walks to the bedroom door before forgetting why she would want to leave.

At some point, Wren must have told the house that Job is in the hospital because she gets texts from almost everyone asking what they can do to help. She previews the messages in the notification bar, so they remain "unread." After ignoring Daniela's response for an hour, the woman texts again to ask what hospital Job is in. Rachel answers immediately.

Forty-one minutes later, there is a knock at the door.

Rachel sits still at her desk, hands poised over the keyboard in a pantomime of work, and wills the person in the hallway to disappear. Thirty seconds are gone before there is another knock, firmer this time. Glaring at the intrusion, Rachel gets up to answer. Daniela, of course, looks more pregnant and more beautiful than ever.

"May I come in?" she asks before sidestepping her way past, which makes Rachel jump back, so she doesn't touch the belly. Now the pregnant lady is standing in the middle of her bedroom with a hand supporting the small of her back. Rachel averts her eyes and wishes she knew what she did to deserve such punishment.

Daniela does not waste words on pleasantries. "I found someone who will look in on Job," she says, brown eyes direct.

Her breath catches in surprise. "Who?"

Daniela hobbles to the desk chair and sinks into it with a huff. "A colleague of a colleague. She's a midwife at a rural clinic a couple of hours outside the city. She said she would go to Chennai to look for Job."

Rachel's whole body alights with fresh breath; the worried, stale air leaves her lungs. Had she been holding it this whole time? Her hands tremble; she's so relieved. She could kiss Daniela. "Really? Oh my god, that would be amazing. Can I have her number? Email?"

"Of course. I have her number." Daniela's sparse brows draw together in concern as she rests a hand on top of her belly. "How are you?"

"I'm fine, I'm fine," she says, waving away the inquiry's implications as she grabs her phone from the desk. "What's the number?"

"Rachel," Daniela says. She looks up in a daze and meets the woman's dark eyes. "You've been up here for a day and a half. Have you eaten anything?"

She blinks. "I had breakfast with everyone yesterday."

The frown deepens, and Rachel realizes that her answer was the wrong one.

"That was *two* days ago."

Two days? "No, it's fine," she insists. "I'm fine. Stressed, but fine."

Daniela reaches for Rachel, but she backs away before contact can be made. She holds the phone close to her like a shield.

Daniela lets her hand fall away, sighing. Some battles aren't worth fighting. "I understand that, but maybe you could have something to drink? Vernon made some hibiscus tea that's very good. Would you like some?"

"Yeah, yeah, sounds great." Rachel shakes the phone screen from side to side at Daniela. "The number?"

After deliberating, Daniela hangs her head over her own phone and sends the contact.

"Thank you for this, Daniela," Rachel says as she adds the unfamiliar name to her address book, assigning the woman a label for ease of contact. Even in a crisis, she understands the importance of organization. "You have no idea how much this means to me."

"You have nothing to thank me for. We're all worried about him." Daniela does reach for Rachel again, her smooth hand curling around Rachel's shoulder to force eye contact. When unprepared, sincerity can be searing. "Come out of your room for a little fresh air. It would make me feel better."

It has been a long time since Rachel has had a family, so long since anyone beyond Job has conjured up this feeling of care, effort, and affection. Now this woman who represents everything Rachel has longed for after all these years offers her help without reservation. It feels natural enough to make her cry. She settles for telling Daniela that she's right.

The pregnant woman smiles. "Come and have some lunch."

"Lunch?" Rachel casts a look out the window, expecting soft morning light.

"It's just past one."

Which means that it's not late enough in India for Rachel to harass a stranger about finding her husband. The room feels small, after all. "Yeah, that's a good idea."

Daniela guides her from the room, casting quick over-the-shoulder looks as though to make sure that Rachel actually follows. At the head of the stairs, the pregnant woman pauses with a hand on her belly again. "Oops. I'll be down in a minute."

Tension seizes Rachel. She has a sinking suspicion that these constant adrenaline spikes will collect their pound of flesh sooner rather than later. "You okay?"

"Nature calls," Daniela replies with a reassuring smile and then glides to the nearest bathroom. Such grace is unnatural in someone so large.

Letting go of a fresh terror, Rachel plods down into the kitchen, where she finds Vernon at the island with a disaster spread before him. Containers of flour and sugar dust the copper top, melted butter drips onto the floor, the large cutting board is covered in the crumbs of two different loaves of bread. The blonde man looks up from chopping up the remains of a roasted ham that Rachel can't remember eating.

"Hey there," Vernon calls before returning to his work. Rachel notices that his beard has grown shaggy.

"Hey," she parrots as she approaches the island, placing her hand against the edge with the least grime. "Where'd that ham come from?"

"Dinner last night. Anabelle's uncle sent it to us a while ago. Francesca found it in the deep freezer and figured it was time to eat it."

Rachel hums.

Vernon pauses chopping, purses his lips, then sighs heavily through his nose. "Is there anything I can do for you?" he asks, glancing at her from the corner of his eye. This is as close to sympathy as he gets; Rachel is sure of that. She appreciates his tact.

She huffs a wry laugh as she plops into a seat at the island. "You know how to make a stiff drink?"

"Yeah, I can do that. I took some bartending classes in college. I can make you something to go with your lunch if you're interested."

Well, at least Rachel can be confident in Wren's secret-keeping abilities. She thinks about her own stomach and its implications before resolving to be responsible, for Job's sake. "On second thought, it seems like a bad time to start drinking on the job."

"How about a non-alcoholic Pimm's Cup and a Monte Cristo?" Her stomach growls in response. Vernon nods and claps once. "It's decided. Give me ten minutes."

"Thank you."

Rachel crosses her arms on the counter to rest her head. Gaze fixed on the cabinets, she notices the oak is grayed, scuffed, peeling in places. Her vision adjusts to the light and sees that the nickel hardware is haggard with age. If he was here, Job would have already been instaling the maple cabinets he'd talked so much about, would have screwed in flat black handles and knobs. After that, of course, he would want to replace the kitchen table, the island, and would work on convincing Ted to redo the floors.

What would it cost to get the wood shipped in? she wonders as the muscles in the left side of her neck stretch. *Fifteen hundred? Two thousand? We could cover that. Should I buy it for him? I've got the list upstairs. Why not? The lumber will get here by the time he comes home.* Because he's coming home. He has to.

"You like cheese, right?" Vernon asks, interrupting her musings.

Rachel sits up and hums again.

He salutes before piling on the Gruyère. Even though Vernon keeps his cards close to the chest, there's no keeping his affinity for fancy cheese a secret. In the time that Rachel has been in the house, she has tried no fewer than two dozen varieties, each one more expensive than the last. Her mouth waters in anticipation. To control the sudden rush of hunger, she twists her fingers together and asks, "So, how are you doing with the whole no contact thing?"

He dips his culinary masterpiece-in-progress into egg wash. "With Markeya? Oh, you know how it is."

Rachel drums the countertop. "Guess so."

"We're used to spending time apart," he says without further explanation. The sandwich sizzles in a hot pan. "How are *you?*"

She shrugs, shoulder muscles resisting motion. "Scared."

Vernon props one hand on his hip and fusses over the pan with the other. "I can sympathize with that. Did Daniela give you that number?"

"Yeah." She flips the phone over; a blank screen stares up at her. "Haven't texted yet, though. It's early there."

Vernon shakes the pan, and then the sandwich lurches into the air before landing on its second side. It's impressive. "Shoot her your info, just in case she's up early to get into the city."

"Good idea." She peers into her messages, thumbs poised. "What do I say? 'Hi, my name is Rachel. My husband's dying, or is maybe already dead. Thanks for checking on him for me'?"

"Worse ways to ask for a favor."

She thinks about it, then starts. "How about: 'Hi. My roommate Daniela gave me your number. My husband Job is the one in Chennai. Please feel free to call me at any time. I cannot express how much I appreciate this. Thank you, thank you, thank you'?"

"Sounds great." Vernon sets a plate in front of her. The sandwich glistens, dappled with powdered sugar, and cut into triangles the way her mother did when she was little. "Bon appétit."

Rachel presses send on the screen and sets her phone aside so she can center herself on a hot butter hill. Whoever Monte Cristo is, he has exquisite taste. Sweet, salty, crunchy, gooey, everything she wants. As she devours her first meal in two days, Vernon takes out a couple of cups then sets about making a drink with strawberries, cucumber skewers, some kind of simple syrup, and a couple cans of ginger beer. Concoction made, he tops one glass with a sprig of mint from a plant on the windowsill then sets in front of her. "And one virgin Pimm's Cup."

Ginger beer bubbles up, tickling Rachel's nose when she sniffs. Inhaling is heaven, but tasting is beyond: fruit, spice, and everything nice. "Wow, this is great."

Vernon hums as he moves to the liquor cabinet, rustling through the bottle collection. Rachel raises an eyebrow when Vernon hauls out the vodka. "Markeya requested a drink for her dinner. Split shift."

Rachel picks up her sandwich, enchanted by the powdered sugar that clings to her fingertips. "Oh, she's up? Good. I wanted to head over to the carriage house and see what I need to order for the cabinets. Wouldn't want to wake her."

He checks the microwave clock. "I'd catch her before too long."

Teeth breach the Monte Cristo's crusted shell into the gooey center. Rachel groans with pleasure; her stomach cheers. Such a decadent treat coupled with the sharp zing of ginger beer is a real balm after a week of fear. After her parents and brothers died, it was days before Job could convince her to eat his home-cooked version of a Waffle House All-Star Special. Something about grease is just good for the soul. After a couple of bites of restorative sandwich, she tilts her chin to the meal being assembled on the counter. "Is that tray for her? I can take it."

"You don't have to," he says as he packages a second sandwich in a plastic container.

"Going over anyway," she replies. Half a sandwich down, and her stomach already aches.

When he places the sprig of mint into the glass, he dusts his hands free of debris. "Knock yourself out, then. Thanks."

Pushing the plate away, she says, "Anything for the maker of such a sick sandwich."

"You're starting to sound like Wren," he teases as he starts in on his mess.

Rachel flushes, though not entirely out of embarrassment. "I'll take it over now."

"I'll wrap the rest up for you," he offers as he picks up the remains of Rachel's meal.

"Thanks," she says as she hops up for the tray. The two exchange a silent nod, and then Rachel heads outside to the carriage house. Despite its being March, the weather is almost warm enough to warrant short sleeves. Rachel takes in a deep breath of heated oak, of her home in Georgia. Shivers of memory run up and down her arms. Mom in the kitchen, Dad in the garden, her brothers playing in the yard. She can hear them. Taking another breath, she centers herself and trips into the unlocked house.

Markeya, dressed for bed in a floral robe, stands at the bar pouring hot water from a kettle into a glass pot that strains coffee through the filter. It's an excellent magic trick.

"Hey," Rachel greets, shouldering the door close.

The other woman freezes, which causes coffee-grind water to overflow onto the counter. She swears before mopping up the mess. "What's up?"

Her tone is brusque enough to make Rachel self-conscious. "Brought you some lunch. Monte Cristo sandwiches, a Pimm's Cup, and a salad, I guess. Or maybe dinner? Whatever meal it is for you." She sets the tray on the counter and steps back quick, closer to Job's equipment in search of comfort. "I was just gonna see what kind of wood we had before I ordered some for the kitchen cabinets."

"I've gotcha." Markeya slides the tray towards herself, picking at the contents. "Thanks for this. But, babe, you can't be in here, especially not without a mask. The whole point was for us to quarantine away from everyone else."

Rachel blushes. "Yeah, got it. Sorry." The chastisement makes her want to lie like a child. "Didn't know you guys were home."

Markeya sees through her bullshit, of course, even as she digs a blue mask out of her robe pocket and covers her face. "Night shift. Anabelle and I put our schedules on the calendar."

"Oh." *That damn calendar.* Looks like she'll have to subscribe after all. "Sorry."

"You okay?" Markeya asks.

Rachel glances over her shoulder at Job's pristine workshop, which strikes her as not quite right. "Not really," she admits. "Worried."

Markeya gives an empathetic nod. "Why don't we video chat about it? Anabelle's upstairs. You go back into the house, and we'll call from out here."

A medical perspective might be nice, or it might break her heart. Either way, knowing is better than not knowing. "Okay," she replies meekly. She doesn't move.

"You really gotta go, babe," Markeya's tone softens, "it's not safe in here for you."

Rachel doesn't want to go, the smell of sawdust is calming, but she knows she must. Back inside the house, she's surprised that the kitchen is empty save for the drying pans. The hall doors are closed, but no noise hums behind them. She walks to the living room to enjoy some of the silence and winds up sitting on the sun-warmed couch with her head in her hands. Her phone starts to ring, but it's not Job. "Fuck," she whispers to herself before attempting a smile and answering the call.

Markeya and Anabelle fill her screen, both dressed for bed with their hair tucked under satin bonnets. "Hey, y'all," Rachel greets.

"Hey, babe," Anabelle's delicate brows draw together, "what's going on?"

She gulps down an anxiety burp to make sure it doesn't become word vomit. "Well, Job, um, we haven't heard from him in thirty-seven hours. I don't know anything, don't know how he's doing, how he's feeling, what he's going through. Nothing. Nobody knows anything about the virus. I mean, I've attended a seminar at work about it." *If doom-watching a fifty-minute panel of old white guys in red ties talking about burgeoning catastrophe counts as a seminar.* "But I thought it was supposed to infect old people and the immunocompromised. I don't understand this. Job, he's just...so healthy. I don't understand."

Markeya winces, rubbing the wrinkles from her forehead with the back of her hand. "I've been working on a unit for two weeks now. If I've learned anything, it's that it can hit anyone."

As if that's comforting. Rachel rests an elbow on the couch arm, pinching the skin between her eyes. "Where do you think he got it?"

"It doesn't really matter. He's in isolation, right?"

"Of course it matters!" she snaps with eyes wide open. Markeya and Anabelle both frown. She needs them to tell her that Job getting sick is all her fault. "Do you think he got it at the embassy? Because he didn't start coughing until after he got to Chennai." This information is very important, for some reason. "And then he was in the waiting room for twelve hours before anyone even saw him." The very idea of her Job sitting in the middle of a sea of coughing faces makes her stomach uneasy.

"Well," Anabelle ventures tenderly, "that wouldn't have helped his condition."

Coolness touches Rachel's chin. When she reaches, she realizes that she's crying. The back of her hand doubles as a handkerchief. "I just want to know if he's okay," she tells them. Her phone slips from her hand, displaying a less than flattering view of her chin. At least anxiety makes it impossible to be vain. A good thing, too, because her hair has an anxious mind of its own outside of its tie. She twirls a free strand around her forefinger and begins to tug. Words spill: "But there's no way for me to even call the hospital. Either the phone just rings and rings, or someone picks up, and we can't understand one another. I've tried over and over and over. I'm on all of these international community boards looking for help, but no one is even in Chennai. Because who the fuck even goes to Chennai?"

"How about we take a breath, babe?" Anabelle encourages.

Rachel sputters but eventually falls back into breath. She rights the phone. Markeya and Anabelle both stare. No doubt they are unmoved by the display. Hard to be empathetic when your heart is asked to break a thousand times a day. They're probably used to this. *And here you are asking for more of their energy, you selfish bitch*, Rachel's self-loathing screams.

"Look," Markeya says, "I won't sugar coat; it's probably bad. I just got off a sixteen-hour shift in a unit full of patients like Job. They can't breathe on their own, so they're intubated. You know what that means?"

Rachel uses the hem of her shirt to wipe her nose. "No."

"Okay, so when you're intubated, you're sedated, and then they feed a tube down your windpipe." Markeya makes a sweeping motion down Anabelle's throat. "Then that's hooked up to a ventilator that breathes for you." She puts her hands in her lap. "So, if he's not calling or texting, then I would assume he's on a ventilator."

Anabelle shoves her elbow into Markeya's ribs, but it's too late to keep the image out of Rachel's mind. She's repeating, "Oh my God."

"Wait, wait," Markeya almost shouts, waving now. "That's not a death sentence!"

White-hot frisson lights up Rachel's skin.

"It's not," Anabelle chimes in, voice pitched for soothing. "Just taxing on the body. If Job is intubated, then he'll stay that way a couple of days, he'll get better, and then he'll wake up no worse for wear."

"Exactly!" Markeya chirps. Her expression is, from what Rachel can make of it through her blurred vision, horrified. "Most of the intubated patients I've seen go home."

"How many go home?" she demands. Her focus returns to latch on Markeya's face.

Both women's eyes widen. Markeya offers cautiously, "Enough to be hopeful."

"How the fuck am I supposed to be hopeful right now?" Rachel snaps.

Anabelle's blue eyes flare and then fill with tears. Her tone turns caustic, "We're trying to be realistic. I know you're stressed, but try to understand where we're coming from. We're exhausted and scared, and we don't know enough about this to know what to do."

Markeya holds Anabelle's shoulder, scolding Rachel for making the red-haired woman cry. "Look, you need to calm down. Getting yourself all worked up isn't gonna help."

Before she can say "fuck you forever," Rachel ends the call, throws the phone down, picks up the nearest pillow, then screams. She screams until all the sound leaves her lungs, and she's left with the harsh burn of breath being forced over her vocal cords. She screams until she's sure that she'll never speak again.

When the rage ebbs from her body, she settles back into the couch and stares up into the ceiling. Shadows play in corners nearest the windows; the outline of branches flicker when clouds obscure the sun. Light in the living room shifts from dusky gray to warmer marigold tones, though the shift is so gradual that her eyes adjust before she can appreciate it. Not that she can appreciate anything right now, not with her mind holding vigil so far away in some conjured hospital room.

Just as she's beginning to make out the tubes protruding from Job's mouth, she is interrupted by a single, "Hey."

Startled, Rachel jumps in her seat and finds Wren without wig, makeup, or platforms standing in the doorway, gripping the doorframe so hard that their knuckles are white. They look very young. Tired, too. Whatever maternal instincts are taking root in her are enough to snap Rachel back into a semblance of self. She smooths her hair back and says, "Hey."

"What's wrong?" they ask.

"Job," she replies. "You?"

Their lower lip trembles. "My-my mom."

Rachel senses pre-emptive loss heavy over Wren. "Oh, yeah?" she asks.

They nod.

She scoots over to make room. "Want to sit with me?"

They nod again and stumble to crash into Rachel, already sniffling. There is no choice but to hold them. Putting one arm around their shoulders and using the other to pull them into a close embrace, she presses her cheek against their soft peach head. The sobbing doesn't come, but tears do; Rachel can feel them as they drop hot on her collarbone. She doesn't know what to say, doesn't know any soothing words to make fear go away, so she settles on shushing.

Eventually, the tears end and Wren eases away from Rachel, eyes fixed. When Rachel mirrors their posture, they reach for her hand.

Side by side on the blue velvet couch, they are silent. Time passes. Rachel knows that from the sound of footsteps leaving makeshift offices on the first floor. No one bothers them.

A little past six, Rachel's phone lights up on the floor. Daniela's colleague of a colleague texts Rachel back, saying that she's finally arrived at the hospital in Chennai. Rachel leans onto her knees, texting furiously:

Thank you, thank you. This means so much. Please, tell me when you find him.

She gives the woman Job's birthday, just in case it is important. She waits, ripping at her cuticles as if they aren't already bloody.

Ten minutes later, each of which feels like an eternity, the woman says that she has found Job. He's been intubated for a day. Her divine relief is swept away when the woman asks if it's possible to video chat.

Stomach in freefall, Rachel looks at Wren. "I need to call her."

"Do you want me to stay?" Wren asks, already starting to stand.

Her eyes flash between the door and her phone. "I don't know."

"I'll sit over here," they conclude, moving to the piano, their back to Rachel.

Their presence gives Rachel enough bravery to call. The woman has a kind enough face, though that doesn't make their news any easier. The doctors are not hopeful. After being put on the ventilator, Job deteriorated quickly. He is very weak, she says. Perhaps, if you think, it would be best to say something to him. Rachel knows what she means.

She isn't ready for this. Hiding from Job, though, isn't possible. She needs to see, one way or another. After biting the back of her hand, she says, "Okay, put him on."

The woman flips the phone and holds it in front of Job. Rachel is confronted with his prone body as a machine breathes for him. She has to swallow bile. "Jesus Christ," she whispers. The piano bench scrapes, and suddenly Wren is there with their hand on her shoulder.

The woman brings the phone closer to his face promising that Job can hear her. His face is yellow in this light, dark purple bags under his eyes, face rough with days of beard and no washing and hollow with illness. He is dying; she knows that all of her worst fears are confirmed at this moment. Through the din in her ears, she can hear the sound of more ventilators, coughing, and voices all intermingling a world away. Her Job is dying, and the world goes on.

What can she say to him, the love of her life? This man who has shored her up through every thin season of their lives together? The father of their children, the one gone and the one not yet born? The man who she knew she would spend forever knowing? Her breath comes faster, bitten by panic. She knows she has to keep it together for him. She will not ruin their last conversation with fear. She has done that too many times to count.

Wren's hand suddenly falls away, and they leave the room with a cell phone pressed up to their ear. The door closes behind them, already speaking in hurried tones. She is alone with Job and the manufactured rise and fall of his chest.

"I love you, Job. I love you so fucking much. And I know it's never been enough, and I'm sorry. I've loved you the best way I've known how, and that's more than I ever thought I could love anyone after my family." Her voice catches, but she pushes through. Because that's what Job deserves, even if his eyes are closed, and her voice is softer than his ventilator.

"When we met, you saw me in a way no one has ever seen me before, and I knew that it made you special to me. That we were meant to be together. You taught me how to be alive again, that life was worth living even though there were so many days and weeks and months when I didn't believe you. You never gave up on me. You never made me feel bad about how much my grief ran my life. Did I ever tell you how important that was? How special it made me feel?"

She slides off the couch to sit on the floor, needing its constancy as she falls into a memory pit. "I'm sorry, you know, for how I acted when I was sad. It made me so angry, and I shouldn't have yelled at you the way I did. Ever. Because you've always been so good to me, baby. I wish I had been as good to you. I wish an apology made it all better. But I promise you to be better now. I'll do better. Try harder to be better."

Words don't quite make sense anymore; she knows that. "I love you, y'know. I've loved you more than I ever thought I could love anyone. I am so grateful for you, my sweet Job. And I'm sorry. Siobhan." Oh, yes, that wound. "I'm so sorry for Siobhan, Job; you could never know how sorry." Her voice falls to a whisper, "But you'll be with her now, and I love you both. So much. So much."

She can't say anything else without sobbing. She kisses the screen, and her watery eyes blur him and blur him and blur him until it's easy enough to hang up.

CHAPTER TWENTY-SIX

BY MORNING, THE MIRRORS in the houses are all covered with whatever fabric can be spared. There will be no funeral. Rachel's never done that before, but the grief part is familiar. The grief that radiates from Wren's body as she holds them against her chest is familiar. Since half-past three, the young person has been curled in the crook of Rachel's arms, shifting between tears and restless sleep. "Mommy. Mommy. I want my mommy." Their voice is so high, so winsome, so resplendent with loss.

There is nothing to say, of course, only soft murmurings into the top of their head. At some point later in the morning, the grief is enough to put Wren down into deeper sleep, which frees Rachel to tuck some blankets around them and get up for the bathroom. Door closed, she takes out her phone to feast on the messages. The colleague of a colleague has been beyond saintly, sending hourly updates and photos of Job. Her latest messages make fresh tears prick.

Job is up and asking for her.

Not wanting to wake Wren with the sound of her voice but unwilling to stray too far, Rachel tiptoes to the shower stall where she sits on the still damp floor and presses the video chat button. Job's face appears two rings later. His face is sunken with illness, eyes dull with whatever medication he's been given to keep him still, but it's him.

"Oh my god. Hi, baby, hi," she croons as she reaches out to touch the screen. Tears and snot begin to readily spill. Her body shakes with joy and fear. "I can't believe you're okay."

"Hi," he wheezes. His voice is raw and looks like it pains him to use.

"I love you so much," is all she can think to say, using the palm of her hand to wipe away the tears that sluice down her wrist.

He nods, smiling some kind of codeine grin. "You, too."

She sniffles and remembers the situation at hand, the fact that Job is in a hospital in India. "Do you need anything? Can I send you anything?"

Job glances off-camera to confirm something, then shakes his head. "We good." A shaky thumbs-up. "Wanted to see you."

"You see me," she says. It's hard to believe how lucky she is.

"I see you. Love you," he croaks. A small plastic cup with a straw is placed to Job's lips. He winces when he swallows.

Heart strings tugged, Rachel wipes the rest of her face with the bottom of her t-shirt before making a shooing motion with her free hand. "Get some rest, okay? Call or text whenever you want. Phone is on full blast."

"Love you," he says again. His brown eyes are rheumy but warm.

"Love you," she echoes with the sweet smile reserved only for Job, then ends the call. Her heart feels like it's in her throat. She climbs out of the shower and stands at the sink to splash water on her face. In the mirror, dark circles and swollen skin peer back at her. She pokes at the bags. It's been a while since she's looked this bad. Since Siobhan? More cold water to clear away those old memories. This is a day for fresh faces.

As she washes away the grime of sorrow, Rachel's 7:30 work alarm goes off. She clicks the snooze button before the music can wake Wren. Once cleared, she can see the group texts have piled in her absence. Sitting on the toilet with a towel in hand, she begins reading.

Daniela has added you to the group "Wren"

Daniela: Hi, all. If you haven't heard yet, Wren's mother, Ted's aunt, passed this morning. Due to the nature of her illness, a traditional funeral and burial will likely not be possible. In observance of their family's faith, we would like to sit Shiva with Wren over the next seven days. We would like to start observing the practice today, if at all possible. You may notice that the mirrors in the common areas have been covered. We ask that they remain that way. More information to follow.

Vernon: Oh no, that's horrible! Is there anything I can do for the Shiva? Is there a food we should make? Or can it be anything they like?

Ted: Any food will do, but boiled eggs for sure. Cycle of life.

Renato: I'll sit with Wren if they need.

Yukiko: I will too

Markeya:	Would if I could. Anything we can do from afar? Anabelle said she'd start making scones. Chocolate or blueberry?
Daniela:	I'm sure either would be appreciated
Markeya:	Who's with Wren now?
Rachel:	I am. They're asleep in my room right now.
Vernon:	Need anything?
Rachel:	Could use some tea or something.
Vernon:	Up with chamomile in a minute.
Ted:	How's Job?
Rachel:	Off the ventilator. Just got off the phone with him. We spoke for a minute. Weak but breathing.
Markeya:	That's GREAT news.
Rachel:	Relieved. Worried about Wren. Didn't get much sleep at all last night.
Daniela:	I don't imagine they did. When's the last time they ate?
Francesca:	Yesterday lunchtime
Markeya:	I'll bring the scones over. Know they like chocolate a lot.
Lorelei:	Tell us if there's anything else we can bring.
Rachel:	Will do. Please don't knock when you come up. Just come in quiet.

Her housemates give the message a tiny heart, and she puts the phone away to tend to her charge. Soft morning light finds its way through the cracks in her curtains, filling the room with gray. Even in the gloom, she can make out Wren staring straight at her. "Hey," she whispers.

They're silent.

Rachel pauses. "Do you want me to get back into bed with you?" Their single nod is easy enough to obey. She pulls back the comforter with its red flowers and packs in against Wren's soft body. The remnants of yesterday's makeup linger on the pillowcase; Rachel struggles to remember that mess is okay in light of mourning. Job wouldn't care, so neither will she. Instead, she tucks the blankets around them both and holds the young person as they tremble.

It's a terrible thing to lose a mother. Maybe loss isn't as hard when prepared for the blow when you've seen age or disease or heartbreak weigh down the face of the person who's supposed to love you most. Maybe loss then is more tinged with relief than pain. Rachel's never said it out loud, but she's always envied people whose mothers died of cancer. Even aggressive forms can give a person a week to prepare, to say their goodbyes. At least then their death is a mercy. In her darkest moments of grief, Rachel imagined a world in which her mother was diagnosed with thyroid cancer.

She imagined being with her when she got the diagnosis. Oh, the hair-pulling and the chest-beating she would have done! She imagined the chemotherapy: her mother's head wrapped in a blue silk scarf they got in Paris while crossing dreams off the bucket list. She imagined writing down recipes that only lived in her mother's head, using a felt-tipped pen and the finest notecards. Alone in her dorm room, she would imagine a million things she would say to her mother as they prepared her eulogy together. She imagined resting her head in her mother's lap and crying like a child as her hair was smoothed and her pain was shushed. She imagined the open-casket funeral, her mother laying with hands, scarred and blunted from years in a kitchen, folded with great peace over her heart. "She's no longer in pain," the mourners would say, and Rachel would nod in agreement, a soft smile on her lips and a sorrowful wrinkle between her eyebrows.

But suddenly, like this? Fine in the morning, dead by dinner? What kind of sick fucking joke is that? Rachel glares at the back of Wren's head, holding them just a little closer, a little tighter, trying to let them know: *This world is a fucked-up place, kiddo, but you aren't alone.*

The door opens to admit Vernon in a disheveled state. Even in the low light, it's apparent that his hair is dirty. Rachel moves to sit up against the headboard but keeps a hand on Wren's shoulder, watching as he sets two cups of tea on her nightstand. Vernon gives glances between the curled-up ball on Rachel's bed then back to her, silently asking for permission to approach. Rachel is the keeper, and what she says goes. Agreeing with a gracious nod, Vernon moves to crouch by Wren's side of the bed, staring at them. After a moment, he reaches out to stroke their face. Wren begins emitting a strange hollow wheeze. He closes his eyes and hums in agreement. He leans closer until the two are so close that their foreheads nearly touch. Wren is the one who leans forward to make the connection, crying when they do. There is a fresh murmured chorus of "Mommy" on their lips. Vernon presses the back of his fingertips to their cheek. It's a tender scene, one that makes Rachel's own eyes burn with empathy.

"Anything you need," he says, standing. "Anything."

Wren rolls over into Rachel's side, which surprises her into gathering up the young person and their rumpled clothes into her arms. Their head is heavy and wet against her chest. She mouths "thank you" to Vernon, and he knows not to linger. There's barely any noise when he closes the door.

When Wren cries into Rachel, all there is to do is to hold on so they don't fly away, the way Rachel would have if it hadn't been for Job. Tears can't last forever, even when it feels like they can, especially without sustenance. After fifteen or twenty minutes, Rachel doesn't know which, Wren begins to settle.

"I can't do this. I really can't," they whisper as they look up at Rachel with all the innocence of a child. Snot flows over their top lip, and their tongue comes out to greet it. Rachel takes a quick sip of tea then uses tissue from the bedside table to clean her charge's face. Eyes red and puffy, Wren reminds her so much of herself that it breaks her heart all over again. She wants to tell them that things get better, but that would feel too close to a lie. She wasn't as strong as the person in her arms. She needed someone like Job, someone who knew what it was like to drown, to pull her out of the waves of grief before she let herself drown. And she would have most certainly let herself drown. Taking another tissue, she wipes away the black smudges from around Wren's eyes until they're clean. She may not be as strong or as eloquent as Job was when she needed it most, but she is here, she promised to be better, and she'll try.

Encouraging Wren to sit up, she places a cup of tea into their hands before doing the same and staring straight ahead at the fireplace. It's a shame that there's no fire laid; there is a story to tell.

"When I was a freshman in college, my dad lost his job. He'd been in cable for, like, twenty years, and they gave him the pink slip because, y'know, drinking on the job is frowned upon. My mom had a really good job at this restaurant in Atlanta, so it wasn't like the end of the world that he even lost his job. Everyone took it in stride but him. My dad was devastated."

From the corner of her eye, she can see Wren's face turn quizzical even as they have some tea. Rachel takes this as a sign to continue. "Normal people would have found a new job, right? Just start hitting the bricks, go to an employment agency, whatever. Hell, a normal person might take some time off to work on a project or hang out with their kids. Not him." Her lip curls; even after all this time, she hasn't been able to let go of this anger. It's too deep, too bitter. That sort of rage is hard to scrub out with therapy.

"No, not my dad. My dad started drinking more by himself, watched a lot of TV. Mostly travel channels, I think. When I went home for a weekend, all he wanted to talk about was renting a car and going on a road trip."

She leans towards Wren to whisper, "He was big into national parks and historical landmarks. And you know what? I thought it was a good idea for him to get out of the house, see some of the world. After hearing about it nonstop for two days, I told him to go for it.

"Three weeks after I got back to school, he somehow convinced my mom to quit her job as an executive chef, pull my brothers out of a great elementary school, buy a used RV, sell my childhood home, and move to Portland, Oregon." Rachel laughs. It's not funny. Her voice softens with memory. "I remember the day he told me they were going. I had just gotten out of my intro theater class—gag—and he was in the drive-thru at McDonald's ordering three Quarter Pounders with cheese, a Big Mac meal with a Diet Coke, two chicken nugget kids' meals with Sprites, and two apple pies. He's rooting around the car for exact change, and he tells me that the whole family is packing up and heading out on a three-month-long road trip across these great United States before finally laying anchor in Portland-fucking-Oregon."

Wren sets their tea aside. "Why Portland?"

"Anybody's guess, really. They didn't know anybody there, had zero job prospects, and I doubt either of them thought about school systems. Seriously, my brothers were, like, nine, and they just pulled them out of school and left me on the other side of the country. We'd spent my whole life in Georgia. Our families lived in the South. Moving to New Orleans would have made sense. Hell, moving to Montgomery woulda made sense. But Portland?" Rachel huffs, trying to get a hold of herself and the story. This isn't about her feeling bitter; it's about Wren feeling better. "Everything happened so fast; I didn't actually think they were going to go through with it. My dad was always kind of a flake. Super into The Grateful Dead, IPAs, weed, and alien conspiracies. Not the type to follow through on a huge project like that immediately."

They snort. "Kinda makes sense why he wanted to move to Portland, huh?"

"In hindsight, yeah." She shrugs. "Anyway, they packed up their lives, put the house on the market, and were out of town a month later. Before they left, me and my mom got into a huge fight about it. She said she was being supportive of my dad. I said she was enabling his midlife crisis. Hurt feelings all around." Rachel remembers her mother's brisk tone with shame. How much easier would it have been to be kind?

"She wouldn't talk to me on the phone alone after that, always used one of the twins as a buffer. They went up through Gettysburg, D.C., Boston, all the way to Acadia National Park. They'd send me postcards wherever they went, and they'd call on Sunday to tell me how great the trip was going. I'd cry for an hour when we'd hang up. I was so pissed that they left me, but I never said anything else about it. After they'd been gone about a month, I called my mom up to ask her how to make gravy. I knew how, but it was a good excuse to talk. That was the only thing we could ever really connect over, so I started cooking more and asking for her advice." Her eyes mist. "It was nice. It really was."

Wren rests their head on Rachel's shoulder, which helps remind her what the point of her story is. She can soldier on with this. "When they were finally ready to go to Portland, they started through the West. Those postcards were gorgeous. Got one from both Dakotas and was halfway convinced to fly out to join them for spring break. They actually sent me a letter with this picture in it." She picks up the framed photo, jostling Wren enough that they sit up. Rachel smiles down all four of their faces before handing them to Wren. "Theodore Roosevelt National Park. It's the last photo I have of them altogether. Didn't get it until after."

Wren traces her brothers' twin faces. "What happened? If I can ask."

"You can ask." She swallows hard. "Um, when they were going through Montana, they got caught in this really bad slush storm. Snow, rain, hail, everything. Detectives told me it was one of the worst storms they'd had in a while." She swallows again, bracing herself for the rest. This part never gets easier.

"No one was ever really able to tell me what happened. They figured my dad must have hit a patch of ice and lost control of the RV because they careened into a ditch. No one even noticed until the weather cleared. Not that it would have mattered. All four of them died on impact. Or at least that's what the detective told me. For a long time, I thought he was lying to spare my feelings."

Wren sniffs then reaches for another tissue. "Holy shit."

Rachel hums her agreement.

"What did you do?"

She shrugs. "Lost it. Like, what else was I supposed to do? I had to fly to Montana to get their ashes. No funeral, y'know?" Rachel wonders if that similarity will make Wren feel better. "Afterwards, I went to stay with my aunt in Alabama for a couple of weeks before going back to school."

"You went back to school?" Wren looks at her with big, red, disbelieving eyes.

"It was the only thing I could think to do, only thing that made sense." She sips her tea as she waits for Wren to speak. She's ready for the question they're bound to ask.

It doesn't take long. "Does it get better?"

Setting the cup aside again, Rachel reclines further into the pillows so she can stare at the chandelier while Wren stares at the photo of her family. "You know, I asked Job the same thing. We met a few weeks after it happened. He'd lost his parents, so he got it. He told me that it doesn't get better; it just gets different. My grief counselors said that you just sorta make room for the pain. I really thought that was bullshit for a long time." Sometimes she still does. "There was no room in me for all my sadness. My family was gone. How could I be anything other than sad? Even with loving Job, there was still so much of it. Until, eventually, I realized that I wasn't making room for my pain; I was making room for anything else that might come into my life." She touches Wren's arm, and the two share a sad smile. "There's a probably healthier way of coping that you know about, but that's how I dealt with it."

"Sounds about right," they say with watery eyes.

"Actually, and stick with me here, I imagined my heart being a subway car during rush hour in a big city. No empty seats, it's hot, and everybody is either playing shitty music on shitty nineties boomboxes or eating tuna sandwiches. Then the subway gets to the next stop, which is just as busy as the one before, but no one gets off. Instead, all of these fancy businesspeople just cram themselves into the car because fuck waiting for the next one. So now there's just a subway car full of tuna sandwiches and Shalimar, and everyone has to deal with it because we're all going somewhere, and nobody is waiting for the next train to come.

"So, you wait on the platform as long as you need to, Wren. Let as many trains go by as you want, and don't listen to security when they tell you not to loiter because you paid for your ticket." Rachel offers her hand, and they take it, clutching with something close to desperation. "But eventually, you will have to get on board. It'll be gross and uncomfortable, and you'll hate every minute, but you've got places to be. And eventually, some of the tuna sandwich eaters will get to their stops. More Shalimar may come onboard. Perhaps even a few of the boomboxes will leave, to the point that your headphones will drown the rest of the noise out. When you get there, at that point of the journey where there's a little more space in the car, you'll know that you can make the whole trip. And if *I* can do that, *you* are more than capable." Rachel hugs Wren into her side. "But you don't have to do anything right now other than be sad."

"Thank you," Wren says. They rest their full weight on Rachel. "And thank you for telling me about your family. It means a lot."

"I don't like to talk about them because it's hard." Rachel reaches for the frame. Her face is transformed by tenderness when she touches the glass. "My brothers, especially. They died so young that it's easy to get lost in the 'what-if' of their lives. Would they have gone to school? Military? Peace Corps?" Her family returns home beside her bed. "You're about how old they would have been. Nineteen in November, now that I think about it." *Ten years gone already?*

"I'm sorry, Rachel," Wren mumbles. Rachel realizes that they are going to sleep.

She pets their hair and rests her head on top of theirs. "I'm sorry for you, too."

CHAPTER TWENTY-SEVEN

AN HOUR LATER, WREN IS still sleeping, so Rachel texts the house for a replacement. Ted's the one who picks up the mantle, arriving moments later to sit at the desk with a book. He looks tired. To both of their surprise, Rachel walks across the room and leans down to hug him. It's a quick thing, but there's no denying the gesture's sweetness. She flushes but doesn't apologize, doesn't actually feel like there is anything to apologize for. That's new.

She scuttles out of the room before either she or Ted can read too much into the gesture. In the hallway with the door flat against her back, Rachel allows herself a breath free of grief. Collecting herself behind closed eyelids, her mind floods with thoughts of Job and Wren and Wren's family and everything that needs to be done for them. After a few cycles of breath that would make her therapist proud, her anxious thoughts recede like the tides. Eyes open again, she takes out her phone to check her messages. There are a few in the group chat, but the one that catches her attention is from Job that just says, "I love you." Rachel feels like melting. She doesn't, of course, because physics and a laundry list worth of tasks get in the way. Oh, yes, there is work to be done, and who better than her to do it? She must for Wren because they are grieving, and she isn't. It's only fair.

Texting Job back, she tucks her phone into her back pocket and rockets downstairs, where she is rushed by Cornelius who gives her a cursory sniff before heading off to the library. A chorus of squeaks follows after. Rachel smiles at that then lets it fall when she sees the bathroom mirror covered in a sheet. A nasty voice in her head says: *Who are you to smile at a time like this? Get in that kitchen and be useful.*

She obeys. When has she ever not listened to that voice? When she enters the kitchen, she's pleased to find the household majority already there with cups of coffee and bowls of oatmeal. Vernon stands up from the island when he sees her. "How's Job?" he asks. Everyone turns to look at her expectantly.

"He's awake and texting. I'll take it as a good sign," Rachel responds quickly, not wanting to linger on her good news when there's so much else to be done. She claps her hands together then rubs vigorously. "Okay, where are we?"

Lorelei quirks a brow. "What do you mean? We're in the kitchen."

Rachel fights to keep from rolling her eyes. "I mean, what have we done so far?" Silence. She struggles for patience by going to grab a cup of coffee. "For Wren? How's their dad? Has anyone checked in with the coroner yet? Called the funeral home?" She pauses before pouring. "Wait, is Wren's mom Jewish?"

"Yes, she converted," Daniela confirms.

Rachel hums as she peers down into that shiny black contents in her cup. "Well, so, how are we supposed to handle this? Aren't there a lot of rules?"

"Yes," Daniela replies. "We should have her buried soon. Within twenty-four hours."

"How are they going to do that?" Markeya's voice pours through a speakerphone. "The morgues are backed up."

Whipping around, warm coffee splashes over Rachel's hand. She doesn't notice. "So, we haven't even called the coroner yet?" There's no hiding the annoyance now. Don't these people care about Wren? "Who's in charge here?" she snaps.

"You, apparently," Renato snaps back.

The room watches her with creases between their eyes. "I can be if needed." *More flies with honey*, she tells herself to soften her tone. This needs to go better. "Wren has older brothers, though, right? Where are they?"

"California," Daniela replies.

"Are they flying in?" Rachel asks as she sweetens her coffee.

"I don't see how they could," Markeya's voice says.

Yukiko glances between Rachel and the phone resting on the island. "Should Wren go home to her father?" she asks cautiously.

"Absolutely not!" Markeya shouts, her voice rattling the phone against the copper top. Everyone freezes. Francesca stops eating mid-bite. "He's been exposed, too. He could get Wren sick!"

"But we want to sit Shiva with them," Vernon says, looking at nothing but the phone. His tone is tense, the first time Rachel has heard him be anything less than perfectly polite. "Isn't that about their family sitting under one roof?"

"Um, okay," Markeya says snidely. "But like, that only applies when there isn't a fucking plague raging. How about this? House rule: No one is going anywhere."

Rachel blushes and looks down at the counter. Tension makes her uncomfortable.

Vernon doesn't make it better when he says, "Markeya, it's a sacred religious custom."

"So is sacrificing a virgin to a volcano so it doesn't blow! Some customs shouldn't be observed. I don't know how on earth y'all think there's going to be any kind of a burial."

The room is silent and seems inclined to remain that way. *We're never going to get anything done like this*, Rachel thinks, which is enough to throw her into action. She looks up to make grim eye contact with Vernon before reaching out for his phone. She can be brave. She can manage this mess. When he hands it to her, she says, "Could you or Anabelle call the coroner? If we can't sit a regular Shiva, the least we can do is have Wren's mother buried today."

Markeya lets loose a sigh that's so exhausted that Rachel wishes she hadn't asked. "I seriously don't know how else to tell you this: It's not gonna happen. I'm sorry."

Daniela gets up to waddle over to the phone. She gives Rachel a nod of solidarity and then says, "We need to try. I don't think Wren observes a lot of Jewish customs, but their mother was very devout."

Francesca starts to eat again. "Huh. A Catholic Jew. Who would have thought?"

Throwing a look over her shoulder, Daniela snaps, "Mama."

The old woman holds out both hands in askance at her daughter. "What?"

"Please don't say things like that!"

The spoon clatters from the old woman's fingers with an indignant clatter. "Why not? I think it's good she was devout even though it wasn't the way she was raised." Francesca retakes the utensil and settles into her oatmeal. "She chose her religion. Not many people do that."

Before things can slip further away from the task at hand, Rachel says, "*Anyway*, we want to honor her as best we can. If we can have her buried today, then all the better. So, Markeya, can you or Anabelle please call the coroner? If having her released today is at all possible, let's go for it. We can find out where she should be buried and let you know."

Daniela gives Rachel a thankful smile. "I'll call their rabbi," she says.

Rachel walks to the fridge, cleans the dry erase board of its grocery list, takes up a pen, and begins to write everyone's name. "Okay, what else needs doing?"

"Music?" Renato asks from his cup of coffee.

"No, no music," Daniela says. "Nothing that makes you feel good. It's disrespectful." When everyone looks at her knowledge blankly, she adds, "My mother-in-law requested I take classes at the synagogue."

"Oh," Renato says glumly. "Well, what are we," he gestures to Yukiko, "supposed to do then? Music is very important to us."

"We'll ask Wren if that's what they want," Daniela decides, and Rachel nods in agreement. "I know they're not devout, but they may want to respect the Shiva."

"How are we going to do that?" Lorelei asks with arms crossed. "No one can come be together right now."

Vernon stands, folding his tablet under his arm. "I'll handle that. I'll start a stream that anyone can log into. I'll keep a camera on in the living room for Wren to meet with 'visitors.'"

Rachel writes down his self-appointed task then asks, "Isn't there a candle that's supposed to stay lit?"

"Yes. A special seven-day candle. I'm not sure where people get them, though. The rabbi, maybe?" Apparently, Daniela's classes haven't gotten this far in the mourning process.

Francesca wipes her mouth and stands. "We have candles downstairs. I'll look."

Daniela touches the old woman's arm. "Mama, wait until everyone has a job."

"She's right," Rachel says. "Let's stay on track. We need to figure out who's doing what. If at all possible, Wren's mother should be buried today, or try," she corrects quickly. "So, um, Markeya, are you going to call?"

"Anabelle definitely has more pull than me." There's murmuring on the line. "She says she'll call. If she can't get it done, we'll figure something out. Who's getting the burial details?"

"I am. I'll text you," Daniela says with her phone already out.

Rachel writes, "Anabelle: Coroner; Daniela: Rabbi." Then she says, "Okay. So, Anabelle is calling the coroner to have Wren's mother's body released today. Daniela, would you and Ted please work with the rabbi? Vernon, you're going to get a Shiva stream up and running that anyone can jump onto. What else is everyone doing?"

"We need a lot of bread," Daniela offers. "Bagels, challah, babka."

"I can do that," Lorelei says, already rolling up her sleeves and heading for the aprons.

"I'll help after I look for that candle." Francesca stands ready at the basement door. "Wait, how much should we make?"

Lorelei replies, "Until we run out of flour." With a fresh fifty-pound bag of flour sitting in the basement, that's quite the challenge.

After noting "Baker" beside the two women's names, Rachel finds the musicians and had no trouble pointing them out. "What about you two?"

Renato's gaze drops as he shrugs sheepishly. "Well, I'm only good at music, so..."

Yukiko is bolder than this, though, and stands with stacked dishes in her hands. A small furrow settles between her brows. It is the fiercest Rachel has seen her so far. "I will cook some dishes. Miso soup and curry will travel well for her father."

Renato's head perks up even as he frowns. "Wait, wait, wait, if you're gonna show off, I'm going to, too."

Yukiko matches his frown. "I'm not showing off, Renato."

He crosses his arms in a pout. "Peruvians make good food, too, you know."

His girlfriend mutters something under her breath, then tries not to shout: "No one's saying they don't!" She doesn't exactly succeed.

Ignoring her, Renato stands and starts for the basement. "We still have that mahi-mahi in the freezer?"

Daniela rolls her eyes at him. "We should."

Rachel hides a smile before assigning the couple new roles. "Bring up all the meat we have, please. It'll help us plan meals." Spotting the single empty spot of the checklist, she calls over her shoulder, "Hey, Markeya, what about you?"

"I've got to go to bed before my next shift, but I can send the scones in ten. Chocolate. Double batch. Tomorrow morning, I can arrange the food train down to Providence."

Rachel writes that down, feeling good for having a full list. This makes sense. She caps the marker. "Okay, good." She says it again and pulls mushrooms from the fridge.

Her spell broken, the crowd begins to move to the beat of its own drum when, as though suddenly realizing, Renato asks, "Wait, what are you going to do?"

Rachel accepts an orange apron from Lorelei, who brings it without being asked. When the strings are tied tautly behind her back, and a recipe pulled up on her phone, she says, "With any luck, I'm going to make Beef Wellington."

CHAPTER TWENTY-EIGHT

DUST TURNS TO MUD WHEN Rachel wipes her hands together. Not that mud matters much with so much dirt already caked into her jeans. In hindsight, taking Daniela up on her glove offer was a better alternative. She wasn't thinking well then, only wanting to help Markeya with clearing the garden beds because time moves too slowly indoors. It moves too slowly out here, but at least there's the benefit of marking time with progress. Early in the morning, when the wind bit instead of pinched, the garden beds were overgrown with whatever hardy weeds that had not been attended to in the fall. Now, each box is clear and covered with last year's compost. Markeya takes great pride in that compost, lets Rachel know that it was her who "cooked" the kitchen scraps and garden foliage until they were nothing but black gold.

They've patched things up since Wren's mom passed. Markeya isn't one to let things stew, she says during a brisk walk around the block with Cornelius. Something about moving forward and picking up dog shit is enough to get them talking. "Might as well air it," Markeya says when Rachel tosses a green bag into a neighbor's trash can. "Too much poison in the world already."

Rachel appreciates her honesty and allows her apology to reflect that. Tensions were high, then, they know that, but apologies should always follow. Since then, the two have spent a little more time texting memes, news reports about case numbers, and the latest YouTube personality's take on *Cats*. Now, side-by-side, they spread the composted dirt and insert signs that distinguish vegetable territory: Squashland, Mount Kale, The Democratic Republic of Snow Peas, and Radish Island. There's a contingency from Tomatoland that Markeya tends under grow lights in the carriage house, so those are an unknown agent for now. Rachel has faith that they will be a valuable addition to the V.U.N. (Vegetable United Nations) come June.

"Hey, later tonight, will you look in the basement to see if there are any pepper seeds?" Markeya asks as she finishes planting a row of snow pea seeds.

"Sure thing." Rachel is pretty sure she already knows where to find the labeled glass jars. Somewhere in the back room with the mysterious shoe that no one seems to ever want to move. It feels good to know things like that.

"Have you seen Wren today?" Markeya asks as they swap spaces, and Rachel saturates the plants with the hose.

She straightens, looks through the kitchen windows that stare back down into the garden but sees no sign of their housemate. Not a surprise, really. Though Wren handled the Shiva with the utmost grace, they had made themself scarce since.

Despite an HR-worthy clash with the mortuary, Anabelle had managed to get Wren's mother's body released for burial in time to observe the appropriate customs. Then, after a burial only attended by the family rabbi and Wren's father, the family took to the screen and stayed there. Twenty-four hours a day for a week, the video vigil was open and available. Vernon had done a great job rigging a spare table plugged into the foyer outlet to film the Shiva candle (though truth be told, it was a purple seven-day candle Markeya bought in Salem a tourist season before and required Francesca to remove a Lilith label with some dish soap and a lot of elbow grease).

Wren played the part of grieving child to perfection, or so Ted told them, by remaining silent as family members talked over one another to the point that the laptop speakers rattled. Every day starting around seven or eight, the screen would fill with the East Coast chapter and would be followed by subsequent time zones well into the evening. At night, Wren was led to bed by someone and quickly fell asleep, usually in their clothes and shoes. The first few times, Rachel stayed with them for an hour after, stroking their soft head, which was quickly growing into a lush carpet. They refused to wear wigs out of respect for their mother. Rachel admired their commitment.

Since the Shiva, Wren spends a lot of time in their room. Catching up on schoolwork, keeping busy, they say, but Rachel knows this game. She can hear them cry through the door on the way back to her room. She doesn't want to press. Grieving is different for everyone. If Wren needs her, they'll say something.

Turning back to the dirt beds, Rachel confirms, "Yeah, I saw them at breakfast."

Markeya stands up straight and wipes the sweat from her forehead into her glove. "How did they look?"

Rachel is starting to understand that this cavalier attitude is a cover for concern. She doesn't say this, though. People who are rough with love don't often seem to like being told when they're soft. She scoops up the winter weeds and dumps them a paper sack. "About the same, honestly. See them at mealtimes, but that's about it. Why do you ask? Something happen to make you think otherwise?"

Markeya grabs another yard bag and flicks it open. "I guess not. They sent me a text at, like, two this morning. Some stupid cat video."

For a second, Rachel's stomach aches with the familiar sting of rejection. She shakes her head to get herself straight. No need for middle school politics at a time like this. *Focus on what you know. Who knows dead parents better than you?* "Well, I think insomnia is to be expected. After my family died, I'm not sure I slept much for a couple of months."

Markeya pauses for a moment, allowing Rachel's words to fill the garden between them. New Rachel realities are planted in the soil with the soybeans. Then, after the moment passes, she picks up weeds and says in a nonplussed tone, "Really?"

Rachel nods, appreciating that cavalier attitude all over again. "Yeah. Grief hits hard, but it always hits different. My whole thing was that I didn't sleep, and I almost exclusively ate Cheetos and watched *SNL* compilation videos." Taking the hand rake, she turns over the soil in the last bed and smiles. "There's this skit where Kate McKinnon and Aidy Bryant are, like, meat farmers who are pushing up against vegans by saying it's okay to eat their animals because they're 'individually stupid and bad.'"

She has to stop what she's doing because the laughter is coming on too strong, shaking her body with absurd memory. Just her laying under her dorm bed with the blanket draped over the side, a dozen empty Coke bottles, countless Cheetos bags in various stages of staling, and her cell phone haloing them all in blue light. "The whole time they're doing the skit, they have this actual basket of meat cuts—chicken, beef, pork, everything—that you can just tell smells disgusting. I'm not even doing it justice, but I swear to God that segment saved my life. Seriously, 'Smokery Farms,' you've gotta watch it."

Markeya blinks. "I'll put it on my list."

"Anyway," Rachel drawls, still chuckling at the thought of animals with "nothing personalities." "It wasn't a great time in my life, but you do what you have to. All things considered, I think Wren is handling everything well."

"Their dad seems to be doing okay, too." Markeya opens the tool shed tucked behind a tall bush for a sack of wildflower seeds. "Saw him outside the other day when I brought him that cauldron of soup."

"Awful nice of you to drive down on your day off."

She tuts. "Too hard to be alone like that. Ted drove down today with the challah and pork chops that Francesca made."

The sad image of Wren's father eating challah in a dark kitchen makes Rachel's heart hurt. If only one of her parents had gone, she doesn't think anything would keep her from being with the last one standing. "Do you think Wren will be able to stay with him soon? It's been over three weeks. It should be okay to go see him now, right? Stay for a while?"

Markeya hums, then sighs. "Hard call."

Rocking back on her heels, Rachel rests her hands in the dirt, gripping through sliding particles in search of some purpose. She thumps onto her backside but doesn't get back up. "Comfort might be more important right now. Besides, neither of them has been outside the house, as far as we know. Maybe going to stay with him for a few weeks would be helpful."

"I just..." Markeya sighs again and sinks down next to Rachel on the ground. The two stare off into the distance. "If something happened..."

Not knowing, that's the killer. "Yeah," Rachel murmurs.

"Well, we should talk about it. As a group," Markeya amends. She pulls her knees close to her chest. "I'd almost feel better if he came to stay with us for a couple of weeks. At least then I would know what he was doing."

A half-smile lifts her cheek. "Illusion of control," she sings.

"Still *feels* like control," Markeya sings back.

"Yeah, well..."

"So, how are *you* doing?" Markeya thumps Rachel on the shoulder. "How's Job?"

Rachel allows the subject to change without argument. "Little better today. He should be able to travel soon. Maybe as early as next week." That's hard to believe.

"Still at the commune?"

"You know it." Rachel leans her head onto her knees and groans. "I wish he'd never left in the first place."

"Come on now, don't do that." Markeya rubs her palm into Rachel's upper back. Hard. Rachel winces and leans away from the pain. "We were all acting in his best interest. Who's to say where he actually got it anyway? The point is, he lived, and he's coming home sooner rather than later. You know what kind of person you are, Rach? You're the kind of person who is predisposed towards guilt. You always try to make yourself feel shitty."

Suddenly, Markeya slings a heated arm around Rachel's shoulders and pulls her in close. She smells like dirt, wildflowers, and onions. "You've suffered enough. Focus on being grateful."

"Y'know," Rachel says dryly, "I don't think telling someone to stop worrying or feeling shitty has ever worked."

"What would help, do you think?"

Some kind of bird flies overhead, but Rachel is too ignorant to know which one. It's not a blue jay, that much is sure. "I'll let you know if I ever figure it out."

"Fair enough."

Rachel scoots back until her spine is flush with the kitchen wall. "So, how are you doing out in the carriage house?"

Markeya snorts. "Anabelle and I are driving each other crazy, but otherwise fine."

"Anything we can do to help?"

"Find a cure for this virus so we can go back to our rooms?" A defeated sigh. "Nothing to be done for it, really. We are both grown adults who like to live our lives a certain way. I don't mind my life being a little cluttered, and she's a neat freak. She's a night owl; I'm an early bird. Love her to death, but I'll be damned if she doesn't annoy the shit out of me."

"Plus, y'all both must be stressed to forever."

"Can't even begin to describe."

"I'm sorry."

"It is what it is. Wish people would stop buying us pizzas, though. Don't get me wrong, I love a free meal as much as the next girl, but my scrubs are a little too tight."

"My jeans, too."

"Stress eating is real."

"Ain't it, though?"

They fall into silence, both heads tilted up towards the sun like seedlings. Clouds drape patterns on their faces then drift out of sight. Rachel's breathing deepens as she closes her eyes. Of course, Job is there with his face covered in tubes, looking so helpless and pale that he might as well be dead. *That was then*, she reminds herself as she opens her eyes. It's better not to court nightmares in the middle of the day.

"Sometimes," she starts on a dehydrated whisper, "I don't know what to say to him. Job, I mean. Like, I'm over here playing in the garden and eating savory crepes for lunch, and he's over there trying to get a full night's sleep."

Markeya hums the way she does when she's thoughtful. "Shared trauma is a real bitch."

"What do you mean?"

"Y'all have been together a long time, right?" Rachel nods. It has been a long time. "Let me guess, you got together right after your whole family died?"

"Pretty much. But, like, he got it. His parents went a couple of years before. We got each other."

"I'm not knocking it, babe, believe me. This isn't a critique; I'm just saying that the two of you get one another in a way that no one else in the world does. It's like how soldiers during war get really close to their unit. No one else gets what happened but the people who were there when shit went sideways. That's how you two were. You understand each other's trauma. But now he's experiencing this new trauma, and you're experiencing yours. See what I mean?"

Rachel's lips purse, and her blood pressure spikes. "So, what, we suffered too differently to 'get' each other now? That's why I can't talk to my husband?"

"Will you calm down? Jesus!" Markeya snaps. "I didn't say anything like that. Stop looking for a reason to be mad. What I'm saying is that you are out of sync with your normal, which is wicked weird for both of you. If you give yourselves some time, acknowledge the awkwardness, and *relax*, it will all sort itself out. Frankly, though, I'm not sure how you've gone on this long with how uptight you are. Surprised you haven't blown up."

"I've got my reasons for being uptight." While talking about her family being gone may have become easier, discussing Job in a different hospital bed is not something she's ready to discuss. "And I'm baseline anxious."

Markeya scoffs. "Obviously."

Huffing in response, Rachel asks, "Well, how do you manage with Vernon? You're out on the frontline every day, and you never get to see him."

"Well, sure, it's hard, but we've had more practice than I'm betting you and Job have. Vern and I don't spend all our time together either. I try to get a travel contract somewhere new every nine or ten months. We're apart for a bit, then we're together again. It's great."

After only a handful of weeks without Job, Rachel can't even begin to fathom that sort of distance. "How does that work?"

Markeya leans forward enough to make eye contact. "With a lot of communication and *honesty*, if you catch my meaning."

She doesn't at first, but then she does. Rachel's face blasts with heat and squeaks, "Oh."

Markeya starts to cackle. It starts as a regular laugh, one that shrugs the shoulders, but then it devolves into gulps of air that work themselves out as wheezes and honks. Pushing tears out of her eyes, she says, "Your face right now. There's that sweet Southern girl I've been waiting to meet. Need some pearls to clutch?"

Shooting up to her knees, Rachel starts vigorously raking around dirt. "No, no, I'm sorry. That was none of my business."

"I'm not ashamed, though I'd much rather you ask your questions than bulldoze that flower bed around all bashful." Markeya stands up to stretch.

"I'm so sorry. Seriously, I'm not judging. I've just never heard of anyone…well, outside of the relationship and it not being a *huge* deal."

Markeya leans down for the seed bag and starts to scatter some into turned-over soil. "It's called polyamory, babe, and it's different for everyone. It can get complicated because humans are going to human, but that's why it takes open lines of communication to make it work."

"I'll be honest, was not expecting to hear about polyamory this afternoon."

"After a couple of months of knowing you, I figured you could hang."

She keeps her eyes fixed in the dirt. "I'm flattered."

"You should be. I don't talk about this stuff with just anyone. Again, not because I'm ashamed, just because it freaks people out." She tuts. "Which is all to say: Even though Vernon and I have some practice, this is still hard. When we video chat, knowing that he's next door makes it worse. Not being able to touch him after a long day? Torture."

That, at least, Rachel can understand. "I'm already dreading Job getting to Boston and having to quarantine for that very reason."

"Babe, let's try to focus on one worry at a time. He's coming home. Celebrate that."

Rachel burns with embarrassment now. "I know. I know. Sorry for being ungrateful."

"You're not ungrateful," Markeya says. "You have a natural proclivity for anxiety."

Rachel laughs as she stands up to dust the dirt from her hands. Again, it does nothing. "You put that on a t-shirt, and I'd wear the shit out of it."

"Now we're talking. Side hustle, baby."

The mudroom door opens, and the two women find themselves joined by Renato, all bundled in his heaviest wool coat despite the warmer than usual temperatures. "We talking about making some money out here? Gonna cut me in?"

Markeya eyes him with a salty frown. "Depends. You helping now that the work is almost done?"

"Depends," he replies slyly as he descends the stairs with the regality of some French aristocrat. "How much do you mean by 'almost'?"

She juts out her pointed chin. "Need help tilling the front garden."

He snaps then smiles. "Damn. Not late enough."

Rachel wipes her hands on her pants, reconciled with the fact that she'll probably have to burn this outfit anyway. "Do you still need my help?"

"No, you're free to go," Markeya says. "You're calling Job in a bit, yeah?"

"Yeah." She checks her phone and ignores all the group chat texts. "Forty-five minutes. His sleep schedule is still outta whack."

"Well, I'm sure you don't want to greet him with a face full of dirt. Go on. I've got most of the help I need with this one."

"Hey!" Renato, forever the showman, places his hands on his hips in a pout.

Markeya isn't having any of it, though. She takes him by the shoulder and starts pushing him out of the garden. "Hey, yourself. Let's go before we lose the sun."

"I can help more tomorrow," Rachel says as she heads for the kitchen stairs.

"Great, thanks. I'm going to make Renato dredge the pond tomorrow. There's definitely a couple of dead squirrels in that bad boy. Don't want to miss that." She stops, which causes Renato to stumble. "Oh, hey, do either of you know what's for dinner?"

Renato shrugs his shoulder away from his captor and says, "Lorelei is making chicken and dumplings."

"Fuck, I love that girl." Markeya grins at Rachel. "Send some my way?"

"Sure thing." Rachel gives a half-hearted salute. Her arms are already sore. "Anabelle around tonight?"

"She's not. Working a twenty-four-hour shift today. Home tomorrow in the morning. Babe, you've got to use the Google Calendar."

"Yeah, yeah." Rachel huffs up the stairs, knowing full well that Markeya is right and that she's still too scared to make the commitment. "We'll save her a plate. Later, y'all." Opening the mudroom door, she's smacked in the face with a scent so rich it makes her mouth water. As soon as she opens into the kitchen, she says, "Holy shit, it smells so good in here."

Lorelei stands at the kitchen island with half a raw chicken in one hand and a cleaver in the other. "Sauté some garlic and onions then suddenly everyone thinks you can cook," she says. "What a magic trick."

"My favorite kind of magic trick," Rachel says as she makes a pass by the range to peer into the Dutch oven. Mirepoix browns and shimmers up at her. *The foundation of anything delicious is carrot, onion, and celery,* her mother says from the heat. Rachel smiles all the way up the hall, where she checks the mail and finds nothing for her but plenty of credit card offers for

Yukiko and Renato. Even during a pandemic, banks gotta try to make a buck. The Devil works hard, but CitiBank works harder.

Catching sight of herself in the hall mirror, Rachel sucks in a horrified breath between her teeth. Somehow, despite the fact that she hadn't dug in the garden with her face, her skin is covered with dirt. Under her eyes, her forehead, chin, cheekbones, it's everywhere—hell, she might as well be *Emperor of the North*. She checks her phone. Only half an hour before it's time to call Job. That might not be enough to start steaming the fucking lithosphere off her face.

She turns for the stairs in a panic, taking them two at a time. As she rounds the corner, Daniela's voice calls from some open door, "Oh, hi, Rachel, would you help me a second?"

Heart in her throat, she reaches for the wall to steady herself but stops midway because she realizes that dirt plus white wall equals a bad time. The motion sends her stumbling then skipping before catching herself. Her room, so close now, seems so far away.

"I'm so sorry. Didn't mean to startle you. Are you okay?" Daniela asks, footsteps close.

After straightening, she finds the pregnant woman there in a black house dress with a smudge of sage green paint on her face. How much would it take for her to look like an actual Madonna? Rachel says, "Yeah. Just my pride. What's up?"

Daniela hooks a thumb over her shoulder. "I'm painting a wall in the nursery but can't quite reach the top. Can I borrow your height?" She may as well have asked Rachel to shovel shit out of the bathroom.

Reading whatever story is on her face, Daniela hastily adds, "But if you're busy..."

"No, no." Rachel swallows her attitude. She made a promise to be better, and by God, she's going to try to be less prickly. Try. "I'll do it. Already need a shower."

Daniela smiles in thanks and waddles back to her room in jeans that still fit. Rachel follows but stops before entering. Everything is perfect: walnut furniture free of scuff marks, pristine white linen, and not a hint of clutter. *How do people live like this?* she wonders.

"Just in here," Daniela says as she gestures to a door swung wide open. Rachel winces at the sight of the cradle draped in plastic. Fire lights down her arms and pools in her fingertips. As she gets closer and sees the changing table, sick swirls in her stomach.

Rachel distracts herself by noting the fact that the nursery is housed in a small walk-in closet. There is a window, though, she notices, that lets in the right amount of light to filter in over the cradle. Oh, yes, the cradle. She averts her gaze.

"Are you okay?" Daniela asks, voice soft.

"Huh? Yeah, fine." The lie is familiar but enough to keep the conversation flowing. She grabs the roller stick off the floor with one hand and looks up at the ceiling. Everything is blocked out in sage green with a perfect hand. "I like this color."

"Thanks. My mom and I are going to paint some sunflowers on later this week."

"That will look cute," she says, then hefts the roller up and lets it fall onto the wall with a wet smack. Of course, Daniela and her mother will hand paint sunflowers in this perfect little nursery. And it will be beautiful, *of course*, and everyone will love it and Daniela and her perfect little baby. *Makes me sick*, Rachel grumbles to herself as she paints over the white remains. The faster she works, the faster she can get to Job. Then she can forget all about this precious room.

"Oh."

"What's wrong?" Rachel asks over her shoulder, not appreciating any critique.

Voice calm as anything, Daniela replies, "My water's breaking."

CHAPTER TWENTY-NINE

RACHEL FEELS THE BLOOD rush out of her face into her feet. The roller handle slides through her fist until its butt hits the floor. "Oh, shit," she says, staring as the pregnant woman strokes her belly in thought. Meanwhile, Rachel runs through a mental checklist of things that need doing: call doctor, pack overnight bags, find Ted, look up the fastest route to the hospital. "So, uh, do we need to go?"

Daniela blinks back to the conversation with a smile that smacks of serenity. "No, it's okay, there's time. Plenty of time to finish up these walls, at least."

Looking between the wall and Daniela a couple of times, Rachel asks incredulously, "Aren't you early? Shouldn't we call your doctor?"

"Anabelle says that it can take some time to go into active labor." Daniela squats to close the open can of paint with a nearby mallet. "Besides, I'd feel better knowing the nursery was more or less done."

Rachel puts a fist on her hip and furrows her brow in confusion. "You seem a little too calm right now. Are you having contractions?"

"Been having them all morning. That's why I started painting, to keep my mind off of them." Plopping some small brushes into a water cup, she continues, "Fortunately, this isn't the first time I've been pregnant, so I knew what would help."

Rachel blinks at this piece of news. "Oh?"

Daniela doesn't look up from her tidying task. "The last time…" she sighs before pushing up to her feet. "Well, the last time the baby didn't make it."

Not quite standing eye to eye, Rachel feels waves of horror and embarrassment wash over her at once. It's a wonder she doesn't topple over. She can't keep from asking, "How far along were you?" Because she needs to know how alike they are.

Daniela dusts her hands together and allows her tender face to turn into one of wistfulness. "A little over thirty weeks."

"Oh, my God. I'm sorry—I thought this was…" She thought that Daniela was the luckiest person on the planet who had never known a day of sorrow. Is it too late to act better? "Well, no wonder you're so calm. Does Anabelle know this isn't your first time?"

Daniela crosses her arms tight across her full chest. At last, she seems concerned. "No, I didn't tell her. Should I have?" Her chestnut brown eyes brim with tears as her confessional flows. "Ted and I don't like to talk about what happened to our son. He had Patau syndrome. We thought everything was fine until it wasn't. We didn't think to…it didn't show up in the scans. But with this one," she places a protective hand over her belly button, "we had all the tests done. Blood work. Ultrasounds. Genetic testing. Everything. She's supposed to be healthy. We did everything right."

Rachel rapidly nods in understanding, rushing to touch Daniela. "Of course you did." It is the first time she has touched the pregnant woman, but she is not surprised by how soft her skin is.

"You know how this feels, don't you?" Daniela covers Rachel's hand with her own. "The fear, I mean. You have the look."

"What look?"

"The 'I didn't get to be happy, so why should you get to be happy?' look."

Why bother denying that truth? Rachel looks away and says, "I'm sorry."

"Don't be. After we lost our first, I looked the same way for a year. All my friends were pregnant and delivering perfectly healthy babies, and all I had was the memory of my son's tiny clenched fist. I've been you, Rachel. You didn't have to tell me; I knew."

"I'm sorry."

Daniela clucks and leads them out of the nursery so the two can sit on the edge of her pristine white bed. They think better of it a moment later and slip down onto the floor, the two women still holding hands. A contraction must overtake Daniela because her grip tightens then relaxes. "When did it happen?" she asks with closed eyes and deepening breath.

Rachel stares up into the corner of the room. "A little over a year ago. Before our trip."

"How far along were you?"

"Thirty-two weeks," she replies in a sigh. Thirty-two long, beautiful weeks. "There was nothing they could do. Lose the baby or lose us both." When it came down to that, Job had made the decision for them both. She still wonders if he regrets that decision.

"No wonder you've—" she starts.

"—been such a bitch?"

" —been in so much pain."

They chuckle. "Yeah," Rachel says, the humor falling away in a pit of murky memory. "Something like that. It's complicated."

Her companion shrugs. "It's always complicated."

"I'm sorry about everything, really," Rachel says, squeezing Daniela's small hand. "After it happened, I couldn't leave the house. I broke down in tears anytime I saw a diaper commercial, y'know? I was just a mess. I still am."

"It gets easier," Daniela promises on another contraction. They seem a little too close. "You don't forget, but it gets easier."

That, at least, she knows is true.

"I'm going to grab a pad out of the bathroom. There isn't a lot of fluid, but it's coming." Daniela struggles to her feet before Rachel can help.

"Sure thing. Shout if you need me."

When the bathroom door closes, Rachel sucks in big gulps of air. "What the fuck," she mouths. She takes out her cell and finds two missed calls and a text from Job.

She calls back. He picks up on the first ring. "Hey," she says.

"Hey. Everything okay?" His voice is still hoarse.

"Um, kinda? Daniela's water just broke."

"Holy shit." He coughs. "Is today the day? Her due date in the calendar isn't for a couple more weeks."

Of course, Job is on the group calendar. She tries not to roll her eyes. *Be grateful for him and every little thing he does*, she tells herself. "It's early. I think we should go to the hospital, but she doesn't seem too worried. Guess we'll wait on Ted."

"Where's Ted?"

"Providence."

"Really? Seems like he should have let someone else do that with Daniela so close to her date," he says gruffly, though it's hard to tell if that's out of displeasure or fatigue. "Well, she should still call her doctor. No such thing as too careful."

"You're right."

The bathroom door swings open, and a wide-eyed Daniela stands at the threshold. "I think I'm in labor."

Finally, it's hitting her, she thinks with relief. Rachel stands with the phone still to her ear. "I know, you said your water broke."

"It did, but I mean that the labor is happening now. I'm *very* dilated."

"Holy shit," Job and Rachel say in unison.

Rachel tells him, "Gotta go."

"Good luck. Love you," he says and then beeps away, which leaves Rachel standing there with a phone perched on her fingertips.

"Well, what do you want to do?" she asks.

Panic distorts Daniela's usual cherub face with a frown and wide eyes. She steadies herself on the doorframe. "I think it's happening. Can you call Anabelle?"

"Not your doctor?"

"He's on vacation."

"Of course. Okay, should I get Francesca?"

"Yes, please."

Rachel runs to the door and shouts, "Francesca!"

Somewhere downstairs, a voice calls back, "Eh?"

"The baby's coming!"

"What?" comes a chorus of voices from behind other doors.

A stampede comes for them, as Rachel calls Anabelle. With each ring, a new roommate appears in the hallway: Wren, Lorelei, Yukiko, then Francesca to bring up the rear. "Is it really D-day?" Wren asks, peeking over Rachel's shoulder.

"Will y'all go in while I get some advice? Make her comfortable, I guess," Rachel says, shooing everyone inside with an aggravated hand.

After the sixth ring, she hears: "Hi, this is Anabelle. I'm sorry I missed your call. I'm probably in the O.R. right now or asleep. Either way, please leave me a message, and I'll get back to you as soon as I can."

Rachel redials and watches as Francesca and Yukiko put towels down on the floor then encourage Daniela to sit. Wren keeps running a nervous hand over their scalp, and Lorelei stands close to the wall with her arms crossed.

Anabelle's voicemail. Rachel redials. "Pick up, pick up, pick up," she whispers.

Finally, she answers and sounds about as tired as a person can. "Hey, what's wrong?"

"She's having a baby?" Rachel says, surprised to find her tone quizzical.

"What? Who's having a baby?"

"Daniela's water broke, and now she's having a baby." The woman in question has a fresh sheen of sweat on her face that her mother mops away with a washcloth.

Rachel hears a light switch flick. "Okay..." There's a slurp from a straw. "When did her water break?"

"Um," Rachel checks her phone, "fifteen or twenty minutes ago?"

"That's it?" Anabelle sounds annoyed. "Let's calm down. Her water *just* broke? There's plenty of time. Call her doctor."

"No!" Rachel shouts. All of the other women look at her. She lowers her voice. "We can't do that because her doctor is on vacation, and she's having the baby right now."

"Rachel, listen to me," Anabelle's voice gets just a little more Southern, "first pregnancies take forever. Your heart is in the right place, sugar, but if she goes to the hospital, they're just going to send her right home. It's a process."

"You're not listening to me. Here, I'm going to put you on speakerphone." She does and walks the phone to the woman on the floor. "Daniela, you talk to her."

Daniela keeps her eyes closed. "Hi, Anabelle."

"Hi. What's going on?"

She takes a deep breath. "I think I'm having the baby now."

"I've got that part. Are you having contractions?"

"Yes, since this morning. But they haven't been bad."

"How far apart are they?"

"Close." Daniela cracks an eye open at Rachel for confirmation. "A minute and a half?" Rachel nods. "A minute and a half."

Anabelle is quiet for a moment. The room exchanges a handful of concerned glances at one another. "Okay," she says at last, "it sounds like things are progressing a little faster than planned. Let's stay calm. You're, what, thirty weeks? Not ideal, but manageable. I'm going to have you come in. Where's Ted?"

Wren says, "Driving back from Providence."

"Okay, let's get you an ambulance then. Is it okay if I call you back after I do that?"

"Sounds great," Daniela replies and lets her head fall back against her mother's chest.

"Call you right back." Anabelle hangs up. Rachel makes sure her ringer is on full volume.

"What do we do?" Yukiko asks with a folded towel between her hands.

Everyone looks at Francesca. When the old woman notices, both of her dark brows shoot up in surprise. "How should I know?"

"You have three kids!" Wren says.

Francesca hikes up her shirt to expose her scarred belly. "All three Caesarean!"

Wren tilts back their head and laughs so hard they fall back onto the bed. They don't bother sitting up and instead speak at the ceiling, "Are you kidding me? You've never seen this done before? I thought you worked on a farm or something."

"A *fish* farm," Francesca clarifies.

"Jesus Christ," Rachel growls. "So none of us know what to do? Lorelei? Yukiko?" Both shake their heads. She tries to think about the birthing classes she took, digging deep into the repressed recesses of her mind, but none of her teachers ever talked about what to do in case of an impromptu bedroom birth. "Well, at least there's going to be an ambulance. I guess we just get some more towels to help with the mess?"

Daniela clears her throat. "I don't think the ambulance is going to get here in time." She pulls up her dress and spreads her legs. "The baby is coming."

Without meaning to look, they all crowd around to look at all that swollen flesh and damp hair. Yukiko gasps. Lorelei asks, "Is that the head?"

Daniela glances anxiously between all of them. "What should I do?"

"I don't know! *She* had Caesareans! Rachel points at Francesca then circles the rest of them with the same frantic finger. "And apparently none of the rest of us attended a halfway decent health education class. The only people who know how to deal with *that* aren't here."

"Should we go get Markeya?" Francesca asks.

Before anyone can weigh in on that, the phone rings.

"Hey," Anabelle says, "so, the ambulance is on its way."

"Hey," Rachel sings as she stares straight between Daniela's legs with the same apprehension one might feel looking down the barrel of a gun, "so I'm looking at hair pushing out of a vagina."

"What?"

"Hair. Vagina. Baby."

"Video call me."

Rachel hangs up and redials with video, which puts her face-to-face with herself. Dirt, paint and sweat mingle together to create some bedtime terror conjured up to scare children. Anabelle meets her with an equally haggard face, though it is clean. "What the fuck are we supposed to do?" Rachel asks.

Anabelle wrinkles her nose. "What happened to you?"

"I've been working in the garden all day. I wasn't expecting to deliver life."

"Okay, first things first: Wash up and get your hair up."

Rachel shoves her phone into Lorelei's hands before muddying up Daniela and Ted's pristine bathroom. The mud she leaves on the hand towel may never come out. As she scrubs, Yukiko comes in and offers to braid her hair. She accepts gratefully, and the young woman whips sweated strands back into a tight queue. The whole of the matter takes less than four minutes, then they're together again

"Should I go get Markeya?" Vernon's voice joins from the doorway.

"Not right now. I'd rather not run an exposure risk, if we can help it," Anabelle replies. "One of you can do this. If you need to go get her, I'll tell you. The ambulance should seriously be there in a few minutes."

"You don't have any experience with delivering babies, do you, Vern?" Wren asks.

"Unfortunately not."

"That surprises me about you," they say.

"Okay," Anabelle snaps, gathering everyone's attention again. "Let me have a look."

Lorelei's face shines red. "Is that okay with you?" she asks their patient.

Daniela throws up her hands. "If everyone else in the house is going to see this, the doctor might as well get a peek."

"Okay..." Lorelei says as she crouches and adjusts the angle.

No one speaks as Anabelle assesses the blood-stained towel and everything on top of it. A second later: "Wow. Cool. So, let's have a baby."

This is not the answer Rachel was hoping for.

"Can't we wait for the ambulance?" Francesca asks.

"Nope," Anabelle replies. "You're gonna have to push, Daniela. Sit up for me a little bit, okay? Yukiko, get some pillows behind her back. Rachel, get in there."

"What, me?" Rachel squawks. "What do I do?"

"Catch it! You can do this. You're delivering a baby, not defusing a bomb."

Rachel scoots closer a little closer, eyeing the tufted head. "Sure about that?"

"Positive. Daniela's body is going to do what women's bodies have done for a very long time. No fuss needed."

"I'm not fussing."

"No, but I can see you're about three steps short of freaking out. Breathe."

"Okay," Rachel says.

"Okay," Anabelle says.

"Okay!" everyone else shouts.

"Lorelei, hold me higher," Anabelle demands. "And can someone get me some light?" Vernon sprints up to the attic and is back down in less than thirty seconds with the lighting rig he used for the memorial candle. The dark-haired head is brought into focus.

"Everyone else, go get some towels, warm water, and some clamps." The general speaks, and they scramble to obey.

"And the tarp from the basement," Daniela calls after.

"Don't worry about that right now," Anabelle chides.

"Do you know how hard it is to get blood out of wood?" Daniela's face is a sweated mirror of Rachel's. "A plastic sheet will take two seconds to put down and will save me a lot of work later."

"How you doing, babe?" Anabelle asks. "Feeling okay?"

"I'm okay," Daniela wheezes. Her faces is two shades past red.

Footsteps rush back up, and Yukiko quickly scoots a black plastic tarp underneath Daniela's bottom, then covers that with a new towel. It seems a silly gesture at this point, but when a woman is in labor, she gets what she wants. Rachel takes a few steadying breaths before kneeling between Daniela's legs. The two women nod at one another.

"Did your doctor say anything about premature birth? Any pre-existing conditions that might have caused this? I'm updating EMS in case this gets complicated."

"This is my second birth. My first was a late-stage stillbirth."

"I see. *Really* wish you would have told me that." Anabelle clears her throat. "The ambulance should be there in ten minutes."

"Ted is en route. About ten minutes. Told him to step on it," Wren announces as they return with a pot of steaming water. "For your hands, I guess?"

"Mama," Daniela whispers.

The older woman sits on the floor next to her daughter. Mother and daughter preparing for the third generation. Rachel wonders what her mother would have done had she had the chance. Would she have fed her daughter ice chips? Would she have held her hand? Would she have cried with joy?

Setting her own ache aside, Rachel poises in front of the hot heat and is ready to catch the fleshy football. At least, if she drops it, it's not a far fall. Babies can bounce a little bit, right? *It's not going to go that way. Everything is fine.* "Ready," she says once, then twice.

"On your next contraction, I want you to push. Can you do that for me?"

Daniela takes her mother's hand, and she does.

Everything happens quickly, then. The head squeezes out, fitting into Rachel's waiting palms. It isn't a football exactly, but the slimy thing has some heft. Anabelle warns not to hold tight, to let the baby shift on its own. The shoulders come one by one, and then she's out covered in God knows what. Rachel holds the buttered noodle with eyes so wide they could roll out of her skull if she sneezes. She's crying already, her lungs tiny but strong. And all that hair! There she is. Just there.

"Where's the cord? Lorelei, move me so I can see!" Anabelle's voice is loud enough to get through the din of wonder. Blinking tears away, Rachel finds the cord wrapped loosely around the baby's neck. With a careful finger, she lifts it over the baby's head and sends her up to Daniela's bare chest.

When Rachel finally takes a look around the room, she finds that there isn't a dry eye in the bunch.

"We're not done. I need everyone to focus," Anabelle says. When Rachel does, she finds that the white towel underneath Daniela has turned a dark red. Wren puts down a fresh sheet. The jubilation of a moment ago passes into unease. "We're going to try and help you pass the placenta as quickly as we can. Okay, Daniela?"

"Okay..." the new mother says in a daze, holding her baby to her breast.

"Is everything okay?" Lorelei asks.

"This is normal. Rachel, I need you to feel around for a hard part on Daniela's stomach. Can you do that?" Rachel reaches up and with new familiarity does as requested, "Start at the top and work your way down. You'll know it when you feel it."

"Got it."

"Great. Now I want you to push down as hard as you can. Someone make sure the doors are unlocked for the EMTs. And get your face masks ready. They'll be there any second."

Rachel pushes and winces when she sees Daniela's face contort. She murmurs an apology but keeps pressing the mass as it slides down. On another contraction, Anabelle tells Daniela to push and push until a disgusting fleshy mass slides out into Rachel's hands.

After everything that's happened today, this is the thing that makes her retch. "Tell me what the fuck to do with this thing!" she demands.

"Put it on a sheet." Rachel tries not to throw the purple and red sac at Yukiko and instead places it gently into the offered sheet. The placenta is lucky that it's still attached to the baby. "We're just going to let it hang out for a couple of minutes before we clamp it off. Anyone find something for that?"

"Will a chip clip do?" Wren asks, producing two bright yellow bag sealers. "It's all I could find. On an unrelated note, the tortilla chips will need to be eaten today or tomorrow."

"Has it been sanitized?"

Wren shrugs. "I dunked it in alcohol."

"It'll have to do. Rachel, let me show you where to clamp—"

She is drowned out by fresh sound. A door bangs open downstairs, followed by the sound of stumbling feet and Ted shouting Daniela's name. Three and half seconds later, a man who looks disheveled and wholly unprepared for parenthood appears in the doorway to take in the chaos. To his credit, his assessment is brief before he falls to his wife's side to kiss her and then his child. "Oh my God," he exclaims, breathless, smiling, and tearful. He pushes Daniela's damp hair aside and asks, "Are you okay?"

She cries and laughs at once. "I'm well. We're both well. Thanks to everyone."

Ted laughs too, the tears and snot streaming. He looks at each person in the room and bows his head. "Words cannot convey how I feel right now," he says, then returns to marvel at his child as she suckles at her mother's breast. He strokes her hair.

As Rachel smiles at the touching tableau, Daniela reaches out to her. When the two clasp hands, one slick with sweat and the other slick with whatever placentas are made of, she echoes her husband, "Words cannot convey."

No, not really.

CHAPTER THIRTY

IT COMES AS NO SURPRISE to anyone that Anabelle is the one to win the baby betting pool (a pool Rachel discovers was laid soon after the pregnancy announcement and promptly forgotten until the slip of paper was found under a crab-shaped fridge magnet). Despite the early due date, the baby comes in at a hefty seven pounds and six ounces. Other than jaundice, she's perfectly healthy. The day after all the birthing sheets are bleached and the floor scrubbed, the twelve housemates, Klimt, and Cornelius convene to greet the newest addition.

"Congratulations," everyone shouts when Ted and Daniela come on-screen, resulting in a pulsating feedback loop that is not muted soon enough.

Vernon mutes all the mics, relishes the silence, then says, "Let's try that again. One at a time, please."

Markeya and Anabelle wave tiny silver pom-poms in their frame. "Where'd you get those?" Renato asks.

"Work," Markeya says. "For morale."

"Do they work?" Lorelei asks.

"Not even a little bit," Anabelle replies on an exhausted sigh. Her face looks gaunt in this light, though maybe it isn't the light at all. After a breath, she brightens, "But enough about that. Congratulations! How are you feeling, Daniela? Doctor come by yet?"

"I'm doing okay. Lots of doctors and nurses. They all heard that I live with you and have been extra attentive. Apparently, you have quite the reputation."

Markeya nods big. "She's a bulldog."

"What do you mean by that?" Anabelle whines.

"It means you'll cause all types of hell if you don't get what you want." Markeya nudges her roommate's shoulder with hers.

Anabelle grins. "Well, that's true. Glad to hear my bad attitude means you're being taken care of. How's Yana doing?"

"She's solid," Ted tells them as he moves his phone closer to Daniela. From her spot in the kitchen, Rachel peeks over Yukiko's head and focuses on Job's face in the video call instead of the happy family. She's not quite ready to look at that particular sun. Looking at it the first time was almost enough to blind her. "We're having a hard time getting her to breastfeed."

"We?" Daniela's tone is not generous, and everyone gets a chuckle out of it. "The nurse said that it's normal. Is that normal, Anabelle?"

"Not ideal, but normal enough. Keep trying! Every little bit helps," she says.

"Any idea when you'll come home?" Renato asks, leaning an elbow into Vernon's shoulder, so he's front and center in the shot. "We want to make sure the nursery is finished."

Yukiko shushes him and yanks the back of his shirt.

Ted grows bashful. "Aw, you guys didn't have to do anything for us."

"Done what?" Renato says, trying to recover when he realizes everyone in the kitchen is glaring at him. "We haven't done anything. We have done zero things in the nursery. We are actually making a room for Cornelius to play in when it snows. Yep, that's what we're doing. Setting up a dog obstacle course."

"Oh, good," Daniela says, playing along. "I would hate to be surprised."

"Speaking of surprises," Vernon leads. "When are you heading out, Job?"

Job says, "Tomorrow morning if you can believe it. Should be in Boston by Friday. Two weeks at the luxurious Hampton Inn, then home." Rachel's eyes burn at the thought. Without saying anything, Wren reaches over and pats her back.

"Do you want someone to pick you up from the airport?" Ted asks.

"No! I'll get there on my own, don't worry."

"Let us know when you land so we can start bringing food," Lorelei says.

Job waves her off. "No, no, you don't have to do that."

The German woman cocks her head to the right and says, "Yes, we do."

And that's that.

"When do you think you guys will be released?" Wren asks the family.

"Not sure. Maybe tomorrow?" Ted shares a look with Daniela. "The baby needs to stay under the heating lamps for a little while."

"Mmm, yes, medium-rare baby." Wren hums in delight and rubs their belly.

"Don't be weird," Yukiko scolds, swatting at them.

Wren sticks their tongue out, and Rachel rolls her eyes. "Children, please," she says.

"They'll probably be able to let you know tomorrow morning," Anabelle interrupts before the main house delegation can devolve further into schoolyard behavior. "A little blood test, and we'll be good to go. Seriously, y'all, the kid is a tank. She's going to be okay."

Even though Rachel can't look at the lump in Daniela's arms, she can't deny that the news makes her happy. "Well, let me know when to come get you from the hospital," Francesca says. "I have the car seat ready. That's all you need, you know, to take a baby home."

"We know, Mama," Daniela says, as a little cry interrupts them all. It is a strangled sound, one that sends a bolt of ice down Rachel's spine. "I'll call you. For now, I think we're going to try to eat a little something. Safe travels tomorrow, Job!"

"Thanks," he says, clearing his throat. "Be sure to get a little something to eat yourself. It's late here, guys, so I'm going to sign off for now."

After their goodbyes and Vernon turns off the video chat, the kitchen crew proceeds to chew Renato out for being a surprise spoiler. To atone, he is put in charge of cleaning all of the paintbrushes. Everyone is sure to help with the nursery then, dirtying as many brushes as possible. Though the plaintiff complains nonstop, there is no arguing with the results. Lorelei's delicate wildflower work on the walls and Francesca's gauzy white blinds transform the room into a tiny garden oasis. When all of the plastic wrap, tape, and tarps are removed, the seven of them take turns peering into the closet and marveling at their handiwork.

"How much do you think they're going to charge the baby for this?" Renato muses. "This would run you, what? Nine hundred?"

"It has a window. Eleven hundred," Vernon quips.

"Damn," Lorelei says. "She should get a job."

Something about her tone makes Rachel laugh so hard that she has to take a knee and cry. Her housemates laugh too, but she's pretty sure it's at her. For once, she doesn't care.

*

Two days later, Ted swings through the mudroom door with a car carrier on his hip. Bags hang heavy under his eyes, but he's as jubilant as ever. "Hello, hello!" he calls into the house. He stops in his tracks when he sees the main house crew waiting for them in the kitchen with congratulatory cakes and bread. He takes a deep inhale. "It's so good to be home!"

"So good to see you," Renato says as he goes to embrace Daniela before taking the baby carrier and placing it on the island.

Rachel catches the woman's eye for a minute but can't maintain the gaze. What do you say to someone after you've seen a human head squeezed out of their vagina? She lets Wren push by so they can grab their cousin in a hearty embrace. "Congratulations, man," they say.

"Thank you, thank you. What's all this?" he asks.

"Some Anabelle-approved snacks for Daniela. *You* get nothing," Wren teases. "Kidding, kidding. Just some stuff the neighbors dropped off. Don't worry, I took names. I knew you'd want to send a thank-you card, Dani." They clap Ted once on the back before pouring their attention over the car seat carrier. "Oh, hey there, baby, look at you."

"Anything else out in the car?" Vernon asks.

"The overnight bags, but I can get them in a minute," Ted says.

Vernon is already outside as Daniela's phone starts to ring. "*Hola*," she answers in a sing-song voice. "Yes, we're fine. Are you home now?" She mouths *Anabelle* to everyone else. "Oh, good. No, we haven't gone upstairs yet. Is this about Cornelius's exercise room? Wait, where's the dog?"

"My room. Didn't want to get him overexcited about the baby," Wren answers. "We put the baby clothes in his bed, though."

"Thank you for that," Daniela says. "What? Okay, okay, be patient. We're going now." She moves the phone to her chest. "Apparently, we need to go upstairs before she goes to work."

"Then, by all means," Ted answers, "lead the way." He picks up the baby carrier and follows the horde out of the room.

Rachel decides not to follow, settling instead at the kitchen table where she waits for Job's "I'm not dead" text. His plane is due any minute now. She takes a deep breath to push the irrational fears away. The plane will not fall out of the sky today. It isn't allowed.

When Vernon enters the room with a clatter, she jumps in her seat. He apologizes and asks where everyone went. She points towards the hall, and the voices tell him everything else he needs to know. A moment later, she's alone again. On the other side of the house, the new parents laugh in delight before lavishing praise on the artists. She should be up there, too, she knows that, but she isn't ready to see the baby, isn't ready to hold it.

Her phone buzzes in her hand. She picks up after the first ring. "Safe and sound?"

Job chuckles. "Safe and sound. Should be off and out in twenty minutes."

"Then only two more weeks." Rachel twirls the salt shaker. "Are you sure I can't come to see you?"

"Positive," he says, tone suddenly grave. "I'm going to my hotel room, and I'm not coming out until I'm cleared to leave."

"But I'm allowed to bring you stuff, right?" Rachel's not sure if she can do that part. Being that close and not able to do anything about it.

"That's what they said." He's silent for a moment, then says in a chipper tone, "It's only two weeks. Plus, my phone reception is going to be way better. You're gonna see this sweet face in some high-def resolution."

"Do you have enough to read? Watch? We could probably get you some games. I know Wren is super into retro Game Boy stuff."

"I'll be okay, sweetheart. Mostly I want to take hot showers and sleep for a really long time. Hell, might even write a little."

"Yeah, I imagine there's a lot to say."

"Yeah…Rachel?"

She sets the salt aside. "Yeah?"

His voice lowers to a whisper, "Are we okay?"

She thinks about what Markeya said about trauma and honesty. "It's a little weird right now, but I think we're going to be okay. A lot has happened." She touches her stomach. "A lot is going to happen. We've just gotta find each other again. That's all."

"I love you," he says, and she knows he means it.

"I love you, too." When they hang up, she feels safe. Her normal anxiety is there but doesn't marshal her heartbeat.

Footsteps come down the stairs before Daniela and Ted return to the kitchen, the baby securely bundled to her mother's chest. Their faces are creased with a seriousness that sweeps away Rachel's previous peace. "Can we talk to you for a minute?" Daniela asks.

"Sure?" She stands in uncertainty. At last, here it is, "the talk." Now they'll finally do what Rachel has expected they'd do since she moved in: kick her out.

Following them, she winds up in the library, where Daniela sits in the wingback chair with the baby. The sight hurts but not as much as before. Rachel averts her gaze to watch Ted close the door. She sinks onto the chaise with hands clasped tight in her lap. Here it is: the big one. At last, she will be called out on her bevy of bullshit and her behaviors and her bad moods, kicked out and searching for a new home right before Job has a chance to enjoy himself. Maybe they'll at least do him the favor of renting out the workshop space. After all, it wasn't his fault. She wants to blurt all this at them, but their identical expressions of serenity creep her out enough to keep quiet on the topic.

"Congratulations," she says, unable to keep from saying something.

"Thank you," Daniela replies as she turns that serene look down at the bundle. Better at the baby instead of her.

"Doctor say everything was...okay?" Rachel asks, gaze shifting between them both. *Is this the part where they tell me this actually is a cult?*

Daniela waves. "Other than some tearing, I'm fine."

She winces and instinctively crosses her legs a little tighter. "Cool. I mean, sorry I wasn't, y'know, a real doctor."

"Rachel, please, you have nothing to apologize for. Really."

Ted sits on the floor next to Daniela's feet and rests an arm over her knees, and smiles a tired smile. Not knowing is killing her, so she blurts, "Are you kicking me out?"

Their eyebrows rise together, a sure sign a couple has been together a long time. Daniela speaks first, "What? No, of course not. Why would you think that?"

She starts at the most obvious, "Because I've been a huge asshole?"

Ted says, "You've been under an extraordinary amount of stress. I don't think anybody would be the pinnacle of amiability at a time like this." He points up at the thing on Daniela's chest. "No, we want to talk to you about the baby."

"What about her?"

"Well...it seems the three of us have more in common than we thought." His expression turns sheepish. "Daniela mentioned that our histories look alike. No specifics, though, I swear."

A hot blush spreads across Rachel's face. "Oh, well, it's...I'm not, like." She doesn't know what to say.

Ted nods in understanding. "It's hard to talk about."

"Yeah."

"Which is why I know what you did was—" Tears fill Ted's bloodshot eyes. He wipes them away with his wrist. "Sorry, I didn't mean to get so emotional."

Daniela reaches down for her husband's shoulder. "What you did for me, for us, it means so much."

This is not the conversation she was expecting to have, and it's hard for her brain to handle. She shakes her head. "Your body was going to do it, one way or another."

"But you were there to help me. Cool as a cucumber."

Rachel snorts. "We were in the same room, weren't we?"

Daniela isn't having these evasive maneuvers. "You helped me when I needed you most. You delivered our child. You took the cord from around her neck. You removed my *placenta*. That's not nothing. From what Anabelle told me, you saved my life. If you hadn't pushed the placenta down, I would have kept bleeding. Who knows if the paramedics would have been able to save me. I could have died. My daughter could be motherless."

Rachel stares at the wall above the couple's head. "I just listened to Anabelle."

"Everyone in that room saved my life. Rachel," Daniela says sharply, forcing her to look at the family. Her tone softens, "You need to know how much that matters to me."

"To both of us." Ted reached up for his wife's hand. "Knowing that Daniela was taken care of while I was away meant so much to me, too." The couple exchanges a look of tenderness before turning it to Rachel. "We need to ask you—"

"Will you meet our daughter?" Daniela finishes.

"What do you mean? I met her." She eyes the bundle.

"No," Daniela says. "When we got here, you looked at the baby carrier, and then you went somewhere else. In your mind. I watched it happen. Whenever you're upset, you go somewhere else. You haven't met her yet."

Sometimes, it isn't fair to be seen.

"I understand," Ted begins gently, "or at least I think I do, why you might have some strong feelings about having a baby around. When I held her for the first time, I was so overwhelmed with love that my heart felt like it was going to actually explode. It was truly the most spiritual moment of my life. The closest I've ever felt to God." Rachel watches as new tears flood his eyes. "But later, when I was holding her while Daniela was asleep, I couldn't stop thinking about our son. Thinking about the baby clothes, the nursery, his heartbeat...his not heartbeat. You know, right?" He lifts to lock his gaze with hers. "Here I am with my precious daughter and thinking about him and the life *he* didn't get to have. So much shame poured over me, Rach. Shame of moving on, shame of being happy, shame of loving this little girl more than I've ever loved anyone in my life."

Oh, shame, I know thee well, Rachel thinks as an empathetic pulse sends her back to a day in a doctor's office that ruined her life. Staring into Ted's memory-slicked eyes, she can almost see his own doctor's office, can almost hear the devastation.

"No one told us how hard it would be," he says, voice rough with emotion. "Everyone always talks about the loss. No one told me how to mourn the what-if."

Daniela kisses the top of Ted's head then says, "We want you to meet her, but only when you're ready."

Rachel can feel her muscles tense to flee, but there's a part—a smaller, braver part—that wants to stay and meet this miracle child. *It's now or never.* "Okay."

They both brighten. "You're sure?" Ted asks. "It doesn't have to be right now."

She stares at the bundle and forces the sick down. "I'm sure."

Without wasting a second, Daniela scoots up to her feet and comes to join Rachel on the chaise. She moves the blanketed heap out of her arms and into Rachel's lap with all the fussiness of a new parent. Resting the baby lengthwise, the baby's little head is supported by Rachel's bony knees and stabilized by her trembling hands. She stares down at the little face as it cracks open its cloudy eyes. The flesh creature sucks its lips in search of sustenance. Daniela offers her pinky tip, and the creature settles back down into sleep after a few sucks.

The baby is not beautiful. It has a squished face, a flat nose, and is covered in eczema. The shape of its skull still hasn't rounded out, leaving it more alien-like than not. But her hair, well, that dark downy stuff covers her head and tufts her ears. It's precious beyond measure and sends warmth from Rachel's heart and into every limb. Snot runs. She snorts it back up. "Hi," she says with a disbelieving laugh.

Babies are not well-known for their conversational skills.

"What's her name again?" Rachel realizes she's forgotten on purpose.

Daniela places a gentle hand on Rachel's shoulder. "Yana Sophia."

She looks at the other woman and sees tears on her face, too. "That's really pretty."

"Named for our grandmothers," Ted says as he comes to sit on the other side. The three of them stare down at the baby.

"Yana Sophia," she greets softly. "It's very nice to see you again. Sorry our first meeting was so awkward. What with me panicking and you being naked. How embarrassing for you?" They all laugh softly. "Gotta say, you look a lot better not covered in cottage cheese. Highly recommend you continue the trend."

"You okay?" Daniela asks.

"Yeah, this is just really weird." She thought it would be harder to sit here holding this baby, thought she might die, but it's easy.

Ted leans over to grab some tissues off the bookcase and doles them out to everyone. "Can we make it weirder?" he asks.

Rachel wipes her face dry. "You can try."

Daniela moves to place her hand on top of Rachel's. Her face is insistent now. "We want to ask you...will you be her godmother?"

Rachel's eyebrows shoot up so fast that they would have skyrocketed into space if they weren't attached to her face. "Her *what now*?"

"Her godmother," Ted repeats.

At this point, the only thing keeping her anchored to the floor is the baby in the lap. "You know, I'm not really religious."

Ted chuckles. "'Mentor' seemed strangely more formal."

Her head swaps from face to face, unsure of herself in a way she didn't think possible. "I don't know what to say. You don't even know me."

Daniela says, "We know what we need to know. You help others. You're honest. You have a kind, overly practical heart. You held her on her first breath. This makes sense to us."

She looks at Yana Sophia, watches as her eyeballs move under the translucent lid skin. Without meaning to, she imagines her at a year, five years, as a little girl with braids and a bad attitude when she's scared, as a teenager with a kindness unmatched by any of her peers. "What...what would I do?"

"Guide her," Ted says as he strokes his daughter's cheek with the backs of his fingers. "Teach her what it means to be a good person. We want you to have an active role in our daughter's life."

After all that has happened over the last couple of months, it seems impossible for her heart to get any bigger, for her to find any more space for affection for these people. Maybe all the tears have been a way for her heart to make room. "This is—I really don't know what to say."

"Don't say anything right now." Daniela pats her hand. "Take some time to think about it. And feel free to say no."

"No." She starts then sputters, "I mean, not *no*. It's just. This is a really big deal. You're asking me to be a part of your family." A lump gets stuck in her throat.

Ted puts his arm around her shoulders then hugs her. "We are, yes."

She's shaking, but her legs are solid. "I can't tell you how much that means to me. It's just been me and Job for such a long time. It feels like forever, really." More tears, more tissues. "When I was eighteen, I lost my whole family. A couple of months later, I met Job. He'd lost his mom and dad, too. It was just us against the world." Yana Sophia squirms in her bundle then settles. What she would have given to see Siobhan do that. "When I got pregnant, we were so happy. We were going to start our own family. But that didn't happen. A few weeks before my due date...she was just gone. A stillbirth. It was—" Ted holds her closer. "It hit Job harder. One day, when I came home from work, I found him in his workshop with all the doors closed and his generators on." Her voice is almost inaudible. "I was almost too late. When he woke up at the hospital, he told me it was an accident. Who's to say if that's bullshit or not?" Daniela's arm hooks around her waist. Rachel lets them hold her. "It's why we went backpacking. Clear our heads, focus on a new future."

"I'm so sorry," Ted says.

"We'd just wanted it so badly, y'know? Wanted to start our own family to get back what we'd lost. Or try to. And now, here you are, asking me to be a part of your lives in this big way."

"Don't feel pressured to do anything right now," Daniela whispers.

"No," she takes Daniela's hand hard into hers, "it's so beautiful and kind. Thank you. It makes me feel like there's a future for us. Makes me feel like we get another chance at a family."

The new mother squeezes back with the same fierceness. They're bound by blood now, and that's inescapable. "You have a big family now. Both of you."

Rachel looks down at her stomach, one that has begun to gently round. A future in front of her and a future inside of her. "How would you feel if there were three of us?" she asks.

"What do you mean?" Ted asks.

"Like, how would you feel if I was pregnant?"

Daniela gasps in delight. "I think that's a wonderful idea. When you're comfortable, we should talk about it at a house meeting."

She nods big and picks Yana Sophia up to cuddle into her chest. "I hear you. But what if this is a 'ask for forgiveness not permission' sort of situation?" They look at her blankly. She decides to spell it out, "I mean, I think I'm pregnant."

Together, they shout, "*What?*"

The baby starts to fuss, but Rachel soothes her with a few shushes. "Yeah. The night I left Cairo.

When I got here, I missed my period, but I thought it was because of the travel. But then there was, is, the morning sickness and the cravings. And then Klimt hasn't left me alone."

"Have you talked to Anabelle yet?" Daniela asks, already reaching for her phone.

"No, not yet. Only Wren knows. And you guys."

"Holy shit," Ted says.

"You're sure?" Daniela asks.

She smiles, feeling for the first time since taking the pregnancy test that everything will be okay. "As sure as someone can be."

"This is amazing!" Daniela kisses her face. "Oh, Rachel, I'm so happy for you! When do you think you'll be due? Oh, who cares? Yana Sophia, you'll have a friend! We'll have two babies. This will be, well," she pauses, then launches back into jubilation, "I don't know how it will be, but we'll figure it out. Amazing. This is a miracle. When are you going to tell Job?"

Rachel sobers. "Not until I can touch him. If I know Job at all, it'll kill him to know and not be able to be here."

Ted whistles. "I can sympathize with that."

"I can't believe this." Daniela reaches for her child, and Rachel gives her willingly. "You're going to have a friend. A little sister!"

"Or brother," Ted tempers.

Daniela throws him a grin. "It's a girl. I can tell already. Can we tell everyone else?"

"Can your mom keep a secret?" Ted asks.

"Of course she can!" Daniela clenches her teeth and sucks in a breath. "But she might tell him anyway because she won't think it's a secret."

Ted gives Rachel a reassuring look. "We'll wait."

The idea of Francesca with her big secret causes a new sort of fear to bury itself in the freshly tilled soil of her irrationality garden. "Thank you."

Daniela kisses her cheek. "Congratulations."

There are a handful of moments that Rachel would keep in specimen jars if she could. Her wedding day, graduating, buying the house in Chicago, and now this. Her face, head, and heart hurt with all the crying, but it's been so long since she's felt this free. The light feeling carries her through dinner, where Job sits on the screen with his mouth open when he sees her holding Yana Sophia. She relishes his shock and the secret that she carries.

At half past three, the baby starts crying. It isn't a soft cry for comfort; it is a full-blown air siren that reaches out across the house and snatches Rachel up and out of sleep. After five minutes of laying in the dark, she realizes it won't stop. Without turning on the light so as to not wake Klimt, who sleeps on the pillow next to her, she throws on a robe and pads up the hallway. The crying is bloodcurdling now. She taps gently on the door. Ted opens it wearily. He's shirtless, and his hair is a disaster.

"Everything okay in here?" she asks, knowing the answer.

"I'm so sorry she woke you," he replies.

"No need." She pushes on the door, forcing him to open. "What can I do?"

Daniela sits in bed, her chest bared as she tries to give her nipple to the squawling infant. Her face is red and wet. "Mom's downstairs making a bottle. My milk won't flow," she admits.

Rachel reaches into her mind for parenting information. It's still there. "Done the nipple thing? Warm compress?"

Ted nods and sweeps a hand over his face. "Everything. They're both so tired."

An old memory floats to the surface: Her mother asleep on the couch with a twin under either arm to breastfeed. How long had it taken her to get them there? How many sleepless nights? "You're both looking a little haggard. Why don't you take a hot bath? I'll feed her."

Daniela says, "We couldn't ask you to do that."

"You did ask me to be her godmother a couple of hours ago. Maybe you can ask me to do this, too? Everyone needs sleep." She starts towards the bed.

Despite her protests, Daniela is already working the baby into a bundle to hand over. "What about you?"

Rachel shrugs that off and picks the crying Yana Sophia up into her arms. "Eh, I got a couple hours; I'm green."

Francesca's slippered feet drag the exhausted-looking woman into the room with a bottle. Striding for the door, Rachel plucks it from her hand and says, "Look, y'all go to bed. I'll take Yana downstairs. We'll drink some milk, chat about politics, and smoke cigars."

"Thank you," Ted says. If he sat down now, she's sure he'd fall asleep.

"I may not have a baby right now," she says, "but I fed my brothers when they were born. I can handle this. Unless there's something very wrong, we'll stay downstairs a couple of hours. Seriously, take a bath, then get into bed. Come on, Yana, we have things to discuss."

The whole way down, the baby cries its choking hysteria. Her face is contorted with pain, painted red and tear-stained. "I know, I know. It's so hard," she murmurs as she enters the informal sitting room and adjusts its lights to the lowest setting. "One minute you're safe, the next you're naked and afraid. Here, let's get the space heater on and my robe off."

Somehow, both tasks are accomplished with minimal jostling. She settles onto the couch and grabs the blanket, draping it over her shoulder. "A little blankie for us. There we go. Isn't that nice? Here we are: one synthetic nipple with some feel-better juice inside." Rubbing the rubber around the baby's gums helps simmer its temper before yielding to its hunger. "That's the way. There you go. You're just hungry. You had all-you-can-eat on tap for the last eight months, and now you've gotta wait for a bunch of adults to figure out what you want. How is that fair, huh?"

Rachel brushes Yana Sophia's thick black hair back then settles for stroking the tops of her ears when the baby scrunches its face in disdain. "It's hard being out here, isn't it? But everyone wants to keep you safe and happy. We know we can't do it forever, but we try. In a couple of months, if we're lucky, you're going to have a friend. I'll be honest with you; the whole prospect scares the shit out of me. You see, the last time I was here, I was so excited to be a mom. I'll tell you when we

were finally ready—that's your Uncle Job and me—to
have a baby, we were ready. We didn't have families
for a really long time, that's the downside of having
only-child parents, but we wanted one."

Yana Sophia's breathing steadies with each
subsequent gulp. Rachel lets the word spill out of her.
"We did have a baby, though. Her name was Siobhan.
She was supposed to be born over a year ago. But she
wasn't. Guess she decided that she wasn't quite ready
yet. It broke my heart, y'know. Literally. Oh," she
whispers conspiratorially, "'literally' is a word that
means something actually happened, but it's kinda
evolved because people say 'literally' when they mean
'figuratively.' People who don't have real lives get really
upset about misuse. 'You literally broke your heart?
Literally? How are you walking around, then?'" She
rolls her eyes. "Like language doesn't evolve? Get off
your high horse."

She takes the bottle away so Yana Sophia can catch
her breath. "Sorry, we drifted. My therapist used to tell
me that I used humor as a coping mechanism. Which…
is fair. I'm glad I do, though. For a long time, feelings
were hard. Every ounce of emotion was gone from me.
The only thing that would make me feel better was
SNL—it's a TV show we'll watch when you're older.
Don't get me wrong, not everything on that show is
funny. But the absurdist shit would always get me.
Because life is absurd sometimes. Mostly it's absurd."
The bottle is returned to the baby who has already
gotten fussy. "But you get it. You were born on your
mother's bedroom floor while a doctor told me what
to do over a video call. Then the paramedics showed
up in full-on hazmat suits and took you to a hospital in

the middle of a global pandemic. That's absurd. Right? You get it."

Yana Sophia looks at her through squinted eyes as she drains the bottle dry. Rachel picks her up and starts to burp her. "You know what else is absurd? I got pregnant the day I left my husband across the world, but he doesn't know yet because we were separated by the aforementioned global pandemic that almost killed him. But then he didn't, and right now he's in a hotel ten minutes away, but we can't see him for twelve more days. That's absurd." The baby lets out a man-sized belch. Rachel laughs and returns her to the blanket. "But you're going to be okay. You live with a bunch of people who are going to watch you grow up and root for you and be in your corner." She strokes her ear again. "I'll always be in your corner."

Wren's voice frightens her. "Talking to yourself in here?"

Rachel's head jerks up and finds Wren standing in the doorway in their ratty star-dappled nightgown. "I have the baby," she explains.

"Oh, shit, there she is." Wren takes a step towards them then pauses. "Are you naked?"

"Kinda." She looks down at her chest, and the baby's soft cheek against it. "Skin-to-skin contact is important. What are you doing up?"

Wren plops onto the other end of the couch. "Can't sleep. Came down for a snack."

"I'm sure there's something in the kitchen."

They loll their head backward. "I'm not actually hungry. Emotional eating."

Rachel nods big. "Gotcha."

"What are you talking about with her?"

"Absurdism."

"Lit." They chuckle. "Fatalists don't make themselves."

"No, not at all. I was telling her that her life is already absurd but that she's going to be okay. There are a lot of people who will be there for her no matter what. That makes her lucky."

"Hard to feel lucky sometimes," they whisper.

"Speaking for yourself or in general?"

"Myself mostly." Wren quiets. Rachel watches them squish their eyes together then open to reveal tears. "I just miss my mom so fucking much."

"I know you do, sweetheart. Wish there was an easier way to get to the part where you have more room for all the missing." She adjusts the baby into her other arm so she can offer her hand to Wren. "The first year is the hardest. Birthdays, holidays, the worst. It doesn't get easier; you just start knowing what to expect."

They start crying in earnest, pressing the heels of their palms into their eyes. "I never thought I'd be nineteen with no mom. No mom to see me walk across the stage for my diploma. No mom to help me through my first bad breakup. No mom to love my first solid partner more than me. No mom to worry about me when I travel the world. No mom."

"Can I tell you something I've learned after all these years of having no mom?"

Wren nods as they wipe their face clean.

Rachel reaches and takes their wet hand. It's hard to see so much of herself in this young person, but she's willing to share herself for their sake. "You will always have a mom. Your mother will always be with you. Call it whatever you want: spiritual connection or just a deep-seated psychological attachment; your mother will always be with you. I hear my mom all the time, especially when food is involved. I know it's crazy, but I hear her telling me what to do, how to take care of something. Hell, sometimes I hear her when I speak. There is no getting rid of mothers." She squeezes Wren's hand hard. "Some of the best advice I ever got from a counselor was to talk to my mom whenever I missed her most. I'd sit down, meditate, and imagine being with her under this oak tree we had in my backyard growing up. I swear to you, it was like she was right there. Maybe, when you're ready, we can do it together."

They lay down to rest their head against Rachel's thigh. "That'd be nice."

She sets the bottle on the table so she can rock the baby with one hand and stroke the lines from Wren's forehead with the other. "You're going to be okay," she says. "Just like this baby, you've got a lot of people in your corner. You're not alone."

CHAPTER THIRTY-ONE

TWO WEEKS LATER, A RED Honda Civic pulls in front of the driveway. Rachel sees a masked man in the back seat whose eyes look a lot like Job's. Jesus, her heart feels like it's going to fly out of her chest and crash into his. The door opens, and a man gets out with a weathered backpack slung over his shoulder. He thanks the driver, closes the door, and the car drives away. He waits. She waits. Her muscles strain with stillness. The months, the distance, and now here they are. Suddenly. Not suddenly.

"Hi," she says. The pain in her throat is exquisite.

Job's eyes water. He removes his surgical mask to reveal a scruffy beard. He's so thin, so frail-looking, but he's Job. "Hi," he says. His voice sounded different on the phone.

When they fall into one another, there's no drama. It is homecoming. Job's chest feels solid against Rachel's, even though she's gained all the weight he's lost. The wide expanse of his hands press against her back, and God, it feels so good to be touched like this. He smells like hotel soap and car air freshener. It's perfect. Tears come, at last, staining his rumpled shirt. "You're here," she whispers.

"You're here," he echoes, handing his head in the crook of her neck.

"I never thought I'd touch you again," she confesses.

"I know, I know," he tells her, grip growing tighter.

Planting a kiss on his cheek, she's not quite ready for lip kisses just yet; she takes him by the hand and laughs through her tears. "But, hey, let's get you off the street. Do you have everything?"

Job looks over his shoulder at the space where the car used to be. "Gosh, I sure hope so."

Rachel feels a grin coming on then spins on her heel. "Let's start in the carriage house."

"Can't believe how big this place is," he comments as they make their way up the drive.

From the corner of her eye, she catches a few faces peering out the house windows. She shoes them away. "Not bad for a Craigslist find. The front yard is big, too. But the first floor of this place is your workshop," she says with a flourish.

Job stops to put his hands on his hips. Rachel relishes his wide eyes and raised brows. He lets loose a low whistle. "Wow."

An odd pit of pride swells in her stomach. "I told you we renovated, right?"

His gaze traces the outline of the house. "In a week or something crazy?"

"It's still a work-in-progress, but it's hospitable," she tells him as she starts to open the door. It creaks its resistance. "You've had worse."

Despite outside appearances, the workshop is clean with nary a speck of sawdust. Every tool in its place.

Beside the giant workbench are stacks and stacks of lumber. Rachel leans over to flick on all the lights, flooding the room in bright white and yellow.

"Oh, yeah, way worse," Job's voice trails. He gives up a goofy chuckle as he wanders closer to the center of the room. "That maker's space in Chicago didn't have heat. *This* is Shangri-La."

"Markeya and Anabelle live up on the top floor at the moment, but they're at work right now." She knows this because she checked the calendar.

Reverent, Job's hands caress the top of his workbench. "This is incredible."

Rachel leans against the wall so he can have all the space he needs. "I'm happy the wood made it in time. Apparently, Vernon placed an order with one of our wholesalers the week we signed our lease. A housewarming gift."

He lifts the blanket covering the lumber and judges it. "High-quality shit."

She smiles at her husband's pleasure and her roommate's thoughtfulness. "Only the best. Vernon can be weird, but he's got good taste."

He turns to face her, beaming with excitement. A shiver of delight causes the hairs on her arms to stand on end. "Rach, I'm going to make the most unnecessarily intricate cabinets you've ever seen. They're gonna make those French Rococo cabinets we saw look like shit." He glances between the pile and the workbench. "But maybe some practice first. My hands need to get back into the habit."

"You'll get there in no time," she assures.

Job's focus gets locked on something on the floor. When Rachel looks, she can't see anything out of the ordinary. Finally, he says, "I missed you."

It almost sounds like a question, a surprise. "I missed you, too," she answers. It's true.

He looks up at her. The space between them widens. "I'm sorry I haven't been here."

"What?" she asks, then laughs. "How was that your fault?"

"Are you kidding?" Job plops down on the lumber and scratches his beard. *When did it get so gray?* "I should have come back with you."

Rachel approaches slowly, placing each step like a tightrope walker so as to not fall in the pit below. "You did what you needed to do. You needed to be alone." When she's close enough, she reaches to touch his shoulder. He jumps at first, then relaxes. "It was my fault you went to Chennai and got sick."

"No, it's not," he tells her as he reaches for the hand on his shoulder and squeezes it. His eyes are so sincere, so easy to believe. "It was going to happen. A bunch of people got sick at the retreat, too. I could have picked it up anywhere. Really. You don't have to blame yourself for that. For anything." He looks at the floor but doesn't let go of her. "I heard, y'know, when I was intubated. On the phone."

The blood drains from her face and pools in her feet. To think about that night ever again is like flaying her back wide open. "Oh."

"You blame yourself for so much, Rachel. So much shit that isn't yours, to begin with. Siobhan." His voice hitches, but he recovers before it turns into anything else. Her heart breaks at the sound. "It wasn't your fault, you know. It wasn't my fault either. It just—"

She sits beside him and finishes, "—happened."

Job leans on his knees, hands clasped tight. "For everything that happened, I'm glad I went to the retreat. There were these dedicated silences for meditation, and I'd sit in this courtyard and disappear into myself. There's so much depth inside a person. Infinite depths of consciousness that can help you become a better person, to help you connect to some higher consciousness. But honestly?" He scoffs. "All I thought about was you and Siobhan. I thought about the day we went to the hospital, seeing her there in that blanket."

Rachel takes a deep breath to steady herself through fresh nausea.

"Remember when we got her ashes?" Of course, she does. "I don't think I slept for two days." It was three. "Life felt so pointless after that. Getting up every day felt pointless. I loved you so much, and I still felt that way. I felt so fucking guilty." Job sweeps his hands through his hair. Rachel brings her knees into her chest to quell her quaking. "I wanted to be there for you because I knew you needed me...but it was so hard. When I woke up in the hospital, I told you it was an accident. That was the truth." He whips his gaze to hers, searing her with his expression. "I didn't do anything on purpose. But there was a part of me that was done living."

She closes her eyes and nods. She knows.

"It wasn't your fault. None of it was your fault. It was just so much heartbreak," he whispers. His finger brushes a tear from her face. He smells like sanitizer. "My teachers told me that I had to let go of the past to

353

live in the present. They really drill that into you. 'The past is the past,'" he intones. "But how can you do that when the past is so much a part of the present?"

Rachel wipes her face dry on her jeans. "I've been thinking about the past a lot, too. About you and Siobhan and how fucking angry everything makes me. When I got here, I couldn't even look at Daniela just because she was pregnant and seemed so happy. Like, who was she that she got to be happy? I hated her so much because she had what I wanted. But then later, when the pregnancy went sideways, I found out that we had a lot in common." She leans closer to whisper, "They lost a baby, too. Almost the same way we did."

Job hums and nods for her to continue.

"When it was finally happening, when that baby's head was sticking out of her, I thought: *This is as close to God as we get in this lifetime.* It was divine to be there with Daniela while she held her mother's hand and pushed. Then, all of a sudden, this ugly red thing just plops out into my hands and is suddenly the most precious thing on the planet. Something then, Job, it just shifted." She shakes her head. "I can't explain it. She was just there. She had all this hair and was screaming so loud it was like she was trying to wake the dead." Rachel smiles softly. "Maybe that scream was for me."

"When I saw you holding that baby the other night," Job tells her, "it made me mad. At first, I thought I was mad at you as if holding a baby was some kind of capital offense. Then I realized that I wasn't mad at you; I was mad at me. Because I wasn't able to give you a baby. Because that wasn't our daughter."

If there's anything Rachel can understand, it's this. She puts her arm around his shoulders and hugs him to her. For a few minutes, they sit in silence. Rachel thinks bittersweet thoughts about their daughter, wishing she was there, but then her mind drifts to the life growing in her womb even now. Now is not the time to tell Job. Soon, though, soon.

"They asked me to be Yana Sophia's godmother," she says.

"Really?" he asks, shocked. She nods, pleased. "How do you feel about that?"

"I thought they were crazy when they asked me, but Daniela was insistent. They asked me to be there for her, to be a part of their family. Just like that." She squishes him for emphasis. The long-dead beacon of hope in her heart threatens to catch flame. Everything is there for them if they are willing to take it. "This thing we've been trying to create for ourselves the last decade, they offered without reservation. We can just have it, Job."

A whoosh of breath leaves him, and he stands up fast. "That's a lot to take in."

Rachel watches him start to pace the room. "It is, but I feel like we've put our lives on hold for long enough." Her voice raises, and Job stops. "We've mourned enough. For our parents, for our child, for ourselves. We should start trying again. We *need* to start trying again."

Rachel doesn't ask Job if he's ready. She knows he's not. She'll ask him tomorrow when he's had the chance to see, to understand what it means to try here. Instead, she witnesses him. At first, the tears trickle one by one, then they sluice, and then they turn into big, wracking sobs. She unfolds herself, gets up, and takes him into her arms. She strokes his hair and lets his beard scratch her neck. This is bloodletting.

Tenderly, she guides them back to the lumber pile so his travel-weary legs won't fail him as he cries. Each tear has a purpose, that much is evident, and soon enough, the purpose exhausts itself. When he pulls away, rubbing his eyes, he looks almost bashful that he unleashed such a tsunami on his wife. Rachel realizes that things are not normal between them.

"This is weird, right?" she asks, thinking of Markeya and what she said about honesty. "Like, really weird."

Job dries his eyes on his shirt. "Why weird?"

"We haven't seen each other in months. A lot has happened. To both of us." She rotates her body so she can face him. "It feels like I'm meeting you for the first time."

He laughs at that. "Not making a great impression, am I?"

Rachel grins. "We're just different than we were."

"Different?"

"Do you really feel like the same person you were in Cairo?"

He thinks about that a moment. "Guess not."

"Job," she says sweetly, "we've spent more than a decade together. This is the longest we've gone without seeing each other. A lot happened in a short amount of time. A lot of new trauma that we didn't process together. We're different people now."

A big worry divot appears between his brows. "Are we okay?"

"What?" She rears back at his nonsense. "Of course we are. I think we just need some time to get reacquainted. That's it. Make sense?"

"Guess so..." He reaches to take her hand. "This okay?"

"Perfect," she replies, lacing their fingers.

"So, tell me," his voice regains some of its regular pep, "what's the scoop? Who's feuding with who? Who's the house villain? What do we wear on Wednesdays? When's the sacrificial brunch? What is the four-one-one?"

"Honestly? It'll be easier if you just meet everyone yourself." Rachel stands up to stretch out the sadness.

Job rises with her, yawning all the same. He looks good like this: red-faced and all. There's a lightness about him that tells Rachel everything is going to be okay. "Oh, yeah?"

"Yeah. Not everyone is here right now, which is good. You can meet everyone in stages." She heads towards the door, places her hand on the doorknob, then stops to beam at him. "We can be a lot all at once."

ACKNOWLEDGMENTS

I TALK ABOUT GRATITUDE a lot in my writing. How grateful I am for this; how grateful I am for that. Honestly? The word doesn't touch the feeling. In thinking about this book, though, and who nurtured it, only a handful of people were there for it in a real, tangible way. For those people, gratitude becomes indebtedness. I am indebted to you for all you did for me.

Richie. Without you, there would be no book. You know that, I know that, the people down the street know that. Thank you for always letting me talk through run-on sentences and bad ideas, for making me hundreds of cups of coffee, for rubbing my shoulders when they got tense, for taking care of the house and pets so I could focus on work, for weathering every storm of self-doubt, for being my champion.

The Bond House. Before you, I didn't know I could love so much. Brennan, Lark, Michael, Claudia, Mara, Josefina, Theresa, Gizem, Bill, Lizzie, Bettina, Sal, Ana, Sergio, Valerie, Shawn, and so many others, you changed me in more ways that you could ever possibly know.

Harriet. For being there when the first book was written and for every story since. You are the best friend anyone could possibly ask for, and I was lucky enough to get you. You're stuck with me now.

Mom. Thank you for always encouraging me to do what I wanted to do. Knowing that I made you cry while reading this book was the highlight of my year.

Lizzie. For telling me, in excruciating detail, what the act of childbirth is like on the delivery side. You made the scenes of motherhood all the more real. Thanks to you, I have no intention of ever having children. I look forward to being a great auntie to your son, though.

Liz Campa. It was the most surreal feeling when you called me to tell me that you liked my book. It was the first time in my life that I felt like a real writer.

Bob. For reading the pages before anyone else.

Brenda, Olivia, and Zara. For treating this story with care, attention, and belief. Your work made this a reality.